Ripples

Children of Y'Dahnndrya, Volume 1

Robin McElveen

Published by MKRM Author, 2025.

This is a work of fiction. Similarities to real people, places, or events are entirely coincidental.

RIPPLES

First edition. November 21, 2025.

Written by Robin McElveen.

Also by Robin McElveen

Children of Y'Dahnndrya
Ripples
Ripples

Tales of Y'Dahnndrya
The Tale of Outh'n Durr

Watch for more at https://www.authorrobinmcelveen.com/.

For Rowan - Joshua 1:9

Introduction

The name Y'Dahnndrya rolled off my tongue one day when I created a piece of perspective art depicting several spaceships hovering over a gas giant. I liked the name so much I used it for the planet in my first novel. Maybe one day, the artwork and the novel will connect, but I sincerely hope not. I always feel a sense of betrayal when novels which start in the fantasy realm suddenly reveal a post-apocalyptic Earth somewhere in the history. I don't want to let that happen with this story.

This is a work of fiction. Any resemblance to one of my fellow human beings is purely coincidental.

Things Readers Should Know

Y'Dahnndrya is a world with two continents and many islands (so far). She orbits twin suns. Her traveling companions are five moons. Time flows differently on Y'Dahnndrya. Six seasons (dahlsikin) comprising three months (minsikin) each make up one Y'Dahnndryan year, called a tsimik. The calendar follows the largest moon's cycle. Each month comprises four weeks, which are each nine days long, hence a nainda. A Y'Dahnndryan year is 648 days. Readers might like to know while Yetsye may only have seen fourteen tsimikin, in Earth years, she's closer to eighteen.

For more information, I've provided an index, a brief pronunciation guide, and a glossary which all wait patiently at the end of the novel for those who crave more knowledge.

So Let's Begin

Dear Reader, thank you for picking up this book and giving it a chance. It is my fervent prayer that the contents enrich your life. If you take one thing away from the reading of it, may it be that even small positive deeds performed by one soul can shake the foundations of our world.

"Finally, brethren, whatsoever things are true, whatsoever things are honest, whatsoever things are just, whatsoever things are pure, whatsoever things are lovely, whatsoever things are of good report; if there be any virtue, and if there be any praise, think on these things."

Philippians 4:8–King James Version Bible

Part 1
M'Neshunnaya

1

Glen

Tsifi'ra and Mit'ra warmed Yetsye Shirasdatir as she jogged down a faint trail. Her classes often overwhelmed her and today was no exception. As soon as possible, she escaped. Her favorite place drew her like still water drew met'cha. A little glade nestled in the quiet wood behind her family's d'gut. The leaves rustled in the light breeze, welcoming her with whispered cheers. Yetsye closed her eyes when she reached the center. It was here that she could open herself to the Creator of Y'Dahnndrya, to Azilet'zal, and to Y'Dahnndrya herself.

Harmonic chirps signaled brightly colored chippits high in the treetops. An el'tekh screeched its freedom cry from the clouds. A quiet rustle and methodical munching nearby announced a shaggy mana. It must have followed her there. Sweet scents of liilum and tseta almost overpowered the milder flowers in Yetsye's natural garden bed, but she could just pick out spicy umb'el and warm, nutty dozhi in the riot of perfumes. A flut'ra teased Yetsye's small, freckled nose and lightly kissed her peachy lips with translucent triplet wings and fragile legs. The heart of Y'Dahnndrya thrummed beneath her as the wind tripped lightly over her, bending the long grasses in its wake. In the glade, she could be herself, immersed in the spirit of Y'Dahnndrya. Yetsye heard Azilet'zal's voice in the wind and felt the pure love for life in the beasts and earth. The Holy Presence was tangible here.

Calming moments like this were precious now that Yetsye was an adult. Well, almost. There was still her Visioning to attend before she could claim official adulthood. Learning the basics of battle tactics, animal husbandry, and sky-dome studies nibbled away at her time. The excitement of being able to join her siblings in warrior training waned. While she studied the basics, they were far more advanced. It comforted her, though, to know they were close by. If a problem arose, they would help.

This dawning had been particularly stressful. Yetsye's inability to grasp the specifics of the tactician's art irritated her teacher. Her choice to remain silent didn't help. It wasn't that she couldn't speak. If she kept her statements simple and short, she did well. But if she couldn't, Yetsye often said things which were easily misunderstood. It seemed safer to stay silent and avoid conflict, even if others thought she was a bumbir. This time, her silence cost an extra hesp of menial chores. It also meant she'd be called on during the next session and treated as an example.

A sudden shudder deep in the ground forced open eyes the color of mineral-rich earth. It was so subtle she almost missed it. Though focused on the strange shift, she still sensed her batir's arrival.

Yuvahl Shirashoneh had seen the dawning of eighteen tsimikin, which meant he was perfect in Yetsye's eyes. The scent of earth and metal that hovered around him betrayed his love for tending plants and tinkering with tools. A deep thinker, his motivation usually came from a sense of justice rooted deep within him. Yetsye had never witnessed Yuvahl fail at anything. She was the only one who knew all of his worries. Because she listened, he happily spun tales of his life to her.

Yetsye placed her hand in Yuvahl's open palm and looked into his troubled eyes. "Are you well, Batir?"

He sighed and rose from his knee. Shaking his head, he pulled Yetsye to her feet. "We need to get home. There's news from D'Koruyi. It's not good."

Yetsye trailed after Yuvahl. No definite paths existed in their territory. The M'Neshunnayans worked hard to preserve their lands as Azilet'zal created them. They knew direction by landmarks, the sky-dome above, and the earth beneath their feet. All younglings learned this skill from the dawning they could walk.

She expected Yuvahl to say a little more, but he kept silent. The only time they heard from other clans was on trading days. Yetsye worried her bottom lip with her teeth, thinking about what could have happened.

As they cleared the tree line, she spotted Ya'el waiting. Her siveh's beautifully coiffed copper hair was a shining beacon above mischievous leaf-green eyes and a dimpled smile. That delicate form and grace deceived many foes. Ya'el's well-spring of words rarely failed her. When Yetsye needed an interpreter, her siveh was more than willing to explain. She was beautiful and sociable. The result was a long list of friends, acquaintances, and would-be life-mates. Some dawnings, Yetsye wished she was more like Ya'el. Then she would recant, horrified that she doubted Azilet'zal who formed her. There was a reason for the current existence that was Yetsye Shirasdatir. She would know it when it was time to know it, and not before.

2

Family

Of the three children of Shira, they shared only two tangible traits in common. First, once a child of Shira decided on a course of action, there was no deviation from it. Second was the red-gold hair they inherited from Bayr'akh, their fatir. She was thankful for both. Otherwise, she felt like she didn't belong.

"Welcome back!" Ya'el's intense hug betrayed the depth of her concern. She always believed every problem had a solution if people bothered to look in the right book. If the news worried Ya'el, it must be terrible indeed.

"Is it really so bad, Ya'el?" Yetsye wished she had stayed in the glade. The knot born in her stomach with Yuvahl's frown grew, threatening to eject the kho'ni nuts she consumed on her way to the glade. The three walked the rest of the way together.

Fatir met them at the door, hugging them as they passed through the arched opening. Matir was probably busy inside preparing the dusking meal. Smoke drifted up through the roof and savory scents hung in the air. Shira Rayasdatir and Bayr'akh Orevshoneh were highly respected elders in the M'Neshunnayan Clan. Shira was the High Priestess of the clan, elected the tsimik before Yetsye's birthing. Bayr'akh's skill as a teacher allowed him to guide students of advanced history for many tsimikin.

When Yetsye's eyes adjusted to the dim interior, the first thing she noticed was Shira seated at the low table in the center of the gathering room. Her head bowed low over her bowl. Work-roughened fingers massaged her temples. Two silvery streaks shimmered above her right eye in the otherwise dark brown tresses as a ray of light shone through an oddly shaped, almost round window.

Shira lifted her head and speared them all with her intense green gaze. "A D'Koruyin messenger arrived earlier." Her deep alto voice resonated in

Yetsye's chest. "D'Koruyi brings troubling news. Please sit. We will offer thanks for the meal and I'll spin the tale for you."

Yetsye took the cushion on her fatir's left and Yuvahl sat on her other side. Ya'el sat across from her. Bayr'akh spoke a simple prayer, then filled his bowl, signaling the others to do the same.

"As you know," Shira began, "the D'Koruyin tribes move with the herds. At this time of the tsimik, they camp near the river Miet're. When a great rumbling struck one of their campsites..." Shira broke off and tears brimmed in her eyes.

"What is it, Matir?" Ya'el prompted when the silence continued.

"I'm sorry." She swallowed and cleared her throat. "The messenger reported, ah, I don't know how else to say it. Y'Dahnndrya swallowed an entire tribe." She paused again to allow the news to sink in. "The thought of such a great blow to one's people, though they aren't my own, it's hard to bear."

"What do you mean, Matir? How can this be?" Yuvahl asked the questions hovering on Yetsye's tongue.

"The messenger said the ground opened up and swallowed one entire tribe. Only five D'Koruyin tribes remain. The survivors now fight to maintain order and move to a safer location. I sent Ranica along with four others to the north-western villages to see how they fare and lay hold on any spins that may reveal more truth about the tragedy. While we wait for answers, I've sent out messengers to the other villages to encourage our people to help in any way they can."

Fatigue etched deep lines in her parents' faces. Yetsye filled her plate with more kho'ni greens, bansan berries, and jiban nuts. What did it mean? Why was this happening now? Why should something like this happen at all? Each question daunted her spirit, though her appetite remained intact.

Shira refilled each of their beakers with warm mana milk. "There's more. The Miet're River shifted its course."

Yetsye's eyes widened, temporarily neglecting the food on her plate. "What do you mean? How?" She looked around the table. The anxious circle of faces worried her.

"I've never heard of such a thing happening in all my tsimikin. The earth of Y'Dahnndrya shuddering? Yes. But to this extent?" Shira shook her head slowly and took a sip of her milk. "Never!" The beaker tapped the table dully as she set it beside her plate.

Bayr'akh lay down his utensils and wiped his mouth and hands. "This is new to me, too. I've studied the Great Cataclysm many times, though this shift seems not at all terrible compared to that. Surely strange things occur, but they won't affect my love for my family, my people, or our world. To keep moving forward, we must know more about this. I'm sure Ranica will bring news as soon as she can. Until then, we'll be patient and continue our work to maintain the delicate balance of life on Y'Dahnndrya."

"It sounds like an interesting adventure to me! I wish I was with Tani Ranica." Ya'el's excitement was normal. Ranica was Shira's younger siveh. She and Ya'el were much alike. The latter speared a forkful of greens and popped them daintily into her mouth. She swallowed before speaking again. "Losing so many lives is tragic. But how exciting to be alive at this moment in time. To witness such a magnificent show of Azilet'zal's power and Y'Dahnndrya's unpredictability, I think it's amazing!" Her smiling face radiated pleasure. Yetsye wasn't sure whether to grin at her siveh's brazen excitement in the face of such horror, or point out her gross insensitivity.

"You would," Yuvahl gently rebuked around a mouthful of berries. He swallowed. "I'm truly at a loss. What should I do? I want to stay with my own people, but should I offer my help to the D'Koruyin? And have you heard anything from Shinnoah?" He wasted no time seeking solutions.

"Once Ranica determines the extent of the damage in our own territory, she'll send word back. I asked her to travel on to Mt. Charan to consult the Guardian of the temple. It's the only place in Shinnoah which an out-clanner can enter unannounced. Seth Yi'in will know anything worth knowing." Shira cupped her hands around the warm beaker and took another sip.

"Our people knew what they were doing when they elected you High Priestess, Matir. Your insight and wisdom are beyond compare!" Ya'el wiped her face and hands and prepared to leave the table.

"Wait! There's more." Ya'el relaxed back onto her cushion. "The timing is regrettable," Yetsye knew what was coming and tensed, "but Yetsye must journey to the Plains of Levanna. The time for her Visioning has come." She paused a moment and her gaze softened. She continued, but turned to Ya'el. "You and Yuvahl should accompany her. I've already spoken to your mentors.

If you agree, we'll prepare on the morrowdawn and the following dawning, the journey must begin."

"Yes, Matir. Of course, I'll go with Yetsye." Ya'el didn't hesitate at all. She cleared her place at the table and flashed a teasing smile at Yetsye as she said, "Who will interpret for her if strangers appear along the way?" Yuvahl looked up with a grin and winked at Yetsye, cooling the temper rising within her. He nodded his own acceptance and quickly finished his meal, clearing his place when he was done.

Yetsye remained at the table, lost in thought as she ate mechanically. What purpose could Azilet'zal have for her? The thought was scary, but also exciting. She'd thought this dawning would never come. Now that it was here, how strange that it should align with such a tragic event! And this wasn't the only strange thing. She'd just started her training. The journey to Levanna would take at least two nainda of travel time. Missing classes would set her back even more in her studies. There was no helping it. The Visioning wasn't optional, though, on rare occasions, postponing it had happened in the past.

She finished her meal and cleared her place. "Matir?" she asked as she cleaned her bowl and utensils.

"Yes?" Shira looked up from storing the leftover food.

"Are you certain I must go now? The timing seems wrong. And I could help here, don't you think?" She finished putting away her dishes, then sat beside the mud-brick oven.

Shira sighed and stored the leftovers in the cooler set into the floor. "You are so young and so caring. I'm proud of the woman I see blooming inside you." She glided on graceful feet to her datir, took her hand, and led her to the brazier. Bayr'akh, who had remained at the table, followed them at Shira's nod. As they sat on the soft rug, she shared more.

"Under other circumstances, I might have agreed with you. However, my own visions have shown me you must go now. There may not be another chance for you. I don't know what this means, though, and to spin the truth, I'm afraid. I don't want to let you go." She reached over to enclose Yetsye in a gentle hug. "You are my youngest, flesh of my flesh, bone of my bone, and heart of my heart. All my children are precious and I would guard you with all I have 'til my very last breath fades away." She released Yetsye from the hug, but gripped her shoulders firmly. Dark green eyes met warm brown orbs intensely. "But protection is a double-edged sword. Too much and, though they exist, the youngling cannot truly live. Too little and the youngling's life may fade too quickly, like a candle set into the middle of a windy lake."

She took Yetsye's small hands in hers. "Do not fear. The prayers of our people go with you to help you. I pray often for your growth and success. Keep faith in Azilet'zal, knowing there is a purpose for your life. And whatever you're shown in Levanna, you can be certain the path is good, for Azilet'zal never leads us down a wrong path." They grinned at each other. Shira's smile revealed little to Yetsye, who knew her own smile betrayed everything.

Bayr'akh patted her shoulder. "You won't know the outcome of the choices you make until you make them," he grinned as he stated the obvious. "But no matter what, you must progress down life's path. This is just one more stretch of that journey. All will be well. You'll see."

Yetsye hugged her matir again, tightly this time. She felt the press of lips on her hair. "Thank you, both," she whispered softly. "I will love you 'til the end of my last tsimik. Maybe beyond!"

Shira pulled back a bit to look into her eyes. "Maybe beyond? Are you losing faith already? You know our spirits will soar freely with Azilet'zal when our earthly vessels can no longer contain them. Never forget what's truly important, though. You are loved, and there are those who believe in you and in what you will become. Don't waste time doubting."

One more tight hug from each of her parents was Yetsye's send-off to the washroom. She cleansed herself and gazed at the dark eyes staring back at her in the mirror. "Do I have what it takes?" she asked the reflection. She felt flawed. If she lacked the courage to speak out against offensive or harmful things, how could she possibly serve others? She asked herself again what kind of purpose could Azilet'zal have for someone like her, then sighed. The morrowdawn would be busy. She didn't have time to worry. Her siblings would be with her, after all. Surely everything would be fine.

She plodded to her room and collapsed onto her mat. She lay there, half praying, half wondering, and well on her way to blissful sleep, when the warmth of an edjig pressed against her left side. Churk curled his long length next to her stomach. She'd rescued him from a thorny bramble vine two tsimikin past, and he'd stayed with her ever since. It was probably best. One wing tore badly in the struggle and he would never glide through the canopy again. She scratched behind his floppy ears and under his square muzzle. A smiled spread over her face as a gurgle of contentment rumbled in his bearded throat.

The ruffed muffit she'd rescued a nainda ago began a rhythmic, chirping song from her cage in the corner. Here was another injured foundling who might never survive in the wild again. Her camouflaged scales would make it easier for her to survive than Churk. But a broken talon and one ruined eye spoke volumes about the viciousness of a tsa'gra's teeth and claws. She just needed time to heal. The test would come sooner than expected, for Yetsye couldn't leave an animal locked in a cage while she traveled. If the muffit chose to stay, she'd name her. And with that thought, she drifted off.

3

Provisions

Light trickled through the curtain of vines outside Yetsye's window two dawnings later, gently rousing her from a deep sleep. "It's already time," she mumbled as she blinked. Last dusking, she and Shira loaded travel sacks with dried fruits, vegetables, and nuts. Almost as an afterthought, Yetsye asked her matir for a pouch of jerked meats, thinking they'd be a pleasant treat on the trail.

Shira tried surprising her by adding a small bag of Yetsye's favorite sweet, too, but Yetsye was too observant. Shinnoahn bon'jiis differed from any other confection. Sweet-tart flavor compacted into a springy outer shell covered a slightly less tart, creamy center, offering a complexity lacking in M'Neshunnayan sweets. Yetsye proclaimed herself an expert on them before she'd seen the dawning of five tsimikin. She smiled as Shira met her eyes and tried to explain away the small indulgence.

This journey was exciting, but Yetsye still took it seriously. Her life paths lay before her. It wasn't choosing a path which was so hard, but the outcome of her choice that bothered her. Her worries remained muted for now, but they lurked at the back of her mind.

Sighing, she quickly offered dawning prayers to the Creator and made her way to the washroom. After cleansing and refreshing herself, she dragged the pik'teh through her thick, curly hair and bound it in two red-gold poofs on top of her head. She mourned the immature appearance in the mirror, but it was the only style she could manage which would keep the unruly mass out of her face. She frowned over her lack of skill. Why hadn't she learned different ways of binding her hair before now?

"Ya'el never has this much trouble," she grumbled to herself. With her hair temporarily tamed, Yetsye scrubbed her face and rinsed her mouth with aljis juice, the super-fine grit in it scrubbing her mouth clean. She glanced once more at her reflection, then turned and headed to the main room.

"You sleep too much, Little Siveh!"

Yetsye sighed. She didn't have time to reply but gave her siveh a half-grin.

"Aren't you excited at all?" Ya'el pressed.

Yetsye preferred to ease slowly into the dawning, but Ya'el always woke instantly. Once again, she wished she was more like the older girl. Most of the classes she had trouble with took place in the early part of the dawning. Now that she thought about it, maybe that's why she had so much trouble with subjects she should know well.

"Good dawning to you, too, Chirpy," she quipped in return. Her quirky humor flew past most people's understanding. Since Ya'el was talkative and cheerful like a singing flyer, this fit. She'd also be the one most often speaking for Yetsye on this journey, should they meet anyone on the way. "And shouldn't you say maiden? That's what I am now."

"Not quite yet. What about your Visioning? Seeing the dawn of fourteen tsimikin isn't all it takes. Besides, 'maiden siveh' sounds like you're tripping over slippery rocks in the stream." Ya'el teased back. Yetsye smiled as she walked over and wrapped Ya'el in a hug.

Azilet'zal's blessing rested on her. Ya'el would be her voice while Yuvahl would faithfully guard them both. They were all capable of handling most dangers well enough on their own, but unexpected things happened. And if necessary, he could also speak for her if Ya'el wasn't able to.

"Kaf'ket for all of you?" asked Shira as she served bowls of homish gruel and leftover kho'ni greens. She was usually at the temple, officiating at early prayers, but the temple assistants offered to guide this dawning's visitors. At the resounding chorus of assent, Shira filled the pottery beakers to the brim with the creamy brew.

Yetsye wrapped her hands around the cup, soaking in the pleasant warmth. She raised it to her face and blew gently across the surface to cool it. As she breathed in the steam, she caught the scent of sharp spices, most notably sitma and jinj. Shira always prepared the favorite dishes of each of her offspring before their Visioning journey began. Matir knew hers well, but these spices were Ya'el's favorites. Something was wrong. No one else seemed to notice, so Yetsye focused on eating. She held her tongue for now, but decided to speak to Matir after the meal.

The family gathered around the table and treasured the last moments before Yetsye took her new path. A lot could happen on a journey like this. A pilgrim could be seriously injured or maybe not even be able to return home. In fact, when Yuvahl took his Visioning journey, one of his closest friends died when the company came upon a family of tsa'gra unexpectedly. Yuvahl still suffered horrible dreams from time to time, but having Matir's tsa'gra companion in the house with them helped.

When Yuvahl and Ya'el finally left the table, Yetsye had her chance. "What's going on?" Ever direct when confronting something unpleasant, she clipped out the whispered words while staring deep into Shira's eyes.

"What do you mean, Yetsye?" asked Bay'rakh, drawing her attention to him.

"Something's wrong. Something besides the shaking of the ground. I can sense it. Please tell me what you can." She folded her hands in her lap and waited.

Shira sighed. She motioned Yetsye to sit on a cushion by the brazier as she and Bay'rakh did the same.

"Many tsimikin ago, when you were born, I received a dusking vision." Yetsye's eyebrows rose in surprise. "A massive lake larger than any I've ever seen spread out before me. Four blurred figures stood on the shore. The calm surface reflected all things around and above its glassy surface. The water was dark, concealing the depth.

"On the shore, the smallest figure stooped to pluck a stone from the ground. She glanced at the stone in her hand and gazed at the lake once more. Drawing back her arm, she threw the stone with all her might. As the stone flew from her hand, it danced across the surface, generating ripples. As it skipped, it grew larger and larger until it was the size of a tsa'gra's head. It jumped higher and higher with each impact until finally it plunged into the center of the lake. When it sank, the small ripples became a great seiche rushing outward. The figures stood and watched the wave tumble and claw its way to the shore, unafraid of the formidable wall of thunder and might. The water crashed upon the shore, swallowing the four figures."

Tears brimmed in her eyes, and Shira's voice shook. She breathed deeply to regain her composure. "When the water receded, the four figures had become three, the smallest no longer among them. I have carried this burden for many tsimikin and only your fatir knows of it. I have an inkling of the meaning, but no prophecy is set in stone.

"All actions create ripples throughout Y'Dahnndrya. These ripples affect all who are part of the tapestry of life, even if the effect is unnoticeable at first. I believe our Creator has a marvelous plan for you. I'm proud of all my children. And I worry about what may one dawning be. Will you continue to walk forward? Which path will you walk? I can only turn the worries over to Azilet'zal, for each of you must make choices."

Yetsye didn't know how to receive such news. Knowing what her matir held close to her heart did nothing to calm the knot in her stomach, either. If anything, the knowledge made it worse. As she looked at her folded hands, her fatir tenderly gripped her shoulder.

"Yetsye," Bay'rakh's rich tenor tones soothed her, "you are a wonderful person, full of life and hope. You must believe in yourself and have faith that Azilet'zal will not guide you down a wrong path. Faith in your family wouldn't be wrong, either," he smiled. "When even the dawning feels dark and it seems there is no one to turn to, we'll be there for you, if not in person, for certain in your heart and in your memories."

"Fatir, is it true there's life after death? Do you really believe that?" Her voice revealed her concern for everything she'd heard.

"Yes, I do. With all my heart, I believe it," he replied. All the confidence in the room must have filled him up because there was none left for Yetsye.

"If you believe, then I will do my best to believe while I search for my own answers. This way, fear won't hinder me. I promise you both, I will never turn away from my purpose, whatever it may be." Yetsye rose and hugged her parents once again. She busied herself clearing away her place setting.

While she cleaned, she pondered. Four people, not three. Who was the fourth? And who'd be washed away by the wave? Ya'el was the smallest in form, but she was the youngest. And why would anyone want to set such a wave stirring, anyway?

She finished her tasks and headed out the front door to where Yuvahl and Ya'el waited with four pack-laden mana. One carried most of the gear, while the other three carried smaller bags filled with snacks and other things they might need on the trail. Yetsye mounted the leading mana, and Ya'el perched elegantly atop the next. Yuvahl brought up the rear, making sure the gear and his siblings were safe.

She stared as her parents said goodbye to Yuvahl and Ya'el. There was nothing unusual in the goodbye to hint at Shira's hunch. She'd have to be patient. No one knew where a particular path would lead in the end, least of all her. She reminded herself to keep a tight hold of her faith. She couldn't falter now, not when she hadn't even started traveling her own path. Ya'el would laugh if she suspected such a fickle attitude lay hidden in her heart. She could see Yuvahl frowning about it, but he'd be more likely to understand. She was more like him than Ya'el. The thought of losing someone would haunt her until she solved the mystery. They clucked to the mana and their friends bore them slowly away to the southern edge of Zulima village.

Yetsye drank it all in. When she returned, everything would be changed. Even if nothing were to change physically in the village, her eyes would never see it the same way again after this journey. She knew this well because of Yuvahl's many tales about his Visioning. Yetsye believed it was healing for him to remember the journey and treasure the memories of his friend, so she always listened.

Now, she yearned for the simple dawnings of her younger tsimikin. This trip presented Yetsye with a mystery which was exactly the opposite of what she longed for. Predictability was a soothing balm to her while it was anathema to her siveh. Ya'el sang brightly behind her, the notes clear and high. Yetsye glanced back to see her wide smile and shining eyes. Then she joined in the song with her rich harmony, doing her best to drop the shroud Matir's revelation cast over her. As they passed into the cover of the familiar woodland, the chippits added their cheerful chirps to the tune. It wasn't long before Yuvahl's rich baritone joined the choir. What a merry bunch of travelers!

4

Surprise

The Kya'al River ran south and filled Lake Mir'ir. The ford was in sight when Yetsye looked up to see Tsifi'ra and Mit'ra floating high above her. Her stomach grumbled, eliciting a chuckle from Yuvahl. She couldn't decide whether to be embarrassed or laugh that he heard it all the way at the end of the line.

"Alright," he announced. "Here is as good a place as any. Let's rest and eat."

The mana grazed on sweet grass and refreshed themselves with cool water. Yetsye and her siblings, lost in their own thoughts, pulled rations from their packs and settled in for a quick meal. A heavy silence, broken only by a stray chirp or swish of leaves, blanketed them, smothering Yetsye's earlier excitement. She expected to encounter another pilgrim or two on this path by now.

"I'm going over there," Yetsye said and pointed to a sunny patch of ground lit by a single ray. It was far enough away from the others for her to concentrate, but close enough if there was a problem. She lay back on the grass and began her calming ritual. It wouldn't be as easy as it was in her little glade back home. But so many worries swam around in her mind, it was necessary to try. Opening her senses lowered the barrier she kept in place between her and other humans. She could be herself with her world. Y'Dahnndrya accepted every inhabitant, despite their flaws. Such peace and belonging so moved her, a tear escaped one eye.

A low rumble vibrated within her before she heard it with her ears. Her eyes snapped open as she bolted up. "Time to move! And quick!" she warned as she jumped up.

Almost immediately, chippits burst out from the nearby treetops, clanging their discordant alarm. Not far behind them, a flurry of edjigs burst out of the underbrush, a dizzying jumble of reds, greens, and blues bumbling as fast as possible on their twelve short legs. They were nearly silent, but their wings flicked in fear. Muffits, flut'ra, wild mana, beasts of all kinds flowed forth from the forest like a waterfall.

"Quickly! They won't stop for us," Yetsye's authority rang out. "This is deep fear! I've never felt anything like it from our animals before." She drew her mana behind a stand of trees, tightened down her pack, and quickly hopped on. It took little effort to urge her friend to follow the fleeing animals. Ya'el and Yuvahl followed close behind her, the extra mana drawn by its reins.

Yuvahl yelled over the stampede. "It's a good thing you read the signs!"

Yetsye waved her reply but kept her attention on the surrounding area. If she'd been any slower, their mana would've scattered with their wild kin. Fleet and vigorous, their paws hit the ground softly and left little trace even when on the move. Their supplies would've disappeared, too. Yetsye kept scanning. What was out there?

In moments, the threat burst out of the trees, the largest bush'ka Yetsye had ever seen. Bush'ka were shy creatures. Yetsye once waited all dawning to catch just a glimpse of one in the wood closest to home.

Standing tall and broad, her blue-green crown rose twenty arm-lengths into the air. Her barrel-shaped body heaved in distress and her enormous eyes rolled around in their sockets, frantically seeking escape. Then another unexpected event crashed upon them as the bush'ka howled her rage to all with ears to hear.

"Pain! Paaaaiiinnn! Pa-in!" she trumpeted from her silvery blue muzzle. Yetsye understood and observed carefully as her mana raced away. The bush'ka shook, twitched, and bucked. Her thick legs pounded off to the left into the forest, desperate for relief.

Yetsye urged her mount to turn around. An animal in pain could always call her a friend. It took three attempts, but finally the mana turned and reluctantly followed the bush'ka. They might be bulky and built like boulders, but a bush'ka's favorite food was the nectar of delicate tseta flowers. Yetsye remembered passing some blooms a short distance from their last stop. If she could find a way to attract the bush'ka to the flowers, the animal would calm long enough for her to find the problem and perhaps lend a hand. Belatedly, she hoped her siblings noticed where she'd gone. There was no time to check.

With much cooing and urging in the mana's silky ear, Yetsye guided him back to the campsite. "Ah!" She loosed a cry of victory at the sight of the tseta. She headed toward the bright blossoms and then stopped. It would be much easier to draw the bush'ka to the flowers and treat her there while she ate. Whistling loudly in a short, sharp flurry of notes too quick for most ears to follow, she achieved her goal. The bush'ka's lumbering gallop slowed as it turned toward Yetsye's call. It took little urging to steer her mount toward the tseta-twined tree. It was harder to stop him but Yetsye managed it and together they waited, she patiently, and her mount tensed to run at a moment's notice.

Closer and closer the bush'ka came, but her gait slowed when she sniffed the sweet scent emanating from the pink blooms. "Ah! Now." Yetsye quickly scanned the beast for the trouble. Silky strands of fur under her left hip held a thorny branch captive. She looked behind her and sure as the two suns' cycling, her siblings were there. She motioned to Yuvahl and urged Ya'el to retreat with the mana. He was allergic to tseta pollen, but he was the only one calm enough to help.

Yuvahl came forward wrapping a cloth around his mouth and nose, careful to stay downwind, and waited while Yetsye made her way to the bush'ka's head. She clambered up the tree it feasted from so she could speak into its tiny ears and look into its large golden eyes. The bush'ka had to focus on her or they'd never be able to remove the prickly sapling.

She reached the top and extended her hands slowly. The giant, soft nose passed over her open palms and rested there for a moment. The golden eyes shifted focus long enough to find out about the being in the tree before her. Yetsye spoke to her in low murmurs and the beast visibly relaxed.

Soon Yetsye climbed down and motioned for Yuvahl to join her. Together, they disentangled the tormentor from the bush'ka's underbelly. It was heavier than she thought. The fur had camouflaged its size. The knowledge that the tseta feast wouldn't last long added to Yetsye's frustration. Yuvahl took a deep, slow breath as the last strand of silky hair came free from the branch. Yetsye and Yuvahl slowly backed away from the bush'ka as she finished the last few blooms.

Before she lumbered off, she turned briefly and nuzzled her rescuers, almost knocking them off their feet in her appreciation. She rumbled and snuffed rhythmically, "Thank you! Thank you!" In return, Yetsye rumbled back courteous replies, punctuated with relieved laughter.

It had been such a long time since Yuvahl helped her with troubled beasts. He was part of the reason she started down that path. She'd always loved them, but when she realized she had a special gift, she determined to do more for them. Yuvahl headed toward Ya'el's hiding place. Yetsye smiled at his back as she trotted happily behind him.

"Thanks, Yuvahl. I wasn't sure you'd notice me peeling away, but I'm glad you did."

He stopped and turned slowly. "Did you fall on your head, Yetsye?" His brows made a deep "v" and his faded green eyes darkened. Her jubilation turned to dismay at the unexpected scolding. He ticked off points on his fingers as he continued. "You didn't count the cost. If you mishandled this, if you weren't in time, if there was even a small miscalculation, you could've been killed."

He grabbed her by the shoulders, forcing her to look him in the eye. Even then, he had to grab her chin, for she was determined he would not see her tears. "I'm sorry to make you cry. But you have got to think ahead. Even a little forethought could go a long way to saving a life. Do you understand my meaning?" She nodded once, but couldn't bring herself to apologize. As soon as the knot in her throat dissolved, she would. He couldn't have known that she had thought things through. She was only sorry she had no words or time to convey that message to them.

The mana stood alert, several strides away. Yuvahl rested an arm around her shoulders and pulled her toward them. She dragged her feet and shuddered. Tears burned hot tracks down her freckled cheeks.

"I'm sorry, Batir, but I couldn't help thinking of the bush'ka's pain." She gave him a wobbly smile, but straightened her shoulders with determination. "I'm certain this gift has something to do with my purpose." Azilet'zal gave her the ability to understand beasts for a reason, surely. "And I know you won't understand, but I did think it through. Really, I did."

Ya'el emerged from the bushes followed by their mounts. She gazed at Yetsye in amazement, for once truly stupefied. Her mouth opened to speak, then closed. She tried again. Still, no words emerged. Puzzled, she simply walked to her siblings, and the three hugged each other tightly, just breathing and shaking with relief. Yetsye tripped over her words in her eagerness to apologize and share the spin of the adventure. She couldn't calm down at all.

They prepared their mounts for camp. "That glade over there will do," Yuvahl announced, waving to his left.

Yetsye followed his finger and scanned the glade for trouble. When a large animal stampeded, there were bound to be casualties in the wake. Scavengers and predators would come, for free food was a rare gift. Closing her eyes, she tried sifting through the atmosphere for hints of killing intent.

Yetsye opened her eyes when she didn't find any and spotted something out of place. Was that a flash of color? It didn't fit with the surroundings. She wandered over to check it out.

"What is it, Yetsye?" Ya'el regained her voice.

"I'm not sure." She crept closer. Her siblings followed. As they neared the spot, curiosity gave way to dread and then to dismay. She jumped back, slamming into Yuvahl's broad chest. He steadied her.

"An arm!" Ya'el exclaimed as she hurried to the shrubs. Boundaries had little meaning to her. Every human was interesting. Quickly parting the bushes, she revealed the form of a young D'Koruyin brave lying beneath them. An obvious injury left his face pale. His long black braids trailed off to one side and his arms sprawled to either side of his head as if taken by surprise from behind. He was well-muscled, though thin. Crimson spattered his hide vest on one side. Beaded leather bracers at his wrists flashed white with glints of green, purple and orange as the suns' light hit them. Those had drawn Yetsye's attention.

Yetsye turned off her clamoring emotions even as the color drained from her cheeks. Her walls against humanity stood firmly in place once more.

Yuvahl stepped forward at Ya'el's beckoning hands, jolting Yetsye from her petrified state. "Yetsye!" She started again at the sound of Ya'el's exasperation. "Please go find some saghitan leaves. This man needs our help!"

Yetsye nodded. She was more than happy to go find the leaves if it meant she didn't have to talk to a stranger. It didn't stop her wondering, though. Why was a D'Koruyin in M'Neshunnayan Territory? Did the bush'ka harm him or was it something else? Was there more danger nearby? Would it harm them, too? This man was a total stranger and a warrior from the look of his weapons. He slept now, but what would happen when he woke?

Her mind kept as busy as her eyes, which sifted through the many ground plants for the diamond-shaped saghitan leaves. The sooner he recovered, the sooner he could be on his way and they could resume their journey. It was ungracious of her, she knew. She prayed Azilet'zal would strengthen her and pined for the dawning when she could easily speak to others.

Sighing, she lifted her eyes to the canopy above. A flut'ra crossed her path, its translucent red and yellow wings fluttering madly in its desire to find the tseta blooms she could smell but not see. It flitted around her head three times before bobbling off deeper into the forest. Yetsye almost followed it. The thought of returning to the camp and facing the stranger set off flut'ras in her stomach. She frowned and continued searching for the leaves, finding them not thirty paces further down the animal track. Carefully harvesting them as only a M'Neshunnayan could, she soon filled the hem of her tunic. Surely that would suffice.

Yetsye's feet pounded into the camp to find food warming over a welcoming fire. She placed the leaves in the stone bowl Yuvahl held out to her and stood for a moment, catching her breath. She looked toward her siveh and the D'Koruyin warrior who reclined on Ya'el's pallet. Ya'el used a moistened cloth to cool his face. His vest was gone, revealing an intricate tattoo.

For a moment, Yetsye lost her fears in the fascinating design. The swirling lines connected all manner of beasts and plants. At the center, a majestic el'tekh spread its wings high, its claws outstretched. Its piercing, golden eye radiated wisdom and knowledge beyond her learning. Time and place didn't matter anymore.

When she finally regained her senses, she stood beside the pallet. Ya'el stared up at her in amazement. She risked a glance at the warrior's face to find icy blue eyes as fierce as the golden one on his chest gazing up at her. Frightened more by her own actions than that gaze, she retreated to Yuvahl and the fire. It was going to be a long dusking.

5

Tsa'gra

Yetsye woke to the rhythm of low voices speaking. The unfamiliar rumble meant the stranger was well enough to talk. She kept still, careful not to betray herself. And though it was rude, she listened.

"...a pilgrimage." The first clear words were Yuvahl's.

"Yes. Now that Yetsye has seen fourteen tsimikin, it's time for her to receive her Visioning. We're traveling with her to the temple in the plains of Levanna. Do you have a similar ritual in the D'Koruyin Clan?" That was Ya'el. Even if the clear feminine tones weren't there, Yetsye would know it was her from the rapid flow of words.

"Ours is a mental and spiritual journey we may experience at anytime." The warrior spoke in flawless Shunya! Yetsye couldn't believe it. There was always a bit of trouble among vendors and customers on trade days because it was hard to decipher the accents, even when everyone spoke Genra. She thought every clan taught their younglings two languages only, their own and the common tongue. How had this stranger mastered theirs? Fear held her tongue hostage, but it couldn't dampen Yetsye's curiosity.

"How interesting! Please spin more of your tale for us," She heard the swish of fabric. Ya'el probably. She could hardly keep from dancing when something new crossed her path. "We never hear anything about how the other clans live. It's a topic I've always wanted to study. Please tell us more."

The warrior tried to move, but grunted. He wasn't doing as well as she thought.

Her siveh hastily apologized. "I'm sorry! I didn't mean to press you. These things are new and exciting to me." Ya'el's clothes rustled as she retreated.

Yetsye's stomach growled at the scent of mash cooking over the fire. Betrayed by her own need for food, she rose slowly from her pallet. While avoiding eye contact, she signaled the others with a brief nod and headed away toward the sound of a stream.

A small pool nestled on one side of the running water, bordered by smooth stones. She knelt and covered her face with her hands. Three shaky breaths ended in sighs and she lifted up a prayer for strength. Any confidence she gained from helping the bush'ka seemed worthless in the face of her hasty retreat.

She frowned and reached her hands toward the fresh, cool water. Splashing her face again and again never failed to energize her. What it couldn't do was wash away irrational fears, no matter how much she wished for it. The man obviously meant no harm.

Yetsye dried her face with the hem of her tunic and released her hair to comb it out. Thank goodness she always carried her pik'teh in her belt pouch! She tugged it through the thick mass of curls and began the painstaking task of taming it once again. When she was done, she checked her reflection. Another person reflected behind her and she jumped to her feet.

Her breathing kept pace with her pounding heart. Fear rooted her to the spot. She tried a calming method her fatir taught her long ago, a manner of conscious breathing in which one focuses on the simple task of taking in air and releasing it again steadily.

After a few moments of complete silence, she found she could move again and turned slowly. He was still there. She could see his feet wrapped in soft hide boots, the hems of his pants and the fringed end of his beaded loincloth. She wanted to look up, but this was her limit.

"I am sorry." His voice was surprisingly low and gentle, as if he knew he was the reason for her fear. How? How could this out-clanner know what remained a mystery to her own villagers? He turned and limped back toward the camp. She looked up then and watched him fade into the leaves. She glanced around. Ya'el popped out from behind a tree and followed her patient back to the fire. A twitch betrayed Yuvahl's position to her right. She frowned again and stalked toward him. He stepped out to meet her.

"Why?" she hissed, seething, hands balled into fists at her sides. He was used to her moods and understood her anger. Their betrayal hurt and she recognized it in her tone. He couldn't have mistaken her if he wanted to.

"I'm sorry, kitling," he blurted and reached out a hand to grasp hers. He lowered himself in front of her, placing gentle hands on her cheeks since she refused to look at him. "I didn't realize he was following you until it was too late." Regret darkened his eyes as he shook his head. "I don't believe he'd harm anyone without a reason or I would've made the noise of the cataclysm to warn you. We took a chance." Her frown faded, and she bobbed her head once.

Yetsye glanced quizzically at him. "How do you know he's not dangerous?" He stood and looked away. She tugged on his sleeve persistently.

"Alright, alright," He swiped at her hands to stop her. "I'll tell you all I know." His grin softened the lines of his face. "His name's Tsadok Akal'a. He says Azilet'zal sent him this way on a quest. His fatir is Zev Zared." Yetsye's jaw dropped to hear they were in the presence of the D'Koruyin Chieftain's kin. Yuvahl nodded and continued. "Using his own words, he's 'disgraced his pareh' and this was a way to earn honor and gain Zev's favor. He also spoke of his Dremsha. It sounds a lot like our Visioning."

Yuvahl stepped over the stream. He knelt and splashed his face, washing away the dust of yesterdawn's travel and the grogginess of sleep. Then he added, "When he spoke the word 'honor', his eyes hardened with determination."

He rose from the stream bank, and they started back to camp. "The man's a truth-speaker, Yetsye. And loyal." He stopped her for a moment and placed his hands on her cheeks again to be sure he had her full attention. "We. Can. Trust. Him. He says his quest lies with us."

She needed that reassurance from Yuvahl. Still, she couldn't help dropping her jaw in dismay when he continued. "Ya'el and I believe it would be a good thing with all that's happening now. An extra pair of hands, eyes, and ears would help. We wanted to let you know before we set out again, so you could prepare yourself." She sighed, knowing she'd have to get used to this new person. But Yuvahl's judgment was sound.

"I'll do my best. I can't promise more than that." Yetsye let out a slow breath. Yuvahl released her and they continued walking.

"He never said why he was a disgrace, though." Yuvahl broke the silence when they were halfway to camp. "That's a puzzle. I can't understand why a fatir would do so, unless it was something unforgivable." They stepped over a fallen sapling and continued toward the orange-red flicker they could now see through the shrubs. "Wouldn't it be better to simply talk out the problem and seek a favorable solution? Perhaps that's one of the differences between our clans."

Yetsye kept her eyes down once they entered the camp. She filled a bowl with mash and sat next to her mana for comfort. To calm herself, she whispered to the creature in between bites. She felt eyes on her and wasn't sure what to do. There was strength in that gaze. What a formidable person he must be!

Yuvahl was right. Why would this man's fatir think him deficient in any way? He earned her siblings' trust so quickly, and Yuvahl was no fool. It was harder to tell with Ya'el. She somehow reserved trust while making others feel welcome and understood.

Thoughts of her must have drawn Ya'el to Yetsye's side, for she soon sat beside her. "I was so preoccupied with Tsadok's wounds, I didn't give yours much thought."

Yetsye kept her eyes on her bowl, but she murmured, "It's alright. I checked my hands carefully and cleansed them with water. I also rubbed a bit of the saghitan juice on them. The scratches still show, but they're healing." She set her bowl down as Ya'el pointed to her left hand. She would check both of them because she was infuriatingly meticulous in healing. It's what made Ya'el so good at it.

"See?" Yetsye was ready to finish the cooling mash. It tasted much better while it was still warm and creamy.

Ya'el grunted and with a quick nod, she released Yetsye's hands and allowed her to finish her meal. "You know, we didn't realize."

"I know." She mumbled between bites. "Yuvahl told me."

"Yes, but I need to offer my own apology." She bowed her head in sincere regret.

"All will be well. I don't hold it against either of you." The words sounded braver than she felt. She set her empty bowl on the ground once more and wrapped an arm around Ya'el's shoulders. "I'm sorry you have to bear so much on my account. I'll work hard to overcome my fears. If he's earned the favor of my kin, I can hardly do the opposite."

Ya'el's eyebrows lifted in surprise, and her lips parted in a crooked smile. These were all the warning Yetsye received. "Well, well! Our little tsa'gra kit is growing!" She didn't bother to lower her voice and Yetsye heard a stirring behind her. Her focus remained on her siveh, unsmiling. Ya'el chuckled and tapped Yetsye's back. "I'm sorry. I couldn't help it. That's the bravest statement I think I've heard from you. I couldn't let you get cocky." Ya'el winked and rose from her patch of earth to break camp. Yetsye swatted playfully at her as she donned a crooked grin.

"One dawning, Ya'el. One dawning..." she trailed off.

"One dawning what, kitling?" Her siveh's feral grin challenged her.

"One dawning, someone will have your tongue for the words you speak too easily. I hope I'm not there to see it. Makes me shudder to think of it!"

"Ah! So you'd leave me to the likes of an enemy?"

"Yep." She'd exchanged the grin for something a bit more solemn. "Whoever tries, they may win. I wouldn't want to see it."

"I can't believe you, Yetsye! Yuvahl, can you believe the audacity of this kitling?" She gestured wildly at Yetsye and looked toward Yuvahl.

Yetsye couldn't hold a straight face any longer and a wide grin broke through. "I wouldn't want to see them get stomped in the mire of their own making!" She laughed. "No one could be victorious over you in a battle of words, Siveh!"

As she laughed, she saw Yuvahl's broad grin and felt her heart swell with his approval. She was so bad at joking. This, too, had been a significant risk for her. One misstep and her siveh, though knowing her well, made her feel two hesps tall. Then, she wouldn't have spoken to her for dawnings.

Lost in her thoughts, she forgot to be careful where she looked and her treacherous gaze landed on the D'Koruyin. He focused all his attention on his bowl of mash. But somehow she knew he understood the exchange and found it amusing. Then, as if he sensed it, he met her eyes boldly. She turned away and finished her mash.

After breaking their fast the next dawning, Ya'el tended Tsadok's wounds. The D'Koruyin stowed his gear in the pack he slung across his body. "Minimal effort with maximum result," Yetsye mumbled as she observed.

The D'Koruyin were a nomadic people, known for their efficiency. Where the herds went, they followed. It intrigued her, but she was far too uneasy with most humans to ask questions. She'd leave that to Ya'el and just listen to the resulting conversation. Yetsye finished loading her gear and joined the others as they returned the campsite to its natural state before resuming their journey.

If she thought conversation would be constant, Yetsye was mistaken. It wasn't because Ya'el didn't try. Rather, the D'Koruyin seemed to be lost in thought. Yetsye could see him clearly, for he rode in front on the spare mana after they'd shared out all the gear. His eyes constantly scanned the sky-dome and the tree-line. Alert might be too mild a word for how aware he was. In a way, the quiet ride through the woods with the stranger ahead of her pleased Yetsye. It was almost like he understood her need for space. But how was that possible?

They continued in silence a long while before Tsadok raised his right arm and loosed a high keening cry. Yetsye yelped and covered her ears until Ya'el tapped her shoulder. A reply sped down out of the sky-dome, followed by a growing black speck. The speck became a majestic el'tekh which alighted on Tsadok's outstretched arm. He clicked at the flier and she clicked back. He clicked again and raised his arm to help her lift off once more into the air.

Then Tsadok did something even more amazing. He bent over his mana... who stopped! The other mana followed the example of the leader. Two breaths passed and Yetsye heard what her thoughts had drowned out, complete and utter silence. Such was not the normal silence of a lively home, but the eerie silence of a forest warning. The air reeked of menace. Tsadok dismounted, closed his eyes and cocked his head to one side. He crouched and touched the ground, eyes still closed.

Yetsye realized she could help. She spoke quickly and softly to her mana. A light snuffle and a couple of clicks told her what she needed to know and what to do. Softly and gently, she motioned the others to quietly and smoothly resume their ride. Tsadok led his mount.

Any sudden motion when invading tsa'gra territory meant instant retaliation. And they were indeed being watched. As they walked their mounts, Yetsye sang using elongated syllables, more sounds than human words.

"*Shraaatze prrraawww.*
Shraaatze prrraawww.
Tsik sharr zet na prrraawww.
Tsik na prrraawww tsrrr grrraaa tze naaaa.
Tsik sharr zet na prrraawww."

She sang it over and over again as they walked. After the second hearing, her siblings joined her in the song. Slow and steady, the tempo was enough to almost put her to sleep, but they made it through without trouble.

Truly, she would have to be more aware. Yetsye had gifts she should use to help those who were kind enough to help her. She couldn't do that if she allowed fear to cloud her vision. Resolving to do better from this point on, she tried thinking of Tsadok as her batir. Maybe that would ease her interaction with him. He hadn't hurt her or her siblings. He was helping them and he wasn't even of their clan. Though he was still healing, with this latest warning, he'd proven himself to be reliable, too.

"I can do this," she mumbled to herself repeatedly. "Surely I can do this. I must." It helped that he seemed to speak to the beasts. She wanted to know more about his abilities.

Yetsye forced herself to look directly at Tsadok. He still faced forward, focused on guiding his mount. She watched as long as she dared, a frown of intensity decorating her brow like a knotted coronet of vines. She almost gave herself a headache with the effort and decided scanning the surrounding forest wouldn't be as hard on her. As they traveled, she cooed sweet words of thanks to her mana friend and offered up silent prayers of thanks to Azilet'zal. Yes, she would definitely defeat this fear. Maybe Tsadok was a helper from Azilet'zal. Maybe.

6

Descent

The suns rose eight times since leaving home. Making and breaking camp got easier every dawning. Tsadok's nomadic life gave him skills she and her siblings didn't have. How had they never learned the things Tsadok taught them? Yuvahl and Ya'el accepted him eagerly, but Yetsye's mind kept her from doing the same. After sharing with her siblings that first dusking, Tsadok said no more about his home. Yetsye sighed as Ya'el pelted him with questions. He was never rude. He simply declined to answer. She made a mental list of his attributes and listed patience at the top.

After his initial apology to her, Tsadok never looked directly at her. He remained alert to their surroundings, making sure they had time to prepare for danger. But he never faced Yetsye and made no sudden moves around her. His care stirred her curiosity, and she studied him when she thought he wasn't looking. He must be a kind person, too. She added it to her list.

The travelers made good progress, reaching Lake Mir'ir in nine dawnings and Hwish'keh Falls on the south shore in five more. Yetsye spoke to her mana when Yuvahl called a halt. She relieved the beast of his burden and set up her pallet. Then, she motioned to Ya'el to say she was going off alone, promising to stay close. Without waiting for a reply, she took a trail leading away from the river. She glanced over her shoulder one last time to see Tsadok look at Yuvahl.

His answer chased after her, fading a little more with each step. "She does that. It's normal for her, but I've never seen anyone else do it. She says emotions build up and overwhelm her. Going off alone to meditate helps. She calls it 'being embraced in the arms of Y'Dahnndrya.'" How could he tell what Tsadok was thinking? She faintly heard the wry chuckle that followed. "If she isn't able to get away, she exhausts easily. The way she describes it makes me jealous."

Yuvahl wasn't in the habit of baring his feelings. His admission of jealousy meant Yetsye needed to redefine her image of him. Pausing just a moment, she peered back through the trees. Ya'el looked up from cooking. A flash of white revealed her smile as her mouth moved. Yuvahl shot her a playful hand-sign, then laughed and patted Ya'el's head roughly. Why couldn't she be more like them?

She took another step but stopped when she heard Tsadok's low rumble. She strained to catch the words. "You are truly honored by Azilet'zal for such a strong bond to exist between you."

Ya'el's voice revealed her surprise. "Isn't this kind of thing normal for families?"

Yetsye's hike had taken her far enough now that her siveh's question was the last thing she heard. She set her mind back on the task at hand. If she didn't take this opportunity, who knew when there would be another? She desperately needed to feel the earth cradling her once again. Besides, she probably shouldn't be listening in.

Twigs and old leaves crunched as her feet carried her deeper into the verdant cover. The woodland sounds drifted to her through the swaying branches, singing her on her way.

Yetsye easily found the perfect spot, a swirling eddy filled with purple, blue-black, and gray stones rounded by rushing water. The rippling stream lapped a pleasant rhythm, and she breathed deep of the forest air. A soft, springy patch of mazh under the chi'cha trees proved a perfect bed. Now she could look up from under the long whip-like branches swaying gently in the light breeze. Scents of heady tseta and spicy jinj hovered in the air and tickled her nose. She sneezed and giggled.

Golden rays pushed through the canopy and danced around the water's edge. She watched as they shot sparks off the glassy wings of dyr'kunfi. The insect hunters zipped, hovered, and twirled in the air around her, hunting tiny met'cha. The soft drone layered beautifully over the water music. High above the chi'cha, chippits nesting in the highest kho'ni branches sang the two suns to sleep.

As Yetsye lay on her spongy, blue-green bed, she inhaled once more the scent of earth and plant and beast. She exhaled slowly, closed her eyes, and opened her other senses to receive the bounty of Y'Dahnndrya. Her nose painted mind pictures of tart, yellow dozhi, Matir's favorite. Liilum reminded her of Matir's beautiful spirit, clean, crisp, and fresh. The clicking and buzzing of the insects crescendoed as she sank deeper into Y'Dahnndrya's embrace. Her mind filled with their glittering mid-air dance.

Suddenly, the scent of leather and raw wood invaded her sanctuary. She frowned. Before she could ponder the intruder's identity, the fur and feathers of an edjig brushed against her, diverting her attention. Without opening her eyes, she raised her hand to scratch behind its long, silky ears. The soft growl of pleasure erased her frown and drew out a smile instead. She growled softly in reply and the edjig moved on to its dusking nest, its many legs tripping lightly through the underbrush.

A cooler rush of air urged her to return. The light faded fast once the suns hung so low. She would have to run. Still, she sat up slowly, reluctant to return to the discomfort of camp. "Oh, well," she thought, rising, "I can only keep going, may Azilet'zal help me!"

She turned to head back and found herself facing Tsadok's back. She gasped and hurried after him, the fire of her anger consuming her fears. Why hadn't her siblings stopped him?

When she burst out of the tree-line and into camp, she stalked straight to Ya'el. The frantic signing motions she chose when words wouldn't come declared her displeasure.

"We didn't!" Ya'el grabbed for her hands, trying to calm her. She pulled away, so Ya'el trapped her face between delicate hands and forced Yetsye to face her. The younger maid stopped fighting and gasped for breath as she listened to Ya'el's words. "He insisted and promised you'd never know he was there. It was his own idea and a simple precaution. I think he'd do that for any of us. And I thought it was a good idea."

"I am sorry." The low voice behind her startled her so violently, she clung to her siveh, hiding her face in Ya'el's shoulder. She shook and hated her weakness and fear and her inability to do anything about either unless her anger blinded her. Soft footsteps retreated slowly. She tilted her head just enough to look at him through one slitted eye. The flash of sorrow in his own filled her heart with regret. It was gone so quickly, though, she might have imagined it. He bowed and sat beside the fire. Yetsye felt Ya'el's apologetic shrug.

"He's not the only one who's sorry, Siveh," she whispered as she wrinkled Ya'el's blouse in her fists. Only then did her hot tears flow.

Heavy emotions always took their toll, and Yetsye's head ached. Ya'el prepared a beaker of strong bil'ti tea for her. She finished it as quickly as possible. The bitter brew worked fast. She was the first to fall asleep under the sparkling stars.

The next dawning, Yetsye woke early enough to witness the rising of Tsifi'Ra and Mit'Ra. The path beside the falls awaited them, offering the reward of rest and refreshment at the bottom. From there, the trail eased into hilly grassland.

They ate a leisurely meal of mash, dried berries, and nuts, then set to work. Each of the travelers pulled lengths of rope from their packs. This stretch of the path was steep and slippery, increasing the risk to the mana and supplies. The faithful beasts would have an easier descent without the added weight.

Ya'el handed Tsadok an extra length to tie the supply sacks together in a long strand. He set the line of sacks close to the trailhead. Yetsye couldn't face him yet. Yesterdawn's scare was too fresh. She stayed busy rolling her blanket and tying it to her pack. Then, she set it near the others and steadied her mind for the grueling hike down the cliff.

"Yetsye!" Yuvahl shouted from the remains of the fire. "Let's go!"

Yetsye obeyed happily. She flung her pack onto her shoulders and spoke to the lead beast. Together, they stepped off into magnificence. The view from the top of the falls stole Yetsye's breath and a lone tear made its way down her cheek. She shook her head. The trail required intense focus and there was no time to marvel.

The mana led the way, placing each taloned paw solidly onto the path before lifting the next. Yetsye did her best to mimic them. The mana needed constant encouragement and Yetsye's chest swelled with the pride of being useful.

Once, Yetsye smelled smoke on the breeze. It wafted away as quickly as it came, but to catch the scent in this location could only mean one thing. When they turned the next sharp curve, Yetsye spotted the garish glow pulsing under black smoke in the distance. They were only half-way to the bottom. She turned to warn the others and lost her footing.

7

Entrance

Time slowed to a crawl as fear stole her voice, and the sky-dome exchanged places with the cliff. Her wrist burned, grasped by a fist of stone which pulled her to safety. An equally solid arm held her against the cliff face as she gulped air into suddenly deprived lungs. The faint tang of leather and wood told her clearly who saved her. How had she been unaware of his presence behind her?

"Thank you," she gasped, hoping he could hear her over the falls, hoping the words might erase her earlier rudeness. He was D'Koruyin, yes. But he was also Y'Dahnndryan. His large hand briefly patted her back. He heard.

Closing her eyes against the spray, she tried again to warn the others. "There's fire! We have to hurry," she yelled.

Speeding up seemed impossible. The few times they could move faster balanced with treacherous places which slowed them again. The acrid scent of burning trees grew stronger with each step. Three turns more, and they'd reach the ground. They passed through several layers of smoke and suddenly the milling beasts could be heard below. Flyers and earthbound, big and small, all gathered at the vast pool below the falls. A family of el'tekh circled above, screeching a warning to all beings. "Fire! Fire!"

Yetsye reached the bottom without further mishap. She looked up to see Yuvahl motion toward the water, then headed immediately for safety. The beasts rushed around her. All were in the same danger and worked together to save each other. Chippits, who couldn't fly through the thick smoke, snagged their claws in the shaggy fur of the wild mana and bush'ka who swam down and to the far side of the river.

A tsa'gra kit sent out its loud, mewling cry. The sire and dam returned the call, but were too far away. In the confusion of bodies and legs, it was impossible for the kit to tell where to go. Yetsye weaved her way to the tiny creature and was almost crushed by a tramping bush'ka. She rolled to the right just in time and restored the kit to her family. For a moment, Yetsye watched as they sprung into the water and swam across.

"Yetsye!" Yuvahl's call spurred her to action again. Fierce fists of heat would knock them over soon. Before she could reach Yuvahl, she spotted a confused bush'ka heading in the wrong direction. She motioned to her batir, and he set her mana to face the same way. She mounted at a run to catch up to the bewildered beast. Once they were beside it, Yetsye bent to her mana's ear. She rose again and, grasping the silky hair of the bush'ka's forelegs, climbed up on its back. Scaling the prominent neck ridges proved easier than she expected. When she neared its ears, she sang soothing, rhythmic tones and the bush'ka slowed. Yetsye motioned to her siblings to go ahead without her, hoping they could see. She'd cross the pool with the bush'ka. A tree crashed behind them. The bush'ka spotted the cool water and broke into a lumbering gait. It splashed into the water and its momentum carried them farther into safety. The frigid pool contrasted so much with the intense heat, Yetsye fought for breath. Waves pushed against her, but she hung on to the bush'ka's backward curving horns.

Finally, they reached the safety of the opposite shore. Her eyes burned and watered, and her nose stung, but Yetsye exchanged thanks with the grateful bush'ka who kept nuzzling her. She grinned, then laughed in relief. Feeling eyes on her, Yetsye glanced around, thinking it was Yuvahl. Her gaze met Tsadok's instead. That piercing, steady gaze caused heat to flood her neck and cheeks. She turned away.

The survivors headed away from the forest fire en masse, following the path of the suns. Animals peeled off from the motley herd, little by little, and within moments, the humans were the only ones on the dirt path. Exhaustion was too mild a word for them, but camping was out of the question. Yetsye knew the wild blud'igs wouldn't go far. Sleeping travelers were too great a temptation for predators, and no one was fit to keep watch right now.

Yetsye motioned to Ya'el, who rode beside her. "Why don't you and Tsadok ride and sleep?"

"That's so tempting." She barked the suggestion to Yuvahl, who was in the lead. He nodded, too tired to speak. They paused only long enough to graze the mana and gather the rope necessary to keep the sleepers astride their mounts. Yetsye jerked herself awake just as Yuvahl urged her to keep working. Fighting stiff muscles, she loaded two packs onto the mana closest to her, then helped the others tie the beasts together with more rope. At least if they all fell asleep, the mana wouldn't wander. She and Yuvahl tied Ya'el and Tsadok to their mana with the rope that remained. Yuvahl took the lead mana's reins in hand and set out again. Yetsye walked beside Ya'el's mount.

When she was sure Tsadok was asleep, Yetsye spoke up. "I'm sorry I'm more of a hindrance than a help. This fear of mine is crippling, I know. I'm working on it." She paused, then added, "I just wanted you to know."

"I know." Yuvahl glanced back at her and nodded. And then they walked. And walked. And walked some more.

After what seemed like a lifetime, Yetsye's stumbling feet jerked her awake for the second time. She regained her balance and looked ahead to see Yuvahl trip over flat ground. It was time to switch.

She pleaded, "Please let's stop, Yuvahl. You can barely stand upright. How will you get us there safely?" He doggedly continued, ignoring her. "Let Ya'el lead for a time. Your pride in a job well done means nothing if you lead us astray because you're exhausted."

That last struck a nerve. He pulled the mana to a halt and turned to glare at her through glassy eyes. He set his jaw as if to argue, but nodded and woke Tsadok. Yetsye woke Ya'el. They shared out a few rations. Finishing that, and with Yetsye and Yuvahl tied on the rested mounts, they continued on. Rhythmic footfalls lulled Yetsye to sweet oblivion.

Yetsye sprung up. The fire beside her pallet licked at small twigs as it warmed her face. Yuvahl walked back into camp with his arms full of firewood. He squatted and fed the greedy flamelets until the fire was ready for cooking. Ya'el rummaged through the food stores. Tsadok was gone. Yetsye took the opportunity to relax and stretch her tense muscles.

"Where are we? And how long did I sleep?" she asked, punctuating the last word with a gaping yawn. She rose slowly, easing her sore body into the dawning.

"We're within three dawnings ride of Levanna Stone Temple." Yuvahl stood up beside his pallet, eager to get moving again. "We'll eat and continue the journey. Quickly now!" He waved at Yetsye. "This place may be safe for the moment, but there are always dangers."

They packed silently. Rhythmic vibrations announced Tsadok's return before he strode into camp, the lifeless body of a long-tailed sich'ik dangling at his hip. It was big enough for the four of them to share. Yetsye stifled the shudder she felt at the thought of the once lively sich'ik cavorting through the treetops with its den mates. The energy the meat would provide was necessary, though. She wondered if D'Koruyin had laws about killing beasts. Maybe Ya'el would ask later. She was still too uncertain of him to pose questions directly.

Warm mash and fresh meat filled and refreshed them. After they cleared the campsite, the westward journey continued. At the time of high suns, the path shifted slightly to the south. The suns would guide them for two more dawnings. A small stream rippled near the trail for a time. The flowing water brimmed with delights, bringing out Yetsye's smile. Blue and green min'gif scales reflected painfully in the bright light as they burst from the surface to snap at the flashing gold streaks zinging above. Her senses feasted on the varied buffet as her smile widened with each discovery. Here was life, displayed in fine form before her. She relaxed as Y'Dahnndrya unfolded wonder after wonder.

Rolling hills gave way to the vast plain of Levanna. To the south-west, mounds rose on the horizon. The Gate Stones! Yetsye's excitement grew the closer they got to the temple. The mana sensed the end of the long journey, perked up their ears, and tapped their talon-tipped toes in a joyous cadence. A patchwork of cobblestones paved a brilliant path of rich blue, gold, crimson, yellow-orange, green, and violet from the monoliths that marked the gate to the main temple. Rounded boulders lay haphazard on either side of the line of road, most the size of a mana. However, a few towered taller than her home.

By the time the suns kissed the horizon, the party reached the main complex. "Tani Zhil'la!" exclaimed Yetsye as she dismounted. Shira's youngest siveh was Guardian here. Zhil'la Rayasdatir met them with arms outstretched. When she encountered Tsadok's straightforward gaze, she turned to Yetsye in surprise.

Zhil'la shook her head slowly as she spoke her thoughts. "Many people come to the temple at Levanna, but all travel with members of their own clan. This is something new."

Yuvahl made the introductions, and they followed Zhil'la into a smaller building on the right. "This is our home. Rather than staying in the lodge, won't you all stay with us?" Her warm smile reminded Yetsye so much of Matir, a knot grew in her throat. She stopped the tears as Yuvahl accepted the invitation and they ascended the wooden staircase.

Yetsye hurried to settle into her room and rushed back to the courtyard. Between the stonework, windows, garden beds, and small animals, everywhere she turned, she saw something fresh. Zhil'la waved from the entrance to the main temple, urging her to hurry. When she arrived at the foot of the steps, she realized the others were already waiting. An embarrassed apology tumbled from her lips.

At the top of the stone steps, they removed their shoes and walked into an entryway. Ornate reliefs cavorted across every stone wall, spinning the story of the plants and animals of Y'Dahnndrya. Yetsye's eyes roved, never pausing for more than a moment. The simple lines and shapes outside the temple deceived the unsuspecting pilgrim.

The dining area opened up on their right, filled with long wooden tables. Yetsye settled on a bench next to Ya'el. She looked forward to her first full meal since leaving home. The kho'ni soup and bansan fruit salad tasted wonderful after trail fare.

She peeked out of the corner of her eye at Yuvahl and Tsadok. The smoke of sweet, woody jin'ya weed filled the room as they lit pipes. Found only in the plain of Levanna, jin'ya was a rare commodity. It would only grow wild, though many attempted to tame it. This pleased the M'Neshunnayans, who believed things flourished best in their most natural habitat. If Azilet'zal had wanted them elsewhere, it would've been so when the tale of Y'Dahnndrya was first spun by that Holy Voice.

Zhil'la bombarded Ya'el and Yetsye with questions about Zulima and their parents, about the quakes, and, of course, Tsadok. Yetsye blushed when Ya'el spun the tale of the poor bush'ka and the thorny sapling caught in its fur. She regaled them with the forest fire adventure next, elaborating on how Yetsye saved the lost kit and the confused bush'ka.

Zhil'la turned to Yetsye, her fine eyebrows arching almost to her silver-streaked hairline. "Your gift is even stronger than when I last saw you. Have you been practicing?" Her face radiated with family pride. To distract Zhil'la, Yetsye spun the tale of finding Tsadok.

"Ya'el immediately tended him and within a dawning, he was almost recovered. I couldn't believe how quickly he healed. After all, he was flung aside by a raging bush'ka."

Recognizing this tactic, Zhil'la gave Ya'el her due praise. "Your knowledge of healing seems to have grown too, Ya'el. I'm certain Shira is deeply honored to have such gifted younglings." Her full lips split into a smile of pure joy and she gave them the official greeting of Levanna Stone Temple.

"Welcome, Pilgrims, to the Stone Temple of Levanna Plains! May our Creator grant you solace and ease in this place. May you find a Visioning to point you on the straight way. And may you ever after follow the Creator's guidance on the path of your life journey. Welcome and well-being be unto you all!"

Later that dusking, Yetsye lay on a sleeping pad covered with a light fabric woven from the fibers of chi'cha bark and stuffed with plush dnag'ze wool. She stared up at the ceiling of gray stone veined with orange that was to be her roof for the next few duskings. Her Visioning Ceremony began on the morrowdawn. What would it be like? What would Azilet'zal reveal? She stared past the filigree windows bordering the top of the wall in her room. Starlight trickled in to tease her eyes. So much happened over the last few nainda. Who knew what more would happen when the next dawning came?

Yetsye drifted to sleep on that thought. She dreamed again, though this time the figure who visited her was shadowy, as if her vision was clouded. The figure urged her closer. She strained to see it clearly, but the more she strained, the fuzzier her vision got. So she stopped trying.

Her vision cleared, and the figure disappeared to be replaced with a magnificent aerial view of M'Neshunnaya and parts of the D'Koruyin and Shinnoahn territories. Though she was far away, she could see it all clearly, as if she had the eyes of an el'tekh, hunting prey far below. A wing flashed into view and she realized she was an el'tekh. She could fly! For a moment, she reveled in the liberty of wings.

A sudden, violent motion below interrupted her wild dance through the clouds. Trees shivered as if from a blast of icy wind. The shivering turned to shuddering, and shuddering to quaking. Horrified, she couldn't tear her eyes away from the gaping holes that appeared where verdant forests once stood. At the edges, she watched boundaries blur as the land transformed. Mountains crumbled to dust and deserts bloomed with lush growth and colors so vibrant she squinted, even from her vantage point. Rivers altered their courses, and the abandoned beds filled with rocks and sand. She raced toward the suns seeking an escape, past the boundary of D'Koruyin country, over the O'Na Sea, to hover over the islands of the Ikhel'dur Clan. Some islands sank below the waves while others rose high above, becoming larger with every flap of her wings.

Yetsye fled further until she reached the territories of the Bot'ha and Genzet. The chaos was equally terrifying, and the suffering left in its wake, as heart-rending. A rift formed at the eastern side of the continent. What had once been one enormous chunk of land was now two portions violently pushing away from each other. Dread settled heavily in the pit of her stomach. She turned her head homeward to see impending doom encroaching upon the unsuspecting souls living on each land mass. There was no way to stop it, and Yetsye shrieked in pain and frustration.

Then, a spark-a tiny orange flame-flickered in M'Neshunnaya. It grew and spread. Soon, tiny orange flames spread to ignite green in D'Koruyi, burn violet in Shinnoah, set islands ablaze with red, and engulf the foreign lands in yellow and blue. Soon tiny tongues of flickering flame were all she could see. All the colors joined to turn brilliant white, burning away darkness from the face of Y'Dahnndrya.

She turned her head and once again saw her own wing. Gone were the earthy browns of the el'tekh's feathers. She was white like the flames. No! She was a flame, a soaring bird of white flame.

8

Preparation

Yetsye woke. Not the reluctant waking of a normal dawning back home, but the waking which is as sure as stone and as certain as the cycling of the suns. She sat up and wondered about the meaning of the dream. The vision was so clear and the color so pure, her eyes watered from the intense memory. She dressed quickly, donning her favorite blue tunic and the matching loose pants that allowed free range of motion. She shunned her traveling boots. The feel of cool, smooth wood beneath her feet quickened her. Nothing in this place would harm her. She lifted up prayers, splashed her face, and combed through her hair. This was a dawning of simplicity, so her hair hung unfettered. She carefully stored her things in her bag and welcomed the first dawning of her Visioning Ceremony, in this place most sacred to the M'Neshunnayan Clan.

Yetsye padded down the hall and stairs as she headed back to the dining hall. Yuvahl and Ya'el sat at a table already with Tsadok. A radiant girl stood nearby, gesturing gracefully with her hands. She seemed close to Ya'el's age and Yetsye could see the flush of excitement on her siveh's cheeks. Yetsye's footsteps faltered at the sight of yet another stranger, but she had prepared herself for this.

She sat on the wooden bench by Ya'el and bowed her head politely to the girl, though she couldn't quite meet her eyes. Black tresses, beautifully curled, and small pink lips wide with laughter caught her attention. The maiden's roomy shirt, full skirt, and fitted vest, all brightly patterned and heavily embroidered, betrayed her as Shinnoahn.

"I bid you good dawning! My name is Leila Muenbrukh. And you are?" Leila looked expectantly at Yetsye, who glanced quickly at her siveh, pinching Ya'el's tunic in a silent plea for help.

"This is my siveh, Yetsye," she smiled and gestured for Leila to join them. "She's shy of strangers and even our own villagers. There are many dawnings in which she doesn't say two words outside our home. She's pleased to meet you, though, or she would've turned 'round and run back to her room." Ya'el's throaty chuckle changed to a quickly drawn breath as Yetsye's gentle pull on her clothes became an almost vicious pinch on her thigh.

"Ah! I understand. My youngest relative is the same. It's very difficult for him, as his babei is an influential leader." The maiden's voice rang with pleasant vibrations, inviting Yetsye's trust. "I've often thought fear of saying the wrong thing held his tongue captive." Leila softly smiled.

Yetsye nodded with heartfelt sympathy. She glanced at Yuvahl and found his gaze riveted on the fair maid. Over time, she'd observed many emotions on his face, but nothing like this. She couldn't remember him ever showing much interest in the females of Zulima. He had complimented them on their skills or morals, but it always ended there.

Her thoughts returned to Leila. What did they know about her? What could they know from such a brief acquaintance? She was obviously friendly and vibrant, apparently brave and self-assured. Though this was all surface observation, Yetsye believed her batir would not be romantically interested in someone who wasn't M'Neshunnayan. He cared too much about the law for that. She looked at him again, a smile pulling at the corner of her mouth and her eyes beginning to sparkle. After a few moments, Yuvahl noticed her teasing grin and frowned. He looked away. That was an interesting response! When an assistant brought Yetsye's meal, she couldn't ask Ya'el anything more.

Since the Visioning ceremony required fasting, Zhil'la prepared a magnificent feast for the pilgrims before they began. Yetsye had trouble knowing where to start. Kho'ni leaves steamed with nuts of the same tree? Or maybe thick slices of rifi bread dotted with the rich, sweet spices of Bot'ha? There were bon'jiis from Shinnoah and sweet, warmed mana milk. The woody scent of khaf'ket wafted out of an earthenware pitcher. Roasted min'gif steaks rounded the meal out with a casserole made of chippit eggs, kart, bet'ihs and tir'peh. The Guardian carefully chose foods which would supply pilgrims with the necessary energy for the ceremony, which could last up to three dawnings.

Yetsye ate steadily, pacing herself to avoid an upset stomach. She savored her meal, eating over two hesps. She cleaned her things when she finished and took three slow, deep breaths.

It was time.

9

Visioning

"**N**o one knows when the first Visioning occurred in this place," Zhil'la answered when Yetsye had asked earlier. "M'Neshunnayans suspect it was before the Great Cataclysm, in a time long forgotten."

Yetsye now stood in the imposing shadow of the main temple. The massive stone blocks enclosing the hall drew her eyes up and up. Last night's vivid dream invaded her mind and planted a knot of apprehension in her belly. She tamped it down. It was time to stop this foolishness. Wasn't she fully grown? The time of path-choosing had come. With her resolve set and her face forward, Yetsye strode through the entrance to discover what paths Azilet'zal offered her.

The hall seemed endless until a fork prodded Yetsye to make her first decision. Left or right? She was right-handed, so she chose that path. On and on she walked. The path sloped down, and she thanked Azilet'zal for the relief. She continued on until the walls closed around her, creating a dim tunnel.

Suddenly, a vast chamber opened up before her. Water bubbled gently in the far left corner, fed by a tiny stream which flowed directly out of a natural crack in the wall. The far side of the pool disappeared into darkness. Water music and cool air currents soothed her chaotic thoughts.

Her bare feet slapped against a man-made mosaic path. Light from high above glinted off a line of brilliant orange, violet, emerald, gold, red, and dark blue tiles. Yetsye took a little time to study them.

"Oh! Beasts playing among the plants of Y'Dahnndrya," she pealed in delight. Her voice echoed in the cavern, reminding her to focus. Sparkling water beckoned, and she continued toward it. Several basins stacked beside the pool bore the mark of D'Koruyin potters. They were the only clan who crafted pottery with such intricate designs. Neatly folded towels filled carved niches above the basins.

Yetsye could go no further. Her gaze traveled up into the recesses of the natural ceiling. Deep blue sky peeked through more hand-carved windows. She knew from the spinnings of other pilgrims that Min and Dahl, the Guide Moons of Y'Dahnndrya, shone through these windows at dusking, leading path-seekers with their light.

Yetsye shook herself and prepared for the moons' arrival in the windows above. First, for the ritual bath she chose a basin carved with leaping mid'jin and plucked a small towel from the wall. Then she climbed into the pool after disrobing, surrendering herself to watery arms warmed by the heart of Y'Dahnndrya. She poured water over herself using the basin, splashed her face briskly, and submerged again. Her red-gold hair fanned out as it soaked in water like a sponge. The soft towel brushed over her skin, cleaning away every speck of grime.

As she purified her body, she purified her mind. Yetsye recalled each selfish act, every word, action, and thought against Azilet'zal's guidance in her life—and acknowledged it before that Holy Voice. Why had she taken those particular paths? Were there different ways she could've handled each? How could she improve? Aloud, she vowed, "I will make wiser choices in the future." Her voice echoed back at her, the statement becoming a mantra.

Yetsye climbed from the pool and snatched at another towel. She dried herself vigorously and continued until there was no trace of moisture. Another dry towel wrapped around her served as a dress. Once she folded her clothing and placed it in a second basin, she was ready, though that was supposed to be done before the ritual bath. She offered a prayer of apology and hoped Azilet'zal wouldn't mind her unintentional misstep.

The glow of the suns faded steadily now as she stepped into the center of the cavern. A solid ring of mazhit stone, blue shot through with shimmering green and gold flecks, marked the place. Two orange circles of strika stone were set into the center, the smaller one having slightly more yellow in it. At equidistant points just inside the ring, the ancient artisan inlaid six different colored gems. Five sentinels of gray-blue yesha stones separated the central stones from the gems. The simple map of Yetsye's universe lay before her—suns, moons, clans, and Y'Dahnndrya all bathed in heavenly light. The maiden stepped into the center and knelt, bowing over her knees. She lifted her torso and sat on folded legs, head bowed and palms pressed together. The ritual chant flowed musically from within her to fill the chamber.

"Here I wait

"Here wait I patiently

"For Azilet'zal's Voice I wait

"The Voice which speaks truthfully."

She clapped three times and continued.

"Show to me

"Reveal to this Seeker

"The path most glorious

"The way I must go."

She clapped three times again before finishing the chant.

"Show this seeker thy will for my life."

With one last clap and a low bow over her knees, Yetsye lay down on her back in the center of the ring. The windows began directly above her and stretched along the ceiling, tracing the sky-dome for ten kez. She closed her eyes and opened herself to Y'Dahnndrya and to the Creator who fashioned them both.

Deep, deep down, the depths of Y'Dahnndrya stirred. She wondered if another quake occurred. A furrow marred her forehead as she worried about her loved ones. Yetsye knew she would have to place this worry before Azilet'zal, too, for worries hindered the Visioning. Her dearest desire was to make the best use of this life. That must be her focus now.

Time passed oddly in the cavern. The rhythmic water splashing into the pool eventually called Yetsye to visit the land of sleep and dreams.

She flew high above Y'Dahnndrya again. Her keen eyes picked out every detail of life. She hovered for a moment, taking in the lively tapestry, ignoring the buffeting winds, steadily focusing on the world below.

Then she dove. Wind shrieked in her ears and skimmed her flaming white wings. The fire within engulfed all she passed over, destroying nothing. She was afraid. And she was fearless. From one corner of Y'Dahnndrya to the other, she flew, setting the tapestry ablaze. Everything kept its original form, but a form made painfully pure. One needed the strength of Azilet'zal to gaze upon it. All stood on equal footing. All of Y'Dahnndrya worked together for the sake of Y'Dahnndrya, beasts and humans alike.

Suddenly, the flames guttered and disappeared. Darkness shrouded all in a cold, inky fog. She was a bird of clacking bones, sucking the life out of all she saw, a harbinger of death. Under her sharp gaze, every living thing withered into dust which drifted away on the slightest breeze, as if their existence was only ever a dream. Y'Dahnndrya lay beneath her, a lifeless ball of rock. Dry, hard, and bitter, was she, filled only with dirt, stone, and sand. Yetsye Deathwing opened her beak and loosed a piercing shriek of pain from the weight of despairing hopelessness.

The dream shifted once again, and she saw her childhood reflection in the surface of Lake Gloush. She wasn't alone. Many humans and beasts crowded the banks, waiting, unmoving, silent.

"Why are you here? Why does only my reflection show?" She wished she hadn't asked when every set of eyes turned toward her. Hope and fear swept over her in rolling waves. Emotions warred within and threatened to suffocate her. Uncertainty froze her mind for a moment.

Then, at her feet, she spied a smooth orange stone. She remembered Fatir's words from long ago. "Even the smallest stone will stir the calmest, deepest lake." His meaning seemed clear now. Yetsye bent and plucked the stone from the earth, rubbing her thumb over its smooth surface. A single scar marred its face, a glaring imperfection, but if she wielded it carefully...

She   skipped   the   stone   across   the   glassy   lake. Pt..........pt........pt......pt.....pt....pt...plunge! Sinking with ten times its weight in the center of the lake, it stirred ripples that became waves. The waves became walls of water bearing down on the souls lining the shore. In horror she watched, unable to tear her eyes away. Fear and regret drove her to her knees. The water loomed closer, and she readied herself for the deadly impact.

Instead, the water surrounded her, wrapping her gently in its embrace. It cleansed her and she could breathe. She opened her eyes to see the beings shining. Their faces glowed orange, violet, green, blue, yellow, and red, and blinding white garments clothed each human. All that remained when the wave ebbed was a growing sense of peace and contentment.

She groaned. Her stiff body protested the extended stay on the hard floor. Rolling onto one side, Yetsye pushed herself into a sitting position, forcing reluctant muscles to obey. She blinked several times to clear blurred and gritty eyes. Her lungs expanded as she breathed deeply, filling them with the cool air of the chamber. Tsifi'Ra and Mit'Ra sent out a shy dawning welcome from the widows high above.

Two paths spread before Yetsye. Choosing would not be difficult. Following the path faithfully worried her more.

She rose first to all fours and then stood. Making her way carefully to the pool, she removed the towel-dress and stepped in. Thoughts swam circles in her mind as she bathed. The warm water might heal stiff muscles, but it did nothing to ease worries. Again, she climbed out and dried herself. In one of the smaller pots, she took some of the running water and drank. The pure liquid slipped easily down her parched throat. Dressed in her own clothes, she retraced her steps to the entrance.

Yetsye squinted in the full light of the suns. When her eyes adjusted, she made her way to the dining hall. Her siblings and their new friends were there, as was Tani Zhil'la's family. She met their amazed stares with confusion. "What is it?"

Ya'el was on her feet, running. "You're glowing, Yetsye! Your hair is on fire, red and gold, and now there's silver, too." She grasped her by the shoulders and checked her for signs of fever. "Are you alright?"

"Yes," she stated and smiled softly, though heaviness marred the moment. Ya'el smiled back. But Yuvahl, who stood nearby, must've caught something in Yetsye's expression. He mouthed, "We will talk later." Yetsye nodded. He would understand.

10

Choices

Finding a moment alone with Yuvahl was harder than Yetsye expected. When Ya'el offered to help Leila clear the leavings after the dusking meal, she found her chance. Tsadok exited through a side entrance and when Yuvahl turned to follow, she tugged on his sleeve and tossed her head toward the main door.

The siblings strolled down the central path until they reached the gardens. Stargazing had been a common interest since Yetsye could remember, and they pointed out favorite constellations as they walked deeper into the lush growth.

Yuvahl suddenly stopped and turned to face Yetsye. He crossed his arms and waited with uncharacteristic impatience. He was definitely worried.

"Easy, Batir!" She began by trying to soothe his worries. "I saw three dreams in this place, one before going through the ritual and two during." She grinned mischievously and raised open hands to the sides of her face, wiggling her fingers. "Of scary and exciting things." Then the smile faded. "Azilet'zal gave me two paths to choose from. I know which one Creator wants me to choose, but the choice is still up to me. I can either light the spark which results in a united Y'Dahnndrya," she paused, her brow furrowed with the gravity of the second option, "or I can snuff the spark and murder the world I love."

"What did you see?" he prompted quietly when she said no more. He led her to a nearby stone bench and urged her to sit. Then, he squatted in front of her as he used to do when she was a hurting child. She looked into his eyes and was relieved when she saw only concern for an equal. Holding his gaze with her own, she relayed her dreams.

"I saw the whole of Y'Dahnndrya, as if I was an el'tekh flying high in the sky-dome, above the clouds. I could clearly see home, Shinnoah, D'Koruyi, the islands of the Ikhel'dur, and even Bot'ha and Genzet. The face of

Y'Dahnndrya changed in magnificent and terrible ways. Rivers altered their courses, deserts bloomed with flowers, and forests burned to deserts. Mountains crumbled to dust. Majestic islands sank beneath waves while new ones sprang above the swells. If the Great Cataclysm was anything like this, I can see why it still lingers in our memories and histories."

She stood and walked a few paces in silence, then stopped. Raising her face to the stars, she suddenly asked, "Why do we have stars?" Her question startled Yuvahl, and he rose.

"To point the straight way in darkness," he answered with certainty.

"And what are stars, really?"

"Fire. What's your point?" He was growing more impatient. She almost laughed at his indignant stance. This role reversal was fun! Now she was the teacher.

"Right. I'm sorry for the confusion, but I'm still working my way through it all. May I continue? I don't want to do this with Ya'el. You know how slow I am and her questions would only make it worse." A rueful grin spread over her face. He nodded and motioned for her to continue.

"What is fire?" She continued where she left off. "What are its properties and uses?"

"Fire is warmth and also light, useful for guidance and keeping warm in the cold seasons. As it eats, it grows. It purifies and refines metals." Yuvahl ticked off each item with his fingers.

"Yes. In my Visioning, I was a flaming el'tekh, at first the orange of M'Neshunnaya. A single flame of orange light in Zulima set more flaming orange tongues aglow. These tongues spread outward to Shinnoah, shining a deep violet there. When the flames reached D'Koruyi, they became green. The flames spread to the west, lighting the other territories red, blue, and yellow. And when all territories blazed with color, the flames flashed brilliant white, along with my own flaming feathers."

Another long pause, abbreviated by a deep sigh, drew Yuvahl's attention away from the stars and he faced her. She sat again as a lone tear trickled down her cheek. The light of the moons must have sparked a glint off it. Yuvahl sat beside her, wrapped an arm around her shoulders, and hugged her lightly. She needed to be strong now. The next part was hard, for it recalled her matir's dream from forever ago. She quietly cried into his tunic and, after a few moments, regained the balance she needed.

"I'm sorry. It's hard," she began. "Matir had a dream. She spun the tale to me before we left, only because I asked. Now I wish I hadn't. It scares me." She paused, took two shaky breaths to slow down the tears, and continued. "In Matir's dream, she saw four figures standing on the shore of Lake Mir'ir." She watched Yuvahl's face closely as she relayed the dream to him.

Yuvahl froze. He guessed the meaning much faster than she had. "One of us won't return home." His familiar, solemn tone rang deeper this time. It made her wonder if he'd ever spoken so seriously to her before. Her eyes scanned him carefully while he thought it over. "You believe Ya'el is the one?" he asked.

She hung her head. "That's the general feeling. Should we tell her? Would it make a difference if we did? I just keep stuffing it down to the bottom of my thoughts so I won't have to deal with it. It's nice that you know now. A burden is more easily carried by two."

"I don't know whether it would make a difference if she knew. No one can know the future with certainty. Even visionings are only possibilities. Our decisions in the moment make the actual difference. We'll just have to pay attention." His practicality soothed her. "You said there was something more?"

Yetsye nodded. "In my third dream, I saw Lake Gloush. Many beings crowded around the shores of the lake. It was a time of waiting and the surface of the lake reflected the sky-dome. I asked two questions and, as one, all eyes turned to me, filled with both hope and fear. It scared and confused me. You know how people and emotions affect me. Anyway, I looked down and saw a smooth, orange stone. I bent and plucked it from the ground. As I ran my fingers over the surface, I found a scar. I thought if I threw it well, it would still achieve its purpose, even flawed. I skipped it across the surface of the lake. When it sank below the center, it sent out ripples which grew to giant walls of water racing toward the shore with fearsome power. I was afraid, and sorry for what I'd started. I sank to my knees, waiting for death. The waves overtook those on the shore but didn't destroy everything. The water embraced and supported me. It cleansed me. My breath came freely and my fears sloughed away. When the waters receded, some of the people and beasts were indeed washed away. But those left standing shone bright. The faces of the people glowed the color of their clans and their garments became radiant white."

Yuvahl took several breaths before he broke the crystalline silence. "Amazing. You know the spin of my visioning tale, and it's nothing like what you've experienced. After all, my appearance didn't change, and I only saw one dream, vivid though it was. What path have you chosen?"

"I will do what I must. Change is difficult for everyone." Yetsye allowed a wry chuckle and rose once again. "I sound like an Ancient, don't I? The intensity of this even alters my words."

She hung her head. "There are some things I must change about myself first. I know there's a task I must perform. I know this task involves contact with other clans. But my first task is finding my balance. To do that, I know I must increase contact with the people around me now. If I can't even talk to them, how will I learn to talk to all of Y'Dahnndrya?"

Yuvahl nodded. "And then? What will you do once you're able to talk to out-clanners?" His expression overflowed with skepticism. She didn't blame him.

As she turned to look at him, she filled her next words with as much determination as possible. "Then comes the move for unity."

His eyebrows shot toward his hairline. "Unity," he whistled softly and shook his head.

His reaction wasn't a surprise. Unity was a touchy subject since it almost destroyed the peoples of Y'Dahnndrya long ago. But that time, the motive was a lust for power and the instigators, two tyrants. This time, it was love for Azilet'zal and Y'Dahnndrya, driving the desire for uniting the clans.

"Unity?" Ya'el's echoing question surprised them both. They'd been so focused on their conversation, she'd been able to join them unnoticed. Yetsye wondered how long she'd been there. Had she heard about Matir's dream? Ignoring that thought was the only way Yetsye could continue.

"Yes." Yetsye's single nod punctuated the word. "I'm glad you're here, Ya'el. Now you'll both know of my destined path."

"The clans don't know enough about each other. And they certainly don't know much about the beasts. Look at how they treat them! We're all scattered and suffer the bane of ignorance. We tolerate each other. But underneath the tolerance is disrespect and an unhealthy pride. It divides us and hinders our care of Y'Dahnndrya."

She paused, then continued. "Azilet'zal smiled on us when Tsadok joined us. And meeting Leila in this place gave us an opportunity to learn about another culture. We can take this knowledge to our own clans. But a stronger push is necessary. For true unity to take place, the clan leaders must agree so they can encourage their people to work with them toward unification."

She exhaled. "I feel like this quest is too big for me. Just thinking about how to get started is exhausting. I need more information. As I am now, none of the other leaders would think twice about any tale I would spin."

"I know where to get that," said Ya'el with sparkling eyes. She wore her mischievous grin and Yetsye cringed inside.

"And where is that?" Yuvahl raised his left eyebrow and his crooked grin revealed his thoughts. Adventure loomed on the horizon and there was no knowing where Ya'el's suggestion would lead them. He was as excited by the thought of the unknown as Ya'el.

"Mt. Charan. The temple at the summit is said to house more knowledge than any of the other clan lib'rari. That should be our first stop." Yetsye opened her mouth to object, but Ya'el interrupted. "No one in our family ever walks alone! You know that well, Yetsye!"

Determination radiated out of Ya'el. How did her siveh know she was going to suggest her siblings return home? "I couldn't ask you to follow me now." She tried to dissuade them, anyway. "Besides, isn't that meant as more of a spiritual togetherness?" Her resolve thawed a little. But only a bit. She couldn't dismiss Matir's dream so easily.

"Just try to keep us from following you wherever you choose to go from here." Ya'el looked at Yuvahl, who nodded.

He continued where she left off, his voice squashing any argument. "We spoke an oath to stay with you. To break it would be death of the worst kind. Breaking family oaths? By Azilet'zal's Voice! I swore long ago to protect my family and protect them, I will. Try stopping me, Yetsye. Ya'el feels the same."

Yetsye looked at her siveh to find her nodding in hearty agreement. Yuvahl continued. "Let's head back now. They'll wonder what happened to us. We can talk more on the morrowdawn."

Yetsye nodded, reluctant to return but knowing the truth of his words. Would this dusking be another full of dreams? Would she be able to rest? Her journey from now on promised to be full of uncertainty. One thing did stand out, though. Many dangers existed in the outside world. Would she and Yuvahl be able to protect Ya'el? Would Matir's dream come true on this quest? Answers eluded her.

When she finally stepped into her room, she sank down on her knees and bent over them, giving her tiredness, worries, and fears to Azilet'zal. She asked for guidance along the path she'd chosen. When she was done, she crawled into the comfortable bedding and curled up on her side.

Before she drifted off, she heard a bell toll in the distance. She wondered at it, but was too tired to do more. Her Visioning ceremony and the emotional and mental strain which followed weighed down her eyes and sapped her strength. She focused on relaxing and sleep welcomed her gently into its peaceful embrace.

11

Onward

The suns stretched long arms across the rolling plains, creating boulder-shaped shadows and reflecting tiny sparks from the dewdrops scattered generously on every surface. The colors from the cobbled path flashed in joyous reply.

Yetsye woke long before the suns made their presence known. Now she strolled in the small courtyard to the right of the temple. Tears streamed down her face at the glorious handiwork of the Creator displayed before her eyes. Offering dawning prayers seemed more appropriate here in the blessed serenity. How would she be able to go back to normal life after witnessing such wonders?

These fancies eventually gave way to more weighty thoughts, and her steps slowed under the burden. Protecting Ya'el would be her most arduous task. Her siveh was unpredictable and often took risks, ignoring her own safety in search of knowledge. Her ability to shut everything out so completely annoyed Yetsye. In ways both spiritual and mental, she fell far behind Ya'el, who amazed everyone, despite her nosy questions and rough teasing. She couldn't stop the smile that pulled at one corner of her mouth at the thought. Her life wouldn't be the same without Ya'el. She'd just have to remain alert to danger.

The path led her deeper into the courtyard, where a beautiful fountain marked the center. Blocks, hewn out of an unfamiliar striated stone, ranged the many shades of green and reminded Yetsye of home. The sculptor carved a tsa'gra dam and two kits. Small streams flowed from each mouth. She walked around the fountain, her eyes transfixed by the intricate sculpture.

When she'd studied it thoroughly, she resumed her stroll, taking a path on her right which was bordered with tall evergreen shrubs. The path turned abruptly and her nose collided with a solid chest. She would've fallen if strong hands hadn't gripped her shoulders. She squeezed her eyes shut.

"Thank you," she squeaked, trying to catch her breath. The scent of wood and leather surrounded her, and she trembled, her old, unwanted fear creeping back. She shook her head in an attempt to dispel it.

"Are you well?" Tsadok's low voice stayed level and quiet. He surely sensed her distress. The warrior was very kind. He didn't deserve her baseless fear.

She blinked her eyes and nodded, opening her mouth to speak. Only a tiny squeak came out. Heat rushed over her face and dread threatened to smother her. She couldn't do this! Why did Azilet'zal choose her? A knot formed in her throat and tears would surely follow if she didn't leave soon. "I'm sorry," she finally managed a creaky whisper and tugged against Tsadok's hold on her shoulders.

He released her slowly, as if he was afraid she would fall. She nodded but couldn't bring herself to meet those icy blue eyes. "I have to go." Her voice was almost back to normal. She turned, and though she wanted to run, forced herself to walk back to her room, muttering to herself. "I will rise above this fear. I will find a way."

Yetsye finished loading her travel sack, checked to be sure her hair remained carefully tucked into the two familiar puffs, stored her pik'teh in her bag, and gave herself a final once-over to be certain all was as it should be. She turned away but quickly glanced again at her reflection.

The two silver stripes of hair, one right in front of each ear, puzzled her. It might have worried her more if she'd never seen similar things before. It wasn't unique, but it was definitely rare. She breathed deeply, gathered her things, and left the comfortable room. Maybe she could visit this place again soon, to bask in the soothing atmosphere. She thumped down the stairs and jogged to join the others at the dawning meal.

Voices warned her before she reached the dining area. "What is going on? Streaks of silver? Does that mean what I think it means?" Yuvahl's voice drifted out, heavy with worry. "Will our youngest siveh be a Guardian? Or a Clan Leader? They're the only ones I know with silver streaks in their hair.

Either way, I'm worried about how to protect her. Guardians and leaders need that more than others."

Yetsye stopped beside the open doorway and leaned back against the wall, still out of sight. She wanted to know their true feelings, which they wouldn't reveal if she joined them. She wasn't as fragile as everyone believed, and their coddling frustrated her now.

"Yuvahl, could you just be still? Have a seat! I'm sure she'll tell us more when she's ready." Ya'el donned the peacemaker role when Yuvahl couldn't or wouldn't. Yetsye could hear his rapid footsteps, a constant, dull thudding of boot heels.

A low, rumbling voice that was hard to decipher floated out to her. Tsadok. Then the steps paused, and a bench creaked, taking on added weight. How strange that Tsadok could accomplish what her siveh could not. She wondered what words he used.

His voice brought back their earlier meeting in the gardens. She could only imagine how he viewed her now after such awkwardness. Heat crept up her neck and face again just as an unfamiliar musical chuckle rang out. Leila must've joined them, too.

After a few moments of nothing but murmurs, Yetsye decided it was time to enter. She sighed, raised her head in determination, and stepped boldly into the dining hall.

"Good dawning to you all!" she said when she reached their table, her cheeriness only somewhat forced. She drew strength from the beautiful atmosphere and infused her speech with as much vibrancy as she could muster. She made her way around the long table to sit next to Ya'el. Beautiful Leila perched daintily across the table from her. Yuvahl hunched over his plate next to Leila, careful not to sit too close.

Tsadok sat on the other side of Ya'el and across from Yuvahl. Yetsye wondered if he did it on purpose so she wouldn't have to see him. A pang of sadness mingled with annoyance and confusion struck at her heart. She determined to work even harder to conquer her fears. At least she could speak in his presence now, just not directly to him yet. Her phobia slowly eroded with each dawning of exposure to this stranger's calm presence. The earlier meeting resulted in a tie between fear and the determination to have the victory over it. She would've fought against him and run at the first chance a nainda ago.

All eyes focused on her as she relished the sweetened grain mash topped with kho'ni nut crumbles, fresh bansan berries, and sweetened and spiced bil'ti tea. Bil'ti trees grew in groves, their leaves harvested often during the seasons of planting, rain, and harvest. Since there was a healthy grove in Zulima, it was yet another reminder of home.

She smiled again and devoured everything set in front of her. The others eventually followed her example and finished their meals, talking between bites and even joking once or twice. She and Ya'el quickly cleared away the dirty plates, beakers, and utensils when everyone finished and rejoined the others at the table.

"I know you're wondering about many things," Yetsye began hesitantly, her head bowed. "To be truthful, so am I." She cocked her head to one side and redoubled her efforts to speak directly to others. "One thing I know, I must go on a quest. It will take me away from all I've known, into places beyond my imagination. I don't know where it will end, how dangerous it may be, or even if I'll succeed. But I've made my decision. I'm going." She inhaled deeply and carefully chose her next words.

"I'll spin for you the tale of my Visioning, but it may take a bit of time. Are you willing to listen?" Tsadok and Leila rose as if they would leave and before she had time to reconsider, Yetsye spoke out.

"Please don't leave!" she exclaimed while looking at a point somewhere between Yuvahl and Leila. Yuvahl understood and motioned for them to stay. With a breath of relief, she smiled, albeit weakly. She did it! She spoke her true feelings to others, though looking at them while doing so was a mountain yet to be scaled. Hurrying, she spun her tale, leaving nothing out. When she was done, she glanced around the table.

Leila clasped her hands together, white knuckles betraying strain. Yuvahl, who had heard the tale already, revealed nothing in his face or manner. Ya'el's mouth curved in a smile of delight, which didn't surprise Yetsye in the least.

And lastly, there was Tsadok. She leaned forward a bit to see what she could discover in his hands, but connected instead with his crisp, cool eyes. She almost looked away but steeled herself to return the gaze. His stony face cracked just a little. She couldn't tell anything about his feelings concerning her Visioning but he was grinning like a self-satisfied tsa'gra. Could it be because she finally had the courage to look him in the eyes? Her brows drew together, and she turned away, feeling the unwanted flush of heat blanketing her face again.

"I don't mind going alone." They'd see through that weak lie meant to protect them. She'd never been good at lying. She never had much need for it. "But I'd be happy to have company and I can think of no better companions than any of you." And with that, she stopped, folded her arms on the tabletop, and dropped her head on top of them. She hadn't done that since she was a youngling.

Ya'el was the first to venture a comment. "Stripes, eh? They're wonderful!"

Her muffled voice crept out from under an elbow. "I don't know how I got them. They weren't there when I went through the purification ritual and my appearance after the ritual wasn't really uppermost in my mind. I had too much trouble sorting my thoughts to consider my reflection."

"Well, it's something connected with your Visioning, then." Ya'el concluded. Her tone said it was simple common sense.

"Obviously," Leila agreed in her velvety soprano. "I cannot go with you on this quest, as I have my own path to follow. But if you're heading toward Shinnoah, I may be of help to you at least part of the way. If you agree, of course." Yetsye liked this person more and more. Her quiet speaking voice made one think of the tinkling bells which hung from the Shinnoahn tents on trade days. Yetsye relaxed a little, for she loved the music of bells.

She peeked at Leila. "I would truly enjoy that." Then Yetsye smiled to be sure Leila would understand her sincerity.

She was waiting for one other, uncertain if he would say anything at all. Ya'el must have sensed something from her. Or maybe she was simply as curious as Yetsye. "Tsadok, what will you do? Will you go with us or go back to your tribe?"

"I have cast my lot in with you all. With Yetsye, I will stay. She will need more sets of watching eyes."

It was the most Yetsye had ever heard him speak in her presence. Maybe he'd been talking like that to her siblings the whole time. An uneasiness built inside her and she wondered what it might be. She pushed the feeling away.

"You know Yuvahl and I go where you go. We promised Matir and Fatir we'd watch over you on your journey. I don't think it matters how long it takes. Family matters most, right?" Ya'el, dear Ya'el! She reached one hand down to grasp Ya'el's under the table. She heard, more than saw, Yuvahl's solid nod of agreement, which rustled his tunic. Now that they'd decided, Zhil'la dispatched her fastest el'tekh messenger to Zulima. Within a dawning, Bay'rakh and Shira would know what their children intended to do.

It was time. Replenished supply sacks nestled against the sides of the mana. The younglings said their farewells and made their way back up the patchwork cobblestone path. As they did, Yetsye once again opened up all her senses to the fullest extent. She wanted to remember the peace and tranquility surrounding this sacred place. It might be a long time before she'd feel it again. The knowledge that it could change before she saw it again urged her even more.

Feeling eyes upon her, she glanced around to meet Tsadok's piercing gaze once again. He didn't look away this time. The time for sparing her was gone, and she was the one who'd opened the door. She steeled herself to squash the irrational fear hovering at the edge of her reason. This person was a friend, a loyal ally, one who'd chosen a dangerous journey to help a stranger rather than return to his own people. He deserved her respect.

And so she nodded, slowly, never allowing her eyes to leave his. He solemnly nodded back, but she thought she detected a sparkle in his eyes. Soon. Soon she would speak to him face to face. She must if she was to continue down this path. Her lungs filled with the fresh air of Levanna once more as she faced forward.

As Yetsye turned, she glanced past her siveh, who beamed. Ya'el's eyes radiated the inner laughter she stifled. Yetsye blushed and frowned. How could her siveh tease her about something that was so difficult? There was so much to learn in this life, so much to see and experience. Was the desire to live this life well a reason to tease anyone?

"Don't worry, Little Siveh! This is a genuine smile of joy." She forgot how easy it was for Ya'el to read her. She nodded and smiled in relief.

As the party crested the nearest hill, the path stretched ahead of them. They looked back at Levanna one last time before heading into the unknown. Leila took the lead, Yuvahl riding at a respectful distance by her side. Yetsye and Ya'el rode together behind them, with Tsadok in the rear.

This would be an uncomfortable ride if she had to feel his eyes burning holes in her back the whole time. She didn't have to worry, though. When she gathered enough courage to look behind her, she saw he took his task as seriously as before, directing his intense gaze to their surroundings. She drew in a deep breath of relief and followed his example.

They retraced the path and where they would've turned east toward home, they instead turned north toward Shinnoah. Yetsye gazed a long time toward the east. Was she really doing the right thing? Did it really have to be her?

She dragged her eyes back to the north and focused on the new vista opening up before them. Why not enjoy it while she could? Only Azilet'zal knew what the future held. Yetsye wasn't certain of much, but whatever lay ahead, they chose to embrace it together.

Part 2
Shinnoah

12

Strange Welcome

The road to Shinnoah led through fragrant, rolling hills. The cheerful clicks of the mana rang in the air even as their bellies filled with each bite of the sweet grasses decorating the landscape with feathery tufts. Yetsye smiled as she remembered how they tossed their heads and bounded from one grazing spot to the next. She basked in the peace herself any time they paused on the trail.

The travelers made excellent time. A thrum grew deep within her as they got closer to the border. It differed from the stampeding beasts, but this mysterious rhythm seemed strangely familiar.

"I don't understand it!" exclaimed Leila as they continued on slowly. An eerie mist blanketed the ground several hundred paces ahead. Leila scanned the horizon, confusion wrinkling her lovely brow. "This wasn't here before." She shook her head and looked at Yuvahl. "Do you hear crackling?"

Yetsye cocked her head to the side as she speared Ya'el with a questioning gaze. Ya'el's eyes sparkled, but her face remained serious. Yetsye watched as she sat straighter in her saddle. Ya'el nodded and before anyone could stop her, she tossed her reins to Tsadok, who was closer, dismounted, and sped straight for the fog.

"Ya'el, what are you doing?" Yetsye never understood the recklessness that drove her siveh to seek knowledge, to the point of risking her life. "Ya'el, come back!" When her siveh disappeared in the mist, Yetsye trotted after her reluctantly. She wanted to know more, but this was not what she had in mind.

The others followed. What else could they do? The stench hit them before the fog, a dizzying blend of char and acidity edged with something like hot, sour spices which burned the nose. It reminded Yetsye of her first cooking lesson, which had gone horribly wrong. She had burned one of

Matir's favorite pots. She grimaced at the painful reminder as she dug in her travel pack for a scarf to cover her mouth and nose.

Yetsye glimpsed Ya'el ahead. Wispy tentacles quested for ways to trap her in their sinister embrace. She heard the others close behind.

"There's a chasm here!" Ya'el yelled back. The reddish glow that faintly tinted the fog emitted intense heat that rolled out in waves. Ya'el wobbled. Yetsye dismounted just as Ya'el's legs gave out and pulled her away from the edge. She half-carried, half-dragged her back toward the others, since Ya'el's strength was failing.

Yuvahl dismounted and reached them as Ya'el fainted. Scooping her into his arms, he trotted back to his mana, hung her over it like a sack of vegetables, and headed away as quickly as possible. Yetsye clicked to her mana and hurried after them.

Once free from the choking fog, Yuvahl gently laid Ya'el on a blanket Leila spread out for her. "What happened?" he asked of no one in particular.

Yetsye offered the only possibility she could think of. "Toxic air? I can hardly believe it, but it must be so. She was the first one through the fog, the first one to the edge, and the only one to peer so long into the rift." A small portion of her preened with the courage she showed to speak her opinion so boldly. But the larger part of her heart rebuked her for being joyful when Ya'el's life might be in danger. If it was in her power at all, no one would be dying on this quest.

Yuvahl gathered Ya'el and the blanket in his arms once more as he laid out a plan. "I think it's dangerous to stay this close to the rift. We'll find a safer place to set up camp and give Ya'el time to rest. I don't know what else to do for her." Worry lined his face and hardened his jaw. Yetsye's eyes burned as tears brimmed behind them. She could only watch as Yuvahl called over to Tsadok.

"Will you help me, my friend?" The warrior nodded and held Ya'el so Yuvahl could mount his mana. Once he cradled the precious bundle in his arms again, he led the way south and east, away from the noxious fog.

When the smell vanished, Yuvahl judged they were far enough away and reined in his mana. He turned to Leila. "Do you think this place is safe enough?"

"As much as any stop along this route," she began with a shrug. "I passed here three nainda ago and there was no fog, no rift. More things could've changed." She spoke as she helped Yetsye prepare a pallet for Ya'el.

"It's ready," Leila beckoned to Yuvahl. He laid Ya'el down gently and almost immediately, she convulsed.

"Turn her!" Yetsye knew little more than the basics of healing, but it was enough to know Ya'el would likely choke if she vomited now. She gently rubbed her siveh's back as tears rolled down her cheeks. Once Ya'el's stomach emptied, the chills started. Yetsye reached behind her, fumbling around for something warm, anything to stop the chills. Leila offered a blanket and a warm, damp cloth that smelled of jinj. Yetsye mumbled thanks as she bathed Ya'el's face.

The chills weren't stopping. "Another blanket, please!" Yetsye wished she had Ya'el's knowledge of healing. All she could do was sit by helplessly, watching and waiting.

Soft steps behind her betrayed Tsadok's presence. He handed her another blanket and helped her wrap it around Ya'el, whose small body shuddered. Yuvahl busied himself starting a fire. Leila calmly took care of the mana, relieving them of their burdens, freeing them to graze.

"Tell me what to do!" Yetsye's desperate plea went out to anyone who could help, but her eyes never left the pale, trembling form of her siveh. Slow, hot tears continually spilled over her cheeks and scorched her chin. She bowed her head and the salty drops seared their way to the tip of her nose, liquid fire bending the blades of grass which cushioned her knees.

A hand on her back startled her. She didn't look to see who it was, but judging from the size and heaviness, it had to be Yuvahl or Tsadok. It didn't matter. Nothing mattered right now except Ya'el. And the security pouring out of that hand was a balm so soothing, it was madness to reject it.

Leila murmured to Yuvahl, who then spoke gently to Yetsye. "We're going to look for healing herbs. Leila knows of a few native to this area. We'll be quick. Will you be alright here with Tsadok? I know you'd be safe, but will you be able to ask for help if you need it?" She raised her head and moved her mouth, but words failed her.

Tsadok looked at her, his stony face revealing none of his thoughts. "Even if she does not speak, we will manage. I will not fail you, my brah'met."

Yetsye flashed tear-blurred eyes from her batir to Tsadok and back again. Since when did Tsadok and Yuvahl claim kinship? Though he used a strange word, the meaning was clear. Yuvahl would have a tale to spin when he returned. Ya'el twitched, reminding her of her task.

Yetsye couldn't access the knowledge locked away in Ya'el's fevered mind. So she spoke to her in low coos and murmurs, as if she tended a beast. Easing a distressed soul went a long way to speed healing, no matter the being. It didn't hurt if you loved them, too. That would have to be enough, at least until Yuvahl and Leila returned with the herbs.

As if thoughts birthed actions, they ran into the camp. A brown, straw-like bundle filled Leila's arms. She and Yuvahl set to work immediately, crushing the stringy stems and globular roots to make a poultice and brew tea. Yetsye silently watched. Doubt gnawed at her resolve. She should've sent them home.

Leila's gentle voice cut through the silence. "I'm not sure this will help, but there is hope. I know of explorers who traveled into the Fyrna Mountains in the north-east corner of our lands. They suffered a similar malady and discovered this remedy. It worked well to ease the symptoms and help the body heal faster." Her hands never paused, even when she raised worried eyes to meet Yetsye's. "This seems similar, but I can't guarantee it will work."

Yuvahl waved away her worry. "You offered a solution when we had none. Ya'el is the plant expert and healer among our family, one of the best in our village. She might've known what to do." Yuvahl's head shook with regret, but his eyes revealed how impressed he was with Leila's knowledge and initiative.

Yetsye couldn't fail to notice Yuvahl binding his heart fast to their new friend. She turned back to Ya'el. The shaking continued despite the blankets and the nearby fire, and her pallor alarmed Yetsye. She squinted and wiped away the remnants of tears, then rose and strode to her travel sack.

"What is it, Yetsye?" Yuvahl asked, jumping up to follow.

"Maybe nothing, but I had a thought. I might know a way to warm Ya'el faster. We can fold up my pallet and blanket underneath her, creating more space between her and the cooler ground. Ah-ha!" she cried aloud in triumph as she dragged the blanket from the sack. She turned around, searching for her rolled up pallet, and found it leaning on a nearby boulder. She hurried back to her siveh's side.

Facing no one in particular, Yetsye requested, "Please lift her so I can arrange the pallet and blanket."

Tsadok, who had stayed near Ya'el, followed her instructions and patiently waited until the pallet and blanket were in place. He gently laid Ya'el on it, and they waited to see if the shivers would subside. "Thank you," she spoke shyly to him. She wasn't brave enough to call his name. Not yet. At least her voice didn't squeak this time.

She watched him bow from the corner of her eye. "I am glad to help."

The moons and stars plodded across the sky-dome. The others encouraged Yetsye to sleep, but she couldn't. Every time she closed her eyes, she saw her siveh crumple and her eyes popped open. Exhaustion was a determined opponent, though. Her head bobbed.

"Yetsye," Leila murmured. "You need to rest. Why not use my pallet?"

Too tired to speak, Yetsye nodded her thanks and lay down. She couldn't have slept long, though. The moons seemed hardly to have moved when she woke again. Leila looked up as Yetsye approached the fire. "Still can't sleep?" she asked. The smile that crept across her face this time was rueful.

Yetsye shook her head. "I keep seeing it. I keep remembering something my matir shared with me before I left home. When I manage to fall into a light sleep, I dream about a long ago memory of my fatir and me. My mind is too busy for sleep." She sank down to sit beside Leila and Ya'el, then sighed. How easy it was to talk to Leila now!

"You shouldn't, you know." Leila's cryptic remark seemed strange. Maybe it was some kind of Shinnoahn saying.

"What?" Yetsye asked hesitantly.

"Sigh like that. You keep all those negative thoughts flowing and it will only make things worse."

"Where did you hear that? It sounds like something Matir would say."

"She's a wise woman, then, for a certain," Leila beamed. "I learned this in our religious teachings. Positive thoughts encourage positive actions. Every action we take causes a reaction somewhere else. If we put in positive thought and action, then we should see a positive result somewhere else." Leila's hands stayed busy. Was she weaving something small?

"I like that!" Yetsye smiled shyly. "Ya'el would, too. I wonder if she hears us talking." Yetsye fell silent and cocked her head up and to the side, looking at the stars above. The smallest of the moons had almost set on the distant horizon. "Actually," she bowed her head with a wry grin, "Ya'el would probably be angry if she knew we talked without her. She loves to hear about the other clans, even though she gets scolded for her curiosity."

"I'm glad you're talking to me." Leila's grin brimmed with happiness this time, and something else Yetsye couldn't put a name to.

"I decided to improve." Yetsye bowed her head as the telltale flush warmed her neck and cheeks. But she continued valiantly, "And you're easy to talk to. I sense no malice in you whatsoever." She paused and weighed her next words. "The reason I stopped talking to my own people is because they have a tendency to not understand me when I do. Once, I stumbled into a violent disturbance at the trading grounds. I was young. A man poked at an edjig with a sharp branch. The edjig cried for help and I couldn't ignore the poor beast. Being a youngling, I threw a handful of dirt on the man and yelled at him. He grabbed my arm in a crushing grip and slapped me hard, raking his nails across my cheek. If Yuvahl and Ya'el hadn't come to my rescue, the injuries would've been worse. It was the last time I took initiative against a fellow human without a direct order from a higher authority. Now I avoid contact as much as I can. But it seems nothing I do turns out as I want it to."

Yetsye bowed her head. Leila reached out to lift her chin so she could look into her eyes. "You are a very interesting person, Yetsye Shirasdatir. Never be afraid to be yourself. And never, ever, *ever* should you lie to yourself about how wonderful you are. Keep believing in yourself, as you believe in Tugansol who made us. The Creator will never steer you down a wrong path."

"No. I hear the Holy Voice in everyone and everything lately." She offered a rueful grin in return and reached over to check on Ya'el. "Ah," she beamed. "No more shivering. It stopped!" She checked Ya'el's temperature. "Her fever's dropping and her heartbeat and breathing have slowed a little. The treatment must be working." She grabbed Leila's outstretched arm in jubilation. "Thank you!" she said while looking her in the eye.

She thought about Tsadok's help earlier. She had to find him. Looking around, she spotted him keeping watch on the southernmost edge of their camp. His head moved when he scanned left and right. Otherwise, he was like a stone statue. She walked over, careful to go just close enough to be heard.

"Tsadok." Her voice almost failed her. It squeaked again. She frowned at herself.

"Yes," he replied without looking at her. He didn't even jump. It seemed nothing surprised him. Since he didn't turn toward her, she walked around to face him. His focus remained on the distant hills. She was torn between relief and a puzzling disappointment.

"I need to tell you something. Well, two things really." His refusal to look at her was not helping. She needed to speak to him face to face to get past this foolish block. He deserved the same treatment from her as Leila received. She hadn't been fair. He'd traveled with them longer than Leila and proven his integrity many times.

Her patience paid off. He turned to face her. In the faint light of the two remaining moons, his tattoo glowed eerily, peeking through the opening of his tunic. She had to force her gaze away from it to meet his eyes. She made it to his unsmiling mouth and couldn't go any further. "I wanted to tell you thank you again for your help. With Ya'el, I mean. I would've had a tough time doing those things on my own." The hard part done, she rushed through the rest. "Also, Ya'el's fever is fading and her breathing and heart rate are slowing. I thought you'd like to know." She paused and looked down again. She didn't leave and Tsadok patiently waited for her to continue.

"I realized earlier it was rude of me to thank you without looking at you. I also realized how I've treated you unfairly." She clasped her hands together so tightly her knuckles turned white. This was so hard! "I talked to Leila so easily and quickly, and we only met a few dawnings ago. I've known you for many dawnings now." She forced her eyes up again. This time, her gaze reached his slightly crooked nose. He must have broken it in the past. "I'm going to get better. I am. Thank you for being patient with me. That's all I wanted to say."

He'd listened intently and now he smiled, his lips parting to reveal beautiful, white teeth. "I never thought I would hear you call my name, much less hear such a speech from you when I am the sole audience." He bowed his head slightly toward her. "I thank you for your report on the health of your siveh. And I thank you for your trust in me. You are most welcome for the little help I could give on your behalf."

"Don't you mean on Ya'el's behalf?" she asked, bewildered.

He just smiled, shook his head slightly, and returned to watching the hills. Now Yetsye was really confused. She was clearly dismissed, though not rudely. Why would he say he'd helped on her behalf when Ya'el was the one he was helping?

13

Tsadok Speaks

The larger of the two suns peeked over the horizon as Yetsye blinked gritty eyes and rose from her half-sleep. She checked on Ya'el, whose eyes popped open at the touch of her cool hand. Her siveh blinked several times.

She forced herself to sit up, winced, and hissed, "Where'd the stampeding bush'ka go?" eliciting a wobbly smile from Yetsye.

Her stirring woke the others. Yuvahl, followed by Leila, hurried to Ya'el's pallet. Yetsye released a breath she wasn't aware she'd been holding and smiled again in relief. Yuvahl's hesitant laughter danced over her shoulder along with Leila's soft, "Ya'el."

"Why are you crowding me? What happened?" Ya'el looked genuinely confused. After yesterdawn's scare, they all had to look haggard. The corner of Yetsye's mouth twitched at the thought. Ya'el frowned when the details didn't come fast enough.

Yetsye grabbed Ya'el's hands in her own, her smile fading to her usual serious cast. "Toxic fumes at the rift." She looked into Ya'el's eyes and whispered, "You almost died." When words failed her, she resorted to using blunt ones. Ya'el's eyebrows rose, and the little color she'd regained drained from her cheeks. "You're going to be alright now, though," she rushed to assure her. "I don't know what I'd have done if you'd gone ahead of me." She hugged her siveh as tightly as she dared. There was no need to fight the tears this time.

Yuvahl and Leila looked on for a moment. Then Yuvahl cleared his throat and spoke up. "I'm glad you're alive. We have Leila to thank for it."

Leila's resulting blush made her look even more ethereal than usual. When Ya'el shivered in the damp dawning air, Yuvahl set to rekindling the fire. Leila headed to the packs to find food for the dawning meal.

"Thank you very much for your care, Leila." Ya'el's gratitude pulled Leila back a step. She nodded and Ya'el continued. "I knew you were a kindred soul from the moment we first spoke. Please teach me this healing technique." Ya'el bowed as low as possible from her place on the pallet.

Her normality eased the tension in Yetsye's shoulders and the labors awaiting her felt lighter. As soon as they finished eating, Yuvahl lifted prayers of thanks to Azilet'zal. They loaded up their mana. Ya'el was still weak, but she refused to be a burden and settled herself astride her mana. Yuvahl refused to move until she agreed to be tied to the saddle. Once the rope was secure, they set off for the southern border of Shinnoah once again.

Yuvahl and Leila worked together to find a safer route. The trail grew more rocky, and the mana plodded along, picking their way carefully around sharp stones.

The further they got from Levanna, the more Yetsye's thoughts wandered. And the deeper she thought, the more negative the thoughts became. Doubts bubbled to the surface of her mind like so many gaseous pockets in a steam swamp. Her brow furrowed and her mana grew restless and hesitated more often. The sudden voice, though it was low and gentle, startled her out of the pit of darkness she'd spiraled into.

"You know, it is a bad thing to think so hard. Unless you wish the wrinkles to stay." Tsadok allowed himself a brief grin. Yetsye blinked and faced forward, uncertain of what to say. "My morah always said my face would freeze like the ice of Nishi if I wore a frown all the time."

"That's kind of ironic, considering your face seems frozen most of the time." The words were out of her mouth before she even had time to think, and she winced. She turned away from him and held her breath. He'd be angry. Anyone would be angry at hearing such harsh words.

For a moment, all she heard was the tapping of claws on the rocky ground. Then Tsadok laughed. Her eyes popped open as she faced him in surprise. The brimming tears dried up. She had just enough time to register the beauty of that hearty rumble before he stifled it.

"Yetsye Shirasdatir, you are an amazing person. Speak truth again to me sometime." She had to look at his face to understand his full meaning, but the tone was gentle.

"I'm sorry. I didn't consider my words well. This is why I don't speak to people." She sensed rather than saw him nod. Just as she took in a breath to thank him for his consideration, he began again, looking everywhere but at her.

"My morah." There was a long pause, as if he chose his words with utmost care. "I have not talked about her since she passed on many tsimikin past. Why now, I wonder?" His brows drew together in thought.

She watched him from the corner of her eyes for a few moments. When he said nothing, she pondered the wisdom of asking a question. She'd insulted him before with her badly chosen words, but she had a feeling even if he didn't want to answer, he wouldn't make her feel bad about asking. She gathered all her courage and began. "What was she like?"

Tsadok studied her without answering. She squirmed uncomfortably. When she couldn't stand the silence any longer, she clarified, "Your morah. What was she like? Um, or if you don't want to answer, you don't have to." She trailed off, bowed her head, and turned her face away from him. She felt the warmth of a blush spread up her neck and across her cheeks. He had to see it, even though she faced away. Keeping her courage up was getting harder and harder. She wanted to run away.

He reached out his hand to her mana's reins. When she jerked back sharply, he hurried to assure her, "I am sorry." He reined in both mounts as Yetsye fought for breath.

"I'm sorry, too!" she blurted, but her voice was small and the others could not have heard her. "I've made you angry?" she whispered and bowed her head. Indeed, she was folding in on herself, trying desperately to hide from that piercing gaze.

"No. Not angry. I am sorry I made you think that." He reached for her shoulder and rested his hand there for a moment before speaking again. "I just wanted to talk to you without the others hearing." He squeezed her shoulder gently, and she risked a glance at him. "You have a sincere wish for knowledge. Ya'el sought general knowledge without deep meaning, making light conversation. The memory of Morah deserves more honor than a passing thought." He released her shoulder, giving her the space she craved.

She returned his gaze with glassy eyes. "Oh!" A bit of a wobble remained in her voice, but she gave a slightly crooked smile. She opened her mouth to defend her siveh, but Tsadok's now open expression arrested the words before they could escape. If his pale blue eyes were like piercing ice before, they were now crystal clear pools of refreshing water, deep and full of life. Pain, sorrow, loss, fear, and worry swam in the depths. But there were also splashes of love and joy, as well as a sense of tranquility. She marveled at his ability to conceal so much.

"Oh!" she whispered again. "How do you do it? How do you keep it all in?" Her eyes, which once had trouble looking at him before, now refused to turn away. They roved over his face, brushing lightly over each revealed emotion. "I can't hide anything from Yuvahl and Ya'el, and if I had to guess, I haven't hidden anything from you, either." She saw a crooked grin appear under his regal nose. "Would you teach me?"

"Come on." And he urged his mana into an easy walk. Yetsye followed, still puzzling over his superior self-control and her unexpected courage to look him in the eyes. The others were far enough ahead they wouldn't hear the conversation behind them. The kind breeze wafting out of the north lent a helping hand to ensure their words wouldn't carry.

They walked several paces before Tsadok spun his tale for Yetsye. "I am Tsadok Akal'a, son of Zev Zared and Mi'yat Akal'a, born of D'Koruyi, Child of Y'Dahnndrya. I exist because Kai'yanga, the Great Creator, is merciful, and for the protection of the Children. Under the dark moon's glow on the thirty-sixth day of the minsik of Ragadi, during the time of wind dances, I was born. My parents rejoiced at my birth, for a robust youngling is an asset to the tribe. Only a powerful son can contend for the position of High Chieftain. And so my training began as soon as I could walk.

"Morah taught me many things before that time, though. She sang and her songs were as beautiful as her heart. She carved and her carvings came to life before my eyes, jumping out of bone and wood alike. The sight of her alone could soften Pareh's face. Years of living and warring fell away from him like the dead leaves of Dishi." He paused as his mana picked its way over a particularly rocky stretch of the path.

"When the time for my intensive training came, excitement pushed me to learn well. My teacher praised me often. Soon I noticed things that felt wrong." Here he frowned. "Older students oppressed younger ones because they were weaker or less accomplished. I wanted very much to right this wrong and sought for ways to do so. I tried talking to the older students, but they scoffed at me. Because my pareh was an elder in our tribe and won much honor on the proving ground, they were not as rough with me, but they did not approve of my efforts to change things. This they perceived to be weakness. Contempt showed in their eyes and words. I tried other ways, and it was not long before the teacher heard of my efforts. He took me aside and spoke to me, heard the words of my tale clearly, and told me I needed to attend more intensive classes. He also spoke to my pareh. When I returned to our orth that dusking, Pareh was waiting for me with Morah seated at his feet, her head bowed. At my arrival, she raised her eyes to meet mine. My heart shook when I saw worry reflected there, but I steadied my gaze to return the hard eyes of Pareh. I went to bed hungry that night. I could not sleep. The image of Morah returned to my mind, her eyes filled with sorrow. The next dawning, she told me something I will never forget. She said to do as my heart bid me, as long as I kept to Kai'yanga's way. She told me I was reckless, but my heart was in the right place.

"Morah's words gave me hope. I endured the hardships of the path of the warrior while seeking ways to improve loyalty within my tribe. I want them to understand. We are strongest when we fight together. We should focus on becoming leaders who are strong in times of both trouble and peace. The strong should encourage the weak. Morah must have known this or she would not have encouraged me. But Pareh disagrees with me." He paused. His jaw clenched, and he simply breathed for a few beats of Yetsye's heart.

Determination etched itself across his face and blazed in his eyes. "That is part of the reason I am here. I seek proof to back up my belief. Pareh thinks I will never find the answer. He believes it is even less likely to find proof outside the clan. So I seek to prove him wrong." He halted his mana and waited for Yetsye to do the same. This time, when he focused that piercing gaze on her, she had no trouble looking back. "Do you think it is wrong of me?"

Yetsye pondered his question in silence. The relief she felt at his patience made thinking easier. Tsadok had to be the epitome of patience. "I think your morah was a wise woman, and she steers you well with her advice. I also think your pareh wants to protect you and your tribe and clan at all costs. It's admirable, but I also believe it may blind him to flaws that could mean harm in the future." She paused, feeling the annoying blush creep up her neck again. She looked away as she continued. "I can't imagine any parent being dissatisfied with you. You've remained steadfast throughout this journey. You're helpful, alert, observant, a truly excellent traveling companion. I've learned to trust you. I wish you could understand how much that actually meant." She shrugged. "I admire you for stepping out on your own and determining your own life path. You inspire me to become a better person for our world and for the honor of Azilet'zal."

They caught up to the others, and bits of conversation floated to them on the fitful breeze.

"...a crack in the ground could be so deep?" Leila's voice chimed out first. "I've seen the flowing rock pools of the Mountains of Fire, but never such a vast fissure here in the plains." Though obviously distressed, her voice never wavered.

"I've never seen such a thing at all," Ya'el answered back. "I'd love to study it some more and see how it affects the surrounding land. If it hurt me, would it hurt Y'Dahnndryan beasts?"

Though the subject was heavy, Yetsye smiled at Ya'el's enthusiasm. Her zest for life never faltered, even after facing almost-death. Yuvahl simply nodded at appropriate points. Yetsye knew they'd hear from him later when they made camp.

When Yetsye and Tsadok drew closer, Ya'el turned toward them. Her broad smile made Yetsye groan in apprehension. "It's about time you two caught up! What in all of Y'Dahnndrya made you so slow?" She punctuated her singsong teasing with a wink and a light laugh.

Yetsye usually loved hearing her laugh, but this time it smudged the precious truths Tsadok shared with her. She paled and frowned at her siveh but said nothing. Yuvahl leveled a stare at her as well. She'd probably have a load of questions to answer when he caught her alone. She nodded at him, wearing grim resignation like a shield.

The suns settled into the blanket of dusking as the travelers made camp. Far in the distance, a high-pitched keening cry rang out, like laughter twisted in despair. As one, all eyes turned to Leila, who might identify the owner of the spine-tingling howl. The color drained from her face. She turned wide, violet eyes toward Yuvahl and recited something that sounded like a childhood chant:

"Beware the Nechna!

Its claws and teeth

They bite and slash.

Its pounding hooves

Do crush to ash.

Its breath so foul

And crying howl

Send all to ever sleep."

Yetsye shivered. Leila's tone held a layer of darkness she'd never expected to hear from the beautiful Shinnoahn. The real thing couldn't be all that bad, could it? She raised an eyebrow in query and pressed a surprised Leila for more information on these new beasts.

"Please tell me more, Leila. If there's a beast involved, I want to help." Her eagerness coaxed the reluctant maid, and she relented.

"The Nechna have plagued my clan for as long as we can remember. They usually travel in packs of three or four, but one is powerful enough to kill a human, even a prepared one. We are five, but it doesn't matter. They'll outnumber and overpower us. They'll attack if they find us here." She shook her head, let out a shaky breath, and continued at Yetsye's urging. "They're stealth hunters. It's unlikely we'd hear them coming and only the most observant person could detect them." At this pronouncement, three pairs of eyes turned to Yetsye, who returned their gazes in confusion. Then she realized they were looking over her shoulder. She turned to see Tsadok kneeling behind her.

Yuvahl took the lead again. "Let's settle in for the night. I'll take the first watch, then Tsadok, then Yetsye. This seems the best way to detect them." Yetsye knew this tactic. People gained confidence when the leader was strong, the plan was definite, and each had a specific job to do.

"Are they poisonous?" she asked.

Leila shook her head. "No. They don't need to be. Their claws and teeth make up for any lack of poison."

"Alright. Then we have a fighting chance." With that, Yuvahl removed a kranj from his belt. The long length of barbed metal cable with three curving hooks woven into the ends was his weapon of choice. It looked menacing enough to deter most human enemies. He rarely pulled his weapon off his belt, but when he did, he meant to walk away at the end. Yetsye smiled at the thought. He was the best kranj wielder in Zulima village, maybe in all of M'Neshunnaya. If the Nechna came with killing in mind, they wouldn't walk away without paying dearly for it.

14

The Nechna

Yetsye woke as Tsadok roughly shook her arm. A gasp of dismay escaped as she jerked away. But he held on while looking away from her into the distance. He hissed her to silence and pressed the air with his free hand, urging her to be calm. Her eyes widened. The menace emanating from that direction was stronger than any she'd ever felt from humans. Weighty, tangible, and overwhelming, it sapped her strength. The air prickled with stinging anger. It must be the Nechna.

She turned to Tsadok for answers. He nodded once. Yuvahl stood nearby, kranj in hand. His stance revealed his mindset, alert and ready for a fight. With his feet set wide and center of gravity low, he reminded Yetsye of the armored pixets of the forest whose plated backs shielded them from predators and whose claws and spikes made even the most desperate beast think twice before attacking.

She steadied her mind and rose to sit on her knees. The oppressive atmosphere weighed her down. Yetsye pushed back against the impressive shield to learn more about the creatures wielding it. Clouds sailed above, hiding the moons, until a gust blew them aside to reveal beasts a little larger than the mana.

The Nechna wore thick, black fur and walked on six padded hooves as large as serving bowls. Their snouts stretched half as long as their shoulders were wide. Slitted nostrils flared with the excitement of the hunt and the sense of righteous victory. Deep aqua eyes, void of pupils, gleamed with a sinister light. Their eagerness to sink teeth into the intruders thrummed with twitching ears and flicking tails. Their movements arrested Yetsye. Something was odd about them, but she couldn't quite figure it out.

"Are we prey or annoying trespassers?" she murmured.

One Nechna stood out, larger than the others. Yetsye pushed at Tsadok's hand and he reluctantly released her. She rose slowly, keeping her eyes on the largest Nechna, and positioned herself in his path. She knew this one was a male from the size of his body and hooves to the profuse mane which fluttered lightly around his face and trailed all the way down his spine, ending in a lush tuft at the tip of his tail. His wide, pointed ears and twitching tail-tip spoke the most often, too. It seemed a mysterious dance to Yetsye's fascinated eyes. If all this didn't mark his status, the single white stripe in his mane was a powerful clue. It fluttered over his left ear.

Yetsye was certain. They were trespassers. Such powerful beasts could've killed them easily by now, as Leila warned. She carefully stepped closer to the leader after sending a reassuring nod back to her companions. Yuvahl looked on in apparent horror, unable to move away from Ya'el, who was still too weak to fight. Leila knelt by Ya'el and wept quietly into her hands.

With each step, Yetsye grew more confident. She reached up and pulled the ties from her hair. Her own mane of curls fell around her face, bouncing in the night breeze, as she tossed her head and spread wide her arms. She couldn't allow the Nechna to see any weakness. Cowardly behavior resulted in death.

Yetsye stepped close enough to smell the foul breath Leila spoke of. When she got as close as she dared, she froze, closed her eyes and awaited judgment.

The dusking brightened now that all Y'Dahnndrya's moons smiled happily upon them, oblivious to the drama far below. Yetsye stood still as stone for what seemed like forever.

"Merrrto of the Plains, I am called." He spoke his name to her mind, a velvety soft bass, slightly muffled.

She jumped in surprise, but recovered quickly. Uncertain whether he'd be able to hear her, she tried replying in kind. "I am Yetsye Shirasdatir. It is an honor to meet you, Merrrto of the Plains. Have we wronged your people?"

The voice in her mind was like deep water, smooth and calm, with a crushing intensity. "You have trrespassed upon ourrr land. Why have you come? What do you seek?" He rolled the r's and lisped the s's. Yetsye marveled at having true conversation with a beast. The musicality of his words stole her own away at first.

"We pass through your land to seek the guidance of the Great Creator at Mt. Charan. We do not wish you or your people any harm." She made her words clear. Misunderstandings would be deadly now.

"We will allow safe passage this time. We see the marrk of the Crreatorrr upon you and know yourrr worrds to be trrue."

Yetsye opened her eyes wide at his pronouncement. What did he mean by 'the Creator's Mark?' It was unimportant right now, though. "If we need to pass this way again, what is the proper way to ask your permission?"

"Await us at the borrderrr. We will know you arre therre and come to you."

"What should we do if time is short?"

"Then come. But prreparre a stone pile, as many layerrs tall as you, having morre stones in the bottom and fewerrr in each successive layerrr. Atop this pile, let the burrning flowerrr bloom. We will see the sign and come."

"How can we thank you for such gracious help?"

"You can learrn ourrr ways. Then, pass on what you learrn. Knowledge is one of the foundation stones of life."

"If I ever need your help again, how should I ask?"

"If everrr you should need the help of the Noble Beasts and you arre away frrom the plains, you should sound the cry which you hearrd earrlierrr tonight. It is a cry of alarrm. We will come when we hearrr it. Ourrr hearring is keen."

"You have my thanks, Merrrto of the noble Nechna, Guardian of the Plains."

Yetsye knew the others heard nothing. She sensed their fear in the stillness. She bowed low to Merrrto, turned, and paced back to the others. Her trust in the beast behind her wouldn't go unnoticed. The pack lowered their powerful bodies to the earth and prepared to watch over Yetsye and her companions.

She reached the campfire and sat beside Ya'el. Leila rekindled the fire but sent wary looks in her direction.

"They'll watch over us. I have Merrrto's word we are safe."

Her companions' faces displayed shock, amazement, awe, and fear, all but Tsadok, whose stony mask held firm. Yetsye looked around at them as she reached for a pouch of kho'ni nuts. "What?" She directed her question to her siblings. "I'd expect disbelief from Leila and Tsadok, who don't know me well, but you two?" Yuvahl just shook his head as he drew in a great breath and Ya'el slumped.

"I'm sorry, Little Siveh. I don't know why this threw me into confusion." Ya'el uttered a wry chuckle. "I guess I just always thought I'd be the one protecting you." She rose shakily and walked to her pack. She pulled out her stiil and pa'pukh. Yetsye nodded when Ya'el turned toward her for a moment. Her eyes followed her siveh as she walked to a small shrub at the edge of the fire-glow and sat down to draw.

Yetsye forced herself to eat, forced the food down her tight throat. The amazing experience with Merrrto was marred. She knew her siblings didn't doubt her abilities, but since her Visioning Ceremony, things were changing. Her old way of communing with the beasts of Y'Dahnndrya was something unheard of, a spin only woven in brakas. No one in Zulima knew of any other person living now who had such a gift. What would they think when she told them her gift had grown stronger?

Yuvahl took Leila's elbow and led her to a rock bench shaped by Azilet'zal's own hand. He settled himself beside her. The presence of the Nechna left her visibly shaken and Yuvahl did his best to comfort her. Yetsye studied the remaining nuts in her hand for a moment before finishing them. She scanned the starry sky dotted with five bright moons and a few wisps of cloud. Her gaze followed the sky-dome down to the horizon and finally settled on Tsadok.

He'd chosen to keep watch over the opposite side of the camp from the Nechna. The corners of her mouth turned up despite the disbelief of her siblings. He saw a need and filled it. She learned a little more about the D'Koruyin warrior with each dawning.

When Ya'el plopped down beside her, Yetsye jumped and stared at her, open-mouthed. She snapped her mouth closed and focused on the leather lacings around her shins. She felt an unnecessary lecture coming.

"You know," Ya'el began, her confidence restored, "you're an amazing person with an amazing gift. When you show another side of this gift, it continues to shock and amaze those who witness it." She paused and shook her head. "You can't avoid strange reactions from people. You need to accept that, as much as you need to accept that you're special," she urged. Yetsye turned to face her, one eyebrow arched. "Keep your humility. But also accept that Azilet'zal has blessed you with this amazing ability. Use it and be certain you use it well."

Yetsye thought for a moment and nodded. It wasn't like she was trying to toss her gift away. How did her siveh see her? Was she considered an equal? Or was she still just a younger sibling?

After a moment, Ya'el mused, "I wonder if they know about the rumblings of Y'Dahnndrya and why they're happening? Could you try to talk to them about it?" The stiil tapped a slow rhythm on the leather cover of her pa'pukh.

Tsadok, who rarely commented on anything, spoke without turning. "You could. If they do not know, they should be informed."

Yetsye nodded and walked away from the fire to stand and bow in front of Merrrto once more. She knew the majestic beast could understand what they said and wondered if the knowledge would unsettle his tribe.

"May I have permission to speak once more to Merrrto of the Nechna?"

"Speak, Yetsye, Chosen of the Crreatorrr."

She sat on her knees before the noble beast, close enough that she could touch his nose if he allowed it. She noted his breath was now sweet and wondered how that was possible.

"Do you know anything about the shaking of Y'Dahnndrya that occurred recently?"

"We arre awarre of it." He inclined his broad face in confirmation.

"Do you know what might have caused it? Our people are worried. Others lost their lives, swallowed by Y'Dahnndrya. A river shifted its course and a large rift now scars Y'Dahnndrya's beautiful face. We are uncertain whether there is anything that can be done." Yetsye shook her head.

"We know not why, but the rrumblings do occurrr frrom time to time. They arre parrt of the cycle of Y'Dahnndrrya. We have lived on the surrface of Y'Dahnndrrya farrr longerrr than yourrr people and ourrr life spans arre worrth five of yourrr own. Ourrr memorries arre passed frrom sirre and dam to kits. The rrumblings come and herrald changes which arre good. All the Crreatorrr does is forrr the good of Crreation. We trrust the judgment of the Crreatorrr. Do you not?" At his question, Merrrto tapped one soft hoof on the ground directly in front of Yetsye, calling her from her deep thoughts.

Yetsye paused before answering with a vigorous nod. "I do. It is my own people I'm uncertain of, I suppose. I need to find a way to unite them, and this is the main reason I travel to Mt. Charan. I've only just reached the fullness of adulthood in my clan. Who will listen to me? What words can I use to make them understand the truth of what I say? But I must look to the Creator for these answers. Thank you for sharing what you know with me. I will share it with my traveling companions, my siblings Yuvahl and Ya'el, Tsadok of the D'Koruyin, and Leila of Shinnoah."

"It is brrave of you, young one, to sharre yourrr trrue-name with us. Do you know therre is a powerrr in names?" Merrrto tossed his head in surprise at the perceived ignorance.

"Yes. My matir taught me this long ago. I sense no falsehood in you and felt my true-name is safe with you. I also trust you with my siblings' names because they trust me. Of the other two, you only have partial names. Thank you again for your teaching. I will return to my companions now and pass on this knowledge." Yetsye bowed over her knees, rose, and bowed again before returning to the fire.

She sat at her former place to share what she'd heard from Merrrto, speaking loud enough for Yuvahl and Leila to hear. "The Nechna will guide and protect us through the plains." The color drained from Leila's face, but Yetsye ignored it and directed her next words to the older girl. "There is a way to become their allies, if your clan-folk want to learn."

The atmosphere surrounding the companions and their fire hummed with the sighs of the great Nechna. Their presence now comforted all but Leila. Yuvahl led the pale maiden to her pallet and sat holding her hand while she fell asleep. Ya'el soon snored softly on the pallet next to her. It was the first time since leaving Levanna that they could sleep in complete safety.

Yetsye stepped to her pallet and scanned the area. Tsadok remained at his chosen post. She picked her way over to his side. "Won't you sleep?"

"I cannot abandon my task." He didn't even twitch.

"What task? Tonight the Nechna keep watch. You don't have to worry. They hear everything in their territory." She reached out a hand to touch his shoulder. Surprised, she caught herself and quickly pulled back. "Please get some rest."

He didn't move from the rock, but kept scanning the horizon.

"If you don't get at least a little rest, you're going to collapse," she urged.

He still ignored her. Annoyance now built to anger. How dare he ignore her when she was making such a great effort? Hadn't she worked hard to talk to him? "Fine!" she sassed. "You sit there and I'll sit here." She flounced to another rock and sat down hard enough to jolt her teeth. "I won't sleep if you don't."

He looked at her now. "You shine very bright when you are... determined." His slight pause made her wonder what he'd really intended to say. Before she could ask his meaning, he said, "I will rest. I thank you for your care." And he bowed his head slightly, never taking his eyes from her.

He walked over to her and offered her his hand. She stared at it, wondering if she dared take it. Looking up, she saw the challenge reflected in his eyes. Azilet'zal help her! She was never good at letting go of a direct challenge. She steeled herself and gripped his hand. He pulled her to her feet. When she would've pulled her hand away, he refused to let go. Fighting him would've proven him right, and she couldn't do that. He led her to her pallet and then released her. She turned to look at him and waited.

"What is it?" Once again, she couldn't read a thing in his now stony face.

Yetsye looked around. "Where's your pallet?" He said nothing, so she offered a reminder. "I told you. If you don't sleep, I won't either."

After a long pause, he pointed to a small boulder at the head of her pallet and said, "I will rest there."

Yetsye's eyebrows shot toward her hairline in surprise. "How will you sleep on a rock?"

"The same way I sleep on my fur and straw at home. The same way I sleep in the saddle at the time of migration."

"The D'Koruyin people are strange." Yetsye whispered. When she realized she spoke aloud, her face fell. "I'm sorry! I didn't mean to be rude. It's just so different from what I know. Amazing is a good word! I should've said 'amazing.'" She tripped over her words in her hurry to reassure the warrior, oblivious to the fact that she'd reached out a hand to his arm.

He placed his own hand over hers and, at her resulting gasp, said, "It is well. I understand what you mean." He gently removed her hand and helped her sit, then leaned back on the rock he'd chosen.

"Are you really going to sleep on a rock?" Concern wrinkled her brow.

"I will sleep. You must also sleep, Yetsye."

She nodded. "May Azilet'zal bless your dreams."

He nudged her shoulder, and she relented, laying her head on her pallet. The events of the dawning exhausted her and as soon as she relaxed, she slept like the Ancients until the suns rose.

15

Surprising Growth

"**M**ay the Grreat Crreatorrr guide you in yourrr trravels, Yetsye Shirrasdatirrr. May Y'Dahnndrrya gift you with benevolent weatherrr and smooth paths. We will keep watch frrom afarrr until you come to the borrderrr of ourrr lands." Merrrto bobbed his magnificent muzzle in farewell.

Yetsye bowed low. "May the Great Creator bless you as you come and go, Merrrto of the honorable Nechna, Guardian of the Plains. May your offspring be strong and plentiful. Thank you once again for your care of us." She straightened to her full height and looked into Merrrto's deep aqua eyes. He blinked.

"You have learrned ourrr ways so quickly, youngling."

"I have a wonderful teacher." Yetsye smiled up at him. Then turned to mount her mana reluctantly. There was so much more she wanted to learn from the Nechna.

The travelers headed north. Yetsye watched the Nechna pack fade into the distance, trusting her mana to follow the others. What an honor to be sent off by such folk! She carefully tucked the memory deep in a corner of her heart, silently vowing to pass on what she had learned from them.

When the Nechna were specks on the horizon, a high keening howl punctuated with surging rumbles cut through the air. The mana broke into a canter. They would have galloped, but their riders checked them. Yetsye allowed her mount to speed to the front of the group, then cooed into his ear to remind him he was safe. He slowed, and the others followed his example.

Yetsye allowed Leila and Yuvahl to pass her and matched her mana's pace to the others. Ya'el rode beside her again. "It was so late when you finished communing with the Nechna we didn't get a chance to hear much about it." She chuckled and continued. "You know, I always knew your gift was unique. How do you do it?"

"I don't know. Before, I'd just sit and listen. Eventually, I could understand what they were trying to say. If I focused well, I could speak back to them. But talking with the Nechna was totally different. They formed complete sentences. With the bush'ka, the chippits, and the mana..." she trailed off, trying to find words to express her thoughts.

"Well?" Ya'el's pushy curiosity frustrated her at the best of times.

"I'm trying to find the words. Give me some time to think!" Yetsye frowned.

Ya'el playfully punched her arm. "You're always so slow," She laughed loudly at her own joke.

Yetsye scowled, and her eyes narrowed to slits. "You know, I don't have to explain it to you," she hissed.

Ya'el examined Yetsye's face closely, lingering on her deep brown eyes. The laughing smile faded to be replaced with a seriousness only seen when Ya'el focused on her work. She stared a long time before she discovered the mischief Yetsye tried to hide. She relaxed a bit, and the smile returned, though diminished and uncharacteristically abashed.

"Oh, Little Siveh," she said with a respect Yetsye had not heard directed at her before, "how much you've grown in such a short time! I forget we are no longer younglings." She took a deep breath, let it out, and changed the subject. Ya'el's beautiful voice, now clouded with doubt, set Yetsye on edge. "We need to find out what's causing the surface of Y'Dahnndrya to shake, whether it's something we need to fix or even can fix." She raised her left hand to her mouth, biting the nails.

"You should stop, Ya'el." Yetsye reached out slowly to tug on her sleeve and bring her back to the present. "Gnawing your nails to nubs won't solve the problem faster. The Nechna told me a little about the rumblings."

Yuvahl and Leila halted their mana, and Tsadok trotted up to meet them. Yetsye didn't realize the effect those few words would have, or even that she spoke so loud.

Once everyone gathered in a tight circle, Yuvahl asked, "So they answered you about the rumblings?"

"In a way, yes." She punctuated her words with a curt nod and a shrug of one shoulder.

"What do you mean?" Tsadok asked calmly from her right. He'd settled his mount between her and Ya'el. He was bold. Her mind flashed back to the dusking before, when he'd insisted he would sleep on the rock nearest her pallet.

Forcing her mind back to the present, she answered, "Merrrto spoke of Y'Dahnndrya rumbling like this in the past, sometimes even more violently. He also said it is the way of this world, that they and their ancestors have experienced it. The Nechna have a strange way of passing down information, almost as if a scroll lives inside them, with information added to it during each lifetime. It's all passed down to their offspring. It's amazing!" In her excitement, her tongue tripped over the words.

"Wait, a bit! Slow down!" Leila frowned. "Do you mean you had an actual conversation with those violent beasts?"

"They aren't violent. I don't think you could call them beasts like you would other non-humans." Yetsye fixed her eyes on Leila's and her stern expression lent weight to her words. "They're territorial and have a strict code of living." Yetsye's matter-of-fact tone, spoken with such a straight face, upset Leila, whose eyes flamed with anger.

"How dare you take the side of a beast," and she stressed the word, "over the people they have oppressed?" Her teeth clenched and her fingers twisted in the fabric of her pale blue over-skirt. "How dare you think so little of our suffering? How dare you speak of such things as if you know it all?" Each question forced its way past her clenched teeth, marring her rosebud lips into an ugly twist.

The bell-like voice which first gained Yetsye's trust now took on a raw quality she'd never expected. Leila urged her mana closer to Yetsye until they sat eye to eye. Yetsye waited and refused to back down.

"I didn't know before last night. They taught me. And I do know what I'm talking about." The younger maid spoke slowly, making certain her words were simple and clear. "And if you will allow me, I'll share my knowledge with you. In those beings who guarded us last dusking, who still guard us even now, you could have a valuable ally. The choice is yours." She paused. The only sound was Leila's ragged breathing and a snuffle from Yuvahl's mount.

When Leila said nothing, she continued. "They are quite comfortable staying in their own land. If you think about it, they never leave the boundaries of their territory. It is we who invade theirs." Yetsye warmed to her argument and raised her chin, feeling an unfamiliar confidence growing inside her.

Ya'el caught her before she continued. Hand upraised, she interjected, "Hey! The rumblings? What about those? I mean, they are what we were talking about first, right?"

Yetsye nodded without taking her eyes from Leila. For the first time in many, many tsimikin, she was not the first to look away. "Yes. We should focus on that for now."

Ya'el continued, "If the rumblings have always occurred from time to time, isn't it safe to assume it's possible Y'Dahnndrya lives as we live, growing, hurting, and healing? Maybe it's some kind of cycle."

"You might be right." Yuvahl nodded thoughtfully, though his eyes continually studied Leila's rapidly changing expressions. "I've often wondered how Azilet'zal formed the mountains and the rivers. Maybe this is the way it was and is done."

"What do you think, Tsadok?" Ya'el asked as Yuvahl urged Leila's mount back a few paces.

Yetsye and Ya'el watched the proud warrior, whose eyes followed the retreating pair as they whispered earnestly.

"Tsadok?" Ya'el called insistently. His head swung around so fast at the sound of her voice, his hair, now loose but for one braid, swished over his shoulder.

"What is it?" He rumbled.

"Do you think these shakings could be the way Azilet'zal shapes our world and encourages her growth?" She stared at him, face full of expectation and the joy of hearing things from an out-clanner's perspective.

"There is a tale which travels among our tribes telling of the Great Cataclysm."

"Yes, we know that one!" Ya'el interjected. Tsadok waited for her to finish before continuing. Yetsye couldn't tell if her interruption bothered him.

"It is told that in the center of a magnificent village, larger than any I or my people have ever seen, a great fire rose from the ground, slowly at first and then more quickly. Soon red stars sprang into the sky-dome. When they rained down again, little fires ignited and gave birth to bigger blazes." He started his horse forward, and the others followed. Yetsye called to Yuvahl, and he and Leila trotted ahead to lead as they all listened to the spinning of Tsadok Akal'a.

"For many dawnings, the sky-dome rained with red stars and fire devoured everything it touched until all that was left was the dust from which Kai'yanga formed the Children. The Ancestors fled, taking all they could carry, supporting the weak who fell along the way.

"After three dawnings, they reached a place of safety, a high flatland the flames did not touch. There they made camp and considered all that had happened. Supplies were few and the time for hard decisions had come. That dusking, they watched as their land smoldered and writhed far below. Flames and smoke smudged the far horizon and laid an indisputable claim to the territory which was once theirs. They decided to keep moving east, leaving only a small group of watchers who would bring word if the fire ever burned out."

He spun his tale magnificently. Yetsye listened, mesmerized by the melodic sing-song of his velvety baritone.

"My people traveled for many dawnings until they reached a great lake. It lay in a lush valley overflowing with sweet flowers, lively beasts, and fresh water. And so the people stayed there for several tsimikin."

He halted. Ya'el turned to face Yetsye, who shrugged and shook her head. Ya'el turned back to Tsadok. "Why did you stop in the middle? Please tell us more." She was practically bouncing in her saddle and Yetsye mentally cringed.

Tsadok frowned in disapproval. Yetsye shot a meaningful glance at her siveh, but since Ya'el's focus remained on the warrior, it did no good. They had asked him seriously what he thought, and he was seriously trying to help.

"I'm sorry!" The words popped out of her mouth as soon as she registered his frown. "It was rude of me to interrupt your thoughts." Ya'el was genuinely sorry, though others failed to see it sometimes. Every word she spoke sounded so light and carefree. Despite that, people usually forgave Ya'el because of her easy-going nature. Yetsye's bluntness and social anxiety insured she never got that luxury.

"I am sorry, too. I was trying to remember if the rest of the story mentioned anything about the rumbling of Y'Dahnndrya. There is another tale of a band of warriors riding to meet with our people, claiming to be descended from those who remained in the Land of Fire. They spoke of the fires burning out. When the smoke cleared away, a lake of hot, bubbling muck had replaced the flames. They also said after many tsimikin, this muck hardened into rock. My people scoffed at their words, finding them hard to believe. My ancestor of five generations past offered to return to the place with them to seek the truth. Because of his courage, when he returned with the news of their truthful tale, my people chose him as High Chieftain. My pareh is named for this ancestor, Zev Zared."

Tsadok took two deep breaths. "I journeyed many dawnings to the land of bubbling rocks when my warrior training had just begun. The strangeness of the landscape startled me. I found the stone bubbles, as the messengers said, and there was no sign of any movement. When I returned, I was confined to our orth for a full nainda because I left without notice. You are probably right, though. I think this is the way Y'Dahnndrya gains more rock. It is created deep within her and then birthed out onto the surface."

Both Ya'el and Yetsye stared at him in awe. Yuvahl was equally impressed. Leila still wore a frown, but her color slowly returned to its normal translucent shade of the early sunrise. She nodded understanding.

"Your people move all the time, don't they?" Ya'el's curiosity meant trouble if Tsadok left because of it. This time when Yetsye shot daggers at Ya'el, her siveh saw the brown eyes slitted with disappointment and tinged with the fear of losing a valuable ally.

"I was just making an observation and thinking aloud. I didn't mean any offense." She turned apologetic eyes to Tsadok as she continued, using her free hand to illustrate the apology with gestures. "I thought your people move around and are used to doing so. But the M'Neshunnayan and Shinnoahn Clans are rooted in place. I wonder what we'd do if we had to find a new home. That's all." Her voice faded away.

"I took no offense. I think you are wise to look at this side of the problem. It is always a good thing to plan ahead for circumstances which alter life."

Ya'el's spirit revived at his kind words, and she smiled. It wasn't long before she was chattering away with Yuvahl on another topic. This left Yetsye to her own musings. It might've been dangerous to think too long and too hard on such a terrifying event, but what else could she do? She had a quest, and it seemed their world was tearing herself apart to build herself up again. The weight of it pressed down on her, threatening suffocation.

A seed of dread germinated in the depths of her mind. If she was to unite the peoples of Y'Dahnndrya so they could escape another Great Cataclysm, what could one person like her do against such overwhelming enemies as Misunderstanding and Prejudice? She wasn't sure, but she was determined to try.

Yetsye's mana kept pace with Tsadok's, the latter choosing the path for a few paces. When she finally noticed his smile, teeth shining blue-white in the dim light of early dusking, she replied with a timid smile and asked, "What is it?"

"Your face is interesting when you are solving a problem." And then he slowed his mana to drop to the rear-guard position once again. She wished he'd stop making such disturbing observations. They distracted her from her purpose. Then again, maybe she should ask him what he meant by those words.

On the morrowdawn.

Then, they would be in sight of Mt. Charan and within another two dawnings, if Leila calculated correctly, they would reach the temple at the summit. Maybe Seth Yi'in could help her find the answers she sought.

16

Mountain Temple

The climb to the temple on Mt. Charan took two and a half tedious dawnings. When they stepped through the impressive stonework gate, Seth Yi'in blocked their path – arms crossed and face grim.

"What took you so long?" He snapped in Genra. His squeaky voice rang with the heavy accent of the Shinnoahn people. His long, thin mustache shivered with the force of his words. Yetsye would've laughed if she'd known him better.

Ya'el followed different rules and her musical chuckles raised thunderclouds on the old man's brow. He breathed slowly and evenly and said nothing further. But his eyes narrowed to slits and the corners of his lips turned down in disapproval.

The travelers dismounted as Yuvahl answered for them. "Deep ruts in the path forced us to slow down. Working our way around them wasn't easy. The quaking of Y'Dahnndrya changed more of her face than we knew, including a giant rift in the land that added two dawnings to our travel time." Yuvahl stood tall, unruffled by the smaller man's ill temper.

Seth Yi'in grunted acknowledgment. When he spoke again, his voice held grudging respect for the tall youngling who didn't waver under his scowl. "Your meal is ready. I'm sure you need refreshment. Once you clean up and eat, we will talk."

Yetsye's hair caught the Guardian's eye when she dismounted. He had turned to go but abruptly changed direction. Stalking toward her before any of the others could react, he grabbed her arm and jerked her around. She tried to wrench her arm free, but couldn't shake off his grip. Who did this stranger think he was? His behavior was not only rude by M'Neshunnayan standards, but she still had a hard time controlling her fear.

"What?" Her tight voice did nothing to disguise the struggle inside.

"Hmmm," was all he said as he searched her face and eyes, ending his inspection at the silver strands in her hair. He released her as abruptly as he'd trapped her and turned to go. As he walked away, he threw over his shoulder, "You and I will need to talk privately before you leave this place."

"I won't speak with you alone. I would have a witness." Her pointed, though shaky, words halted his purposeful stride. He turned slowly. Yetsye's stomach twisted.

He laughed, an unpleasant sound without mirth. "I frighten you, then? Hmmm. That's a good thing, I suppose. Bring your D'Koruyin guard along. He, at least, will not interrupt."

Now she was angry. This little man seemed to want to irritate her, but she refused to give in. "He's not my guard. He's my friend and I will ask him. If he's unwilling, then my batir, Yuvahl, will join us. He's the one you insulted first." With each word she spoke, she gained more confidence. Azilet'zal only knew where it came from, but she no longer had any fear of this small man, no matter what he said.

Seth Yi'in laughed, and this time it was genuine. When he could speak again, his tone was almost normal. "As long as they don't interrupt, I don't care who it is." And the audacious Guardian sped ahead of them to the dining hall.

Whoever designed Mt. Charan Temple focused on simplicity, from the lines of its walls to its furnishings. The stones composing the structure were of native graida, the brown, tan, and gold variations giving it all the decoration a temple could need. Where Levanna's stones were intricately carved, Charan's were devoid of such adornment. Wall torches spaced close together held back the shadows.

Furniture followed the same rules. Neutral colors of sand, bone, beige, and gray worked along with natural fiber rugs to create an airy, soothing atmosphere. Yetsye felt very much at home here, despite their dubious welcome.

The dining space was smaller than the one at Levanna, but still large enough to feed two hundred people at once if the need arose. Candle lanterns hung from the low ceiling, and a large, round fire pit smoldered in the center under a square hole in the roof. It reminded Yetsye of her family's gathering room. The rectangular tables sat low to the ground, four of which were surrounded by large, colorful cushions. A veritable feast, charmingly arranged, spilled across the center of the table closest to the entrance.

And then she spotted them, "Bon'jiis!" Yetsye's jubilant cry echoed loudly in the vast room, and all eyes turned to her. A blush heated her face, and she bowed her head, though her lips turned up in a crooked grin. Her outburst about something so insignificant surprised her.

Tsadok stepped up to the table and reached for the platter topped with the delightful spheres. He studied the colorful pile and plucked a pale green one from the silver platter. He carried it to Yetsye. The unfamiliar grin on his face set off all kinds of alarm bells. When she didn't move, he took up her hand and placed the bon'jii in the center of her palm. She managed a crooked grin. He chose another, a pale orange, from the pyramid and popped it into his own mouth. She watched, curious, as his eyebrows rose. He grabbed the nearest goblet and guzzled its contents.

When he finished, he turned puzzled eyes to Yetsye. "How can you relish something so very sweet?"

Yetsye laughed. Her emotions had a mind of their own when she let them build up. If given the choice between releasing it in laughter or tears, laughter was better. It was the first time her restraint had broken since leaving home, and it danced around the others like a carefree zephyr. All but Seth Yi'in joined in the merriment. The Guardian observed the traveling companions in silence, giving no sign their merriment affected him.

"May we eat?" Yetsye asked when she caught her breath. She was suddenly ravenous, and the mountain of food looked delicious after the trail fare. At Seth Yi'in's nod, she popped her bon'jii into her mouth and smiled at Ya'el. She chose a leaf green cushion beside the laden table. They offered thanks to Azilet'zal for the magnificent feast and pounced on the platters in front of them.

"There's something wondrous about a table full of food," Ya'el pronounced around the bansan berries she'd just popped into her mouth. "When the belly is satisfied, hearts become lighter and conversation flows more easily."

Yetsye nodded. Smiles blossomed around her. Gentle teasing flitted through the air like so many flut'ra taking wing. She basked in the garden of joy her companions planted in front of her, savoring the momentary peace and tranquility, all the while knowing it wouldn't last forever. She turned and met Tsadok's steady azure gaze. He cocked an eyebrow in question. Did he expect her to say something? What?'

If her stare bothered him, he didn't show it. Her eyes traveled inexorably to the tattoo covering his torso. As Yetsye gazed at the intricate designs, the el'tekh in the center came to life, drawing her in. The designs behind the el'tekh moved as well, swirling and twisting as if ripples started in many places on the surface of a lake. Her hand suddenly burned, and she shook her head. When she came out of the trance, she discovered the source of the heat. Her hand spread over the el'tekh at the center of his chest, trapped beneath Tsadok's. She blushed, and though troubled, she knew it wouldn't do any good to pull away. Tsadok nodded, not daring even the smallest smile. Maybe he thought she'd run away again. She frowned and bowed her head.

"Something happened," she whispered as she raised her eyes again, the others around the table momentarily forgotten. He nodded again, still holding her hand captive. "Your el'tekh flew and the lines of your markings swirled and turned as if stirred by the flapping wings, so many ripples on a vast lake." She paused and took a deep breath before continuing in an excited rush. "If one stone can create ripples that affect the entire lake, many stones could cause more ripples, stirring the lake even faster!" Her face radiated heat. She watched as Tsadok paled and he released her hand slowly.

Seth Yi'in stood up before she could say anything else and beckoned Yetsye to follow him. Tsadok rose as well and trailed respectfully behind them, his expression blank once again, though his color hadn't yet returned to the normal tan.

They walked deep into the heart of the temple. The heavy silence spread like a shroud over them and made the trek seem longer. Had she offended Tsadok? Even worse, had she disgusted him? Was it fear she read on his face? She must ask later. She had to know.

As the trio traveled the stone pathways, Yetsye wondered what it was Seth Yi'in had to say to her. What was so important he wanted her to hear it alone? As they turned the next right, she stepped into a torch-lit room furnished with a luxurious rug of the softest d'nagze wool and several more cushions like those in the dining hall. A small altar nestled against the back wall. Yetsye quirked an eyebrow at Seth Yi'in, confused.

"This altar holds the traditional elemental symbols, reminders of how the Creator birthed a world of balance and order. One does not bow or kneel here. The items in the bowls are tangible samples of earth, fire, air, and water, which increase the ability to focus. The air around us fills with the scents of ynthe and jinj root coals. Fountain water drips rhythmically into the last bowl." Seth Yi'in's love of his studies showed clearly in his desire to acquaint his guests with Shinnoahn religious beliefs. A genuine scholar was he, one who didn't mind sharing his knowledge with anyone who showed an interest.

Yetsye nodded and murmured her thanks as she bowed her head in respect. When the three seated themselves on cushions in the center of the room, Seth Yi'in plunged into conversation. "You bear the sign," he said. He was serenity incarnate, pausing for effect.

"What do you mean by that?" Yetsye remembered the Guardian's vexing attitude and wondered if he wasn't playing some strange game. It was as if he deliberately tried to make everyone around him angry, punctuating his speech with barbed words and riddles.

"Temper, temper, youngling." He kept poking at chinks in her armor. "Your hair. It wasn't always like that, was it?" He must think her some kind of fool.

"No." She snapped the answer and felt heat flood her neck and move up into her cheeks. Would he ever speak clearly?

"How old are you?" He snapped back. She sighed inwardly and was certain it showed in her manner. She needed to humor him. They had to have Seth's help.

"In the month of Memma, I met the dawn of my fourteenth tsimik. What does that have to do with anything?" She clasped her hands together, her uneasiness growing with each of the questions he barked at her.

"If you have seen fourteen tsimikin, and you are M'Neshunnayan? Am I correct?" At her nod, he continued, switching effortlessly to M'Neshunnayan dialect. "You have just come from Levanna, having experienced your Visioning ceremony."

She nodded again, deciding this man might not be worth all the angry energy he piled up inside her. "Azilet'zal help me," she whispered.

He continued in his pompous manner, "Am I also correct in believing your hair changed at that moment?" She nodded again, though she wasn't certain exactly when her hair changed. It could only have happened during the ceremony.

"The Shinnoahn Clan has passed down a prophecy that a messenger would come, recognizable in several ways. The first would be the flaming hair and the silver streaks which ran through it. Every child of Shinnoah learns about the Messenger sent by Azilet'zal, who would bring about extraordinary change. I believe you, Yetsye, could be..." He paused before speaking the last two words in a softer tone than before. "The Messenger."

Yetsye moved her jaw, but no words came. She looked at Tsadok and felt like a min'gif out of water. She was certain the warrior could clearly see her confusion.

"Yetsye," her attention returned to the Guardian, "something profound happened on your journey and again here, did it not? Tell me about it." He was snapping at her again. She thought she might understand his manner better now, his way of first needling with contempt, then snapping commands or observations. "I can understand Shunya, as well as I can speak it. Sometimes words get lost in translation when one speaks Genra." He then sat and waited.

Yetsye focused on breathing to gather her thoughts. She spun the tale of her visions and their journey to Mt. Charan, including the rift blocking their path and Ya'el's resulting sickness. She paused and then added, "Oh! And we met the Nechna. I spoke with Merrrto. You might be happy to know there are ways your clansmen can cross their territory safely." Seth Yi'in's eyebrows shot up in surprise. She tied off the threads of her spin with Tsadok's 'living' tattoo.

He bowed his head when Yetsye stopped. When the Guardian raised his head, admiration flickered in his eyes. "I have never heard of such a thing, humans physically speaking with the beasts. Well, not in our living existence, and I have lived for many, many tsimikin now. I do recall a dusty tale of one person in the ancient scrolls who did so. This is another sign of The Messenger. If you wish, you may read the scroll yourself in our lib'rarum. You may also stay here as long as you feel there is something for you to learn. This temple is dedicated to deeper knowledge of our world. May you find the answers you seek." With that, he rose, motioning for her to stay or go as she wished. He barely acknowledged Tsadok's presence.

When Seth Yi'in's strident steps became tiny taps in the distance, she turned to Tsadok. "What do you think?"

He was silent for a long time. She bowed her head, wondering if she shouldn't have spoken. When he finally answered, his low tone soothed Yetsye's nervousness. "I think you should listen. Azilet'zal speaks most often in simple ways. If you listen for the Holy Voice, you will hear it resonating within."

He was right. She was worrying over nothing. She nodded her thanks and turned her focus to the task at hand.

Together, they rose from their cushions and returned to the dining hall to find the others had already gone to their rooms. One of the temple stewards met them at the entrance to the hall and led them to the sleeping quarters. Yetsye was happy to have a room next to Ya'el. Tsadok moved on down the hall to enter the room on her other side. She nodded to him and entered the room that would be her home for now. On the morrowdawn, she would need orderly thoughts and clear focus. A peaceful sleep would help. She climbed onto the pallet situated under a colorful, glashiin-paned window and fell asleep.

17

Seeking Answers

The lib'rarum of Mt. Charan Temple amazed visitors with its lofty ceiling supported by massive stone arches. Yetsye marveled at silvery veins splintering the shiny black surface and noted three men wouldn't be able to join hands around the columns. The dining hall and main temple might be plain, but the lib'rarum housed enough color for three temples.

Shinnoahns favored squares, lines, and intersections. They even used them in their written language. Mosaic tiles covered the ceiling in several shades of purple, though brilliant splashes of other colors varied the pattern. Yetsye thought the art form suited them well when she considered their love of knowledge and order.

The history of Y'Dahnndrya meandered around the edges of the ceiling, while in the center, a giant hand holding a green and blue ball nestled in a wavy violet field. Yetsye strolled around the room and studied the pictures. Tsadok walked with her, a silent shadow. She found what seemed to be the beginning of the story and gasped.

"Look! The fire your people speak of in the spinning of your tales? It's here." She'd spoken over her shoulder in Tsadok's direction, but she barely looked at him. He rumbled an affirmative. "They're beautiful, aren't they? There's even a spin for the beasts." Her voice softened as she absorbed pictures of beasts she'd never seen before.

"Yes." Seth Yi'in answered at her other side, startling her. Yetsye grimaced because Tsadok seemed impossible to surprise. "Would you like to know why?" Yetsye nodded, listening carefully as Seth Yi'in spun his tale. Despite the Guardian's eccentricity, Yetsye sensed he was one of the wisest people she would ever meet.

"Long, long ago, before the time you can remember, before the time your zat'matir and even her matir can remember, there was a great fire which consumed the land. The people of the land fled before its ferocity, fainting from the strength of its blaze. They reached a safe place after many hard dawnings of travel." As he spoke, they strolled beside the mural.

"Along the way, many loved ones succumbed to the heat, smoke, and flames. The people, once many, were reduced by two-thirds of their number. The remainder did all in their power to nurture the gift of their Creator, this treasure of the heavens we call Y'Dahnndrya.

"In order to serve Tugansol well and nurture the whole of Creation, the people also separated into six clans. Those who loved the cold winter, who loved the crisp music of mountain streams and breezes, who sought to preserve knowledge and wisdom in the people were called 'Shinnoahn', 'Lovers of Knowledge.'"

They moved further down the mural to a section with hints of the clan colors in the background. "Those who loved the flora and fauna and wished to immerse themselves in that warmth called themselves 'M'Neshunnayan', 'Those Who Nurture', and 'Bot'ha', 'To Cleanse and Purify.' There were those who sought to protect all the people of Y'Dahnndrya, even at the cost of their own lives. They chose the names 'D'Koruyin', 'Protectors of the People', and 'Genzet', 'Those Who Guard All Life'. The people who loved most the sea breezes and the frolicking ocean beasts, who sought to care for them and nurture them, chose the name 'Ikhel'dur', 'Guardians of the Waters.'"

"Over time, the threads which connected our peoples thinned and frayed. The meanings of glorious names faded away and the people gradually strayed from their original purpose. Suspicion and dissatisfaction led to mistrust and greed. Slow and insidious is the infection of such sickness, so that no one understood what was happening until it was too late."

They paused while the Guardian continued. "The masses often hold those who recognize it for what it is, the brave souls who speak out against it, in contempt. Dissenters do not understand the significant damage they do to all life on Y'Dahnndrya. The earth, water, and air suffer and the fires of Y'Dahnndrya's heart burn hot. Somehow, what happens to us affects our world and what happens to our world affects us."

"The smallest stone still has the power to stir the calmest lake." The words Yetsye whispered reminded her of a long ago memory. Her family had gone to the lake to celebrate the dawning of Yetsye's fifth tsimik. As soon as they arrived, she scampered to the shore, fell on her hands and knees, and gazed into the glassy surface. Her freckled reflection stared back at her until she placed her palm on the surface. Then a whole new world opened to Yetsye's eyes as she saw the water-folk swaying, dancing, and glinting below. Fatir asked if she was alright and she nodded enthusiastically, urging him to look at the water-folk himself. He shook his head when he tried and failed, but told her she had an amazing gift. Then he plucked a small pebble from the ground and called Yuvahl and Ya'el over. He skipped the pebble over the lake and pointed out the ripples it caused.

"The smallest stone has much power. It can move the calmest lake." Fatir's words still rang within her.

The Guardian carried on, lost in his own telling, oblivious to Yetsye's momentary lapse of attention. "This portion," he said while pointing toward the end, "shows the faithful servants of Tugansol, tending to the needs of Y'Dahnndrya and all the living beings which exist here. There are still faithful servants and you will know them by their deeds. Among those who see the danger of imbalance and disunity are the Temple Guardians and Clan Leaders. These people will be your allies. They are able guides and mentors, should you ever have a need."

He stopped and the chamber seemed void without his lilting chant. Yetsye held her breath, afraid she would crack the glass of truth she was peering through. Seth Yi'in waited patiently. When she collected her thoughts, Yetsye asked, "If all our esteemed leaders know the importance of unity and harmony between the clans, why have our peoples fallen so far away from the truth?"

Seth Yi'in took a deep breath and thought for a minute. "I think if you look deep within yourself, you will find the answer to that question. But I will give you one word to start you on the path. Pride."

Yetsye thought hard for a moment and nodded. She hadn't been certain of his help before. But after such a tale, she felt she knew him a bit better. As a Guardian of Y'Dahnndrya, he might have a lofty attitude, but he was a truth-speaker and worthy of her trust.

She thought of her Visioning, then said, "I'm not sure how to do it, but I am certain of my task. I know I must encourage unity between the clans. We'll make a greater impact if we work together for the good of Y'Dahnndrya. Right now, M'Neshunnayans are simply tolerant of strangers.

Intermarriage and even simple visits with out-clanners are discouraged. I don't know how things work in other clans, but what I've heard from Tsadok and Leila tells me their beliefs are similar. We need to regain the unity that was lost to restore balance to our world."

"I believe you are correct." The pomposity was back in Seth Yi'in's voice. "Would you like some advice?" Without waiting for her answer, he continued, "Of course you would! You should stay here and search the scrolls. I'm quite certain you'll find many helpful articles in our collection."

Yetsye's crooked smile revealed her understanding of his manner. She bowed her head, hoping to mask the laughter which threatened to erupt, and quietly offered him her thanks. She composed herself and raised her head. "Your lib'rarum is so magnificent! Where do you suggest I start my search?"

"Come! Come! I will take you to the proper section." His sandaled feet tapped quickly against the tiles. In his excitement to show off the wonderful collection, he tripped on a stone which had turned up its nose a bit from the rest of the floor. Yetsye almost giggled at the irony, but Tsadok's knuckles tapping her shoulder saved her.

They made it to the shelf with no further missteps. When Yetsye saw the massive amount of scrolls she'd have to go through, she sent a request for Ya'el to join her. Her siveh excelled at this type of task, never missing the smallest detail and committing all the vital parts to memory as quickly as she read them. It was almost always fun to have her siveh with her, but for something like this, Ya'el's particular talents were invaluable.

Tsadok gently pulled the scrolls from their square nooks as Seth Yi'in pointed them out. Yetsye took them from him and placed them in order on the nearest table. When her siveh joined them, she'd have an excellent selection to start with.

Ya'el arrived, rosy-cheeked and breathing rapidly. "Where do we start?" Her eyes sparkled. Yetsye knew she couldn't resist the lure of fresh knowledge. As soon as Ya'el spotted the pile of scrolls on the table, she selected the first one, unrolling it before she even sat fully on the bench.

"These are the scrolls which are most likely to contain the information you seek. From this point on, you may choose a scroll from any shelf." Seth Yi'in was being so cooperative, Yetsye could hardly believe it. He was practically dancing. "I remember how much fun I had when my quest began.

Oh, the excitement! The intrigue! Isn't it wonderful to solve puzzles? Would you care for some khaf'ket? It may help to keep your senses alert while you search."

She looked to Tsadok, who kept silent and Ya'el, who was already fading from view behind a growing pile of finished scrolls, and answered for all of them. "Yes, please. Thank you very much for your kind offer and for all your help. It's most appreciated." She infused as much respect as possible into her tone and bowed for good measure. She thought she'd figured out the old Guardian, but his rapid subject changes still made her dizzy.

Seth Yi'in walked to the nearest attendant and sent her for the khaf'ket. He turned around and gave a slight bow of his own. "It seems I have a bit of business to see to. I'll leave you to your research. If you have questions or run into a problem, you need only ask one of the stewards who will notify me." Without waiting for a reply, he spun on his heel and tapped his way off to another section of the great lib'rarum.

Yetsye turned to Tsadok. "Do you know where Yuvahl and Leila are?" He nodded once. "Do you think you could bring at least Yuvahl here? I'd like to talk to him for a moment. I think he'll be reluctant to leave Leila's side, though. He's grown to like her very much."

Tsadok nodded again and headed off toward the lib'rarum entrance. Something was wrong. Something had bothered him enough to set him back to the stone statue he resembled when he first joined them on their journey. She was determined to find out what. But the research should come first, at least for a little while. She didn't intend to wait too long, though, especially if it meant one of her friends was suffering. She had so few friends, after all.

Yuvahl entered the room, followed closely by Leila. Tsadok entered soon after them, his brow furrowed. "What is it, Yetsye?" Yuvahl bit out the words. It was so unlike him. She hardly knew what to do.

She gripped the hem of her tunic in her hands. "I'm sorry! Is my timing bad? I just wanted to see if you or Leila were interested in reading through some of these scrolls." Agitation burned in her belly. She didn't want to cause problems. She raised her hands, palms out, and added, "If not, that's fine. I just hadn't talked to you in a while and I felt like you might want to know what's going on." Her last few words trailed off, clouded by uncertainty. She clasped her hands together and dipped her chin, hardly daring to look at this unfamiliar Yuvahl.

"It's fine," he replied stiffly. "I can help on the morrowdawn. I have much to think about this dusking." With that, he turned abruptly and left. Leila followed him out, looking worried.

Yuvahl had never spoken to her that way before. At the thought of his sharp words, her hand wandered up to clutch at her heart. Ya'el, buried further in the scrolls, noticed nothing at all. Yetsye turned to Tsadok in confusion, but the mosaic mural overhead held him captive. She let out a wobbly breath, dragged in another and forced down the knot lodged in her throat. She would not cry over this. Her family's love for her was strong. Nothing would sway that for long, even if the present was painful.

Yetsye sat down opposite Ya'el to sift through the vast wealth of knowledge Mt. Charan Temple preserved within its walls. Never mind the blurriness that kept her sifting through scrolls longer than usual until her vision cleared.

18

Finding Risk

Scouring each scroll disguised the passage of time. Tsadok stood silent and still at Yetsye's side, keeping watch. If she took time to think about it, she would have wondered what could harm them in the temple. Twice they thought of the need for water, only to find he'd already placed it there for them. At the slightest hint of hunger, they looked up from their research to find a platter of fruit or nuts nearby. Not a word passed his lips, though, and Yetsye wondered what he was thinking.

Near the close of the second dawning, the suns sank low on the horizon when Ya'el finally put down her last scroll and stretched. "I think we'll do better if we stop for now. The suns are setting. We should rest," she sang, "while the star lights burn bright in the sky-dome."

Yetsye nodded. Her dry, gritty eyes and aching back pleaded for relief. Tightness at the top of her neck and across her shoulders heralded stiffness when she woke on the morrow. She followed close behind Ya'el, dragging heavy feet toward the arched entrance. Though tired, Yetsye giggled. With Tsadok close behind her, she was certain they looked like a tsa'gra dam herding her kits.

Ya'el entered her room. Yetsye waited until she'd closed the door, then turned around and headed back outside. She knew Tsadok would stay with her. She wondered whether she could crack his stony exterior and get to the root of the problem. Was it even safe to try, especially considering their exhaustion? She knew he was trustworthy and a friend. Treasuring that precious connection encouraged her to offer any help within her power.

Yetsye led the way to a fountain in the middle of the courtyard. Water spewed from a central spout amid three frolicking draconisi. She stared at them, wondering what it would be like to see the flashy, long-bodied water-folk in their ocean home.

"Have you ever seen one?" Random curiosity took over for a moment. When Tsadok didn't answer, Yetsye turned to face him and sat on the stone wall surrounding the fountain. He shook his head and her brow wrinkled in concern. "Please talk to me. We only just started speaking as friends and now you won't say anything at all. To anyone."

Tsadok dropped toward the ground in a squat that would allow him to move quickly if necessary. He bowed his head, and she studied the single complex braid with her eyes. He took a deep breath and raised his face. She could see him clearly thanks to the two brightest moons peeking over the garden wall. The weather-roughened features so close to her own allowed her to chip away at the layers of armor masking his thoughts. He closed his eyes so suddenly she flinched.

When he opened them again, he also cracked open the door of his soul. The force of so many conflicting emotions washed over her like the rushing wave of her Visioning. It almost toppled her from her perch and stole her breath. The desire to help him carry those chaotic emotions off-set the intense need to save herself from the flood.

He nodded as a tear slid down her cheek. An unspoken apology flitted over his features. When she could speak, she shook her head and half whispered, "You have nothing to apologize for. You haven't done anything wrong." His apology confused her. Hadn't she asked?

At least she knew now he wasn't upset with her. Or was he? It was almost impossible to sort through such an immense wave of emotion. "I think I might have to apologize to you, though. Maybe it was rude of me to press you into sharing." She looked up and simply breathed for a moment. Then, she closed her eyes and listened, extended her senses to the maximum to feel deeply all that lay around her. She needed to center her focus so she wouldn't mar this friendship with careless words. Her heartbeat slowed to normal and her breathing evened out.

She turned toward Tsadok and found only the garden path edged with pretty shrubs. He'd moved to sit beside her on the edge of the fountain, close enough to talk to but out of her reach. He was always so considerate. Placing her head in her hands, waves of uncertainty once again overwhelmed her.

"Have I hurt you? Angered you?" she directed to her knees. She couldn't look at him this time. She couldn't bear to see disgust or disappointment on his face.

"No." Who knew such relief nestled in so negative a word? She gasped in its wake. He heard it, though she tried to hold it in. He exhaled, as if a heavy regret weighed him down.

"Thank you for speaking to me." Yetsye got up and turned to go. She felt a tug at her belt and turned. His face was open again. He wasn't ready to leave and didn't want her to go alone. For this selfless friend, she stayed.

"I won't leave, but I need to walk a bit. I have too much energy pent up inside." He released her.

She paced in silence, then decided since he wouldn't talk, she might as well attempt another calming exercise. It had been too long since she last felt the refreshing embrace of her dear Y'Dahnndrya.

She lay face up beside the gravel pathway, letting her entire weight press her down into the soft cushion of grass. Before her eyes closed, she caught a flash of movement on her right. Tsadok followed her example.

He turned his head to look at her. "How do you do this? If it calms, I will try."

"Face the stars. Close your eyes. Feel your weight pressing into the arms of Y'Dahnndrya. And breathe slowly, deeply, steadily." With soothing words, she explained. "Choose a sense. I usually go with sound first. What can you hear? There are so many sounds around us. We hardly notice them in our busy lives. Stretch your hearing to the limit. As you do, the other senses will open up. You'll be able to sense things in ways you usually don't." She wondered if her eagerness to share this precious gift was too much. Everyone back home looked at her strangely when she tried to explain it.

For several heartbeats, there was only the breathing of two human Y'Dahnndryans and the night sounds of the garden's met'cha, the splashing fountain, an unfamiliar cooing in the distance, and a light breeze stirring the leaves.

"Do you-" "We have-" they began together.

"Please go ahead." Yetsye puzzled herself. She never talked during her calming ritual. Why did she try now? And he was going to speak, too? She frowned, wondering if he would continue.

"No. You should go first."

She sighed. Oh, well. Maybe he'd answer her question. She could only try.

"Do you have a place like Levanna in D'Koruyi? I've often wondered what life is like in other clans. What animals live there? And what kind of music dances on the breezes of your home?"

"Hold! I can only answer each question in turn." The hint of a smile danced in his voice now. "For inspiration and to search for the Voice of Kai'yanga within us, we visit Mesna'ya, The Singing Canyon."

"Do you sing there?"

"Sometimes. But it is called Mesna'ya because it is the wind who sings through the canyon. Holes of all sizes and shapes cover the walls and as the wind passes by, the song it sings is like a band of pipers rousing the spirits of the Children."

Yetsye totally forgot about the calming ritual, turned on her side and propped her head on her hand so she could hear him clearly. She couldn't imagine the sounds, but she tried. How wonderful it would be to experience it in person!

He remained on his back, eyes closed. "We go there once a tsimik, as a people. But anyone can visit the canyon any time they need deeper guidance. I visited a few nainda before you found me in the forest. It was then that I received this tattoo. It sounds to me like your Visioning ceremony and my visit to Mesna'ya work the same way. While I waited at the edge of the canyon to hear the voice of Kai'yanga, I saw a dream. Will you listen to it?"

She nodded slowly, fearing her voice would break the fragile connection forming between them. He must've heard her movement because he continued.

"I stood on the canyon and it fell away beneath my feet. I should have jumped, but I did not. Nor was I afraid. I watched all of D'Koruyin Territory grow smaller and smaller beneath me. Gold-flecked wings unfurled from my back and I opened my mouth to cry out in pain. All that came forth was the cry of the hawikh. Calling. Calling for..." His voice trailed away for a moment. "I am uncertain, but a question rang in the cry. I flew in ever-widening circles and as I flew, more of my people came to join me in the sky-dome, golden feathers flashing green in the light of Tsifi'ra and Mit'ra, the Glorious Lights. A black line which began at the horizon came closer, growing wider and thicker. Soon, more fliers joined us in the air, brown-gold feathers flashing the colors of their clans. We soared high in the sky-dome, rejoicing in the freedom of flight.

"To my right, an el'tekh flashed white, and orange flames fluttered along the wingtips and trailed behind the tail. This el'tekh wore a tall crest upon the head, also tipped with orange flame. As it flew, it ignited the two on either side of it. This fire did not kill. It quickened. Then the flaming el'tekh flew toward me. I backed away in surprise, but was unafraid. I let it come closer and soon my gold-flecked feathers were alight with green flames which did not burn me. Instead, I felt stronger and lighter. Invincible." He paused.

Yetsye was so caught up in the spinning of his tale she had missed the tears streaming down his temples. Now that she noticed them, she sat up, knees curled to the side, and reached out a hand cautiously toward him. When she would've touched his shoulder, he opened his mouth to continue, and she quickly pulled back.

"When I woke, this tattoo marked my chest, a tattoo not of my choosing. I believe it is the way Kai'yanga has spoken to me. In this way, I cannot forget the purpose for my existence." He sat up, still not looking at her. "You are the white el'tekh, Yetsye Shirasdatir. As soon as I saw your changed appearance at Levanna, it confirmed what I already believed. It was you I searched for. But it seems it was you who found me," he asked as he turned toward her, "was it not?"

Piercing blue eyes cut straight through soft brown ones, driving deep into her soul. She nodded because words refused to form.

"I knew I had to find you, and I know what I must do now. I will help you with your task, even if it takes all of your given tsimikin to accomplish it."

Yetsye sat up sharply on her knees and gasped in dismay. "No! You can't do that. What about your own life? Your clan? What about the special person you'll choose for your life-mate?" Yetsye shook her head slowly in disbelief. "Why would you risk all those things to stay with me? I'm just a stranger and not even one of your people."

"You are of my people if you are Y'Dahnndryan. Have you not worked out your purpose yet?"

Affronted, she quickly snapped, "I can't help it if it takes a while for me to catch on to things!"

Looking away from her, he muttered, "Maybe that's why Azilet'zal had to show you three times." She thought she heard an edge of disappointment in his low voice.

Anger ignited in Yetsye. Rising stiffly, she stalked away, tears brimming. She didn't get five paces before he grabbed her elbow and turned her around. One eyebrow rose and his smile confused her. When he saw her brimming tears, apology took the place of humor. "I am sorry. My teasing was too harsh." He dropped his hand to his side, allowing her space and time to choose what she would do next.

She was torn between walking away and staying. She'd got what she wanted, the assurance of friendship. They were talking again. She inhaled deeply and nodded once. They continued walking toward the living quarters, but at a much slower pace.

"I was only angry because you're right." She was bad at admitting her faults, but she didn't want to leave things as they were. Positive deeds cleansed negative energy, as her matir often reminded her. "I'm sorry for my anger. Ya'el says I always take things too seriously."

He inclined his dark head in understanding.

"You're certain your task is to help me with mine?" He nodded again. "Then I guess we're both working toward the unification of the people because I'm more and more certain that's where my dreams are pointing. I think it's going to take more courage than I have, though. And maybe that's why you saw the dream which came to you. I also know that if I need them, Yuvahl and Ya'el will be with me."

They were almost at the entrance now. Yetsye stopped and turned confused eyes to Tsadok. "Have you noticed how Yuvahl stays close to Leila?" The openness of before disappeared from his face completely, but she continued. "I hope beyond hope we succeed. I wouldn't wish my batir to live in agony for the rest of his life."

Tsadok returned her gaze with raised eyebrows.

"He loves her," Yetsye announced. "He's finally decided and chosen her as his life-mate." She clasped her hands together under her chin and mused, "But I doubt he's mentioned that to her yet. Quietly supporting her is his way of showing love and care. Few people catch on, but I bet Leila sees it in some small way. I wonder if she feels the same."

When his eyes didn't stray from her face, she explained a bit more. "You see, when we children of Shira decide on something, there's no going back, no other path but the one. We are determined." He nodded again at her explanation. His silent answers made her remember why she originally came out to the courtyard.

"You never answered my question. What's bothering you?" She hoped her sincere concern showed on her face.

He turned away and kept silent. Yetsye counted eight rapid heartbeats, wondering if he'd answer. When he finally faced her again, his eyes hardened with resolve. He took a deep breath and looked directly into her eyes. Yetsye waited, wondering what required so much courage to say to someone like her who was small and totally harmless compared to someone like him.

"The best way to explain is to compare my situation to that of Yuvahl, but with a much heavier weight of responsibility." His eyes never left hers and he never moved, but Yetsye felt as if she was nose to nose with him.

She turned away first, confused by his words. She was sure of one thing, though. He loved someone deeply, possibly someone he shouldn't. And what did he mean by responsibility? Was having a life-mate such a heavy burden? A foreign twinge struck her chest. She finally nodded slowly.

"I think I understand. I'll do my best on this quest. Maybe one dawning, the obstacles will shatter. I'll work hard for both you and Yuvahl to live in happiness with those you love." She smiled gently up at him. He nodded without taking his eyes away, but his emotions remained locked inside again and their connection severed. Was she not a good enough friend? The thought saddened her.

Yetsye spun on her heel and led the way to their rooms. She might not be sure about many things, but one thing she knew. Sleep wouldn't be easy this dusking.

19

Forbidden Place

Three dawnings eased along at Mt. Charan Temple. The quiet of the cavernous lib'rarum allowed Yetsye and Ya'el to study in peace. They'd fallen into a comfortable routine — rise, dawning meal, study, middawnding meal, study, quick break, cleansing, dusking meal, study, stroll in the courtyard, and sleep.

As each dawning passed, the need to take action with no clear direction increased Yetsye's agitation. Her heel bounced as it tapped out a frantic rhythm. Ya'el tried to relieve her restlessness.

"I guess it's time to gather all we've learned together and see what we can do with it." Yetsye fixed her eyes on Ya'el, ready to take the next step.

After a quick inhale, Ya'el shared her findings. "Concerning Y'Dahnndrya's trembling, I've only found legends surrounding the Great Cataclysm. There are six different spins, one from each clan. Though the tales have some minor variations, there are more similarities. In all of them, the ground of Y'Dahnndrya shook and rifts opened, revealing a sea of glowing liquid fire. Another similarity in each was people becoming sick or dying from the strange mists that rose from the fiery rivers. And the liquid fire burned anything it touched to ash." She paused for a moment. Her color faded a bit more with each reminder of her brush with death. Yetsye reached out a hand to grasp Ya'el's, finding it cold as ice. Ya'el smiled her thanks.

She gathered herself, rearranged two of the scrolls, and continued. "It looks like these are based on eyewitness accounts. More disturbing than anything else, there doesn't seem to be a way to stop this fiery mass from going wherever it wills. When scouts returned to sites where the fiery rivers once flowed, they saw only black stone in its place. Some of the stone was shiny, like glashiin. Holes and bumps textured other spots. No one seems to know how this happened or what caused it. Whatever the differences in texture, the stone was cool to the touch, and no mists rose from it. They deemed it safe to explore and scholars studied it without learning much." She paused for breath.

"As far as I can tell from my reading, the study continues today in the Fyrna Mountains of Shinnoah and in parts of Genzet. There are those who consider one other place an excellent school for learning about the Great Cataclysm." She looked around the table at Yuvahl, Leila, Tsadok, and finally Yetsye, where she allowed her eyes to linger. She grinned, quirked an eyebrow, and stared Yetsye down in challenge.

Yetsye had enough of her ill-timed teasing. "Come on. Tell us!"

"Yacan."

Her fireball exploded exactly as expected. Ya'el smiled in triumph as everyone gasped. Everyone but Tsadok.

"Yacan?" Yuvahl had always held a troublesome interest in the forbidden place, and Yetsye frowned at the excitement in his words. "Are you suggesting we travel there to find out more?"

Yetsye squirmed in dismay. She had no desire to go there. If Ya'el's life was in danger, Yacan would be the most likely place for her to lose it.

"But what of Yetsye's quest?" Tsadok interrupted. "Have you not promised to help her?" Tsadok rarely voiced his opinions and Yetsye was just as surprised as the others when he spoke in her defense.

"Yes. And we are." Ya'el's eyes darkened toward him for the first time since he'd joined them. Her voice oozed indignation. Rising to her full height, which was no taller than a mana's back, she shook off Yetsye's hand and asked, "Did you think M'Neshunnayans are oath-breakers?" Yetsye stiffened, but Ya'el reined in her temper to explain. "I believe her quest and Y'Dahnndrya's shaking may be connected. It's worth investigating." She turned an expectant face to Yetsye.

Why did she have to decide? No one liked her decisions. Ever. The harsh tang of dismay soured her stomach when they pushed her into making one. She gulped and clasped her hands together in her lap.

"What?" The word was a hot coal forced painfully from her mouth. Her heart beat frantically against the cage which trapped it.

"What does the group leader think? Have you learned anything?" Ya'el pushed for an answer.

"Yes." She struggled to put her knowledge in order and continued, though her voice faltered a little. "I read about the Great Cataclysm and its effects, but found nothing more than what you've already shared." She stopped there, hoping Ya'el would drop the other question.

"And about Yacan?" Ya'el was pushy when she really wanted something, and Yacan offered an irresistible adventure. No one could miss how the lure of mystery set her green eyes aglow. Yetsye remembered all the warnings uttered by every Guardian, the spins concerning those who visited the island and never returned.

"What about Serafin? They say she's the most fierce of all the Ikhel'dur and the strictest Guardian. She won't let you break the rules of Yacan. The penalty is death." Yetsye raised watery eyes to Ya'el and then to Yuvahl. "Please forget it. It's too risky," she pleaded.

Ya'el shook her head, determined. "I know about Serafin. I also know she's not the only Guardian on the island. It was said that long ago, before the Great Cataclysm, trees and other plants were different, sentient in strange ways. They could defend themselves. After the Great Cataclysm, humans began caring for the plants and they calmly allowed this. All but one. She is Edrea."

Seth Yi'in entered as Ya'el finished. "Are you thinking of going to Yacan? How foolish! You'd never survive." His long mustache danced as he shook his head.

"Would you tell us what you know about Edrea, Guardian?" Yetsye hoped his spin would stop them. Leila wouldn't continue the journey with them, but Yetsye had still seen her face pale at the mention of Yacan. Tsadok had his mask on again. Seth Yi'in might be her only hope.

The Guardian began the tale after a long moment spent stroking his mustache. "Edrea, the Great Tree, is reputed to be the oldest kho'ni tree in all of Y'Dahnndrya."

Since kho'ni trees grew taller and wider than any other tree she knew, Yetsye couldn't imagine the size of Edrea after she'd been alive for so many hundreds of tsimikin.

"Edrea chooses the Guardian of her island. No one knows how. She also passes judgment on those who set foot on the island, deciding who should live and return and who should disappear from the face of Y'Dahnndrya forever. She is thought to be the first test of worthiness and Serafin sees to all the other tests." He glanced around the circle of travelers, measuring the effect of his words.

"I don't want to go. It scares me." Yetsye decided bluntness was her best weapon this time. She was right. Seth Yi'in nodded sagely. The smug look he usually wore changed to a concerned frown.

But Ya'el's face darkened again. Instead of backing down, she pushed harder. "We have a legitimate chance to visit one of the most wondrous places in the world and you would let fear be your guide?" Her calm voice fooled no one who caught the daggers shooting from her eyes.

"Seriously, Yetsye. You should accept more challenges in your lifetime. How will you ever gain the courage to chase after what you truly want in this life?" If Ya'el saw how her words affected Yetsye, she was too angry to care. Yetsye trembled inside, but she wouldn't give Ya'el the satisfaction of seeing her break.

Ya'el's tirade continued, taking a vicious twist. "How will you ever win a life-mate with such a cowardly heart? I thought we were trying to solve problems here. I thought we were going to change our world. Do you think we'll accomplish it by cowering in safe corners?"

She was now as red as the runner in the center of the table, seeing Yetsye as an obstacle in the way of her research. Normally, she wasn't this harsh and each word cut Yetsye like a ki'fi, re-opening the floodgates of her tears. She clamped her mouth shut, though, ensuring the hot words straining for release remained caged. This Ya'el, drunk on the thought of adventure, was not her caring siveh.

"Ya'el. That's enough." Yuvahl stepped in between them calmly. He was slow to react, probably from the same dismay as the others. Ya'el's vehemence shocked them all. Yetsye breathed a shaky sigh of relief and nodded her thanks.

Tears still falling, Yetsye controlled her voice enough to answer. She turned her head left, then right, not knowing a safe direction to plant her gaze. "You don't know what you're asking, Ya'el." The tremulous words were simple enough. Tsadok placed his hand next to hers on the bench, lightly brushing against her white-knuckled grip. She took another shaky breath. "I will think on this. I need..." She rose quickly and stepped back from the bench, still uncertain where to look. Shaking her head, she turned and ran, leaving the others to deal with the aftermath.

Yetsye flew through the lib'rarum entrance, her loose outer tunic flowing behind her. Her breathing grew more ragged with each pounding step. Desires and doubts waged war within her.

Should she yield to Ya'el, only to find it caused her death? Would it make her even angrier to take away what might be the only opportunity to explore a place she and Yuvahl always studied? What should she do?

Yetsye ran until the air was fire in her lungs. Every muscle shook, threatening to drop her to the ground if she stopped. When she could no longer see through the tears, she fell to her hands and knees, gasping for breath, sobbing until the tears ran dry.

20

Lady Aflame

Slowly, Yetsye raised herself to sit on the cold stone pathway. Even though she and Tsadok had been visiting the gardens each dusking, this area was unfamiliar. An interesting sculpture carved from shiny black stone stood in front of her, surrounded by fyryan shrubs. The flame-colored flora drew her gaze upward. The artisan had carved a woman with long, flowing hair. Her tattered tunic showed much of her flawless body through ragged holes. She walked on tongues of flame. The brilliant orange fyryan blossoms added a visual effect unlike anything Yetsye had seen. The woman's arms rose in front of her, as if to welcome all of Y'Dahnndrya.

As Yetsye stared, the woman's hair rippled, as if stirred by the breeze. The flames at her feet danced, and the torn hem of her tunic flipped and fluttered to avoid them. This woman walked with purpose. Her eyes blazed, golden stars of fierce determination. But the smile beneath the strong yet dainty nose revealed a gentle spirit.

Yetsye couldn't tear her eyes away. As she stared, the woman came fully to life, glowing gold and orange. She looked down at Yetsye, who sensed rather than saw the woman's smile widen. Though her mouth didn't move, the woman's voice rang clear in the young maid's mind. Her deep, rich alto held a tone of authority.

"Do not be afraid! You will find courage is there when you need it most. This courage will not depend on those around you. It will come from within, placed there by the Source of all creation. Do not fear going where the shadows grow long and dark, for there will your courage and strength be honed for the times ahead."

A hand on her back brought Yetsye forcefully to the present. The statue stood lifeless on its pedestal once more. Yetsye's cheeks were cold, and she realized she was crying again. The hand moved from her back a bit uncertainly to wrap her shoulders in consolation. The comforting scent of wood and leather surrounded her. Tsadok.

She whispered brokenly, "H-how can I let my s-siveh die! How... can I en-encourage them to g-go?"

She buried her face in his shoulder and wept until her throat was raw. When tears gave way to shuddering breaths and shuddering breaths became soft sniffles, she finally stirred and would have moved, but the arm at her shoulders held her in place.

"Just for a moment, please listen." She relaxed a little, and he slowly released her. He cupped her cheeks with his hands, capturing her eyes with his own, and continued. "You have a great heart for your family, wishing to protect them at all costs, even to sacrifice your own desires. The depth of your care is apparent. But there is a flaw. To protect someone from experience is to hinder their growth. Ya'el may not die there. Why would you say this? Why could it not be Yuvahl or me?" He paused for her answer.

Yetsye uttered hoarsely, "Matir saw it in a dream long before I left for my Visioning."

He nodded. "Your siveh does not know this?" When Yetsye shook her head, he continued. "Even if she did, do you think she would change her mind? What was it you told me when first we visited this garden? When the children of Shira decide on something, the decision is made and there is no going back, no other path but the one. They are determined."

She nodded and pulled at his arms. He set her free. "Thank you, Tsadok, for reminding me," she said, bowing her head. "I'll tell the others." She looked up at him again. Her watery smile snapped his mask back into place. She winced, afraid she'd offended him. She stood to return, and he followed.

In the lib'rarum, they found the others still gathered around the table. A huge map opened before them, showing all the land masses and oceans of Y'Dahnndrya. Yetsye followed Yuvahl's arm with her eyes until she ended at his finger resting on Yacan. Her eyes brimmed once more. Even if she decided against it, those two would likely override her decision. The thought of it cut her deeply.

She bowed her head. It seemed she did nothing but hide and cry lately. A lonely tear made a slow path down her right cheek to drip off her chin.

When she raised her head again, her bruised spirit didn't hinder the words which burst unwanted from between trembling lips. "We'll go. Azilet'zal help me live with myself! But we'll go."

She stared at Yuvahl until he bowed his head, understanding only now the depth of risk in going this direction. How had her level-headed batir forgotten something so important, all for a selfish desire? He wasn't himself either. This quest was changing all of them.

Her shaky sigh hung heavy in the air as she turned on her heel and left the lib'rarum for the last time that dusking. Tsadok stayed with the others and his absence affected her more than she expected. Was she depending on him?

Instead of heading to her quarters, she visited the stables. She was used to visiting the mana often back home. The path they followed now allowed very few visits with her dear friends. The mana whistled and cooed as they recognized Yetsye, excited to see a familiar friend again. She patted each of them and uttered soft, encouraging clicks and coos, speaking in the manner of their kind.

By the time she finished this process with the last mana, tears were once again rolling down her cheeks. She brushed at them angrily. She'd decided. There was no going back. No matter what, she'd see this quest through to its end.

The mana in front of her sensed her distress and nibbled at the closest puff of hair. The tie broke, spilling one half of her hair down her neck and across her eyes. This had the desired effect, and a watery chuckle escaped her lips at the obvious ploy. The mana rumbled his approval. Her softened eyes gazed in wonder at the playful beast.

"Thank you," she whispered, looking directly into his eyes. He bowed his head toward her and she placed her forehead against his and whispered again, "Thank you very much."

When she raised her head, Tsadok stood at her elbow with a look she'd never seen directed at her before. If she was to name it, she'd think he was furious. When he spoke, she knew she was right.

"Why did you not go to your room?" The quiet words seemed chipped from ice.

She flinched and backed away. "I needed more time. I was in no mood to sleep." She shook her head. The fallen portion of her hair swayed and reminded her of her disheveled state. She blushed. She must look utterly ridiculous! Bowing her head, she frantically tried to remove the other tie, turning away as she did so. He caught her hands and forced her to look at him.

"Your hair is not as important as your safety. Do not leave again without telling me where you are going."

Yetsye's temper flared. She'd had enough of being trampled on this dawning. She yanked her hands down quickly and her skull crashed into his nose, stunning the unprepared D'Koruyin. He released her, and she backed up against the stall door. She reached behind her back and fumbled nervously with the catch as she hastily apologized. "I'm sorry. But I'm tired of everyone forcing me into hard decisions. And I'm tired of being treated like a piece of precious jewelry. I can protect myself if the need arises."

Tsadok shook his head to clear it, then focused his eyes upon her, now several paces away. The catch released, and she stumbled out of the stall. He stalked toward her. She nearly tripped and fell, but regained her balance and raced to the stable door. She made it to the third stall before he caught her around the waist, trapping her arms at her side. Her heart threatened to fly away in fear. Why were the mana so calm?

"You cannot run from this." The flat voice in her ear revealed none of his intentions and she struggled. "This is the consequence of making me worry. Now stand still."

"But you're angry with me! Why should I stand here and listen to more words that slash my soul to shreds?"

"I will not do that. I swear it on my honor as a warrior and a D'Koruyin. I will not raise my voice. I am not here to discipline a youngling. Will you listen calmly?"

She stilled and eventually nodded, so he relaxed his grip. "I want you to trust me and rely on me for help." Her only response was a jerky nod. He released her completely, but she still couldn't face him. Her spirit was in no condition to allow words past her lips right now.

"Would you like to know how D'Koruyin women wear their hair?"

His abrupt change of the subject caught her off guard and she spun around to stare at him, her mouth gaping. He had to ask her again before she could answer, and still her answer came in a daze.

"I th-think I'd like that." Having got those few, small words out, she felt more able to deal with the storm raging inside her. Hairstyles seemed a safe enough topic.

He held out his hand, and she stared at it for a long moment. Slowly, she reached out her own and cautiously placed it in his. He led her back to the garden and directed her to sit on a bench near their usual spot. But instead of sitting beside her, he stood behind her. Startled, she bent to move away, but he placed a hand on her shoulder.

"I didn't think you were going to fix my hair!" She fought off his hands in protest. "It's really hard to work with," she protested as she dodged and attempted to cover her hair.

Her argument fell on deaf ears, and he firmly moved her hands out of his way. He placed her hands at her sides and reminded her, "I want you to trust me." At the sound of his voice, she jumped, but his conversation was so normal she soon relaxed. His fingers removed the last hair tie easily.

"You worry about strange things. Your hair, for instance. Do not. I am as determined as you. I will work at it until it is done. Why is your hair always bound in this way?"

"Because it's easy and secure," she retorted.

"Yes, but there are other ways to bind hair easily and securely. I know it is important to you to keep your hair from blocking your eyes or ears. These things are also important to my people. We travel often and many times the move is sudden. The D'Koruyin have perfected many ways of binding the hair to keep it out of their way and still keep the length."

As he spoke, he brushed his fingers through her hair. Yetsye winced, hissing in a quick breath. He didn't apologize. Maybe he didn't notice.

"You are right about this beautiful hair," he continued. "It is difficult to manage. I will win, though." She blushed in surprise and grinned at the declaration. She winced again as he loosened another knot.

While working on her hair, Tsadok spoke of his childhood adventures living with the Gahl Tribe, Mesna'ya, life on the plains, life in the mountains, anything but the previous topic which caused such chaos.

"The tam'na of the plains are shy. You would like them, I think. They rumble loudly when they are pleased and growl low when they are not. When they are happy, they hop on their four paws like the d'nagze of the mountains. When they hunt mijiwa, you cannot see them at all, for their coats blend well with the golden grasses of the plain. Their eyes are a deeper gold."

He was talking so much! She'd read about tam'na in the lib'rarum at Zulima, but she'd never seen living ones. Animal spins always improved her mood. Yetsye drank in the soothing balm.

"Can you make friends with them?"

"Yes. I once befriended a female with two kits. She followed me home, the two kits tumbling after her. My morah smiled but said they must live in their own den, for ours was too small for all of us."

Yetsye chuckled, a low musical sound. She felt a light tug on her tunic. Tsadok backed away and stepped around the bench to face her. He nodded in satisfaction.

Yetsye couldn't look away from the proud smile on his face. It didn't stop her curiosity, though. "But how will I accomplish this style? I couldn't see what you were doing or even tell from the movement of your hands." Though thankful for his help, his actions confused her.

"It is alright if you do not know the how. I will help you whenever you wish."

"But what if you're not there?"

"I will be there."

"Then you'll need to help me on the morrowdawn, I guess?" She was uncertain about this new bend in her path.

"If you wish it, then I will. However, this style is for travel and will hold for many dawnings without the need to take it down and put it up again. It is much more efficient than your previous style and I think it suits you better."

Running her hands over her hair, she discovered braids gathered at the nape. She bowed her head to hide the blush she could feel warming her cheeks. It was impossible, though. The moons shone brightly. There was no hope of hiding it.

She rose quickly and walked ahead of him back to their sleeping quarters, pondering the strange ache in her chest. When had it begun? She shoved the question aside, afraid of the possibilities. They'd be preparing for the trip to Yacan on the morrowdawn. She hadn't thought of it before, but she dreaded what Seth Yi'in would say when he learned they were disregarding his warning.

At the door to her room, Tsadok tugged at her elbow, drawing her attention. "Please do not leave us again without letting us know where you are going. You are too important." He waited for her answer, his eyes never leaving hers.

"I give you my word. I'll let someone know. Thank you, Tsadok, for everything you've done this dusking. You helped me so much." She started into her room and turned back. "Is your nose alright? I'm really sorry if I hurt you." She bowed her head to hide her shame at the memory.

"I think I will live. I should have expected it. You were cornered and, like the beasts you love, you do not react well when cornered."

She nodded her thanks and entered her room.

21

Determined Shadow

Tsifi'ra's face peeked over the horizon when Yetsye hurried back to the secluded niche she stumbled into yesterdusk. But first, she placed a written note on top of her table where one of her siblings, or Tsadok, would find it. She really needed some time alone to focus on her purpose.

A roughly hewn bench she hadn't seen the dusking before faced the alcove where the Lady stood. She shook her head. This really wasn't the best place for her to focus, but she eventually spotted a shwi'ich tree, its long tendrils blooming with tiny white tubular blossoms. Their soft perfume lured her. She parted the dangling branches and raised her hand to the trunk. The harsh, stringy bark tickled her palm.

A small spring near the roots of the tree, bubbled over and around three specially placed stones. Yetsye wondered at the strength of those roots. In the dahlsik of Ikishi, when storms raged, these trees whipped around wildly. After the storms passed, they leafed and bloomed again, twice as lush. She couldn't think of a more perfect example of how she should live — pliable enough to bend and twist with the stormy trials of life, warmth and strength enough in her core to withstand the frigidity of loss, and able to bloom beautifully in seasons of plenty.

Yetsye's eyes followed the trunk up through the verdant cover to the sky-dome above. Dawning came gently, first deep blue, then pale purple. A few stars still winked at her, but the moons had long since set. The silence of the garden was broken only by the laughing spring and a few early-rising insects and beasts. She sat on a flat rock beneath the tree and leaned her back against the trunk, rather than lying on the dewy grass.

Her eyes fluttered closed as she opened her senses to immerse herself in the beauty of this place. Krichte fiddled their merry tunes, serenading mates. Himmers darted here and there, their hide wings beating the air only a few times as they flitted and glided, flitted and glided their way around the tree-tops. The scent of freshly washed earth and grass surrounded her, mingled with aromatic saghitan, grekh, and sweet chimah.

Something cold pushed against her fingers. She waited. The brush of soft, fuzzy warmth snuggling against her hands rewarded her patience. A bizhal! She'd only seen them once before, at a vendor's stall. Their loving natures enriched the spirit, and many people enjoyed adding them to their households. She kept still, and the bizhal clawed its way around her lap and settled its round body in her loosely clasped hands. When the bizhal no longer fidgeted, Yetsye opened her eyes.

Yetsye found, not the two sets of icy blue eyes she expected, but three staring back at her. Had it not been for the bizhal in her lap, she would've darted away from the scowl that was entirely too close. She blinked and lowered her eyes, then flipped over one hand for the bizhal's inspection. It bowed its head and nuzzled her palm, begging for a good scratch behind its tiny, round ears. She couldn't help smiling at the palm-sized ball of fluff. She picked it up carefully, cupping it in her hands, and ignored the thunderclouds darkening Tsadok's brow.

"Are you lost?" she asked it, delaying her scolding. "Lonely? Separated from family? I wish I knew its language." She'd search for a scroll on bizhals as soon as possible. The bizhal didn't mind as she raised it up. She brushed her cheek against its black down and admired its two iridescent antennae. "Aren't you beautiful?" The bizhal nuzzled back, and she reluctantly set it softly on the ground.

"Alright. Is it time to return, then?" She asked without taking her eyes off the bizhal who bobbled away into the shrubs.

"Yes." His voice revealed only slight annoyance. She wondered why she hadn't smelled the wood and leather she associated with Tsadok.

Yetsye sought the light breeze. The trunk had been shielding her from it. "You tricked my senses," she chuckled wryly as she glanced at him from the corner of her eyes. Her grin faded. The scowl hadn't disappeared. A deep sigh escaped. "You found my note?" Resignation crept into her tone as she broached the subject she least wanted to discuss. She had kept her promise. What more did he want?

"Yes," came the sharp reply.

"Then why are you scowling?" She had a feeling she knew, but she asked anyway. If he wanted her to do something specific, he really should've said that from the beginning. Her contrary behavior confused her. Maybe she was more like Ya'el than she thought.

"Why did you not tell me in person where you were going?" Yes, there was exasperation, but a certain weightiness hinted at an emotional complexity she couldn't quite grasp.

She finally faced him. His bowed head and tense muscles revealed his disappointment and spurred her to make things right. Reaching out hesitantly, she apologized. "I'm sorry. Please believe I was not trying to hurt you. I had to be alone for this."

"And did you accomplish what you set out to do?" The words escaped through his clenched jaws and rapped against her ears like her teacher's scroll.

"No," she mumbled and averted her eyes nervously. She pushed herself up and walked over to the bench she'd shunned before. How could she tell him he was part of the reason the connection failed?

"Humph!" he grunted. "There must be a reason you did not tell me in person." The scowl softened, and he shook his head as if he thought he might reveal too much.

Yetsye covered her face with both hands, trying to think fast. She rubbed her eyes. If she explained the reason she needed to be alone, would it hurt him even more? Bluntness might be best, since it would be the most honest. She was a terrible liar, anyway, thank Azilet'zal.

"Please try to understand. It's harder for me to concentrate when people are around." She couldn't stop the jerkiness of the words she forced from her mouth. "I think it's even harder if I sense you nearby. I don't know why." Her hands took on a life of their own in a curious dance of gestures.

"Even if I am quiet and you cannot sense me?" She looked up at the whispered syllables and took in his bowed head and slumped shoulders. What happened to the proud warrior? What had she done? He released his breath in a rush and she jumped. Tossing his long braids over one shoulder, he intoned, "I understand." He turned and walked silently away.

"Wait! I don't think you do." She jumped to her feet and called after him, desperate to repair the broken connection.

He ignored her. Stunned, she followed him, slowly at first, then half-running to match his stride. She had to clear up this misunderstanding.

"Please wait, Tsadok!" As she grabbed for his arm to stop him, he suddenly braked. She slammed into his back, full force, almost knocking them both to the ground and scratching his elbow with her thumbnail. When she righted herself and caught her breath, she faced him.

"You really don't understand. Your actions just now, your feelings, were very clear. You're disappointed and hurt and I'm the reason. I don't want that." She was almost pleading with him now. Without realizing, she placed her hand on his shoulder and looked up into his eyes. "I enjoy your presence, your friendship. No one else has ever taken such care of me besides my family. The experience is new to me."

She paused, and he turned his head slightly to look past her shoulder. She couldn't allow that yet. Yetsye groaned inwardly at the sudden role reversal. She moved into his line of sight again to finish, looking up at him, still pleading. "But even Yuvahl and Ya'el understand I need this time alone to focus my thoughts."

He snorted and tossed his head again. If this wasn't so serious, she'd have compared him to the mana. He would've walked away, but she grabbed for his other arm before he could fully turn. He stopped but refused to look at her. She positioned herself in front of him again. Her brows drawn and hard, intent on his face, she dared him to keep looking away.

When he finally gave in, his expressionless mask was firmly in place. Her spirits dipped a bit, but she bravely continued. "Please don't stop coming to gardens like this with me after our dusking meal. That time is precious to me. There's no one I can share this with. Even my siblings are too restless to stay for long, though they have tried." She smirked at the irony, since she was usually the most restless of the three. "But you distract me. I don't understand why yet." He averted his eyes again, but she finished anyway. "I'm trying. Maybe if I know the why, I can learn of a way to focus which would allow me to concentrate no matter what."

She lowered her arms to her sides and fidgeted. Too much hinged on the success of her terribly worded argument. Yetsye held her breath, eager to hear his answer. His sharp nod rewarded her patience.

He took a deep breath and in a quiet voice, almost a whisper, she heard, "Alright. I dislike it, but I will leave you during the early dawning time." His voice was as stony as his expression. His eyes flashed blue fire as he continued, "But do not do me the dishonor of telling me with writing. Tell me with your voice." By the last word, his tone had softened and the flames in his eyes cooled.

She nodded agreement as one enchanted, then dragged her eyes away and severed the connection.

"Are you hungry?" she asked, not knowing a safer topic.

He grunted a 'yes' and they walked in silence to the dining hall.

Yetsye and Tsadok found the others already gathered at a table. An enormous platter of fruits and nuts, two kinds of fruit juices, bix'n milk, khaf'ket, and fresh flat bread rounds drizzled with hahne'en covered the center of the table. Yetsye's stomach loudly protested its empty state and all but Tsadok looked at her in surprise. Ya'el giggled while Yuvahl and Leila hid grins. Embarrassed heat spread up her neck and face.

"What? I woke before Tsifi'ra this dawning!" And she set out to empty her share of the platter, fueled by nervous energy. When she glanced at the others again, it was to find her siblings staring at her awestruck. "What have I done now?" Ya'el just grinned again and Yuvahl shook his head. Ya'el quiet? This was strange behavior for her siveh, though considering Yetsye's manner, she was hardly one to talk.

The dark shadow sitting next to her chose a mug of khaf'ket and a flat-bread, which he folded in half and ate in silence. This wasn't much different from the usual Tsadok. Maybe it was the hard set of his face, or the extreme economy of his movements that betrayed the tension of their conversation.

Yuvahl sensed it and tried drawing him out. "Tsadok, how did you sleep?"

"Well," was the clipped reply.

"Is something bothering you?" he tried again.

Tsadok's hand stopped half-way to his mouth, his bread with hahne'en glistening on it hanging in mid-air. He turned hard eyes to Yuvahl and slowly took a bite. Yuvahl's eyebrows shot upward, and Leila gasped at the blatant challenge. No matter what Tsadok did, it always delighted Ya'el, who found every quirk interesting. She still thought of him as a "new friend" and studied the things he said and did with her usual thirst for knowledge.

"He was only concerned," Ya'el explained to Tsadok. "No need to glare."

Yetsye suddenly felt the weight of the three flat-breads, the hahne'en, the khaf'ket and the handful of kho'ni nuts like so many rocks in her stomach. She bowed her head.

"I'm sorry. Please excuse me." She glanced at Ya'el before leaving the table. She shouldn't have. Ya'el followed her after quickly throwing a questioning glance at Yuvahl.

When she caught up to Yetsye in the hallway, the inquisition began, despite Yetsye's obvious distress. "What was all that about?" She grasped Yetsye gently by the shoulders. When she didn't answer, Ya'el tried again. "What is going on? What happened between you and Tsadok?" Ya'el peppered Yetsye with questions faster than she could form answers. Yetsye leaned back on the wall and slid down to sit on the floor. She looked up at Ya'el in time to see her green eyes harden to flashing gems. She squatted beside Yetsye. "Has he hurt you?"

Yetsye waved an open hand in front of her face, as if warding off a cloud of met'cha. "Slow down, Siveh. I can only answer one question at a time, and even then, I have to have time to think." The dawning had hardly begun, and she was already worn down. She took a deep breath, rose slowly, and continued walking toward the stable.

"To answer the first, I'm not entirely certain." Yetsye's voice started softly but grew stronger with rising annoyance. "I thought things were taken care of when we talked earlier. In answer to the second and third, we talked about a lot of things. I don't have his permission to share it with anyone. As for the last question, no. He would not ever do that. I know it for certain now." By the time she reached the end, energy flooded into her. She looked at Ya'el, waiting for the usual retort. When it never came, she whispered a soft thank you and ran for the peace and comfort of the mana.

Those serene creatures cooed softly and whistled to each other, excited to visit with their friend again. Yetsye found her favorite mount still in the last stall. She'd known for a long time his name was Fhoowhsh, but hadn't called him by it in the hearing of others. She wasn't sure whether they would tease her or question her and she was too tired for either. At least Tsadok wouldn't laugh or run away.

She sighed and took a brush from the wall. Walking into Fhoowhsh's stall, she greeted him with the usual cooing. Then she sang to him as she groomed his shaggy mane, thick coat, and tail.

"The morning suns rise high in the sky.
They beam a dawning joy.
The Children below
Bask in the glow"
"The mid-dawn suns are highest of all.
Their glory warms the soul.
The Children will sing.
Their voices do ring."
"The sleepy suns are settling down.
Their glow begins to dim.
The Children content,
To sleep they consent."
"Beautiful."

The brush flipped out of her hands and she turned to find Tsadok leaning against the wall. She was so immersed in her tune and task she'd become oblivious to everything else. She wondered how many others heard her childhood tune. After quickly glancing around the stable and finding no one else there, she bent to retrieve the brush.

"What are you doing here, Tsadok?" she asked wearily as she resumed her work. "I thought you weren't talking to me."

"You left without saying anything again."

"Ya'el knew. It's the same place I always go when I can't focus enough to do a calming."

He grunted an acknowledgment. She sneaked a glance at him where he now stood next to Fhoowhsh's stall door. He looked as tired as she felt. She'd finished grooming her mount, but she wasn't ready to leave the stall.

So she talked instead. Fhoowhsh happily tolerated her small hands working non-existent knots out of his mane and tail.

"I've been thinking." She wasn't sure if these were the right words, but she'd try. "If we are to unite the Children, I need to try to find friends in the other clans. I'm not sure how to do that. I don't have a way to cross the ocean to visit the Ikhel'dur, Bot'ha, and Genzet. Even if I did, would they welcome me? Or would they send me away? I met some of the Bot'ha at the last Great Gathering."

Tsadok turned his head, raising a disbelieving eyebrow. "Alright. I admit it. I didn't talk to them. Ya'el did. But I was with her. The Bot'ha have always been friendly with us but the Genzet are aloof and hard to approach, even for my siveh who never meets a stranger." She grinned and her hands stilled at the memory. "She tried very hard, though."

She caught his thoughtful nod in her peripheral vision as he opened his mouth to speak. "Yes. We have traded with the Ikhel'dur on many occasions. I have a friend there." He paused and focused on his fingers resting on the stall door, lost in thought. "Pareh disapproved," he said with a crooked grin. "I just stopped telling him when I did get a chance to visit with Mikot." Yetsye turned at the name. He paused again and this time when he spoke his smile showed even rows of white teeth and his eyes softened a bit. "She taught me many things."

Yetsye's hands slowed while she watched the different emotions flicker across Tsadok's face. She'd never seen such a beautiful display from him. A strange pang struck her chest, and she feared the meaning. She suddenly felt the need to renew her efforts with Fhoowhsh by checking his paws carefully for wounds. She wasn't sure what emotion showed on her face but she was certain she didn't want Tsadok to see it.

He continued, unaware of her distress. "Mikot would be a valuable ally. One of her parents is a village elder and another of her relatives is a Master Fisher."

Yetsye fought against the lump forming in her throat and finally squashed it viciously. "How can we get a message to this friend of yours?" Her voice cracked despite her efforts.

"I will see to that if you believe it will help."

"Yes, please." Her voice was barely above a whisper. She heard the stall door rattle. When she rose from her inspection of Fhoowhsh's right front paw, she found herself face to face with Tasdok. She paused, dropped her eyes, and whispered, "Thank you."

Turning to the mana, Yetsye sought the only escape available to her. She grasped his head in her hands and placed her forehead between his eyes. After a few moments, she raised her head, turning wide eyes to Tsadok. "I talked to him."

"To whom?"

"Fhoowhsh."

"Who is Fhoowhsh?"

"This mana is Fhoowhsh. And this is new. I thought the Nechna were the only beasts I'd be able to have conversations with. I should tell the others. What could it mean?"

22

Ancestor's Child

Discussing the new revelation was difficult. Yetsye could hardly believe how her gift had blossomed. Why should others believe her? And if they believed her, how would they look at her from now on? The questions swirled in her mind without answers.

She knelt on the beautiful rug where the rest reclined after the evening meal and spun her tale. The colorful threads she spoke wove an intricate pattern of fear, awe, confusion, and excitement on the familiar faces surrounding her. All but Tsadok's.

Yuvahl questioned her first. "You say you can talk to all animals. Couldn't you already do that?" Yetsye saw the uncertainty clouding his eyes. He looked down at his folded hands. "Isn't that what you did with the Nechna?" Why wouldn't he look at her?

"It's not the same," she stressed. She closed her eyes and took a deep breath, letting it out slowly. "That's what I'm trying to say. I can talk to the Nechna and mana like I'm talking to you. Maybe talking with the Nechna awoke something inside me. I don't know," she trailed off, then came back strong. "But now I can have an actual conversation with a mana." She clasped her hands together in a white-knuckled grip. Their faith in her was important.

"I know it's incredible. I know I sound crazy." Her voice lowered to just above a whisper, but her conviction lent strength to the words. "I know I spoke to my mount in the stable a few moments ago. I also know he thanked me and told me I was kind to care for him so well. Maybe I didn't hide my anxiety as well as I thought because he told me not to worry, that my quest would surely be successful. I didn't know mana were optimists but I guess that fits their good-natured spirits."

Leila chimed in with a cautious smile. "It reminds me of a childhood tale my moyri used to tell me before I would go to sleep."

Yetsye nodded, urging Leila to continue. "There was once an outstanding leader in the history of our world. Her name was Sharl." At the name, Yuvahl, Ya'el and Yetsye glanced at each other. "This woman was a great and wise warrior. She led the Children of Y'Dahnndrya to safety during the Great Cataclysm. No one was sure how or why, but beasts suddenly came to help. Nechna, bush'ka, d'nagze, bix'n, the tsa'gra (who were larger then), and many other beasts offered their strength to carry the wounded or packs of supplies. It is said that Sharl could speak to the animals in ways others couldn't.

"When you came out of the Visioning chamber, Yetsye, your countenance brought this story to mind. I didn't know the tale of your journey yet, but your hair and your face, they are very like the description of Sharl. Perhaps there is some connection?"

Yetsye beamed. "She was our ancestor. In M'Neshunnaya, we call her Shar'yll, datir of Ched'ra. There is a braka written about her, but this part, I've never heard before. Have you, Batir?" If a record of this existed in the lib'rarum at Zulima, Yuvahl would know. Shar'yll's braka had always been his favorite. He opened his mouth to speak when Ya'el cut in.

"How amazing!" Ya'el's smile outshone Tsifi'ra and her eyes sparkled. She sat forward on her knees. "To think we have similar spins in our countries, both telling of the same time viewed through various eyes!"

Yetsye's own eyes strayed to Tsadok, who stared at the entrance. She rose to join him and scanned the doorway. Nothing seemed out of the ordinary.

"Tsadok?" When he didn't reply, she touched his elbow lightly. He flinched as if burned and seared her with an accusing glare.

Yetsye jerked her hand away, fear and regret clear on her face. "I'm sorry! I didn't mean to hurt you." She was also confused. That was definitely pain he felt, but why? She barely touched him. She stared at the offending hand as if it had grown fangs and claws. His words shattered her tension.

"I am sorry, as well. You did nothing wrong. I was trapped within my thoughts." She barely registered his soothing words as she pondered what happened.

When he glanced at the others' obvious shock, his mask slid back into place. It was so unlike the Tsadok they knew for something so simple to disturb him so badly. What was wrong? He bowed low in apology, which added to Yetsye's confusion. "I am sorry to have startled you all. It was unintentional."

Yetsye tried her question again. "Tsadok?" When he turned to face her, she plunged ahead, stamping on her apprehensions as she would stamp on a slitchit's head. "Is there a tale told in your tribe about a woman leader who spoke to beasts?"

He thought for a moment and nodded slowly. Then his own eyes fastened on Yetsye's and he smiled. His smile was beautiful and somehow frightening.

"Will you spin this tale for us?" she asked hesitantly.

He nodded and sat on knees spread wide in the center of the rug. As he carefully placed his palms on his thighs, he said, "It is too long to tell it all, but I will try to share the main points." Tsadok's words took on a sing-song lilt.

"Many tsimikin ago
A brave warrior lived
whose name is etched in time
Sari'i, the 'Beast Speaker'
Strode fierce and proud
Her voice of determination
Poured forth words of wisdom.
"Fiery Cataclysm burned
Our world to ash.
She led the people to safety.
She chose Five Victors
Rulers of the Clans,
With her, also etched in time.
"The decision made
to travel, they must
Away from ash, fire, and smoke
Away from the home, that was no more
The home lost to time.
"Sari'i, pathfinder, found a way.
The beasts, she befriended.
They came at her call

To aid those in need.

The call etched in time."

He dropped the chant but continued the summary. "In appearance, it is said she shone like the suns, from her red-gold hair streaked with five silvery stripes, to the golden tan of her skin. Her golden eyes radiated kindness and fierce loyalty. She was a beautiful woman with a heart of strength. It is not surprising the beasts of Y'Dahnndrya came at the call of such a person. No one knew exactly how she accomplished it. No one knows to this dawning."

"Amazing, indeed!" The silence stretched too long for Ya'el. Yetsye jumped at her outburst and observed how she took expert advantage of the opening. She included everyone by directing her words around the group. "Isn't it? I think it's wonderful that our clans have so much in common. Though, I guess it's equally terrible that we didn't even know about this until now. I really wish our clans would interact more and be less concerned about petty things."

She stood and walked to the table near the entrance, where one of the temple attendants left refreshments. Grabbing a handful of kho'ni nuts, she strolled back to reclaim her spot on the shiny, orange cushion. "I keep telling Matir we need more clan gatherings for this reason. Wouldn't things be much better if we worked together to care for our world?"

"I like your thoughts," Leila clapped and encouraged Ya'el with a broad smile, "and agree whole-heartedly. Do you think the Lady High Priestess will urge the others to do it?" The mention of Shira's lofty title, used only by out-clanners, startled Yetsye. Was she thinking of Leila as family now?

"I'm not sure," Ya'el replied, "but if she would, it would be one way Yetsye could begin uniting the peoples of Y'Dahnndrya." She and Leila looked at Yetsye, who could only stare back. It was unfair of Ya'el to offer another option now that they'd decided. Only a miscreant would go back on their word.

When she realized they were waiting for her to answer, she dropped her gaze. "I'm not sure that's how it's going to happen. I could try that, I suppose, if we weren't already going to Yacan. There's a temple there and another Guardian. Perhaps Serafin will have some words of guidance for us. I really thought I should tell you about my new ability to talk to animals because I might learn some things from them about the different places we visit. But

I'll have to figure out the ways of speaking with them as we travel. I had to place my forehead on Fhoowhsh's. I didn't have to touch the Nechna at all."

They'd forgotten all about Yacan in their excitement about the tales of Shar'yll. At the reminder, Ya'el and Yuvahl brightened up, and Leila frowned. Tsadok reinforced his mask.

"Leila," Yetsye began, "will you go with us?"

Leila looked toward the window high above the main door. Yetsye followed her gaze to find colorful art-glashiin depicting flame and stone. "I want more than anything to go with you," she began wistfully, "but I must return to my home. I've been gone too long and my people will worry. You should go with me to Chefvna. We're on the northern coast and I can help you borrow a skiiv to carry you over to Yacan. You can replenish your supplies and refresh yourselves before going to the forbidden place." The color drained from her rosy cheeks as she spoke the last two words. "I would continue on with you, but I won't be allowed to do so. I'm still a daula in my babeiya's home and should obey him." She nodded solemnly, as if to reassure herself, her hands clasped tightly in her lap.

Yetsye was certain Yuvahl would rather keep Leila with them, too. She risked a glance at him and found his eyes riveted on Leila's bowed head. Yes, his feelings for her were strong. She wondered how he would fare when they had no choice but to leave her behind.

Yetsye rose. "We should prepare if we're leaving within two dawnings. Our mounts are well refreshed, and so are our bodies and minds. We should go as soon as the preparations are complete." No one was more surprised than she at the orders pouring boldly from her mouth.

It took a complete nainda to finish preparing. Seth Yi'in sent an el'tekh messenger to Chefvna to prepare them for out-clan visitors. He couldn't resist requesting some last-minute favors.

"Be sure to note any more rifts you find. And any strange recent occurrences. You can keep a written record on these blank scrolls." He passed the writing materials to Ya'el, then paused half-way. "You can write?" he asked in the condescending tone they expected from him.

"Yes. I. Can." Ya'el was well beyond her limit with this little man. She wore the smile Yetsye associated with the imminent defeat of her opponents in martial arts tournaments. She watched in open-mouthed amazement as Ya'el snatched the scrolls and pouch from the diminutive Guardian and snapped, "You might want to believe better of your fellow Y'Dahnndryans. We aren't ignorant or unconcerned." Her hazel eyes flashed green fire and a flood of red spread from the base of his neck to the top of his bald head. Yetsye couldn't tell if it was anger or surprise or something else. When his expression changed to remorse, she knew it was embarrassment. She bowed her head to mask her ill-timed grin and busied herself checking the gear on her mana.

When Yetsye composed herself, she grasped the reins and walked her mana close to Seth Yi'in. She would never have done such a thing before her Visioning. "Thank you for sharing your knowledge, wisdom, food, and home with us. We're stronger for visiting this place." She bowed her head in respect. The others followed her example before turning their mana to head back down the mountain trail they'd followed only sixteen dawnings ago. It seemed she'd lived a lifetime during their stay. Yetsye had grown, but surely more trials lay ahead.

When they reached the bottom of Mt. Charan's trail, she motioned for Leila and Yuvahl to take the lead. Leila would know best where to go from here. Ya'el rifled through the pouch Seth Yi'in had given her, her expression that of a child offered a plate full of bon'jiis. Yetsye couldn't stop a grin from spreading across her face.

The companions rode north and west. Wispy clouds drifted high above, shielding them from the suns every now and again. The cooler breezes wafting past made the heat bearable but dried up any moisture. Yetsye patted her full flasks, thankful for the promise of a refreshing drink when they stopped.

It wasn't long before Yetsye felt his eyes upon her. No other gaze burned her this way. She frowned. Tsadok presented a puzzle she wasn't ready to solve. Her feelings for the stoic warrior grew stronger every day. It was unlikely they could be anything more than friends.

Besides, didn't he have Mikot? Too many questions and not enough answers kept her frown firmly in place. If this Mikot person turned out to be someone she couldn't respect, would she have the courage to fight for his affection? Until then, she'd have to improve her mask-wearing skills. Besides, this quest was too important to risk failing because of changeable human desires. Without a doubt, she could not fail. She did her best to ignore the burning sensation.

Keeping her back straight, she mumbled encouragement to herself. "Eyes forward, Yetsye. Forward."

23

Deafening Trial

"Oh! A pitikeli!" Yetsye wasn't sure when Ya'el started calling out the names of every new plant she spotted. But her outbursts only happened when conversation lagged. If she didn't know better, she'd think her siveh was nervous. She watched from behind as Ya'el carefully sketched the gray-green blades tipped with clusters of fuzzy white orbs. That pa'pukh hadn't left Ya'el's side since she bought it two tsimikin ago. Every time Yetsye spotted it, she was positive it grew thicker. Ya'el gleaned linnel scraps from the lib'rarum scroll room whenever she got a chance.

"It's a good thing we're not being hunted," Yetsye grumbled and sighed. The slow pace gnawed at her. Would they ever make it to the end of these rock-strewn paths? Twists and curves led them between high, rocky hills. The sparse, stunted vegetation left Yetsye feeling exposed. The clever mana had no trouble. They easily side-stepped the rocks they couldn't sweep out of their way.

And always the wind blew. It didn't whisper in this place. It screeched and howled, a fierce attack on her ears. When she winced for the third time and hunched over her saddle, she felt more than heard Tsadok's mount approach.

She looked up at him from her crouched position, eyes watering from the pain. "How can I make it stop?" Yetsye's tears blurred Tsadok's face into a ghastly caricature.

"I will speak to Yuvahl. We will find a way to mute the sound." He urged his mount forward.

They stopped in a dimly lit canyon with high walls. Yetsye wasn't the only one afflicted by the shrill keening, which crescendoed in the smaller space. All but Tsadok and Leila ransacked the travel bags for anything that would bring even a small measure of relief. She couldn't tell if that was because

Tsadok was determined to show no pain or if he actually felt no pain. Who could know with Leila?

She set her mind back on her search and drew out a finely woven scarf. Winding it around her hair and ears didn't help. The fierce sounds pierced the cloth easily. She looked toward the others and saw Leila gazing at the canyon's exit. How was she able to stand this? Was all of Shinnoah afflicted with this cursed wind? Taking up her mana's reins, she joined the older maiden.

"Why didn't you tell us about this wind?" Yetsye spoke loudly over the noise. "I can't afford to lose my hearing."

"What? I can't quite hear you?" Her perplexed face revealed the truth of her words. Yetsye's eyes slid to her siveh, who eased in on Leila's right.

Ya'el reached out a hand to one of Leila's long, thick braids and moved it aside. Eyes shooting fire, Ya'el spat, "Has our pain entertained you enough?" She viciously threw the end of the braid down. It stung Leila, who jumped in shock. Ya'el stalked off to rummage through her pack again. She found a small cleaning cloth coated with orif for shining hide boots. Ripping it into strips, she stuffed bits of it into every ear, saving her own for last. Leila apologized over and over the whole time. Yetsye offered a prayer of thanks when the blessed muffling cloth nestled snugly in her ears. It didn't cut out all sound, but at least the noise was bearable.

The interminable ride through the pass continued. Only Tsadok still sat tall and proud. If Yetsye hadn't been able to talk with him so often, she'd continue to believe that nothing ever affected him. She wished she had his control instead of feeling so vulnerable.

Once started, the doubts wouldn't stop hounding her. Maybe Azilet'zal did make a mistake. Maybe Tsadok should be the one going on this quest. The fact remained that he wasn't the one. And she knew very well her Creator was incapable of making mistakes. Everything existed as it was for a reason and everything happened as it did for a reason. Above all, she knew even if circumstances seemed terrible in the present, Azilet'zal's reason was a good one.

When they finally reached the end of the canyon, Yuvahl dismounted and yelled to Leila, "Can we camp here?"

At her nod, he gestured an order to the others to dismount and set up the camp. Huddled around Leila's small flame-globe, they gobbled down a hasty meal of dried fruit, nuts, and smoked fish. Yuvahl signaled for them to rest and offered to take the first watch.

Yetsye huddled close to Fhoowhsh's warm side and laid her head on the soft fur. He whistled and cooed in contentment and nuzzled her hair with his nose. She'd noticed the mana keeping their ears low and wondered if they would be alright. It was one thing to stuff fabric in her ears, but impossible to risk the same with a mana.

Yetsye closed her eyes and, though surrounded by Fhoowhsh's warmth, she felt as if her senses had frozen. She missed her connection with Azilet'zal and Y'Dahnndrya. Her siblings must feel the same, for they buried themselves in their own thoughts and deeds, not noticing her struggle. Faint vibrations were the only warning she had before Tsadok sat down next to her. They couldn't really speak because of the stuffing in their ears. He simply sat down and she noticed she was warming up. The wind seemed to have died down, too. That small bit of relief was all she needed to rest her eyes. Her last thought before drifting off was of how she should thank him when she woke.

Dawnings heralded the grueling trek ahead of them, but they gradually grew accustomed to the plodding pace during the dawning and the cold air of dusking. Tsadok settled into a routine, too, joining her before taking his shift at the watch. His open clothing didn't seem to bother him at all. Yetsye knew by now, though, none of them would ever know if anything bothered him if he didn't want them to. So she made sure his blanket was nearby when she settled for sleep. At least he'd have a way to keep warm. His smile, gone almost as soon as it appeared, told her she'd done the right thing for a change.

Yetsye had never felt so useless as she did now. There wasn't much for her to do except ride, eat, and sleep. Ya'el and Leila passed out food at mealtimes. Yuvahl always built the fire or lit the flame-globes when they made camp. Tsadok kept watch. There was little else to do but calm the mana and try to keep warm despite the shrieking gale.

One thing she had was time to think. In fact, the thoughts wouldn't stop. They kept circling through her mind, constant, relentless. Doubts clouded her thoughts more often than ever. Where she'd been full of hope a few dawnings ago, the dreariness of this place ate away at it like orphaned tsa'gra kits at a plate of mana milk. Her face grew pale and her sleep restless, even with Tsadok blocking the wind.

On the fifth dawning, they cleared the pass and bid a joyous farewell to the baleful gusts and the stuffing in their ears. The mountain valley they now crossed sported a close crop of short-bladed bluish grass and brightly colored wildflowers, which looked as if even the lightest breeze would blow them away. Yetsye marveled at the beauty hidden here, but Ya'el basked in it. She watched as her siveh turned to a clean scrap in the pa'pukh, giving her mana free rein so she could sketch pictures of all she saw. Yetsye urged Fhoowhsh alongside.

"It's beautiful here."

"Mmhm," came Ya'el's preoccupied affirmative.

"I've never seen flowers so dainty, or so brightly colored." No response. "Do you think it's because their roots are strong?"

"Maybe," came the one word acknowledgment. Yetsye knew she'd be pushing it if she continued. Ya'el didn't like to be interrupted while she was working. She tried again anyway.

"What about the color? Do you think they're so bright because of the gray pass? Or is it something to do with where they grow?"

"Ugh, Yetsye."

"I'm sorry! I just know you enjoy these things and we haven't talked much lately, not since the discussion about Yacan."

"I'm sorry, too." She paused and sighed before bending once again to her task. Yetsye hoped she wasn't being dismissed. To her surprise, Ya'el spoke. "I'm uncertain about anything concerning these mountain plants. I'm sketching only because I can't hold us up to get the closer look I really want."

Yetsye nodded in understanding. "I know what you mean. I've seen several kinds of flyers, but none have come close enough to study."

"So how do you like your new guardian?"

Yetsye's stiffening drew a giggle from Ya'el. "What do you mean?" she asked, annoyed.

"Tsadok is always near you. Anytime you need anything, it's there, as if he reads your mind." The grin she wore now would stretch across the O'Na Sea.

Yetsye's brow wrinkled in thought. "You're right. I guess any woman would feel honored by such treatment." It felt strange to refer to herself as a woman, since she didn't feel all that different. "And now I'm able to talk to him freely. Finding the right words isn't always easy, though." She scowled.

"Why the frown? This is good news!" A confused smirk tilted Ya'el's lips as she set her sketching aside. "Didn't you want to talk to others like you talk to Yuvahl and me?"

"Yes. I'm just uncertain."

Ya'el's disgruntled sigh made her wince. "Uncertain of what? Yetsye! You're fully grown. When will you let go of all these crazy worries that hold you back?"

The gentle hand on her shoulder soothed even as it weighed her down. Yetsye wasn't sure she could drop the worries of a lifetime as if they never existed. "I'm not like you. It's not so easy for me," she whispered. The hand jerked away and Yetsye looked up to find Ya'el's eyes on fire once again.

"What do you mean?" Her tone was much quieter than usual, but that only meant Yetsye offended her somehow. "Yetsye, do you think life is easy for me? For anyone?" She waited, but Yetsye couldn't bring herself to answer the questions. "Let me share the yellow strands*[1] with you, Little Siveh. Life is tough for everyone, though not always in the same way. You have so much to learn, but you could see this much more easily if you just tried. Do you really think Yuvahl is having an easy time?" Ya'el hissed the last sentence.

"No." That was a simple question to answer, considering his affection for Leila and his choice to do nothing about it. "No, I noticed that. And I'm sorry for my thoughtless words. I know life brings trouble for everyone. I just seem to have a hearty share and always have."

"Are you complaining?"

"Hmmm, I guess I am. And I should stop. I know." She held up a hand to forestall the lecture brewing in Ya'el's mind. "Alright. So I was wrong to imply you had no worries. I'm so sorry for speaking carelessly." She paused, then continued with, "And I have a real problem that I'll need to work on."

Ya'el studied her long enough to make her squirm. She cocked her head to one side. "Tsadok?" She all but whispered the name.

"Mmhm." Yetsye knew she was blushing, but she couldn't stop the flow of heat spreading from her neck to her ears, both of which were clearly visible thanks to the way Tsadok styled her hair. But she couldn't bring herself to voice any certainties about their new friend. If she ever revealed the depth of her attraction, Ya'el wouldn't stop teasing and pushing her toward decisions she wasn't ready to make.

Conversation lagged when the party stopped for a quick break. A scan of the area revealed a pool of water from which a clear stream gently flowed. They refreshed their mounts and quenched their own thirst. Before moving on again, Yetsye wanted to see the silver stripes in her hair. Gazing into the pool, she found Tsadok's word to be true. The simple style he used to bind her hair held up despite the vicious wind and made her look very different. Several small braids woven close to her scalp swept up to the crown of her head and fountained out into loops. She wasn't even sure how he secured them. Her new stripes almost hid. Black circles under her eyes stood out.

She patted at them as she rose, sighed, and turned from the pool, almost colliding with Tsadok's el'tekh tattoo again. She looked up at him, wondering why he was there and so close. His sharp gaze wasn't on her, but on the far side of the pool. She turned around slowly. The dreaded word set her heart pounding.

"Whe'evet!"

24

Messenger's Light

The whe'evet pack closed ranks on the far side of the pool. So close! She could've been devoured already and no one would have known. Like the gateway stones of Levanna, they stood. Still. Silent. Were it not for the wind stirring their rope-like fur, they could be mistaken for carvings cut away from the stone they stood upon. Angry silence pressed in on Yetsye, squeezing the breath from her lungs.

Whe'evet were pack hunters of the northern mountain ranges. Three rows of needle-like fangs and a single, curving horn were all the weaponry they needed to overcome almost any enemy. But Azilet'zal thought to add a stinger on the ends of their prehensile tails. Coarse, woolly coats of mottled gray blended so well with their surroundings it was impossible to spot them before they charged. So vicious were they, their infamy spread far and wide.

Tsadok's mask intensified, but otherwise he gave nothing away. Yuvahl readied his kranj for battle and placed himself and his deadly barbed chain between the whe'evet and Leila. Ya'el stood a little behind and to the side of him, a ki'fi in each hand and a kranj at her hip.

Yetsye studied the whe'evet closest to her. Judging from its size and place slightly ahead of the pack, it must be the leader. She took a step forward and felt a tug on her elbow. She carefully turned baleful eyes to Tsadok. He let go slowly, but returned glare for glare. She refocused on the pack leader. Its gray coat was so matted, full of knots and twigs, she could barely see its six dark eyes through the mop of fur atop its head.

They stared at each other for a long time. The whe'evet suddenly tossed its horned head and let out its blood-curdling cry. Yetsye winced. Pebbles rattled behind her. She held her open hand out to the side to stop the others from moving. She walked forward into the pool, two careful steps, never taking her eyes from the whe'evet. The beast uttered a watery growl and stepped quietly forward on four padded hoofs the size of feasting platters.

Yetsye continued through the water and onto the other side. She hoped the others would not move. This challenge was hers alone.

The two Y'Dahnndryans met face to long-nosed muzzle. Yetsye now had to look up to meet the whe'evet's many eyes. It tilted its nose ground-ward. Foul air wafted toward her with each breath it released. She slowly lifted her hands upward, palms out, silent and smooth, taking care not to startle the pack. After a few moments, she hummed sweet and low, a tune of her childhood about the beasts of Y'Dahnndrya. The whe'evet tilted its head to listen and twitched its cloven ears. The others exchanged a high pitched, up-and-down whine quietly amongst themselves, as if whispering and wondering.

Risking a little more, Yetsye reached her hands forward toward the whe'evet's enormous head. She never wavered when the leader lowered her horn toward her. She walked forward slowly until the horn touched one of her hands.

Never in all her life would she have described the whe'evet as gentle creatures. All the stories painted them as vicious fighters. Yet this creature touched her as lightly as a flut'ra. She released the breath she'd been holding and curled her fingers around the short horn.

Images flowed into her mind. Faster and faster, they came so quickly she couldn't keep up. Instead, she gathered a very basic understanding of the whe'evet mind and memory. It differed from the Nechna — primitive, if she compared the two. She had the feeling these animals were even more ancient, having roamed their mountains far longer than the Nechna had guarded the plains.

When the images slowed, she intensified her focus. New scenes appeared — the whe'evet running in a pack, chasing down prey. She felt their pride in victory, their fear and sorrow in defeat, their worry in times of scarcity. She saw life through their eyes and understood how they felt about who they were and their purpose in the world. Without them, vermin would take over the mountains. Their keen vision saw all movement. And all moving things were prey, for they couldn't see anything but a blur of colors, darker ones showing life forms and lighter ones showing plants, rocks, or earth.

It was unlike anything Yetsye had ever experienced, and she wondered how to communicate her own experiences to this noble creature. She allowed images of family to come to mind, how they worked together to keep Y'Dahnndrya healthy. She thought of her classes and her desire to learn new things.

The whe'evet jerked its head back unexpectedly, taking Yetsye with her, flinging her onto the matriarch's back. She nimbly twisted in the air to land facing forward and motioned to the others that all was well. They accepted her. The pack intended to carry her to safety. Her companions were safe as well.

As one, the pack turned to leave the small pool. Movement further up the trail caused a ripple of alarm among them.

"Intruders!"

Yetsye placed a hand on the beast's head behind its uppermost eye and calmed it, which calmed the others. The word spread through the pack through low, almost indiscernible tones, breaths, and a series of dull taps. She clasped the horn in front of her and tried to explain how she needed her companions and would like for them to move in among the pack. Her host tossed her massive head and Yetsye motioned for the others to come forward.

Tenseness fled as understanding was born, and the mana strode confidently into the middle of the pack. Yuvahl rode up on Yetsye's left. Leila stirred from sleep in his arms. Now was not the time to ask. Ya'el soaked in everything with wide eyes and beamed at Yetsye from the other side of Yuvahl. Yetsye smiled back, then, seeing Ya'el's raised eyebrow, rolled her eyes. She now knew where Tsadok was. She was really going to hate all the teasing that eyebrow promised.

They rounded a bend in the path and suddenly came face to face with the source of the whe'evet's worries.

"What business do you have here, strangers?" shouted the first man to walk toward them. A heavy jacket made of a patchwork of gray furs disguised his true form. He blended well into the background. His stance meant trouble. Leila stirred and clumsily donned her hood.

"We travel to Chefvna." Yetsye's bold answer surprised even herself. She wondered why Leila hid. Weren't these men of her own clan? Were they dangerous?

"What business do you have there?" The man wouldn't let them pass easily. He eyed the whe'evet with blatant malice. Yetsye didn't want trouble. Honesty and simplicity would serve her best here.

"I am Yetsye. My home is in Zulima, in M'Neshunnayan Territory. I have visited Levanna for my Visioning and Mt. Charan for knowledge concerning my purpose and quest. My search has led me here. These Children with me offered help and guidance, among them one of your own."

She motioned for Leila to come forward. Yuvahl helped Leila dismount and she crept to the front of the whe'evet pack. When she removed the hood, the man from the Shinnoahn band came forward two steps before remembering the vicious beasts. He stopped.

"What is this? You would hold my own daula as a prisoner?" His impotent rage was palpable.

"Babeiya!" cried Leila and ran into the man's embrace. He towered over her.

"Is this why were you gone so long? Taken prisoner? We despaired of seeing you again."

"No, Babeiya," Leila corrected him gently. "These are my friends. Why would they allow this if I was a prisoner?"

Yetsye watched tears of joy stream unashamedly down the man's bearded face. What stormy emotions these Shinnoahns harbored! No one existed for this man besides Leila.

Leila turned back, her face bright with happiness. "This is my babeiya, Kven Muenbrukh, Senya. He and the others will help us reach home safely." She missed the frown on Kven's face, and when she spun, he erased it. She continued the introductions, oblivious to Kven's thinly veiled anger. "Babeiya, these are friends from M'Neshunnaya and D'Koruyi. They need to find a skiiv that will carry them to Yacan."

Kven paled at the mention of Yacan and when he turned his scowl toward them, Yetsye's stomach churned. The man said nothing, but nodded. Yetsye wasn't fooled. His suspicions sat rooted in place. She flicked her eyes to Yuvahl, and he gestured with his fingers. The feeling was mutual. Some strange undercurrent stirred the air.

Leila continued with a wave toward Yetsye, who still sat astride the lead whe'evet. "Yetsye is a messenger, sent this way with Seth Yi'in's blessing. An el'tekh left Mt. Charan at the same time we did to alert you to our coming. Did you not receive it?"

"I know not," came the curt reply. "Our band has been out for twice a nainda. Scouting. We just heard the whe'evet howl and came this way."

"Ah, then you won't be able to go with us to Chefvna?" This exchange between fatir and datir was strange. Something wasn't quite right, but Yetsye couldn't see it clearly.

Kven looked thoughtfully at his youngling, then walked away to talk with the other members of the scouting party. He returned, his expression grim. "We cannot go with you. The grumblings of Y'Dahnndrya take precedence."

Leila nodded slowly and looked at Yetsye. A gentle smile spread over her features. "She's the one, Babeiya." Yetsye could feel the familiar heat rising once again up her neck and ears.

Kven's eyebrows shot up. Then, just as quickly, he flashed a scowl back to Yetsye. She focused her attention onto the whe'evet to hide her nerves.

"Her?!" Contempt dripped off his tongue and the sharp word echoed through the rocks surrounding them. Yetsye winced. The whe'evet's ears twitched.

"Yes, Babeiya. I know you were hoping it would be me, but Yetsye is best suited to this task. I believe you can see why." They both gazed at her. Leila's deep purple eyes radiated gentle confidence, while Kven's black set smoldered. Yetsye sharpened her resolve. To show weakness now would mean losing this battle.

"She's unlike anyone else I've ever met," Leila continued. "I heard tales of her calming a raging bush'ka. She also saved a tsa'gra kit and another bush'ka from a forest fire. Her communion with the Nechna of the plains, I witnessed myself—"

"The Nechna?" Kven snorted in disbelief as he cut in.

"Yes. She is truly amazing, but still young. There's much for her to learn. She must go to Yacan." She turned pleading eyes up to her babeiya, whose countenance softened for an instant before hardening once more.

Yetsye steeled herself and raised her gaze toward them. She focused, a piercing glare straight into their hard eyes. Kven stepped back. Leila's words invigorated her and spurred her on to succeed in her task.

"You may be right." He mumbled, and his awe stubbornly returned to skepticism. "Even so, I'll wait for the High Consulate's decision on that. Why should I take the word of a M'Neshunnayan whelp? She's barely old enough to choose a life-mate, and we are supposed to follow her? What could she possibly do?"

What a rude man! When he turned to look in her direction again, he nearly jumped out of his fur-trimmed boots. Yetsye stood next to him, her self-appointed D'Koruyin guard slightly behind her, probably wearing his most ominous scowl. Behind Tsadok, the horned muzzle of a whe'evet rose above them all. Kven's contemptuous conversation with Leila had given Yetsye the opportunity she needed to gather her courage and join them.

Shinnoahns didn't back down, and Kven continued without mercy. A sharp grin pulled at one corner of his wide mouth in derision. "Whelp," he sneered, "what do you have that none of the rest of the Children of Y'Dahnndrya have? Why would the great Tugansol choose you over any of the rest of us? Surely, you can see the reason for my disbelief. You are an untrained, unlearned, unseasoned babete. You're no leader! If you can answer my questions, I will submit to you. If you cannot, then I will wait for the true Messenger the prophecy speaks of."

Yetsye bowed her head, his valid questions stabbing at her faith. "You're right. Why me?" she murmured. "The answer to that is," she raised her head suddenly, "I don't know. I've turned over possibility after possibility and tossed them aside one after the other. The only special thing I can do is talk to the beasts and Y'Dahnndrya. But is it because others are incapable? Or is it because they have no desire to do so? Is it that they have no love for the forgotten Children of Y'Dahnndrya, those whose skin is different? Who stand on a different number of legs? Who wear branches instead of arms? I really don't know."

His humorless chuckle cut through the heavy atmosphere and Yetsye felt Tsadok tense at her side. She raised her voice to finish. "So I travel to Yacan. If I cannot find an answer there, I probably won't find one at all. It's the only reason I consented to this part of our journey."

Kven shook his head. "What you propose is madness." He gestured to Tsadok, Ya'el and Yuvahl. "Do you all owe her a life-debt? Otherwise, I can't understand why you run so eagerly to your deaths."

Yetsye cut in, drawing herself up to her full height. Her eyebrows lowered and her voice sharpened with each successive word. "I have also observed that when people know much, they are less inclined to learn from others. When one becomes a master of some skill, one does not easily accept a teaching from others, even to shunning the Holy Voice of Azilet'zal. Perhaps this is why I was chosen, for if nothing else, I am willing to learn." And with that, she turned on her heel and walked back to Fhoowhsh, who had been waiting patiently. She leaned into his side and steadied her breath. Her body shook from this confrontation she never wanted to have. Tsadok was there, his warm hand solid and soothing at the small of her back.

"You did well." He murmured for her ears only.

"No. I lost my temper." Her quiet reply shook.

"No. You did well. Your meaning was clear. You did not strike out at him physically. You did very well."

"Will everyone be like that? Will I have to go through it again and again?" She looked up at him from her resting place on Fhoowhsh's side, her eyes brimming once again with tears.

"You may." At her heavy sigh, he continued. "You may, but you will not be alone. I make my vow in the presence of Kai'yanga. You will never be alone in this fight."

She straightened and turned to face him. "Thank you," she whispered. She reached out toward him but thought better of it and dropped her hand.

He snatched it in both of his. "I will be with you to the end of this journey."

She hung her head, so he couldn't see the worry in her eyes at the repeated promise. "Thank you, Tsadok, but I can't ask you to sacrifice so much. You have your own life. Your own clan. Your own friends and family you need to get back to." She wondered about Mikot, but could never ask him that. Never.

"Have I not told you before? This is my task, given to me by Kai'yanga. I am to protect you. And I will do that. It is my joy to do that. Why do you refuse to understand?" He allowed a hint of frustration to enter his voice, and she looked at him. He gripped her hand for a moment longer and then released it, though his eyes held hers captive. Only the shriek of a whe'evet broke the connection.

Yetsye turned to see the Shinnoahn band crowding the pack, not liking the menace in their stance. "No," she whispered when she saw the weapons in their hands. She threw herself onto Fhoowhsh and together they ran.

"Stop!" she yelled, and her voice cut through the tiny valley like the fiercest blade. All eyes turned to her, some in anger. "Why are you threatening them?" She raged at them and fought to contain her anger at their foolishness.

"Threatening?" Kven guffawed without humor. "We? Threaten them? They are the ones always hunting us! We are natural enemies. Why should we leave them alone based on the word of a whelp, not even of our clan?"

"Yuvahl." Yetsye's call drew him to her side.

"I'm here."

"So am I," blazed Ya'el's clear voice right behind him.

"Tsadok," she called, and he stepped closer. "Please help me."

"With anything."

Yetsye took a deep breath and raised her chin. "We will defend all of Y'Dahnndrya's Children, whether they wear hair, leaves, fur, feathers, or scales. We were all fashioned by the hand of Azilet'zal, all equally loved by the Creator who fashioned us. You will not be allowed to harm these whe'evet who so kindly offered to lead us safely through the mountain passes." Yetsye's voice rang out, keeping pace with her convictions. "You believe yourselves to be superior to these beasts. I tell you plainly you are not."

The Shinnoahns grumbled and would've surged forward if not for Leila, who came forward to stand between them and Yetsye.

"Harming me will only cause more strife between the clans, for my mother is Shira Rayasdatir, Lady High Priestess of the M'Neshunnayan Clan. She will not let the death of one of her children go unpunished." Yetsye stood in the stirrups of her mount and the suns glared down upon her head.

"Besides that, do you believe needlessly harming a beast is going to win you honor? It will not! Shame is the only reward for such reckless behavior. Do you think harming a youngling from another clan will bring you honor?" She shook her head slowly. "You have insulted me. You've tried to break my spirit with your wealth of knowledge, your words that bite, and your tsimikin. I thought Shinnoahns were something more." The pack and mana stirred with the power surging from her rising anger. Tsadok rested a warning hand lightly on her back. She calmed enough to ease the restless beasts around her.

"A Child who belittles others and seeks the path of destruction is a disgrace to the parents who birthed him and least among all living things. I cannot speak for others. But for myself, I will follow the pattern Azilet'zal has woven for me. I'm fortunate to have the support of family and friends. I believe with all that I am, our Creator wishes us to care for the plants and beasts as well as we care for ourselves. It's just as clear to me our purpose is to take care of each other, regardless of clan.

"You will not hinder me from completing my quest. And if you try to harm one of these furry Children, there will be four more two-legged Children you will have to contend with. I have chosen my path. Which path will you choose?"

Her question echoed before fading into the mountains. Silence reigned in the valley. She forced her small body to stand as straight as the shi'iket tree with its spiky leaves that slice the unsuspecting soul who wanders too close.

Silence dragged on. The Shinnoahn band waited and watched to see what Kven would do. He raised the metal-tipped club that was poised over his shoulder and slid it into his belt. The others also lowered their weapons. Suddenly, almost nonchalantly, he spoke. "You speak well for a young one. Make no mistake, though. I still reserve judgment. But what you say, I must admit there is the ring of truth in it. And M'Neshunnayans are well-known as truth-speakers."

The Shinnoahns trooped back into the mountain pass. Over his shoulder, Kven tossed, "You will find a cold welcome in Chefvna because of the shakings. Though, if you persist in this insanity, I believe they will listen. Eventually." He tossed the last word over his shoulder, laughing.

"Thank you, Kven. I will remember what you say." Yetsye barely got the words out in her relief. When the last Shinnoahn faded into the mountains, her determination diffused. Her strength faded with it, dropping her into powerful arms and oblivion.

25

Chefvna's Welcome

Yetsye woke to the rhythmic patting of mana paws and the feeling of something not quite right. Why was she waking while moving? She pushed away, but someone's arms kept her in place. She looked up to see Tsadok's jaw silhouetted against the starry sky-dome. With intense concentration, he guided his mana carefully around a tricky part of the trail. He only glanced down when it was safely through. Thank Azilet'zal he couldn't see the rush of color she felt flooding her neck and cheeks! The moons must've set already.

"How long was I asleep?" She murmured under her breath. He heard anyway.

"The moons rose and set."

"And you carried me all this time?" He nodded. She tensed. "Why?"

"Back in the valley, you would have fallen from your mount if I had not caught you."

"But why did you continue to carry me? Yuvahl could have done it or you could've tied me to Fhoowhsh."

"This was more efficient."

"Oh." His detachment chased away all the warmth. She was more determined than ever to move to her own mount. "Well, I'm awake now. Fully awake. I can ride on my own."

"No. We cannot stop here."

"Why not?" she asked, growing annoyed with his clipped answers.

"Look around." He helped her sit up straighter so she could peek over his shoulder. The mountainous landscape spread far below them, a dark patchwork in shades of blue, gray, and black opened out beneath her. Jagged, twisting ridges plunged into dark valleys. She gasped and clung to his tunic, accidentally scratching him. He hissed.

"I'm sorry!" She wailed and searched frantically for the mark.

"Yetsye." She stopped upon hearing the velvety tone. She forced herself to sit still and stared at the clasped hands in her lap. "It is alright. It was only unexpected. Do you not like the beauty of this view?"

"I'd like it better from the top of a firm mountain and not from a twisted and cracked mountain path," she grumbled.

He chuckled, and she felt the pleasant rumble through his chest. A strange sense of calm filled Yetsye as that small sound danced around her ears. "You remind me of Chi'che," he said suddenly and chuckled again.

"Who is Chi'che?"

He was silent so long she thought he wouldn't answer. She shifted her eyes to face the rock wall and nestled into the crook of Tsadok's arm. If she had to stay, she might as well be as comfortable as possible.

When he spoke again, a hint of sorrow shadowed his spin. "When I was very young and Morah was still with us, I returned home from a hunting trip with a friend. We came upon a tuft of grass. One blade was larger than the others and sandy brown instead of sandy green. As we passed the tuft, a ball of fur ferociously attacked our feet. We scanned the nearby area for other tam'na but when a tam'na does not want to be seen..." He left the threads of his spin hanging loose, but Yetsye understood. "We kept walking and ignored the small kit. She chased after our feet and we had to step carefully or walk on her.

"We made our way back to the tribe and when my friend and I parted ways, the kit followed me. At the door to my home, Morah sat outside carving bone jewelry. I stood before her, waiting. The kit hid behind my ankle and pounced upon the ball of knotted cord at Morah's foot. She acknowledged me and I asked if the kit could stay. Her serene acceptance surprised me. Pareh was not so eager, but Morah convinced him it would help me learn the path of responsibility.

"I named her Chi'che for her curiosity. She followed me everywhere and curled beside me while I slept. I thought I received the greatest honor the dawning she followed me home."

Yetsye waited, but he kept silent. She looked up, the tense concentration of his face revealing a rough patch in the path. When he relaxed again, she asked, "Is she waiting for you at home?"

He shook his head. His long braids scuffed against the back of his vest.

"Oh." Yetsye was quiet. She thought of the friend who'd chosen to stay with her. Churk's friendship made life more full. If he and the muffit stayed beside her forever, nothing would please her more. Thoughts of them stirred up thoughts of Matir and Fatir, which then reminded her of the terrible dream. Tears rolled silently down Yetsye's cheeks and she wished the thoughts would stop.

She took a shaky breath. "Please keep talking. I don't want to think of anything right now." She shivered.

"Are you cold?" Yetsye shook her head. "What do you want me to talk about?"

"Tell me more about the tam'na and the other beasts of D'Koruyi." Her voice brightened a bit at the thought of learning about creatures she'd never seen. As he told her of the many beasts of his homeland, she closed her eyes to see it more clearly. The golden fur of the pouncing tam'na, as soft as their teeth and claws were hard. The screeching cry of the hawikh as it flew high in the sky-dome, its keen vision revealing prey far below. He told of the shiitha's four squat legs scuffling along the ground, foraging for insects, the poison of its bite deadly to small creatures and excruciatingly painful to those unfortunate enough to encounter one of the unfriendly little things.

As he talked on and on, she relaxed more and more. The rhythmic patting of the mana's paws and Tsadok's rumbling baritone soon lulled Yetsye back to sleep.

Within two dawnings, the village of Chefvna rose out of the mist. After collapsing in the mountain valley, Yetsye made rest and food her priority. She'd been a burden long enough. The fears that once rose before her like an impassable mountain range now looked more like the northern plains. But when she considered what happened at the mountain pool, it seemed these changes were not without side effects. There would be no more fainting if she could help it. It was hard enough trying to keep her focus on this quest without having to field more questions about her ability to carry out her task. And it wouldn't help at all to add an impossible attachment to that chaos.

They rode into the small village as the suns touched the nearest mountain peak. Yetsye stared at the strange wooden houses painted bright colors and capped with pointed, rectangular roofs. As Leila called out greetings in Oahn, the language of her clan, Yetsye scanned left and right. Chefvna appeared empty. She wasn't sure what to expect, but the eerie quiet that met them was beyond anything she imagined.

As Kven predicted, there was no warm welcome waiting for them. Even with Leila leading the travelers, the villagers remained hidden. Yetsye saw a face or two at windows but they withdrew so quickly she couldn't be certain they were real.

The village center boasted the largest wooden building set in a grove of pinya trees. Leila stopped them in front of the double doors made of solid wooden planks and hung with intricate, soot-colored hinges. Walls built of logs stacked atop each other reached high enough to create two floors. The artisans of Shinnoah must be masters indeed. Yetsye had seen nothing like it, nor had she read about it in the lib'rarum.

"This is our gathering hall." Leila's explanation drew Yetsye's attention. "The council meets here to pass judgment. Religious rituals also happen here. We hold anzha, vocal performances, and iscael, community dances, here, as well."

As she explained, a boulder of a man ducked out through the door. His frizzy gray beard reached to his belted waist. Grizzled, black eyebrows over eyes the gray of stormy skies gave him an air of ferocity, despite the smile he wore. Fur adorned his tunic and pants at the hems and cuffs, following the gray theme. He wore a cap of animal fur and a bone pipe jutted out of one side of his mouth.

"Leila!" His booming voice was as grizzled as his hair. "You've been gone a long time. And who are these scrawny strangers?" Scrawny? Yetsye could clearly see Yuvahl's well-muscled form ahead. The urge to look behind her to Tsadok's muscular form pulled at her. She resisted, though. Shinnoahns seemed bent on goading others.

"Bazhbet Mehya, Senya," Leila greeted him with a quick nod, "these are my friends who've journeyed with me from the plains of Levanna." She introduced Yetsye and the others, being careful not to linger over Yuvahl. "They're on a quest and need help accomplishing it. They helped me and I wish to return the favor. Will Chefvna allow it?" Her voice rang out in the common tongue so everyone could understand. Yetsye wondered, though, if there was still some hidden meaning within them.

Bazhbet pondered. Yetsye refused to look away from him. She wasn't sure she could trust him. A slight movement out of the corner of her eye tempted her, but still she focused on Bazhbet.

"Well, Chefvna? Will we help these scrawny out-clanners on their quest?"

His voice boomed around the gathering place and rumbled down the cobbled streets. A murmur sprouted, grew to a hum, and crescendoed, surging and ebbing around them. Bazhbet raised his hands for silence and the noise subsided. "Will we help these travelers? It is a simple question."

"What do they need?" The question rang from the back of the crowd and spawned similar comments.

Bazhbet scanned them, and his eyes settled on Yetsye. "Well? You look a likely young maid. What is it you require?" he asked Yetsye as if he spoke to a youngling. She felt a warm presence as Tsadok's mana stepped up beside hers.

She hoped her gaze didn't betray surprise at being addressed in such a way. Even though she was obviously the youngest, she didn't want to show how much the barb hurt. Then she realized her stare might present a challenge to Bazhbet. She bowed her head in respect.

"We need to restock our supplies. We also need a sailing vessel to carry us north."

"Do any of you know how to sail?" He was less contemptuous now, but still skeptical. Having met Kven, it was a little easier to handle the man's strange behavior. Yetsye silently thanked Azilet'zal for preparing them.

Yuvahl spoke up, "Yes, Senya. I do." Yetsye watched as he bowed his head to the big man.

"As do I." Tsadok surprised them all. The warrior did not bow, but honor rang in his simple words and straightforward manner.

The Senya stared hard at Tsadok as he walked toward him. "I believe we've met, young D'Koruyin. If I'm correct, your pareh and I battled in the Great Gathering kashklav tournament many tsimikin ago. Zev Zared is a man of great honor and courage."

"I thank you for that, Honorable Senya."

Bazhbet nodded and turned to the throng. "I say we help these younglings on their quest. It's rare to see such comradeship and I would like to see more of it between our clans." Nods and murmurs met the senya's statement, most in agreement. Turning to Yetsye again, Bazhbet said with a warmer smile, "You will have your sailing vessel and the supplies you need."

"I thank you very much, Senya." Yetsye bowed once again. She wasn't sure what drove these Shinnoahns, but she was thankful they agreed. She wondered if their answer would've been the same if they specified their destination. Surely they knew the forbidden place was their goal. It was the only land to the north which showed on any of the maps they studied at Mt. Charan. She hoped they wouldn't change their minds.

26

Gift Betrays

Leila dismounted, motioning for Yetsye and the others to do the same. Two younglings stepped forward and led their mana to a stable behind the central building. Yetsye looked longingly after them. She shook her head before following Leila through the door and marveled at the magnificent proportions.

"Rooms are available for you up the stairs." Leila waved her arm toward wooden planks spiraling up, which were neatly tucked into a back corner of the room. Yetsye studied them. She'd seen steps made of tree roots and stones. She'd also seen steps carved out of rock with wooden planks set atop them, but she'd never seen such beautifully simplistic steps made entirely of wood.

"Thank you," Ya'el replied.

A warm and cheery fire crackled on the outer wall, sending the dusky, sweet scent of pinya around the room. A long, thin, oval table sat off to one side of the main room set with khaf'ket, fluffy bread, and bowls of steaming stew. High-backed chairs decorated with rippling carvings on the arm rests faithfully guarded their posts around the table. Bazhbet Mehya dropped into the most ornate chair at one end of the table and invited them to join him.

"Tell me of your travels. From the looks of you all, it's got to be an interesting tale." He propped his elbows on the table and set his chin in his hands expectantly.

Yetsye would've giggled if she knew him better, but the man still scared her. She looked at Ya'el, who nodded, and with wide eyes and a pasted-on smile, she began the spin of all that happened to them.

"Nechna! You spent the dusking with the fierce plains beasts and lived to tell the tale?" Bazhbet's whistle stirred the hair of his beard. His eyebrows nearly touched his hairline as he growled, "I am truly amazed."

When he heard of their encounter with the whe'evet pack and the Shinnoahn scouts, he was even more shocked and laughed at the reaction of his fellow clansmen. "Kven is a good man. His judgment was sound. I will tell him so when he and the others return."

The talk around the table centered on their quest and the supplies needed for the rest of the journey. Yetsye couldn't help wondering what the Shinnoahns valued. Did they have a system of honor? If so, how did it work? Were they rude on purpose, seeking to provoke a fight? She considered how her blunt words caused so many problems at home and wondered whether she'd fit in better here.

"So you are heading to Yacan?" Bazhbet's growl drew her attention. The companions glanced at each other and then stared at the senya. No one had spoken of the island in particular. No, he'd simply made the connection Yetsye was expecting.

She decided to trust this man. "Yes. Our search is pointing us in that direction. I have a personal quest which my siblings and our friend Tsadok have pledged to help me with. But we're also seeking reasons for the shaking of Y'Dahnndrya and possible solutions."

"And you believe you'll find answers in the forbidden place?" Skepticism rang in his tone.

She watched him closely without moving, without blinking. Slowly, deliberately, she nodded.

"You are aware I could stop you." He scowled and his eyebrows drew together. He had the look of a whe'evet. His words offered a challenge, not a question.

"Yes, I am. But you have also given your pledge to help us. Would you now break faith with us?" Yetsye cocked her head to one side and one eyebrow rose with her question. "I had thought the people of Shinnoah held pledges as sacred as D'Koruyin warriors. Even my people speak highly of the honor of these two clans. Our parents taught us to work hard to attain such a level of honor based on your clan."

He stared into her eyes for a moment, then lowered his head with a sigh. "I see you are determined."

"Yes. There's no going back. If you choose to deny us help, we'll find another way." Her chin jutted out and her nose titled upward. Yetsye hoped she was the picture of a determined woman. Attitude was important, after all.

"Very well. Your supplies will be ready two dawnings from now, at the rising of the suns. You could not have chosen a better time to sail the northern ocean waters. O'zi's currents will guide you there with little effort on your part. The return journey won't be so easy."

"Is there any other information that might help us?" Yuvahl was thinking ahead. Yetsye thanked Azilet'zal for her batir's sharp mind. She missed so much when she was nervous.

Bazhbet thought for a moment. "Really, I should say nothing. Anyone who has gone to the island and is allowed to return is sworn to secrecy. But I suppose there is a small bit which would be good advice no matter where a traveler goes."

"You've been to Yacan?" Ya'el leaned forward in her eagerness to know more.

The senya closed his eyes and sat back in his tall chair. He propped his elbows on the decorative wooden arms and steepled his fingers in front of his nose. Suddenly, his eyes flicked open. The stormy gray gaze bore into Yetsye's soul for several long moments before he spoke.

"Watch.

"Your.

"Step."

They waited for more, but Bazhbet was done. Yetsye nodded solemnly once. Tsadok shifted and broke the connection. Yetsye dropped her eyes and inhaled deeply, unaware she'd been holding her breath. When she looked up again, Bazhbet's eyes still bored through her.

"Is there a place outside where I might view the sky-dome?"

He nodded and rose from his seat. "If you're all ready, I'll show you your rooms and then the viewing area you seek."

"Thank you." She murmured. How tired she was now! The march up Mt. Charan seemed much easier than this conversation had been.

As soon as she knew where to go, Yetsye changed out of her traveling clothes for a long, flowing tunic with wide sleeves. The warm, though lightweight, fabric suited her needs for both a comfortable calming experience and peaceful sleep. She rushed out of her room and crossed to

Tsadok's. She knocked softly, then waited, toes tapping impatiently. The door swung open. He waited for her to speak.

"I'm going to go to the viewing area now." She bowed her head and murmured, "You said I should let you know. I'm doing so, as promised." And she spun away. His door closed behind her and the sound of soft footsteps followed closely. She stopped.

Without turning around, she said, "You don't have to come with me. I think it's safe enough here."

"It is a strange place. I will go. If you wish me to remain unseen, I can do that as well."

Turning up one corner of her mouth in a crooked grin, she replied, "Well, it would've been better if I didn't know you were coming. You might as well stay where I can see you. Otherwise, I won't be able to calm at all."

"Does my presence yet bother you?" There was a sharpness in his tone that cut through her.

"Not at all. Not anymore. It's just harder to focus when I feel like I'm being watched." They continued down the spiral stairs and out the front entrance. Tsadok followed her down the thin foot-path to the small garden Bazhbet had shown her through the windows of the upper level.

"Isn't it a beautiful place?" She was staring up into one of the pinya trees. Its tufted branches were home to a flock of hon'chi. The white flyers were no bigger than the palm of an adult's hand, but they sported five-feathered crests tipped in shades of green. Their dawning song spread joy to any ear touched by the harmonic chimes. Now, though, the flyers were settling to sleep. Their chirps came in staccato bursts, as if to say, "To bed! To bed! Time to sleep!"

"This tree will do very well." Yetsye smiled and sighed in relief. Five steps brought her to the trunk of the tree and she placed her palm upon its wrinkly surface. When she closed her eyes, she opened up her other senses.

"Hngh!" She winced and hunched her shoulders. This time, the sounds, scents, and feelings poured into her like a pounding waterfall. Her consciousness tumbled, powerless. The raging flow overwhelmed her. She could think of nothing but the sharp pain of the shrieking hon'chi songs, the high-pitched howling of the zephyr, and the roaring of a nearby stream. The whe'evet screeches and the lowing of the bix'n shattered her eardrums and pressed in on her as if she sank to the bottom of the deepest lake. The cloying scent of strange fruit nauseated her and the liilum at the village entrance choked her with their cloying fragrance. The next attack crashed in on her, the acrid, harsh scent she'd encountered only once before at the rift. She pushed back, trying to force it away. But the insidious odor invaded her nose and mouth, as if she'd swallowed an army of stinging met'cha.

"Wait! Wait! I can't!"

The connection ripped, and she whimpered. Blinding waves of tears streamed down her face. Her nose closed up and the only feeling she sensed was the extreme loneliness of tragic loss. She crumpled.

"Yetsye."

The first thing she heard was Tsadok whispering her name. She tried opening her eyes, but the lids refused to cooperate. She tried speaking, but all that came out were low mumbles and groans. Picking herself up proved as impossible as moving one of Levanna's gateway stones. Her temples were once again drenched in tears of helplessness. Would her well of tears ever run dry? Blessed darkness overtook her again.

The song of the hon'chi wafted softly through Yetsye's window on the gentle breeze. The light of the suns warmed and quickened her spirit. This time when she tried to open her eyes, the lids parted. But she almost wished they hadn't. Yuvahl and Ya'el knelt by her bed, the welcome familiarity of their faces tainted by the worry she saw etched there. Pale, Tsadok hovered by the door. She tried her voice again.

"I'm sorry," she swallowed, but her voice was working, even if it cracked. She tried again, "I'm s-sorry to w-worry you. Could I p-please have some water?"

Tsadok immediately left to find it. Ya'el grasped her hand. "I'm so glad," she whispered. "I'm so glad you're still with us." Yetsye saw tear tracks on her siveh's cheeks and smiled sadly.

Yuvahl, always practical, asked what everyone wanted to know. "What in the name of Azilet'zal happened?" His voice was deathly quiet and Yetsye knew he was keeping rigid control over his emotions.

She shook her head. "I don't know. I was in the garden for calming. I used my usual method. I don't know." She paused for breath and a drink of the water Tsadok brought. She tried holding the cup, but her weakened muscles shook too much. Tsadok supported her head and helped her drink.

The cool liquid rushed down her throat, refreshing her, strengthening her. He gently laid her head back on the pillow Ya'el had plumped up behind her. He backed away again. "My thanks, Tsadok." She took as deep a breath as her sore muscles would allow. They needed to know what happened. How would she explain it, though?

"I'll try to weave the spin for you. I placed my palm against the bark of the pinya tree. When I closed my eyes and opened up my other senses, I was," she paused, seeking a word that fit, "flooded. That's what it was like. Waves and waves of sounds, scents, and feelings rushing over me in a never-ending flood." She coughed a little and Tsadok gave her another sip of the water. She smiled her thanks. "So many senses constantly shrieked in my ears, seared my nose, clawed at my mouth and throat. My heart shattered into shards and tore me apart from the inside out." She stopped and just breathed for a few moments. Even thinking about the experience brought back the feeling of excruciating pain.

She looked to the side where Tsadok knelt. "Is there any more water in the cup?" At his nod, she whispered, "Please." After a long draught, she picked up her spin where she'd let the threads hang loose.

"In the chaos, I could pick out a few things, one interesting thing in particular. I smelled the foul air of the rift we passed before our arrival at Mt. Charan. I think we need to ask if a rift has opened up here. If not, where did the scent come from? Bazhbet might know." The uncertainty in her voice made Ya'el grab her hand once again.

"It'll be fine, Yetsye. We'll figure all this out." Ya'el was always concerned for the sick. If it wasn't Yetsye laying in the bed, if it was Tsadok or Yuvahl, or even the senya, her focus would shift to them. Ya'el knew her calling, her purpose. Yetsye wished she could see her own way as clearly.

Yuvahl added, "Yes. But until then, how will you calm?"

Yetsye hesitated only a moment before answering. "I don't know. But I'll have to try. You know I can't function as well if I don't go through my calming ritual. Maybe I opened myself up too much?"

"It's possible. Or maybe it has something to do with your Visioning enhancing more than just your skill with the beasts." Yuvahl's idea carried the ring of truth, but Yetsye's eyelids grew heavy.

"Yuvahl's probably right," inserted Ya'el, not to be outdone in a conversation. "The next time you go, we'll go with you." She raised a delicate hand to halt Yetsye's rising indignation. "Please. I know you don't like it, but maybe we can help. It's at least worth a try."

27

Pressing On

Yetsye's recovery took time, but within two dawnings, she could walk short paths. She met with Bazhbet Mehya to discuss what she saw, but it only raised more questions.

"The only place that fits your description is deep in the heart of the Fyrna Mountains. I know of no rifts like you described in our area."

How Yetsye sensed something from so far away was a complete mystery. Just how much was she changing? Yuvahl's insight had always been strangely accurate.

"We should prepare a little more before sailing to Yacan." Yuvahl's bowed head didn't hinder his voice coming through clearly.

After their meeting, her siblings took Yetsye for a stroll. The intense greenish blue sky-dome burned her eyes. Each step reverberated within her. Could it be a residual effect from her not-so-calming experience in the garden? She desperately wanted to try again, for the need to focus her thoughts and refresh her soul mounted steadily. Fear was the only thing holding her back. She didn't want to waste any more time. To be fair, she was unprepared for the sudden flood overwhelming her sense. Maybe she could control it now that she knew what to expect. But she couldn't be certain. She sighed.

"What is it?"

Yetsye glanced at Ya'el. "There's so much I need to sort through and it's difficult to focus. I want to go to the garden." She hated the distress tainting her voice. "But I don't want to risk wasting time, either. If I have to take another dawning or two to recover, it would set us back even more. I think it's best to wait."

"If you think so." Concern wrinkled Ya'el's brow, but she nodded.

They strolled to the stable to visit their mounts. Yetsye spotted Fhoowhsh at the same time he saw her. He tossed his head, whistled, and cooed in excitement. She replied in kind as she hurried to his stall and rested her head on his. Communing with him was just what she needed right now. He was a simple beast, very practical.

"Bright colors! Happy visit! Time to go?"

"Not yet. Happy. Warmth. Orange, yellow, and gold." She returned.

"Gray. Sadness. Ready to go. Belly is full. Energy is full. No need to wait!"

"Soon, I promise, Friend. Blue. Purple." His thoughts helped her focus on the important things, and she thanked him for his unwitting reminder of Azilet'zal's provision. The mana's eagerness encouraged her.

She backed away from Fhoowhsh, enough to look into the big brown eyes for a few moments before releasing his head. When she turned, the others were watching her closely. "I'm fine. I did this before and nothing happened."

"How do you feel?" Ya'el donned her healer's hands now, poking and prodding with them and her words. "Any dizziness? Shortness of breath?"

"I said I was fine, Ya'el. I feel refreshed, actually." Saying this, her eyes widened, and she turned to Yuvahl. "Batir! I think..."

"There's your answer," Yuvahl nodded as he cut in, speaking her thoughts back to her.

"Yes! I can calm with the beasts." Eyes alight, she continued. "The mana's thoughts are simple and focused. It should be enough until I can figure out how to control the flow through Y'Dahnndrya."

"But there's got to be a reason you experienced all of Y'Dahnndrya's life force." Yuvahl frowned. "Think about it. You received a lot of information about this area, but it reached much farther than ever before. You felt and saw more than you ever have. That's important. I think you should still practice. It might be handy on our journey and your quest."

Yetsye nodded. He was right. She must master this new twist on an old gift. "Come on. Let's get ready. The mana are eager to go and the hesps turn. [2] We've lingered long enough."

The next dawning, they loaded the mana onto a skiiv. The long-bodied sea-going vessel boasted two masts with triangular sails. Two oars nestled in racks, one on each side, in the event the winds died down or one had to sail against them.

The senya pointed to a round metal box embellished with filigree sea folk. "This is a dirksh'n. Make sure the arrow points to the star at the top. You will come upon Yacan within two dawnings if the winds hold. This skiiv is not equipped with an anchor. You'll have to moor it somewhere once you reach the shore. Be certain to secure it well at both the fore and aft. The tides are strange on the island, so moor her accordingly." Yuvahl and Tsadok nodded.

"Is there really nothing else you can tell us, Senya Bazhbet?" The more Yetsye knew, the better she could protect Ya'el.

"Only that it's best to wait for Serafin to come to you. And come she will. She has a strange connection with Edrea. She will know you're there." Bazhbet wore a slight smile and his gray eyes softened. Yetsye thought she understood him a little better now after their discussions.

"Thank you very much, Honorable Senya," she said, drawing herself up to her full height. "Your kindnesses will not be forgotten." Her formal speech surprised Bazhbet, but she couldn't tell if it offended or impressed him.

"You are most welcome. I'll pray for your safe return." He bowed low before Yetsye, catching the youngling off guard. For a moment, she wasn't sure what to do, but when he raised his head once again, his grin reassured her. She offered him a smile in return. Tsadok took her hand to help first her, then Ya'el board the skiiv. They shoved off and once out of the small bay, a stronger sea-wind filled the sails.

The skiiv flew over the cooperative O'zi Ocean. They reached Yacan as Tsifi'ra touched the horizon at the close of the second dawning. From nine skiiv-lengths away, they could see the great roots which grew more and more impressive the closer they came. Shira's progeny only experienced the ocean during inter-clan trading. But none of them knew of trees that thrived on salty water.

Edrea impressed them with her collection of trunk-sized branches that twisted and snaked everywhere. Platter-sized leaves ranged in color from vibrant cerulean to dark green and the singular, rounded fans grew everywhere. The blossoms were almost the same size as the giant leaves. Milk-white conical blooms darkening to brilliant yellow at their centers set the stage for the bright pink double pistils. Their orange, pollen-tipped partners danced to the music of the ocean breezes. Edrea might be a kho'ni tree, but she was unlike any other specimen Yetsye had ever seen.

The high grating warning of an unknown flyer resounded overhead as the being swooped over the newcomers and was gone before they could identify it. Its cry echoed into the depths of the island and with its retreat, it stole all sounds except the rhythmic waves kissing the Great Tree's feet. In the eerie silence, Tsadok and Yuvahl continued unloading only the items they needed during their visit. They stored the rest in the skiiv's trunks. The skittish mana tapped their wide paws and used their blunt claws to navigate the roots of Edrea.

"How long do you think we'll have to wait?" Yuvahl asked Tsadok, which annoyed Yetsye at first. Then she sighed. It was unthinkable that her batir relied on her judgment after he'd helped raise her from the dawning of her birth. After all, she couldn't even control her gifts yet. She watched Tsadok shake his head and caught Ya'el's attempt to inch her way toward a blossom out of the corner of her eye.

"Ya'el, don't!" Ya'el glared at her outburst, surprise and frustration waging war across her lovely features.

"Why not? It's not like I'm going further into the island's terrain."

"No, but we're strangers here and the laws of Yacan are likely different."

Yuvahl came to Yetsye's aid. "She's right. We need to wait for Serafin. You can ask her your questions, then."

"But will she answer all my questions?" Hands on her hips, Ya'el stood defiant and indignant.

"How do you know she won't?" Yuvahl returned with raised eyebrows. He waited for Ya'el to comply. "She'll probably be here sooner than we expect. Would you anger her before we even get to talk to her?"

Sighing, Ya'el bobbed a reluctant nod. "You're right, though I hate to admit it."

They sat together on one of the large roots. Yetsye wanted to touch her palm to Edrea, but she felt it would be intrusive. She didn't know how to ask for permission.

While they waited, she listened to the murmurs of the others and the soft voices of the mana. It didn't take long for her head to droop. Before it hit the root beneath her, her head lifted and gentle hands laid her down. She murmured her thanks and received a low chuckle in return. Tsadok. But she was too tired to move.

When she woke, wedged between Tsadok and Ya'el, Yetsye's head rested in the crook of the more muscular arm. She raised her chin to find his clear eyes open, but revealing none of his feelings. She sat up and looked around. Motes of light trickled down through the canopy.

She rose and scanned the roots they nestled in, almost missing the glimmer of metallic green-gold in the shadows. Tsadok tensed, but anyone glancing at him wouldn't be able to see any difference. She refocused on the spot to find it gone. A flicker off to her right drew her gaze. It was closer now and a human form slowly materialized.

"Serafin," she barely whispered, and felt rather than saw Tsadok nod. They watched as the slender form disappeared into the branches above her. Though she searched, Yetsye couldn't see or hear anything betraying the Guardian's position. That thought alone was daunting.

Tsadok's presence beside her was doubly reassuring. He must've sensed her uncertainty, for he placed a hand on her shoulder. Courage and strength poured into her through the connection and it startled her, for she wasn't seeking it. Was this what it felt like for her beast friends when she connected with them?

"How are you doing that?" she asked softly, her eyes scanning the branches above.

"Doing what?"

Now she did turn to face him. "Pouring into me the energy I needed most right now. How are you doing it?"

He cocked his head to the side, a question hovering in his eyes for a moment before he shuttered them again. "I did not realize it was happening. Is it unpleasant?" He shifted his hand.

"No!" Her bark of protest woke the others. They rose quickly, blinking sleep from their eyes as their hands groped for weapons.

"I'm sorry," Yetsye did her best to ease their fears and tried to explain what she and Tsadok saw.

"So Serafin visited us?" Yuvahl's wrinkled brow betrayed confusion and disbelief. "If she did, then why didn't she say something or stay here?"

"I don't know. She jumped into the branches and we haven't seen her since." After a moment, Yetsye continued in a thoughtful murmur. "Maybe it's some kind of test. Maybe she wants to see how strong our determination is."

Tsadok nodded but said nothing. Yetsye smiled her thanks for his support.

"Well, I'm tired of waiting." Ya'el would normally have stamped to emphasize her words, but the roots of Edrea were not the most stable floor. The magnificent tree provided a comfortable nesting spot for them, but in other places, it was impossible to see solid ground through the significant gaps. Who knew what lay beneath the root floor?

Keeping Ya'el from bolting off to explore on her own was exhausting. It was now early dusking and Yetsye tried once again to keep her talking while they waited for Serafin to return.

"Ya'el?"

"What is it now, Yetsye?" Having to sit in one place while there was so much to see chaffed. Ya'el's fingertips were in danger of being eradicated.

Yetsye gently took Ya'el's hands and clasped them together between her own. "I know it's hard for you. I'm sorry. Have you drawn everything you've seen here?"

Ya'el jerked her hands away and stalked over to her pack. She yanked her pa'pukh out and threw it to Yetsye, who caught it awkwardly. "Look at it!" Ya'el demanded.

Confused, Yetsye did as she was told and flipped through the beautiful illustrations of the people, places, beasts, and plants they'd encountered on their journey. Everything Yetsye barely glanced at while traveling, Ya'el had documented down to the finest detail. Yetsye stared at her siveh, more aware now of the struggle within her.

"But there's nothing in here from Yacan."

"There's not supposed to be. Don't you remember the warnings?" Ya'el snapped. Yetsye couldn't understand why she was so angry.

Yetsye carefully picked her way over to where Ya'el stood with one booted leg propped on a jutting knot. Her thunderous face spoke eloquently of her desire to throttle Serafin for making them wait so long.

"I don't think she'll come before the moons rise. Rest, Ya'el. Let's sleep while we can." She placed a gentle hand on her siveh's shoulder and said, "Surely adventure awaits."

Ya'el scowled, grabbed the pa'pukh out of Yetsye's hands, and stalked back to the sleeping nest. Yetsye watched as she stepped down into it. Her eyes burned. She'd meant to calm the storm, but she'd never been as good with humans as she was with beasts. She bowed her head in defeat and raised it slowly when the scent of wood and leather settled around her.

"Tsadok?"

"What is it?"

"Azilet'zal really doesn't make mistakes, right?"

"You speak the truth."

"Then why can't I make a positive difference in the lives of my own kyn?" She raised troubled eyes brimming with tears and he hesitantly wiped away the few which fell.

"You will learn." He paused and grinned crookedly before asking, "You can learn, can you not?"

She scowled at him, but couldn't stop the grin tugging at the corner of her mouth. He took her hand and led her to Ya'el and Yuvahl, who had already settled in. Ya'el had situated herself between the edge of the nest and

Yuvahl. What was this? Was she trying to force a bond to grow between her own siveh and an out-clanner?

"Is something wrong?" Tsadok asked.

Yetsye shook her head and settled close to Yuvahl. "A good sleep to you Yuvahl, Ya'el." Yuvahl grunted a reply, but Ya'el remained stubbornly silent.

Yetsye sighed and lay back, facing the canopy. She could just make out a few dots of light high above. The tension between her and Ya'el, and the uncomfortable knot at the back of her neck, kept her awake far longer than she would've thought possible. For such a long and tiresome dawning, shouldn't sleep come quickly?

Tsadok had not lain back, but kept watch. When Ya'el's gentle breathing and Yuvahl's soft snuffles were the only sounds, Tsadok spoke.

"If it is helpful, I can be a sleeping mat again."

If she hadn't looked up to see his grin, she'd never have realized he was teasing her. She replied stiffly, "No, thank you. I'll be fine." She hated the strange weakness which only showed up around him. She regretted having to answer that way, too. Though he was solid, he was much more comfortable than Edrea was proving to be. "I'd wish you a good sleep, but you won't, will you?"

He shook his head. "Sleep now, Yetsye." It was a long time coming, but the curtain of sleep finally descended.

28

Serafin's Way

The light of the suns pushed against Yetsye's closed eyes, waking her before anyone but Tsadok. His tenseness alarmed her. A pair of bent knees clad in a strangely mottled brown fabric wrapped with vine-like cords met her gaze as Yetsye rose from the root-bed. There was no escape from such a close encounter. She forced her blinking eyes upward, noting slender but well-muscled arms tanned by the suns and the most pale eyes she'd ever seen. Though Tsadok's were icy blue, these were paler still, like clear water from a deep well. Pure. Sharp. A shock of close-cropped, sun-streaked blond hair framed the delicate face. Thin lips parted in a feral smile, revealing even white teeth under a small but strong nose.

"Have you finished your inspection?" Serafin's voice was like waves on a windy day. Yetsye caught the hint of power barely controlled. A short, thin club studded with prongs rested across the Guardian's bent knees. It amazed her to find the woman wasn't angry with them, just curious.

Yetsye nodded, which stirred Tsadok from his frozen state. As always, he hid his thoughts well.

"Are you afraid?" There was a hint of laughter in the Guardian's voice, as if taunting fool-hardy strangers.

"Yes." Yetsye frowned, but this was the best answer. Such a person would respect honesty and bravery. Admitting fear wasn't a sign of cowardice, as Yuvahl often reminded her.

"Why have you come here?"

"We are," Yetsye began, but the words suddenly died in her throat. She swallowed hard and tried again. "I am seeking a path. Three dreams came to me, one the dusking before my Visioning ceremony at Levanna and two during the rite. I believe I know what the dreams mean, but I'm not sure how to accomplish my task. I have questions without answers."

Serafin nodded solemnly. Yetsye risked speaking once more. "We are all seeking answers concerning the shaking of Y'Dahnndrya. Why are there two rifts opening up in the surface, and why did Y'Dahnndrya swallow one D'Koruyin tribe."

Again Serafin nodded. She closed her eyes for a moment. Was this how she spoke to Edrea? The pause offered her an opportunity to see if Yuvahl and Ya'el were hearing this. Her jaw dropped when she found them still asleep. She turned to find Serafin's eyes open and staring back at her. "Edrea will permit you to stay. I will guide you. You will obey my instructions. If you do not, you will die."

Her deadpan delivery left no room for argument. Yetsye paled as she wondered how often someone broke the rules. "We will do as you say. My siveh has some questions. Would you permit her to ask? She is very curious, interested in plants and different cultures. Yacan and Edrea have always fascinated her."

"Your siveh, I have watched. Edrea has watched and spoken of her. You were wise to stop her." Yetsye's eyebrows shot upward and Serafin explained. "The blossoms of Edrea, though beautiful, send out a poison so strong it puts even large animals to sleep, a sleep from which they never awaken. Edrea decides when to send out the toxin. She keeps close watch on your siveh." Serafin took a deep breath, then continued briskly, "Wake your siblings. We must go to the temple. You may find the answers you seek there. The mana must remain on your vessel. The dangers increase further in."

Yetsye followed Serafin's instructions exactly. She had no wish to lose any lives on Yacan. She picked her way carefully to Fhoowhsh and whispered to him. With his help, the other mana quickly returned to the skiiv. All the time, Serafin's eyes burned into her back. Before allowing Fhoowhsh to board, she communed with him to calm herself. It might be a while before she'd be able to do so again. By the time she finished, Tsadok had awakened Yuvahl and Ya'el and told them what was happening.

"Your weapons are not allowed." Serafin motioned for them to leave their hunting gear.

Ya'el opened her mouth to question, but Yetsye frowned at her. Her siveh snapped her lips together and shed her pair of ki'fi, tossing them to Yuvahl, who was closest to the skiiv. Yetsye did the same with the ki'fi she kept hidden in the folds of her tunic. When they were done, Serafin beckoned them into the jumble of roots and branches.

She tossed over her shoulder, "Touch nothing except the wooden arms of Edrea and be mindful of how you do that. Do not scan the area. Your questions I will answer at the temple."

They walked for such a long time that Yetsye's calves and lungs burned. The humidity weighed on her chest, making every breath a fight for life. The roots and branches sprawling everywhere, always the same, made it impossible to decipher direction. If they lost sight of Serafin, would they ever find the way home? It was no wonder so many never returned from this place.

In the distance, a gold spark caught Yetsye's eye, though she was careful not to let her vision linger there for long. They must be close to the temple. She felt they were climbing now, though the terrain didn't look or feel so very different. When they tumbled over a large root, a bright white rotunda with a roof of shimmering golden metal straight ahead confirmed her suspicions. Yetsye almost cried in relief. The end of their trek was near.

Though they could see the temple, they didn't walk straight toward it. Yetsye wondered if this was one of the tests Bazhbet warned them of. She sighed and determined to see it through. When they finally stepped through the temple arch, she collapsed on the steps, panting, sweat dripping from the tip of her nose and the rounded point of her chin. Her drenched clothes weighed her down. Her hair had come loose in places, framing her face in dripping ringlets. She raised herself up on her hands and knees to see Serafin's legs and dragged her eyes upward to meet that sharp gaze.

"May I please have some water?" she asked between wheezing gasps. At Serafin's nod, she whimpered in relief. Tsadok's brown hands placed a cup into hers as he lifted and supported her. She was at once thankful and annoyed. How was it possible she'd grown so weak? She took a long draught.

When she quenched her thirst, she looked at him. "Thank you." She set down the beaker. "How are you still able to move so easily?" Without waiting for an answer, she looked around for Yuvahl and Ya'el. They looked cool and refreshed. Why was she the only one fighting to breathe and dripping with sweat?

Frowning, she turned to Serafin again. She forced herself to her feet and faced the Guardian with as much courage as she could muster.

"This is the beginning of my test, then?" This Guardian was a talker, but a simple nod was the only reply she received. "Are there more tests?" Again Serafin nodded. The menacing grin slowly spreading over Serafin's face angered Yetsye. "Fine. Let's get it over with." She met Serafin's contempt with a ferocity so hot she surprised herself.

Serafin looked long and hard at her. "Come with me." The words chipped from ice allowed no room for argument or hesitation. Yetsye followed stiffly, pulling her damp clothing away from her sticky skin. She was cooling and feeling more uncomfortable with every heartbeat. Serafin stooped and disappeared through a small doorway on the right side of the entry room and led her down a dimly lit hallway. Yetsye observed the temple as she walked and made an interesting discovery. This place wasn't made of stone, but of ivory wood. And the roof wasn't bright metal, as first thought. Living, golden leaves shut out direct light and fluttered in a light breeze.

Serafin took her into the first chamber they came to. Inside, a pallet and trunk rested against opposing walls. A small rug made of vines and bright leaves covered the center of the floor, adding a bit of frivolity to the otherwise spartan surroundings. Serafin motioned for Yetsye to open the trunk. She stared at the Guardian for a long while, trying to read her intentions. The silver streaks in Serafin's hair mimicked all the other Guardians and clan leaders Yetsye had seen. But Serafin also wore a fine silver facial tattoo, which made her think of Tsadok's golden-eyed el'tekh. This tattoo, decorated with dots and leaves, outlined her brow ridge and cheekbones, though. There was nothing to be read on that cold but beautiful face, no matter how long she stared. There was no other choice but to trust.

Yetsye walked to the ornately carved wooden trunk. With shaking hands, she twisted the golden clasp and lifted the heavy lid. Bits of fabric filled the cavity. She pulled out a small wad of cloth in her favorite leaf green. It was a cropped vest-like top. A long length of fabric in a deep sea blue followed. A skirt? Both fabrics shimmered as she turned them in her hands.

A smaller carved box nestled inside the trunk on the left. She pointed at it and Serafin nodded. Ropes in different shades of blue, red, and gold lay coiled inside. She chose the pale gold and pulled it out, careful not to take the others. What she thought was one rope was a knotted cluster of several.

Serafin helped her out of her sweat-soaked clothing and into the new things she'd be wearing. "These clothes are more suitable for Yacan." Her clipped words were a surprising contrast to her gentle hands. She moved as she spoke, with great economy, winding the blue cloth skillfully around her legs and hips. "You can move easily in these. They are cooler, too."

"I don't understand. The scrolls always painted this place as a cold and desolate island full of monsters, snow, and ice." Yetsye's confusion seemed to amuse Serafin, who just looked at her and smiled happily.

"Ah. To keep people away." Yetsye nodded as she finally made the connection. "To be honest, I didn't want to come here. If there was any other way, I would've chosen it." She wondered how much she could tell this Guardian, deciding if Edrea chose her, she must be trustworthy. "I fear for my siveh's life in this place."

Serafin nodded, and a thoughtful frown marred the smooth forehead. "You should. Curious people do not fare well here."

Yetsye swallowed hard as Serafin finished twining the rope around her legs. She handed the shortest length of rope to Yetsye and motioned for her to lace up the vest. When she was done, Serafin directed her to take down her hair.

"I'm not sure I can." At Serafin's look of disbelief, she explained, "Tsadok arranged it in a way I'm not familiar with, so it wouldn't hamper me while I travel."

Serafin left the room at a sprint and when she returned to the shocked Yetsye a moment later, Tsadok was with her. "Take it down," she ordered, pointing at Yetsye's hair. He bowed and moved to Yetsye's back. His hands gently removed the intricate braids he'd woven. What surprised her more, she didn't know — her sorrow to see the braids go, or how comforting Tsadok's presence was.

"When you are done, I will decide what to do with it." But for that command, Serafin stood in silence for the duration. When the arduous task was finally complete, Yetsye's back and neck had stiffened. She groaned, unable to trap the sound before it escaped. To stretch out stiff muscles, she bent over her knees. Then she sat up straight once she felt able.

Serafin moved to inspect her hair. The Guardian grunted as she ran her fingers over the silvery strands and separated them from the rest. With those, she made two braids. With the red-gold waves, she made five larger braids that hugged her head and ran down her back. Once done, she bound the five braids together with another piece of the gold rope. "If the rope fails, the braids will not. This hairstyle will allow your scalp to breathe. With such thick hair, you will thank me."

"I almost wish I could cut it like yours," Yetsye lamented. " But it took so long for my hair to grow to this length, I would regret losing it."

"Flattery?" Serafin frowned and her words sharpened with displeasure.

"Not at all!" Yetsye put as much sincerity into her words and posture as she could.

Serafin placed her forehead to Yetsye's, surprising both her and Tsadok. Yetsye felt a slight push against her mind and when Serafin moved away again, she nodded. "You are truthful. Come."

Yetsye rose from her knees and stood. She turned wide eyes to Tsadok, who hurried to support her while she waited for the blood to flow in her legs again. When she could walk, they left the room. Serafin motioned for Tsadok to return to the others. He contemplated Yetsye before heading back down the hallway at her nod.

"He is loyal." Serafin's monotonous words gave Yetsye no idea what she meant.

"Yes, he's been a faithful companion since we met him."

"Are you life-mated?"

In surprise, Yetsye blurted out, "No!" Was this another test?

Serafin stared at her a long time before the Guardian shrugged and led the way down the passage. Yetsye shook her head and followed. She noticed the lights weren't torches like those at Mt. Charan. And they weren't filled with glowing miritasi, like the lamps at home. These seemed to be composed of luminescent flowers. Ya'el would love them. She focused on Serafin. Failing these tests wasn't an option.

The passageway seemed unending. In time, they came to a round room from which two paths branched off left and right. The path they were on continued straight on the other side of a pool gurgling with fresh water.

"Refresh yourself."

Yetsye needed no second urging. Her throat was once again parched and her muscles were still stiff and sore. She gulped three handfuls of the most crisp water she'd ever tasted. After she drank as much as she dared, she stood again and noticed her reflection, not recognizing herself at first. The change in hairstyle and clothing made a such a drastic difference. She wasn't sure whether she liked the change.

"Choose a path." Serafin barked the order in her stormy voice, recalling Yetsye's attention. "Left. Right. Straight. These ways lead to a test. You need only pass one of them to leave this island with your life. If you fail the first, you can try again with the next, and again with the last. But if you fail all three..." Serafin's eyes never left Yetsye's. Under that gaze, she felt weak and as vulnerable as a fresh-born mana. "I will wait for you here. Your companions will be safe as long as they stay where we left them. Focus on the task before you and remember your lessons. You will be fine."

"What lessons?" Yetsye was on the verge of panic. Her breathing quickened and her heart throbbed. She knew of no lessons on how to pass the tests of Guardians.

"Life lessons." And with that, Serafin turned to sit on a convenient vine bench Yetsye hadn't seen when they walked in. Steeling herself, the young maid from M'Neshunnaya offered a silent prayer and chose the path to her left. Azilet'zal would not steer her wrong and would see her through this as through all trials, right?

29

Trial Within

Five steps down the passageway, a sharp blast of air hit Yetsye. It stopped as unexpectedly as it started. The heat and humidity came back twice as strong. Something was wrong and she stopped to scan the area. A wall now sealed off the entrance. The blocked passage shouldn't bother her. She made a decision and going back wasn't an option. She swallowed her fear and strode forward with renewed determination.

Yetsye sped on as fast as she dared to the center of another chamber. Loud clicks and creaks heralded a pedestal ascending from the floor. A square pillow made of shiny gold cloth perched atop it. In the center of the pillow, a clear vial nestled. The mechanical noises stopped when the pedestal locked into place with a final loud click. Hesitantly, she walked to the pedestal and reached out a shaking hand to the spherical container of clear orange liquid, labeled with the number three. Had she chosen the wrong pathway?

Her brow furrowed as she tried to puzzle it all out. She touched the glashiin vial. "No, not glashiin. This is precious opin'e of Genzet," she marveled, breathlessly. She'd never seen it before, but somehow she knew. She lifted the vial reverently and the room, the pedestal, and the pillow disappeared. A dense curtain of fog obscured everything. She could barely see her own feet. Clammy air left her bare arms sticky and dampened her clothes. She shivered.

The cork popped out of the bottle easily when she prodded it with her thumb. A sniff of the orange stuff reminded her vaguely of bansan berries. She sniffed again. And bon'jiis! Maybe this liquid was a refreshing drink, fortifying her for the test. Since nothing else was happening, she took a sip.

Her hand shook slightly as she raised the bottle to her lips. A small sip chased a little of the fog away. She took a larger sip, and the fog dissipated completely. As the syrupy liquid coated her throat, it left a cooling stream of lightness in its wake.

Yetsye was flying through her village. Past her home. Then past Matir praying in the temple and, further along, Fatir teaching his students. When she came to her favorite glen, she smiled. Familiar beast-friends she'd helped during her life ate and slept contentedly beneath her. Her feet touched the ground.

Suddenly, the calm animals attacked her, enraged. Shielding her face and stomach with her arms, she tried defending herself without hurting her friends. Claws ripped at her clothing and skin, drawing blood. Teeth gnawed on her arms and spittle flew into her eyes, coating her cheeks and hands with a slimy film. When she opened her mouth, all that came out was a cry of surprise and disgust. So fierce was the attack and so unexpected that all thoughts raced from her mind except those needed for survival. She cried out again, this time for Churk. It did no good. He, too, was beating at her with his dainty, broken wings.

Her arms and face burned with fever-heat. She ached all over. Chills wracked her bones and muscles. Was it poison? How? She crumpled to the ground and rolled onto her back. A blud'ig moved in for a killing chomp at her throat as the bush'ka she'd saved from a fiery death slowly reared up on its hind legs to trample her. The longer the attack went on, the more order came to her chaotic thoughts.

"Focus, Yetsye!" Finally, she could tell herself something positive. Maybe no one had to die here. She lowered her arms and let the beasts throw their full fury upon her. She opened herself up to Y'Dahnndrya and to the beasts she loved. Swirling down, down, down, with dizzying speed, she almost fainted when the feeling of sudden weightlessness hit her.

Anger. Hatred. Confusion. Fear. Injustice. Negative feelings clamored so loudly they drowned out all others, and it was difficult to find a common thought to share with any of her beast friends. Slogging through the mire of emotions, she finally found what she sought, a small light of hope deep in the core of her dearest beast-friend.

She pushed her mind toward it, and through sheer determination, she reached the tiny flame. Stretching out her spirit hand, she gently cupped it and joined her own flame of hope to it, brightening the light and dulling the sharp edges of painful feelings swirling inside Churk. She blew on the little flame, encouraging it to grow brighter still, her breath so soft it wouldn't knock a met'cha from its pond blossom perch. Any youngling knew that the harsher the breath, the easier it was to extinguish a flame. As the flame grew, the negative emotions diminished. The fog reached in with long, thin fingers and Churk, the beasts, and her glen faded to gray.

Aching, Yetsye dragged herself up onto her hands and knees, then sat for a moment to catch her breath. She felt for the scratches and bites, but her skin was whole. Fog once again shrouded the room, so thick she couldn't see past it. Her trial wasn't over yet. She painfully drew herself up to her full height.

Drawing in a deep breath, she took another sip of the orange liquid, larger than the last one. The syrup ran down her throat and again the fog retreated. She stepped carefully in the direction it drifted until she found herself in a deep canyon of unfamiliar red stone.

Wind buffeted her as it whistled through the canyon. The whistling crescendoed until the discordant shrieks sliced through her ears like ice shards. Yetsye covered them with her hands, but even skin and bones were no match for the penetrating keen. She hunkered down and crept forward slowly, determined to get away from the noise but found her path blocked by beasts she only knew from books and Tsadok's spins. Tam'na hunkered down with claws out and fangs bared. Hawikh, with talons outstretched, poised in the air to strike from above. The solitary shiitha scratched at the dirt and hissed as its tail flipped back and forth. She could try climbing. The holes would help her if she could ignore the shards of sound ripping into her ears.

"Focus, Yetsye!" Why did she have to keep reminding herself to focus? "I'm such a failure! Such a youngling!" As soon as those thoughts came to mind, the wind and noise doubled and she wailed in agony. Hesitating no longer, the beasts charged. Keeping her eyes focused on them, she coiled her silver braids around her ears, stuffed the tails in, and began the grueling climb up the canyon wall.

"If the beasts charge and the wind grows louder when I don't believe in myself, the reverse should apply." She forced her thoughts toward the positive. "I can do this. I am a datir of Shira and a Child of Y'Dahnndrya, beloved of Azilet'zal. No one is more determined than I am. There's no going back. I will succeed." With each positive thought she forced through her mind, the wind lessened and the beasts calmed. By the time she reached the top of the canyon, the wind died altogether. The beasts which had menaced her at the bottom of the canyon now waited patiently for her as she pulled herself over the top. The sudden stillness was mind-numbing and almost as painful as the cacophony of before.

"Who are you and why are you here auzi'ide?"

She turned at the voice. A long barb-topped pole hovered entirely too close to her right eye. She followed the length of it to meet the eyes of—

"Zev Zared!" she burst out.

"How is it you know my name?" Neither his face nor his voice betrayed any emotion, but there was no doubt of his suspicion.

"But you are the pareh of my friend." She was genuinely confused. From the formality of speech, to the timbre and tone of his voice, he was exactly as Tsadok described, even to the hair styled in a bundle of braids. She looked into his eyes and there was an unnatural hardness in them. She faced a fearsome opponent.

"Who are you? Why have you called these beasts to this place?" He wouldn't wait much longer and her previous answer wasn't acceptable.

"I am Yetsye Shirasdatir of the M'Neshunnayan Clan. I seek to encourage unity of purpose between the beasts and clans of Y'Dahnndrya." She paused, uncertain of what to say next, all the time knowing Zev would need more to believe her. She raised brown eyes wide with questions to meet cold blue eyes of determination. A brief flicker betrayed intense thought on the otherwise stony face. It gave her the courage to continue. "Will you help me? I cannot do this alone."

He shifted the barbed pole menacingly, but she stood her ground, her eyes never leaving his. Yetsye counted fourteen rapid heartbeats before he lowered the end to the ground and the fog closed in upon her once more.

The pain was milder this time. Perhaps she was getting used to these trials. With growing confidence, she gulped the last bit of the orange liquid and waited for what would come.

This time, the fog shredded in the face of searing heat. Flames raged around her, searing tongues licking at her exposed skin. She hung, tied at her wrists and ankles between two posts. Blood trickled in rivulets down her arms and back. Her own sweat attacked her through slight cuts on her face, stinging like a swarm of angry met'cha. Once again, a cry of pain forced its way past her cracked lips. Her joints ached and her arms and feet were bound in a way which added to her pain. She could hardly breathe.

Vague shapes swam closer until she could distinguish faces through the veil of flame surrounding her. Disbelief and a crushing sense of betrayal threatened to drown her as faces she knew well jeered at her and called for her death. Yuvahl, Tsadok, and others she knew floated just out of reach of the flames.

It was the last two who shattered her. Matir and Fatir pointed at her. Disappointment twisted their faces as they raged. "It's your fault! Ya'el is dead, and it's your fault! How dare you come back alive while she is no longer among the living? How dare you breathe the air of Y'Dahnndrya while your siveh lies broken in a far land?"

"No!" she screamed back, though her throat was dry and as cracked as her lips from the heat. "It's not my fault! I tried to stop it. I did all I could!" She begged them to understand. Hot tears flowed freely, for she feared the truth in their words.

"Then why is she dead? It's your fault. It's your fault. Your. Fault!"

Yetsye hung her head in despair and whispered, "Maybe you're right. Maybe there was more I could've done. I don't know. Maybe I deserve to die."

As she resigned herself to death, the flames cooled a bit. She raised her head to see the people milling about. Some still jeered, but most returned to their daily routines. Was she going to live?

"Hello?" she asked tentatively.

"Yes?" The voice came from behind her.

"Hello. Can you help me? I want to be free!"

"Can't you free yourself?" came the soft reply.

"How? All my limbs are bound?"

"Mmmm," The voice was wind through dancing leaves.

"So, I must free myself without using my hands and feet." The pain muddled her thoughts. By the Holy Voice, it hurt so much! All she wanted was to ease the pain. If immersing herself in the hope of the beasts and in the positive truths of the canyon worked before, maybe she could immerse herself in something here. What was there, though? The people were too far away and the flames searing her flesh were far too fickle to grasp. There was only one thing she could think of — herself.

"Wait! I must immerse myself in myself? I don't even know how to begin!"

"If you do not, then you will fail this test. But I believe in you."

"Who are you?"

"Don't you know?"

Yetsye paused and thought of all the people who had the ability to speak to her mind. "Edrea?"

"It is as you say. Now, Yetsye Shirasdatir, finish this as a Chosen One of The Creator."

Yetsye nodded and closed her eyes. She receded down deep within herself, down to the tiny flame of hope she'd shared with Churk and further to the glowing ember, the core of her being. Pausing before it, she reached out a tentative finger to it, only to find it growing in size until it engulfed her. She burned, but wasn't consumed. This was the flame of eternal energy, the piece of herself that was born of Azilet'zal. This tiny burning ember would either light flames of unification and purification, or incinerate the hope of all living things. Which would she choose? Yetsye filled her consciousness with the ember. Her confidence grew as she renewed her connection to Azilet'zal once more.

When she opened her eyes, the passageway lay clear before her and the vial, shattered at her feet. In distress, she knelt to gather the precious shards, but they disappeared before she touched them. Standing again, she walked back toward the fountain. This time, the blast of cold air on her skin refreshed and cleansed her body as the testing had done for her mind and spirit.

She came upon Serafin unexpectedly. The bench had been on her left when she'd entered the left passageway. Now they were in front of her, still on her left. How was that possible? She'd taken all three paths?

Serafin's eyes were closed, so Yetsye knelt by her side and waited patiently. It didn't take long.

"What are you doing?" Her harsh words grated against Yetsye's nerves.

"I'm sorry. I didn't want to wake you."

The softening was barely perceptible, but Yetsye caught it before Serafin's mask solidified. "I was not asleep but speaking with Edrea."

"I wouldn't have wished to disturb either of you, then."

Serafin barked a short laugh, grinned awkwardly. Was she out of practice? The Guardian motioned for Yetsye to follow her to the pool. "Drink and refresh yourself once more. Take a long look at your reflection. It may be quite some time before you get another chance to see yourself this way again."

It was the most human the Guardian seemed since they'd arrived at Yacan. Her behavior made Yetsye feel as if she was on equal footing with her. But that couldn't be. Could it?

She rose slowly, walked over to the fountain, and leaned over the edge. She backed away immediately, scared of the dimin staring back at her. When she turned confused eyes to Serafin, the Guardian urged her to look again.

What she saw looking back at her was a red-gold light with two blinding silvery streaks and red-gold stars where eyes should be. Even her clothing glowed as if she'd been refined to the highest purity.

"The pool reveals the image of your spirit. You cannot see it anywhere else that I know of."

"Do you see me this way?" Yetsye thought of all the times her siblings told her she glowed. Was this what they saw?

Serafin's slow nod confirmed her fears. She bowed her head with the weight of this knowledge.

"Edrea approves of your spirit." Yacan's Guardian surprised Yetsye again, drawing her attention away from the pool.

"May I speak to Edrea again?"

Serafin paused, a frown of thoughtfulness wrinkling her brow. "I am uncertain. I can ask her if she is willing."

"There is something I wish to know. When I was growing up in Zulima, I regularly performed a calming ritual at the end of every dawning and sometimes, more often during a stressful day. The last time I tried, I ended up hurt and bedridden. I wondered why and if it has something to do with my Visioning experience and my quest. Maybe you know, Serafin?"

"I am certain it is a part of who you truly are. This gift is only now coming into maturity. That you could do this before in a diminished way shows how strong your gift truly is. It will take time to adjust. You will need helpers to care for you when your body and mind become overwhelmed. You will need proper rest."

Yetsye nodded. "This is what Yuvahl and Ya'el suggested. I was reluctant at first, but I saw the wisdom of their words after pondering them."

Serafin motioned for Yetsye to follow her back to the temple entrance hall. "Your companions grow restless and Ya'el especially finds it hard to wait."

Yetsye doubled her pace to match Serafin's long strides. Leaving Yacan would be more difficult for her than deciding to come. As forbidding as it first seemed, Yacan's present tranquility washed all her fears and worries away. She longed to bask in that peace.

They arrived in the entrance hall to find Yuvahl and Tsadok deep in conversation.

"Where is Ya'el?" Threads of worry laced Yetsye's voice as she searched the entrance hall. But it was no use. Ya'el had vanished.

30

Trial Without

Splitting up wasn't an option. Yetsye's words erupted as babbled nonsense. The others grabbed her arms to keep her from rushing into Edrea's depths. Once they helped calm her, they set off. Every place they inspected revealed only roots, branches, and vines. The suns slipped ever lower on their downward path, shooting helpful rays through the canopy.

A tiny spark of red-gold winked back from far away. Suddenly the helpful lights winked out and fat raindrops splatted on leaves, sending them into a frenzied dance.

"Ya'el!" Yetsye shrieked and would've sprinted toward her had not Tsadok and Yuvahl captured her again. Serafin sprang ahead and Yetsye shook off the hands which trapped her. The three followed, carefully mimicking the Guardian's steps.

"Yetsye, no!" The return cry, so filled with anguish, ripped at Yetsye's heart, drawing great sobs from deep within her. Yetsye stumbled and Tsadok, who was closest, grabbed her up and swung her onto his back. She wadded his vest into her fists.

Serafin reached Ya'el first. She knelt beside Ya'el and Yetsye watched the Guardian's hands brush over bits of brown roots that entwined her siveh. One arm was free and Ya'el used it to wave frantically. Closer in, she could hear Serafin singing softly in a strange tongue. The haunting melody permeated every sense, and Yetsye fought against drooping eyelids. Tsadok's pace never faltered. Yetsye's last thought lingered on why he could fight the sleep-song and she couldn't.

Yetsye woke from Serafin's trance too late. The rain had slowed to an uncomfortable drizzle. She rose from the spot where Tsadok placed her and trudged to the open space between him and Yuvahl. Serafin still knelt by the jumble of Ya'el's clothing, singing a different song this time.

Ya'el was gone again. Forever.

Serafin murmured again in the strange language, but this time it sounded more like a chant. What was going on? That was just a pile of clothing, wasn't it? The fabric entwined in the branches was twisted into unbelievable knots. Edrea's roots were already at work expelling them from Yacan, as if they were repulsive.

Tsadok and Yuvahl grabbed for her again, but they were too slow. Yetsye fell on her knees beside the jumbled mass, scrabbling at the immovable roots. The smooth branches became rough, slicing through the skin of her work-hardened hands with ease. Still, she kept on.

"No," she murmured brokenly, repeating the sorrowful mantra. "No. No. Ya'el, you can't leave yet! You can't! I still need you!" Hysteria drove her on. She fought against the gentle arms reaching for her hands and wailed as they gripped each wrist tightly. They were taking her away! No! She had to get Ya'el out of there! Didn't they know? Didn't they want to save her, too?

"What do we do?" She barely registered Tsadok's voice above her head. Why was it always Tsadok? Yuvahl must be seeing to Ya'el. That must be it. She stopped struggling at the comforting thought, though her tears threatened to drown her in waves of grief. She felt herself lifted and hid her face in Tsadok's tunic. Would her tears drown him, too?

When she woke, Yetsye's first sensation was of warmth and light. The suns? The second was the sensation of sleeping in a nest like their first two duskings on Yacan. And the third was the feeling of a heavy weight, making breathing more difficult than usual. She forced open eyes encrusted with dried tears and tried to sit up. Finding herself trapped, she panicked. She turned her head to see Tsadok's clear and steady gaze on her face. She assumed Yuvahl was on the other side of her, but it wasn't his arm which trapped her. The heat of a blush crept up her neck and cheeks. "Please let me up," she whispered desperately.

If he understood her discomfort, he ignored it. "I cannot do that."

"Why not?"

"I cannot allow you to harm yourself."

"What do you mean? I wouldn't." He shifted so they could both sit propped on the edge of the root nest, though he kept a firm hold on her. He cradled one of her hands in his, drawing her attention to the white binding stained brown-red in places. Yetsye stared at her hand, so much smaller than his, unsure whether it was his fingers or the stained cloth winding around her arms up to her elbows which mesmerized her. Realization dawned.

It was a long while before she could speak again. "I thought it was a nightmare." Her voice broke on the painful words. She cried softly, trying desperately not to wake Yuvahl, whose blessed oblivion she envied. She buried her face in Tsadok's shoulder, wishing no one could see her this way, yet thankful she wasn't alone. Grief washed over her in agonizing waves. She lost track of time and place, and nothing mattered anymore.

"It is hard, but you will heal." Tsadok spoke low and soft, as her sobs subsided into sniffles and hitching breaths. "Your siveh will live in your memory and in the spin you create for the memorial of her life. It is good for the tears to be freed now so your spirit can live free on the morrowdawn."

When even the sniffles faded, Yetsye willed her shoulders to relax. It was strange to be wrapped with arms instead of a blanket. It wasn't the same as sleeping with her animal friends nestled beside her or resting in the stables beside the mana. She felt safe, like she belonged. "Thank you, Tsadok. You are kind."

"I am not that kind." His wry chuckle rumbled in his chest, against Yetsye's cheek. "But I am well acquainted with this kind of pain."

"Well, thank you for being kind to me and to my siblings."

"Your family was kind to me first. I cannot be certain I would have done the same if the positions were reversed." He sounded as if some monumental regret haunted him.

"I know you're here because you feel this is your quest from Azilet'zal," Yetsye's certainty faltered, "but..."

"Yetsye, I am sorry I could not protect Ya'el. As strong as I am, I cannot be in two places at once. And despite my efforts, Serafin's ability to lull visitors to sleep is like nothing I have ever seen. I could not fight it. If I could, I would have saved her."

"What ifs are dangerous, aren't they?" Yetsye murmured, staring into the distance. "I could ask 'what if' questions until the end of all tsimikin and it wouldn't change one thing that happened. What was Ya'el doing?" Her voice caught on the question.

"I do not know. She did not speak to us before leaving. Ya'el did not speak to us at all while you were gone. I caught her murmuring to herself once. When she noticed me watching, she stopped."

"That's so strange! She loves to ask questions. I-" She broke off because speculation led down dark paths. She'd rather remember the good things about Ya'el and keep her memory happy. Unknowns and shattered dreams would taint her mem'ram spin.

She took several shaky breaths. Tsadok spoke again, "You should rest while you can. We will leave this place soon."

She nodded and nestled into his shoulder once again. In this place, Yetsye forgot everything — fears, social taboos. She was warm and safe, surrounded by the scent of wood, leather, and green growing things. For a moment, her willingness to be there, so close to another human besides family, sparked a fresh worry. She thought too long on it and tensed.

"If you sing, would you sing something for me? My thoughts won't be still. Sleep won't come." She'd never be able to rest while thinking of Ya'el.

In a strange lilting rhythm, Tsadok sang, and his smooth baritone worked its magic.

"Softly set the suns
Softly rise the moons
Softly blow the winds
Ever home to me"
"Gently graze the mid'jin
Gently flows the stream
Gently hold my loved one
Ever close to me"
Lightly blow the embers
Lightly walk the ways
Lightly dance the stories

Ever within me"
Quiet sleeps the baby
Quiet tam'na hunts
Quiet stars are shining
Ever over me."

A pricking root jolted Yetsye out of sound sleep. She opened her eyes to find Serafin's staring back at her, unblinking. "Come with me."

Yetsye rose from the root bed, noting Tsadok's arm had fallen away from her. She moved cautiously so the others wouldn't wake.

"Do not worry. They will not know you are gone." Serafin smiled, and it reminded Yetsye of a tsa'gra. They were beautiful beasts. You could never be sure where you stood with the wild ones. She looked at Yuvahl and Tsadok and worried the hem of her vest. Was this really wise? If they woke while she was gone, they'd be angry with her for leaving, especially after what happened to Ya'el.

"I really shouldn't, not without telling them."

"Even if you wanted to do so, they will not wake until long after our business is done."

Yetsye's heart fluttered. She tried to curl her fingers into fists at her sides, but the bandages pinched her wounds and reminded her how she got them. Ya'el surrendered her life to this journey. She would be angry if Yetsye didn't see it through to the end.

"For Ya'el, then," she murmured, and despite her trepidation, she nodded firmly and followed as the Guardian led her back to the temple. They returned to the room with the trunk first.

"Take your clothing." Yetsye picked up the neatly folded stack of clothes she'd worn only yesterdawn. Serafin led the way from the room to the round chamber where the fountain showed Yetsye her spirit form. "Give me your hands."

"What?"

"You are wounded. Trust in Edrea and in me." Serafin reached for Yetsye's hands, which the latter pulled just out of her reach.

"Why should I trust Edrea? She took my siveh from me! From us! And now I'm alone." Fresh tears brimmed in Yetsye's eyes and overflowed. The rivulets burned the memories of yesterdawn into her skin once more.

"Yetsye Shirasdatir!" The once soothing waves of Serafin's voice now violently crashed into the shore of Yetsye's mind. "Yetsye," she said, slightly calmer, "neither Edrea nor I have betrayed you. Nor have we deceived you. You knew there was danger in this place. So did the others who joined you." She reached once again for Yetsye's hands and this time, she didn't fight. "And how can you lie? You say you are alone when it is obvious to anyone with eyes you are not," she hissed. Yetsye winced at the truth of her words.

"You're right." Yetsye hung her head in shame. "I'm sorry for trying to blame anyone but myself. The fault is mine. She wouldn't have needed to come if I wasn't so fearful. I should've taken this entire journey alone." She heard the wobble in her voice and fought against it.

Serafin clicked her tongue as she removed the bandages. She clutched Yetsye's wrists and drew her closer to the fountain. "Lower your arms. Allow the water to embrace your wounds."

Yetsye did as she was told, only to find the water stung like the flames of yesterdawn's test. She tried pulling back, but Serafin stood behind her, hands planted on Yetsye's shoulders, and the water in the fountain refused to release her arms. Serafin's voice turned sibilant, like waves crashing on the rocks of Chefvna. "Such pain should be expected for serious wounds. Bear it, Child of Y'Dahnndrya, Chosen One of the Creator. This pain will fade, but you must trust, if not in us, then in the One who created us."

The icy water turned red and Yetsye moaned. It scoured her wounds. Serafin's voice continued in her ear. "You spoke of fault, but I must speak truth. No one knows all but the Creator. No one can predict the future. We who see visions and dreams must realize these are only a glimpse of what might be. A person must walk the path they choose with boldness in order to live a fulfilling life. If one chooses carefully, there are no regrets, even in death." As Serafin promised, the pain dulled to an ache.

"You may remove them now." Serafin let go of her shoulders and moved aside to finish her speech. "I would think a child of Shira would know best about making choices and following through." Serafin's voice softened toward the end and the smile she offered to Yetsye hinted at friendship and encouragement. She gestured toward Yetsye's hands.

Yetsye raised them in front of her, mouth agape in disbelief. "What?!"

"Edrea told me to bring you here, to bathe your hands in Y'Dahnndrya's lifeblood." This new perspective on water surprised Yetsye almost as much as the fresh new skin on her hands and arms, but before she could comment, Serafin continued. "Edrea also wished you to know Ya'el is not gone forever. She is here," the Guardian gestured to her own heart and to the fountain, "and here within Edrea, too. We will keep her spirit alive until the time is right."

"I don't understand," Yetsye squeaked out.

"We know. One dawning you will. Share this knowledge with Shira. It will ease the pain of losing her, even if only a bit." Her smile limned with sadness now, as if Serafin mourned with her. "We will return now. You need to rest, for the others will wake soon."

"I didn't know you knew Matir."

"I have known Shira for many tsimikin."

The walk back gave Yetsye time to think about all she'd heard and experienced. She and Serafin arrived at the root bed to find a thunderstorm awaiting them. Tsadok was not pleased. The light of the moons revealed obvious surprise in the Guardian's eyes. "Why are you awake?"

"Why did you take Yetsye without telling us?" He tossed the words like stones. The bold anger shocked Yetsye.

"You should not have awoken. I am sorry. Our intent was to heal, not to cause more pain." Serafin's voice displayed the only sign of apology. Her eyes were glashiin pebbles.

"Tsadok, I'm healed. Look." She held out her arms for his inspection. He barely glanced at the creamy new skin, but he nodded.

"Now you should both return to sleep. When the suns rise, you will leave." With only that, Serafin walked five paces and jumped up into Edrea's waiting arms.

"Come." Tsadok tried to hide his ire but Yetsye knew if she could detect it at all, it was intense. She nodded and quickly climbed into the root nest next to Yuvahl. To attempt explanations now would probably make things worse. Tsadok followed. As soon as she laid her head against the roots, she fell asleep.

31

Breaking Down

"**I**s it true, Fatir?" Yetsye heard the words faintly, as if they came through dense fog. "Is it true that there's life after death?"

"With all my heart I believe it," she heard Fatir's reply more clearly as the fog of sleep lifted. She dragged her eyelids open and blinked them several times to relieve the gritty dryness gifted by restless sleep. The darkness confused Yetsye for a moment as she sat up and looked around. Tsadok squatted beside the root nest and Yuvahl sat on the edge next to him. The light of the moons peeked through the canopy and glinted off tear-tracks on his cheeks.

Yuvahl's overflow of emotion sparked against the tinder of Yetsye's memories like a bolt of lightning. She jumped when the wailing began, not at first realizing the keening of the tsa'gra mourn-song was spilling from her own broken heart. Ya'el was gone and no one could understand the depth of her despair, except for Yuvahl. The dirge rose through the treetops of the forbidden place, crashing down again onto the beasts hiding below.

A tsa'gra family crept from the undergrowth. Leading them was a brindle male twice the size of any Yetsye had ever seen back home. His black tail did not swish, as it normally would, but hung low and curved up at the end. Behind him came his mate and their two kits. They surprised Yuvahl. Tsadok simply watched, motionless. Many eyes glittered in the shadows.

The tsa'gra family made their way to Yetsye's side, the male and female nuzzling her face and neck. The kits followed the lead of their sire and dam and nuzzled her sides. Yetsye buried her face in her hands and curled in a ball as the tsa'gra family joined in her song. Their powerful harmonies intensified as the hidden watchers added their own croaks, whines, keens, and whirs.

She felt Yuvahl's presence at her side rather than saw him. The overflow of tears blinded her. So caught up in her grief, she forgot he would understand, forgot he was grieving, too. She'd forgotten everything except the gaping, jagged loss of Ya'el.

Her siveh. Her vibrant siveh, so full of life, so curious about everything, and no longer able to live. Was she in Shinahli? Had Azilet'zal and their ancestors already welcomed her? Was there life after death? Fatir said there was, and he was no liar.

That was it, wasn't it? Shouldn't she go to meet Ya'el in Shinahli? Yes. Where was the ki'fi? Her pocket? A whimper escaped when she couldn't find it, tainting her mourn-song.

She sensed rather than saw Tsadok move. The tsa'gra parted for him but stayed close to her. He took her frantic hands and held them, gently but firmly, lest she skitter away as she would have long ago. Once she calmed, he clasped them together firmly between his and added his voice to the song swelling through Yacan. She looked at him then and fixed her blurry vision on those blue pools, cool relief for her seared soul. For long moments she gazed and crooned, and slowly she relaxed. As she did, she recognized Yuvahl's hands resting on her shoulders and the warmth of the tsa'gra family pressing against her. How long they stayed like this, she never knew, but she did know the memory of that moment would stay with her until the end of her last tsimik.

Tsadok deliberately shuttered his eyes. Yetsye shifted position. And that quickly, the spell broke. As if realizing she no longer needed them, the tsa'gra family faded into the underbrush with a touching farewell.

"Tsik sharr zet na frrraawww."

"Honor to you, Chosen One," she repeated brokenly for the others. A last, lonely tear rolled down Yetsye's cheek. Tsadok still knelt in front of her. She focused her gaze on him, full of determination. The way she'd treated him in the beginning wasn't worthy of her family line, of her clan, of her Creator. He remained by her side, no matter the danger. And she finally admitted to herself she cared deeply for him, though she'd have to keep her distance. He was here, right in front of her, filling her gaze as he had filled a hole in her heart. Would she ever be able to crack open the door of possibilities?

"Thank you very much, Tsadok." Her voice shook and cracked, but she courageously pressed on. "Though that seems so inadequate. How can I tell you everything I wanted to say up to now?" She bowed her head and sighed.

"Say what you wish to say, Yetsye. I am always ready to hear you speak truth to me."

She took a deep breath and felt Yuvahl's hands tighten on her shoulders, encouraging her. Maybe he was. He could always read her well. She took another slow breath and began before her courage failed.

"You are marvelous!" His eyebrows shot up at the candid praise. "You understand me when I don't speak, even when you don't look at me. How do you do that? You know exactly what I need when I don't even know myself. Are you a messenger of Azilet'zal, too, sent to guide me? Will you disappear from my life now that I feel so close to you and have put my trust in this friendship?" She stopped when she realized what she'd just asked of him.

"I will not disappear," was the simple reply, but his beaming face stole her breath away.

She disentangled her hands from Tsadok's and patted Yuvahl's. Her batir loosened his grip on her shoulders and she climbed out of the nest. Yetsye faced Serafin, who'd been watching everything from the branches above. She announced, "My name is Yetsye Shirasdatir. I am the third child born of Shira Rayasdatir and Bayr'akh Orevshoneh, born on the dusking of the single moon. It is my honor and pleasure to have met you, Serafin, Guardian of Yacan, and a personal victory to stand boldly before you.

"And to Edrea who took Ya'el," she paused for a fortifying breath and continued, subdued. "To Edrea, if I held a grudge, I would die miserable and you would outlive me in contentment. It's hard, but I know I am stronger for having met you. And I know I can live a better life than that."

Turning to face Tsadok again, she continued. "And to you, Tsadok Akal'a, son of Zev Zared of the D'Koruyin, I must indeed be blessed of Azilet'zal to have such an ally. Even when I treated you unfairly, you never failed in your calling. I'm proud to call you my friend."

Yuvahl had moved to Tsadok's left shoulder as she talked, so Yetsye had full view of his face. The light of pride shone in his eyes and in his grin, shredding the veil of grief, at least for the moment.

"Yetsye Shirasdatir, you do me great honor indeed," Tsadok began, "for I know the courage it took for you to speak these things aloud, face to face. It is you who are marvelous. I have never seen anyone with the skill of speaking to animals until I met you. I find it easy to speak the tongues of men. Do you think I could learn?"

In the long ago time, the lifetime before this journey took place, if one of her classmates had asked her the same question, she'd have danced with joy. Now, she simply smiled and nodded, her old enthusiasm dimmed by grief. "Yes, I'll teach you."

Serafin jumped down from the branches, startling Yetsye. "It is time for you to leave this place. I will lead you to your vessel. You are not to speak of anything you saw or heard here. Nor are you to speak of anything that occurred to anyone except your clan leaders or another Guardian. Do you understand?" Yetsye and Yuvahl slammed closed fists to their hearts, then lightly tapped their lips with open hands, repeating it once more. Tsadok bowed his head slightly in agreement.

They gathered everything, then followed Serafin as she led them quickly to the shore.

"How long to reach the skiiv?" Yetsye asked.

Yuvahl heard and answered. Tsadok steadied her when her foot slipped.

"Only one turn of the suns, I think. What do you say, Tsadok?"

An affirmative grunt was all they got in reply. His focus remained on the task at hand. Yetsye doubted they would get more words out of him. He grabbed her hand, and for a moment, she panicked. He sensed it and patiently waited. When the words she wanted to say wouldn't form, she clicked and chirped a quick rhythm of notes.

"What is that?" Tsadok asked.

"Sometimes, the messages of beasts come easier to me than my native tongue. I can teach you the song of the chippits back home in Zulima. Learning their complicated song is one of my favorite challenges." And she spent the next hour tutoring a D'Koruyin warrior about the intricacies of chippit-song. That he might never see them long enough to practice didn't seem to matter. Yetsye was grateful for the mental distraction. She couldn't allow herself to think about Ya'el or the reason the happiness song of the chippits was the one that sprang to mind at the touch of his hand. And she certainly couldn't tell him that's what he was learning. At least, not right now.

They followed the treacherous path for another hesp. Tsadok proved a quick student and mastered two more of the chippit songs before they reached the skiiv. The lessons had to be set aside to focus on their footing when the roots grew more twisted.

Yetsye had nothing to think on now except how every nook in Edrea's roots and branches reminded her of the place where they lost Ya'el. Her muscles tensed and her back and neck ached more and more the longer they hiked. Here was yet another obstacle to overcome. She was so tired of tears, questing, trials, and fear. So tired of everything. She yearned for the solace of home and the warm hearth-fire, for Matir and Fatir laughing and talking at the table. Oh, to feel her own pallet beneath her and breathe in the sweet scent of meadow grass! She missed the comfort of her glade.

Churk surely missed her. Had the muffit chosen to stay or go? If she stayed, her name would be Na'ag unless she shared her true name with Yetsye.

Thinking of home took her mind away from the terrible trials and losses of Yacan. When she came out of her reverie, the shore spread out ahead of them. The sound of waves lapping at Edrea's roots echoed off the leaves and the scent of salt-water sent a tang into the air.

When she saw the skiiv moored on Edrea's roots, Yetsye recoiled in sudden panic. "No, we can't!" Yuvahl and Tsadok, who had both swung their packs off, turned at her outburst. Questions and worry shadowed Yuvahl's eyes. Yetsye pleaded with him. "How can we carry this news to Matir and Fatir? And it's my fault. I can't bear their disappointment, though I certainly deserve it for making such a terrible mistake. I can't do it, can't bear the thought of the accusations." And she burst into tears again at the unfairness.

Tsadok clicked at her again and cooed, this time as if he dealt with a skittish mana. He patted her knee, for she squatted on one of the protruding roots. He knelt in front of her until she calmed again. "Listen carefully. Life is full of riddles and truths. Some of them we will not understand until we meet Azilet'zal. The hard times of life come to teach us about ourselves. This part of the quest, though it is hard, will strengthen the Yetsye of this dawning for the morrowdawn and for the rest of your tsimikin. Would you toss aside your purpose so easily? Did you not choose this path?" At her slow nod, he continued. "Then follow it to the glorious end, believing in yourself as you believe in Azilet'zal, who appointed you to this task. Believe in yourself as we believe in you." His eyes sought hers. Though his voice remained gentle, she knew he was chiding her.

Yetsye hung her head, refusing to meet his gaze while she fought her tears. This man had lost an entire tribe of neighbors and friends. When she raised her head, she still couldn't quite meet his eyes. His selfless words forced her to stop and think. She should be ashamed. Doubting her purpose was the same as doubting Azilet'zal. That was not the path she wished to travel. She finally raised her head.

"Thank you, Tsadok. Speak truth again to me sometime," she spoke his own words back to him.

He smiled as he stood, offered her his hand, and pulled her to her feet. Tsadok helped Yuvahl stow the gear in the skiiv while Yetsye greeted the mana. She made up fresh pallets for them from the store of straw and pinya branches, and refilled the long troughs with fresh fodder. Their appreciation for the refreshments and bedding was so overwhelming, it brought tears to her eyes, as did their plea to return to green pastures. She apologized for taking so long to return to them. Serafin showed them where to collect fresh water. Once they filled the pots, Yuvahl and Tsadok loosed the ropes mooring the skiiv. Serafin watched them sail away for a time and then vanished into the green.

Yetsye had time to think on the return voyage. Thoughts of Ya'el would be raw wounds for a long while. Together they traveled to Levanna and listened to her Visioning and the wisdom of Zhil'la. Together they traveled to the temple at Mt. Charan and feasted with Seth Yi'in on the knowledge within its walls. They faced the great Nechna and the fierce whe'evet together. And together they sailed the northern ocean to Yacan Island, to traverse the treacherous roots of Edrea and learn from the Great Tree and Serafin. Now, they would return to the beginning with unwelcome news in place of her beautiful siveh.

But Yuvahl and Tsadok remained by her side. Through all this, they fought together. Through much more, together, they would stand. The bond formed by the series of events they'd gone through wouldn't break so easily. At least, until the quest ended.

The breeze that sprang up pushed the skiiv southward. Though Bazhbet Mehya predicted rough seas, the calm water that carried them made his words seem like a jest. The suns sank on their right while the moons rose on their left. Yuvahl aligned the bow with the faint star bridge spanning the sky-dome. The sailor's friend, he said, would help them find the way home. Yetsye could only wonder what would happen next.

32

Flaming Farewell

Yetsye struggled to open her eyes the next dawning. Life loomed bleak ahead of her, as if Ya'el took half of the suns' light with her. Yuvahl and Tsadok offered steady support, but she hated being a burden. If only she had a rope to pull herself out of this pit of sadness.

The work load was heavier with fewer hands, so she shook herself, shut the door tightly on her emotions, and helped. When she could bear the grief no longer, she talked to the others. Tears washed her soul of doubts and loneliness, and her broken heart mended, bit by bit.

Healing did not mean forgetting in the M'Neshunnayan Clan. Memories were treasures that carried loved ones through trying times. They also served as learning tales teaching the young how to live. M'Neshunnayans never died in vain. Traditionally, they held a memorial spinning in honor of those who passed on to Shinahli. Yetsye mentally composed a portion of her perspective of Ya'el's spin while watching the prow of the skiiv nose its way toward the port of Chefvna, which was little more than a handful of wood plank piers. The beauty of the rocky shoreline, complete with round geilin rolling and squealing in the swells, lit a spark of hope in her soul.

Yuvahl's arm rested lightly around her shoulders, and she sighed in relief. Encouragement flowed into her through the connection.

"You must be enjoying the view for a different reason, eh, Batir?" Yetsye smiled softly, only lightly teasing. She watched his eyes darken with determination.

He nodded and grunted, "You miss a lot of obvious things, but you never fail to see the ones I try to hide." He'd see her again, his dark beauty, Leila. His strength and determination amazed Yetsye. She didn't know if she'd have the courage to give up everything to choose an out-clanner for her life-mate. There could be no mistaking Yuvahl as Shira's son. Once he made this life altering decision, that was it. If he couldn't convince the elders at home to allow it, he'd never choose another. His line would end. It was a sobering thought. Yetsye had never thought much about her own life-mating until this journey. She always assumed no one would accept her quirks and awful social skills. Tsadok's smile flashed into her mind. She pushed the vision aside and saved her worry for Yuvahl.

The arms of the bay opened wide to receive them. The skiiv skimmed the surface and was soon bobbing near one of the rock walls. Tsadok looped and tied the ropes to the mooring rings at the first pier. There were very few people out this early, but perhaps it was the light fog, lifting even as they docked, which kept them inside.

Yetsye and Yuvahl disembarked, their arms laden with gear. Tsadok remained aboard to pass the remaining gear out to them. Yetsye groaned when they were done and stretched out the kinks in her stiff muscles. The men had done most of the work while they made the crossing, allowing her time to adjust. Grief settled uncomfortably in her mind. Why had she thought the effects on her body would be different? Only now did she realize how pampered she'd been on this journey. Stiff muscles hadn't been a problem for her before.

A figure hurrying toward the bay caught Yetsye's eye. She whistled and Yuvahl hurried to her side, Tsadok on his heels. Together, they watched the figure approach. The shadowy blur stumbled once as if a hole in the path surprised them. Now there was no mistake. The outline of her skirt fluttered and her long braids flew as she tripped and regained her balance. Yuvahl took a hesitant step forward toward the woman. Before Yetsye could take it in, he was running. Running was Yuvahl's least favorite activity. His body was sturdy, built more for endurance and strength than speed. Only Leila could've inspired him to go to that extreme. They stopped within arm's reach of each other. Yetsye beckoned Tsadok silently to follow her up the hill.

"It's been terrible," Leila said softly. She wrung her hands. "While you were gone, our three clans called a special gathering. Such strange groaning from the heart of Y'Dahnndrya caused fear and panic everywhere. People are saying it's the second Great Cataclysm crashing down upon us. Most of our folk have gone to Kitra. The rest of us stay and wait for news." Leila's wrinkled brow and the gray shadows under her eyes worried Yetsye.

"We'll be heading to Kitra, then," Yuvahl decided immediately. "If the clans called for a gathering, Matir and Fatir will be there."

Leila looked around and back toward the mooring. "Where is Ya'el?" Silence fell, and she paled. Leila hung her head, but Yetsye had seen the tears pooling in her eyes. "My heart cries with you for the loss of your siveh. May her memory hover near and grant you joy in the remembering." Leila was one of the most beautiful people Yetsye had ever met, kind and thoughtful. Words of encouragement rolled graciously off her tongue. Yuvahl couldn't have given his love to a more worthy person. Yetsye set her mind to craft a change which would help him achieve happiness.

Her own tears rolled slowly down her cheeks. She bowed her head and shifted position to hide them. Tsadok stepped directly behind Yetsye and she was grateful for the quiet reassurance. He always stepped in when Yuvahl was busy. But he was careful to let her have her space. When her emotions were safely under control, she raised her head to find Leila's eyes riveted on her. When they first met, Yetsye had kept her head bowed most of the time. But now, she stood firm, returning Leila's gaze steadily. Leila smiled, and the suns shone full force, robbing the fog of its gloom.

"You've done well. You are making good progress." She turned eagerly to Yuvahl. "See how she boldly returns my gaze?" Her laughter rang out in the otherwise silent bay. The friendly teasing, so like Ya'el's, surprised Yetsye. She raised her head to the sky-dome and closed her eyes. To Azilet'zal, she gave thanks for the memory of Ya'el and the times they shared.

When she was done, she felt more than saw the confused stares. "Praying," she explained, shortly. Didn't they pray, too? Had she done something wrong? She raised a questioning eyebrow because they still hadn't turned away. If anything, their faces grew even more grave. She turned slowly to see the hulking mass of Bazhbet Mehya who had been so hard for her to read. His steps pounded into the chill, wet grasses and she shrank away. A strangled cry of fear escaped her lips. In her haste to get away, she collided with Tsadok. Close contact with a faithful friend seemed preferable to the mountain lumbering toward them.

"Do not fear, Little One." Bazhbet's apologetic voice wheezed. "Your coming means change, as do all the rumblings of Y'Dahnndrya. Change is never easy, never eagerly accepted, least of all by the elder folk. I have a request to make."

His announcement puzzled them all. The Senya turned to Yuvahl and continued. "Leila stayed behind but I believe she would be a great help to her babeiya, who is now at Kitra. If you're going that way, would you be so kind as to escort her? We will replenish your supplies and grant you another two mounts to ease your journey. Have we a pact?" While saying this, he held out his right arm, hand open, and palm upward.

Yuvahl waited to see what Leila wished to do. At her slight nod, he clasped the man's forearm, signaling the promise of a M'Neshunnayan defender, the strongest pledge. He masked his eagerness. Yetsye only sensed it because she knew her batir well. His stance went from tense and tired to tense and alert.

Leila hid nothing. Yetsye took in her smile and sparkling eyes, so like Ya'el's in liveliness, they tugged on her heart. She reached behind her, seeking solid support. Tsadok grasped her seeking hand and cradled it, as she struggled to keep the sorrow under control. When all this business at Kitra was done, then she would focus on the healing.

Bazhbet, his business with Yuvahl completed, plodded back up the hill to the village. As they watched him go, Leila broke the silence. She turned eagerly to Yuvahl and almost squeaked in her excitement. "To travel with you once again, to see unknown places and meet new people, it's unbelievable! I'm excited, but I fear for the state of Y'Dahnndrya." She bounced with the overwhelming surge of emotion. Leila turned on her heel and tossed over her shoulder, "Come on! I'll prepare a meal and we'll get ready for the morrowdawn." She raced ahead, but the others lagged. Yuvahl, who had seemed so eager before, now wore a serious expression, brows low, eyes focused intently forward, and mouth a grim line.

"What's wrong, Batir? Won't it be nice to travel with Leila?" Her confusion was genuine for a moment. And then she realized the terrible truth, even as the careless words flew from her traitorous mouth.

"Being with her will be like visiting Shinahli! And it will also be like wallowing in the torments of Skal'kekt. I will be with her, but I won't be able to touch her heart or make any promises to her. I'd rather not get her hopes up. Would I ever be able to smile again if we fail in this quest to join the peoples of Y'Dahnndrya? If I knew I was responsible for her pain?" He stalked ahead with bowed shoulders, his troubles a visible burden. Leila's house peeked over a hill in the path when he turned back to Yetsye and tossed a command over his shoulder. "Not a word of this to her, eiya?"

This was no request, but a demand carved in stone. "Alright. Not a word." Yetsye agreed. Tsadok bowed his head solemnly.

The tasty meal Leila cooked warmed Yetsye. Bon'jiis appeared before her on a small pottery plate edged with blue flowers and vines. The mound of colorful sweets worked its magic and Yetsye smiled. It didn't quite reach her eyes, but she was grateful for Leila's thoughtfulness.

With her thumb and forefinger, she daintily plucked a pale blue one from the top of the mound and popped it into her mouth in one large bite. She glanced at Tsadok with a raised eyebrow and a crooked grin, daring him to do the same. With a feral smile, he accepted the challenge and popped two into his mouth at once. She chuckled at the memory of his first taste of the round sweets. Seeing him more relaxed than usual affected the others, like the thawing of the ice at the end of Domiki. They laughed and talked long into the dusking, making plans on how to approach the leaders of each clan. Yetsye was glad for the discussion, but her heart shuddered at the thought of the battle ahead.

Long after the moons had begun their downward slide, Yetsye slipped out the door of Leila's home and strolled down the pathway. In moments, she felt another presence. And another. Yuvahl and Tsadok. None of them could forget what had happened the last time they were here.

"Where is our hostess?" Yetsye asked.

"Asleep. I believe preparing such a grand meal for us exhausted her, not to mention our long discussion." Yuvahl kept glancing back to the house built up off the ground. The solid structure of logs wore its wooden shingles like a rotund, pointed hat.

"You should go back to her." Yetsye grinned, though he couldn't see it. She really wished for her batir to push this, to push for change with her. Oh, if only they could break down the barrier that would allow him to stay with his love!

He grunted, aware of his duty. Yetsye couldn't leave it alone. "I'll be fine. Tsadok will stay, won't you?" And she turned questioning eyes up to him. He nodded.

"I will make certain she comes to no harm."

Yuvahl hesitated only a moment before turning and jogging back to the house. Yetsye smiled and turned her face back to Tsadok. "Thank you for helping him."

"I did not."

"What do you mean?"

"That is not help. Your batir loves one from another clan. You know that is strongly forbidden." He sighed and tossed his braids back over his shoulder. She heard him murmur, "It is not a kindness."

Yetsye knew he was right. She knew her own predicament came close to Yuvahl's, but she and Tsadok never spoke of anything but home and their pasts. Love or the possibility of a life together were topics which never arose. She determined to tamp down her emotions until something more lasting was possible. She shook her head, unable to see any other path for herself. As for Yuvahl, who'd decided, there must be something they could do to smooth his path.

Yetsye stopped. "How can we fix this?" Tsadok looked down at her in silence. "I mean, how can we make a future in which they can be happy together? He's helped me through so many things, lost so much. I want him to be happy." She hung her head and when she spoke again, her voice was low and wobbly, "At least I can still help him, though doing the same for Ya'el is impossible."

She raised her face to the sky-dome. The stars sparkled so brilliantly. Their cheerful light blurred and burned through the brimming tears. She dropped her eyes to the surrounding land, scanning first left, then right.

"All of this beauty, all our peoples, all the beast-folk, are more alike than different, I think. Why can't we learn to accept the differences as beautiful and interesting? It's the truth, after all. No one is trying to start a war. No one person is trying to gain dominion over the others. I know of no clan with this intention, either, though I admit no one really tells me much about inter-clan talks. In the ancient past, there were conflicts over who would control our world. Haven't we learned from that? Isn't our present society such that we could share clan-ship as well? Wouldn't sharing our knowledge, as Ya'el desired, benefit Y'Dahnndrya?"

She moved forward again, this time toward a small stone bench under a pinya, Tsadok, her close shadow. When she remembered the other tree, she jerked to a halt and Tsadok stopped behind her. She gulped, remembering the painful experience she'd had the last time she was here. Resolutely, she stepped forward, her eyes never leaving the spot, finding her way to the bench with her hands. Tsadok helped her sit and stood to her right. "There is room for you, too. Won't you sit?"

He looked at her for a long moment. She held her breath, wondering if he'd accept her invitation or ignore it. She wouldn't act on her feelings, but she still wanted his friendship. After scanning the sky-dome, he let out a gusty sigh that surprised her and sat on the bench. He leaned over and rested his elbows on his knees, setting his chin atop his folded hands.

"Is there a way for us to make this happen?" She couldn't just drop the question. Yetsye was determined to find a way, if she had to travel to every island of the Ikhel'dur, or cross over the ocean to Bot'ha and Genzet. So many things happened, her daily life before her Visioning seemed a faint dream. "Ya'el was always the one for crazy ideas that actually worked." She bowed her head once again. The passing of her siveh was a persistent wound tearing away at her inner peace. "I wish she was here." Her voice cracked and Tsadok spoke.

"If she was here, do you not think your constant flow of tears would disturb her?" He reached out a hand to raise her chin so that her eyes met his. "If there is a way, you will be the one to find it. And I will help you, as will Yuvahl and, perhaps, Leila. Even my friend, Mikot, may wish to help in this matter. If you wish it, I will send out a message." He lowered his hand, and she kept her eyes on his.

"I think I'm supposed to speak to your," she searched her memory for the right word, "pareh? Do you think he'll talk to me?"

He dipped his head toward her and said, "It is good that you remembered one of our words. Thank you." Then he turned to face forward and answered her question. "As for Pareh, I am uncertain. I think it will depend on the atmosphere in this meeting of the clans."

"I'm worried about that. With so many people there, how will they hear my message? Do I talk to all of them at once? Or do I spread the word from person to person? Which way would be best?" She rose quickly to her feet and almost lost her balance. She steadied herself, though Tsadok had reached out a hand to her. "Argh! I'm so confused!" and she flung herself around to face Tsadok, who had also stood, concern etching his face with worry lines. "I don't understand why Azilet'zal chose me for this. I'm a young maid who knows nothing of life, has no experience in living alone, without the wisdom of tsimikin." she trailed off, forlorn. "Why me? What kind of influence can I have over such a large amount of people?" She turned away and hugged herself. Softly, she said, "I'm afraid, Tsadok."

"Of what?"

"Failing. Making a mistake. Speaking the words the wrong way. I always do!" She gestured wildly with her hands.

"Does Azilet'zal make mistakes?"

"No! Never!" Yetsye was adamant as she turned again to face him, pounding one thigh with her fist as she spoke each word.

"Then Azilet'zal is not wrong now and you were the one the Creator chose. You will have what you need when the time comes. Would you spit on the honor you have been so graciously given?"

She looked at him and shook her head slowly. Then she whispered, "No. No matter how much I want to run away, I won't do that." She dropped to the ground and hugged her knees to her chest. She was still in the clothing Serafin gave her at Yacan, and the vine ropes wound around her arms and legs pressed into her skin. This was no dream.

Tsadok squatted down in front of her, waiting until she looked at him. "Yetsye," she watched her name dance across his lips, "you will be fine. And you will do well. You must believe in yourself and in your purpose."

She stared at him for a long time, then nodded firmly, resolve flooding her again. Tsadok looked out toward the village as he stood and held out his hand to her. She put her hand in his and gasped as he pulled her fiercely to her feet. She did lose her balance this time and slammed into him.

"What?" His tenseness worried her.

"Hush a moment and listen."

Then she heard it. Angry sounds clattered and clashed off the surrounding mountains. Yetsye heard the clank of metal and the roaring voices grew louder bit by bit. "We must return quickly." She nodded at the terse command.

When they reached Leila's home, Yuvahl and she were already preparing to leave. "There are two bix'n in our barn, but they aren't fast enough to outrun the villagers." Leila's voice, thick with worry, set a river of ice flowing in Yetsye's veins.

"What makes you think they're angry with us?" Yetsye couldn't comprehend it. They hadn't done anything wrong. They were careful to obey all the rules of this town exactly as they were told. What was their crime?

"We are out-clanners here, during dark and uncertain times. Strangers are easy targets." Tsadok's words matched his eyes, as hard and sharp as a ki'fi blade.

"You've seen this before?" At his nod, Yetsye continued. "And they won't listen to us at all?" He shook his head. "This is so unlike anything I ever learned about Shinnoahn society. I thought all Shinnoahns wished for mutual understanding between the clans and a sharing of knowledge. This doesn't make sense!" Yetsye quickly added travel food into a sack.

"Humans do horrible things during hard times. It has always been so and probably always will be." Tsadok took a deep breath and let it out in a long sigh. "Yetsye, we must do as Leila says and leave quickly."

"But we have no provisions, no transport!"

"We will manage with our mana and we will forage along the way. I will show you how to use your knowledge of plants to your advantage. Take only those things we cannot do without. Traveling lightly means traveling faster." Tsadok took charge, and they left the warm log home before the glow of torches peeked over the hill in front of Leila's home.

There were only three mana now. Two were in the village stable because there wasn't enough room at Leila's. Tsadok hoisted a reluctant Yetsye onto his own mana without asking or being told, allowing no argument. Yuvahl motioned for Leila to take the lead. Before the suns rose over the mountains, Chefvna and the angry crowd were far behind them.

Part 3
D'Koruyi

33

Heading to Kitra

People treated truth like a vapor, a thing subject to the mind of the interpreter. This one thought kept running through Yetsye's mind, doing nothing to reassure her. How was she to tell so many people the truths she had discovered? What could she say to make them believe her? How could she convince them some changes were good and change itself was inevitable? Besides, wasn't that something everyone knew already? She sighed.

"What is it, Little One?"

Her eyebrows shot up. Why was he calling her that? "I was thinking about truth," she murmured.

"Mmm," Tsadok rumbled. "A deep topic."

"How far is Kitra?" She wasn't sure she was ready to discuss the 'deep topic' with him.

"At least three dawnings, even at the fastest pace."

"Are you going to carry me the entire time?"

"Unless you can summon another mount." His grin dared her. She almost preferred the quiet statue he used to be when they first met. The constant play of emotions across his handsome face was almost her undoing. She held herself together and played along.

"Is that a challenge?" It had been so long since someone had challenged her. Ya'el was usually the instigator.

Tsadok looked down. Happy surprise danced in his eyes at the mischief she knew glittered in her own. He didn't know everything about her. She wondered at her bravery, and a frown marred the moment.

"Yes." His resounding affirmative drew her thoughts back to the challenge. The menacing tone was at odds with the broad grin splitting his face.

"I accept!" A smile pulled at the corners of her mouth.

When the four reached a small valley, they stopped to refresh the mana and themselves. Yuvahl, Leila, and Tsadok set to the tasks required and Yetsye wandered over to a large pool of water fed and emptied by laughing streams. She bent over the rippling surface, staring into the gray-blue depths. Life thrived beneath the surface.

Thinking of ways she could summon a mount, she reached out a hand to touch the pool. Tsadok grabbed the wayward appendage just before it breached the barrier. She jumped and yanked her arm, but he refused to let go.

"What are you doing?" His voice was thunder and his eyes, lightning, a promise of the chiding to come.

Yetsye cringed, then sputtered. "You're the one who challenged me. I'm going to call a mount. I don't know any other way to do it. Since I was a small child, I've been able to see the water folk." Confusion clouded her brow only a moment before the memory of the pinya tree in Chefvna invaded her thoughts. She paled, then asked, "Will you help me?"

He frowned and cocked his head to one side, making an uncharacteristic show of inner debate. Suddenly, he agreed. "What do you need me to do?"

"I'm not sure." At his snort, she continued quickly, "If you could just pull me away, if it looks like I'm in pain, that might help."

"But you did not show evidence of pain before. How will I know?"

"I'm not sure. I wonder if you kept your hand on my back or even over my hand, if you would feel a difference." She trailed off, hopeful. Oh, to feel that glorious connection again! She missed the calming embrace of Y'Dahnndrya so much.

Tsadok called to Yuvahl. "Yetsye wishes to try using her gift. I will try to help her. If you feel something is wrong, you must pull us away. She almost tried alone without thinking." He sighed again, shaking his head. "We will have to watch her closely, I think, this Little One."

"Yes," said Yuvahl, a smile lurking in the words. "She's always in need of looking after."

"What?!" Yetsye turned first to Yuvahl, then to Tsadok in indignation, eyes burning with anger.

The two men chuckled. Then Tsadok's smile faded. "You were right to try." He turned her to look into the pool. The person reflected back at her glowed with flickering ruby eyes, flaming hair, and jewel-like clothing. Serafin was wrong. She could clearly see her spirit and the others must be able to, as well. She nodded, unable to speak.

Tsadok placed his palm at the back of Yetsye's hand and together they lowered their hands to the pool so that her palm rested lightly upon the surface. Immediately, Yetsye could see everything under the water. She could also sense Tsadok's spirit with her. Scanning, she found his face close by. His astonishment amused her. She refocused on the depths of the pool and started searching. A section of the water glowed golden orange, and a picture formed within.

Tsadok's muted voice wavered through the water. "This is Kitra." So he could see. At last, someone could truly experience what she saw and felt. Her heart swelled with joy. Perhaps now others could understand, too. As she focused on the golden circle, a low rumble reverberated between her ears, rising to a loud groan.

"What's happening?" she asked.

"I do not know. I cannot see clearly," was the concerned reply.

They watched the picture shake. The crowd in the golden frame ran screaming in all directions. Confusion and chaos reigned. The people turned on each other in their haste to get away from the invisible foe. "No!" Yetsye's cry fell on deaf ears. It was no use. They couldn't hear her.

But she could hear them all too well. The pounding of many heartbeats, the panic of their thoughts, she gasped for breath with them, as if the water closed in on her.

"Call them." Yetsye didn't know where the whisper came from or who it was that spoke. *"Call them. You know who to call. They will help you."*

"But how do I do it?"

"Do what?" Yetsye hadn't realized she'd spoken aloud until Tsadok responded. She shook her head and focused inward, seeking the tiny flame at her center once again.

"You know how to do it. You've always known. Reach down deep within you to find the common bond. Then follow along the connection."

Yetsye nodded her head once and spread her free hand on the earth beside her knees. Warmth covered it from above as Yuvahl joined the connection, he too could see the blur of gold, which was all that remained of the vision of Kitra.

"By the Holy Voice," he murmured.

Yetsye plunged, her perception diving deep into Y'Dahnndrya. Without warning, she jerked to a halt. When her spirit no longer shook with the impact, she sent her mind out, seeking the threads she shared with the Nechna, the el'tekh and the whe'evet. Through Tsadok, she also sought for a bond with the tam'na. Each bond snapped taut as she connected, and when all the threads solidified, she sent out her cry for help.

She was free, so suddenly the shock caused her to gasp and shiver. Leila wrapped a blanket around her and rubbed her shoulders. When she could raise her head, she saw Yuvahl and Tsadok helping each other walk to the packs. She rose from the rock where Leila settled her to walk hesitantly toward them.

"Yuvahl? Tsadok?" Was that tiny voice hers? Had she harmed them? Had she made a terrible error in judgment?

Tsadok raised wide eyes to hers in amazement. "How do you do this? How can you withstand the overwhelming flow?" he gasped. She'd never seen him worn out like this, and it scared her even more. Yuvahl didn't speak at all, though he seemed well enough. She knelt by his side, looking him over intently. Then she checked over Tsadok. Everything was normal but for their gasping breaths.

Yetsye bowed her head and quickly apologized. "You won't have to do that again. I didn't realize you'd feel or see anything like that. I only thought you'd be able to feel if I tensed up. My apologies, Tsadok, Batir. I should've stopped when I realized you were seeing as I saw things." When she would have risen, the warrior grabbed her arm, stopping her.

"You misunderstand. I am not angry. I am only lost in the wonder of it."

Yetsye nodded, "I would love to tell you this didn't overwhelm me, but in a way, it did. This was unlike any water calming I've ever done. I usually see the water folk swimming around or skulking on the bottom. I've never seen different places or felt individual thoughts or heartbeats before. And I've never called the beasts to help me this way before, either."

"You what?" Leila hovered close to Yuvahl with wide eyes.

"I could call for help from the beast-folk." She shook her head. "Look, I have a feeling what we saw was a symbolic picture of Kitra, though I only knew it by that name because Tsadok told me. The people gathered there and everything shook. A loud groan sounded again and again. They were so afraid they turned on each other in their mad rush to save themselves from disaster."

"Yes," added Tsadok, "that is also what I saw."

"Yetsye, how is this different from what you used to do during your calming ritual?" Yuvahl finally looked at her, and the look in his eyes made her tremble.

"I used to get only a sense of what I could physically hear, smell or feel. Now I can see faces and places and even feel what those people in the vision are feeling. I don't think it's that I'm seeing the future, but more like undercurrents of what's happening to the spirit of Y'Dahnndrya. I think." She trailed off, but remembered and added, "And now I know how to talk to beasts who are far away, too, I guess."

"I knew it! I knew you were the Messenger." Leila looked at each one of them. "Should we continue on to Kitra?"

They all looked at each other and, almost as one, nodded agreement. Chaos must turn back to order. If Yetsye could help start it, maybe others would take up this calling and fight the chaos threatening to burst Y'Dahnndrya at the seams.

Once their mounts rested, they continued south and west toward Kitra. Distracted from the challenge by her vision, Yetsye ended up sharing a mount once again.

She heard the encampment before it came into view. Tsifi'ra and Mit'ra rode high in the sky as they trotted over the sandy red rock of D'Koruyin canyon country. They'd run out of water early that dawning and had no time to find more. Despite that, the rest of the journey seemed to speed by as if Azilet'zal approved of Yetsye's determination.

Sensing humans and others of their kind, the mana's spirits improved. They pranced, eager to meet their fellow herdlings. Tsadok surprised his companions by whistling two shrill notes that carried on the wind. A reply whistle flew back over the red hills only moments before a rider pounded over the closest.

Yetsye looked up at Tsadok. "How did they know to come this way?"

Tsadok kept his eyes on the rider and his reply was short, "I told them."

Yetsye's nervousness grew as she felt Tsadok tense. "Why are you worried?"

"I carry a M'Neshunnayan *gelte* in my lap, one who has a tendency to glow like the suns at unexpected times."

"I guess that might be troublesome." She felt a pang in her chest. She didn't want to lose this friendship. His worry was justified, considering the vision they saw in the mountain pool. "You could transfer me to Yuvahl's mana so that I'm no longer a trouble to you." She refused to look at him and looked instead toward the rider whose mount was kicking up great clouds of dust in his haste.

"You are not a trouble or a burden. You are," he stopped as if searching for the right word. "Special." She sighed. His words told her nothing of his own thoughts. She glowed. No one else she knew glowed. That made her special.

Suddenly, Tsadok sat ramrod straight, a new level of intensity which scared her. "What is it? What's wrong?"

"It is Pareh," he spoke through clenched teeth.

As sure as the seasons, the D'Koruyin High Chieftain reined in his mid'jin as he met the newcomers. Standing in his saddle, he bellowed in a deeper version of Tsadok's voice, "Why have you come here? What is your business?" He glared at Tsadok, as if he was a stranger.

Yetsye looked up at her friend, taking in his clenched jaw. She moved to dismount and his attention shifted to her. She motioned, and with his help, set her feet on the red earth of D'Koruyi. Squaring her shoulders, she walked to Zev Zared and spoke to him the words of her testing on Yacan.

"I am Yetsye Shirasdatir of the M'Neshunnayan Clan. My purpose is to encourage more unity between the Children of Y'Dahnndrya. Chaos threatens to once again tear our world apart. Will you help me, Zev Zared?

For I cannot do this alone." Her gaze never wavered. And though the arid air burned her eyes, she refused to blink. She waited for the expected threat.

It never came. Zev dismounted and knelt before her, surprising them all. When he raised his head, she saw tears in his shadowed eyes. "I thought your existence was a dream, a symbolic example of what we were all supposed to do. I saw you long, long ago, before you could have been born. When I was a young warrior, my Dremsha, you would call it Visioning, showed me many things. You were one of them. My azho was another." He looked up at Tsadok, who stood beside Yetsye, ready to defend her if necessary.

"Please stand up! You don't have to kneel for me. I'm just a messenger." Yetsye felt the telltale heat of a blush spreading up her neck and cheeks again.

Zev shook his head, but he stood and reached out a hand to Tsadok. "When in my anger I allowed you to leave without saying a word, I did not know you would return with her. Kai'yanga is good! All praise be to the Creator!" He stared into his azho's unflinching visage. "You have grown and there is much you must tell me." It wasn't a question and Tsadok nodded once. "You will all follow me. I will lead you safely to your clans."

Tsadok nudged Yetsye toward his mana but followed his pareh to the mid'jin. She couldn't understand any of their quiet discussion. The D'Koruyin tongue was too brisk. She looked on as Zev froze, then nodded slowly. As Tsadok strode back to his mana, he wore once again the stony mask from days forever ago.

"What's wrong?" She wrinkled her brow in concern.

"Nothing more than before."

"Then why are you changed?" She reached out a tentative hand to his arm and thought better of it. She pulled it back quickly as he replied.

"The hardest part follows. Are you ready to fight this battle? I will be ready when the time comes." With his gentle reminder ringing in her ears, he remounted the mana and hauled Yetsye up after him and encouraged her to hang on. "You need to be prepared if I need the use of my arms. I do not want you to fall."

Yetsye nodded, but indignation marred her brow. She'd been riding mana since she could walk. She could mount and dismount at a gallop without a flaw. Then she realized he couldn't possibly know this and her behavior had only shown him her weaknesses. She would not fall and he would learn she had other strengths.

34

Oh the Heaviness

Zev led them through the encampment. Fear, anger, and confusion hung in the air like the mist of the rift smothering Yetsye. She fought for each breath. Tsadok had seemed a statue before, but now he was a featureless mountain, all sharp angles. The mana's hesitant steps didn't help. Waves of sound, undulating first loud then soft, crashed around her like an uneasy sea.

Yetsye risked another glance up at Tsadok. He stared ahead, keeping Zev in view and only now and again scanning side to side for any hint of danger. The surrounding discussions grew more heated, the voices harsher and more accusatory. By the time they reached Shira and Bay'rakh's tent, Yetsye was exhausted and pale. The emotional attack hit harder and deeper in ways she couldn't yet describe.

Tsadok helped her down from the mana and had Bay'rakh not been there to steady her, she would've fallen. Tsadok dismounted quickly and motioned to Zev. The High Chieftain shook his head and dismounted, leaving his mid'jin to graze freely while he joined them. Yetsye was so tired, but she knew there was at least one thing she needed to make clear to her astonished parents.

Standing to her full height, she waved a hand toward Tsadok. "This is Tsadok Akal'a, azho of the D'Koruyin High Chieftain, Zev Zared." Her parents greeted them properly, though still confused. "He is a man of integrity and honor, a friend who supported us from the time we found him wounded in Yu'ul Forest until now. He has helped me overcome during trials and encouraged me in my darkest hour." She looked up at him, tears threatening, and Tsadok stepped closer to her, nodding. Yuvahl had joined them, standing at her left, and rested a hand lightly on her shoulder. Their presence strengthened her for the rest of the spin.

"Ya'el..." she broke off as closed her eyes. Her voice cracked when she tried again. "Ya'el is gone. Embraced by Edrea. Serafin said to tell you Ya'el will always be within Edrea and within her." Grief closed her throat. Tears flowed freely. She crumpled and would've fallen, but Tsadok caught her up in his arms and looked to her family, waiting for direction.

"I will take her Tsadok," Bay'rakh's voice rang with unfamiliar trepidation, setting flut'ra loose in her stomach.

"Please tell me where to place her. It is more efficient this way." Zev snorted in disgust at his azho's stubbornness and snapped at him in D'Koruyin. Yetsye shrank away from the sound. Tsadok simply stood for a moment, his determination to follow this path clear in his stance.

"This way, please." Bay'rakh broke the strained silence and led the way to Shira's pallet in the comfortably furnished tent. Yetsye hated being a burden and turned her face away as soon as she was free, ashamed at her weakness. She was careful to murmur her thanks, though, and listened to their conversation on the other side of the flap.

"I am sorry if my behavior was rude," Tsadok murmured, "but she is my charge. My pareh will not like it, but I will stay close to her, if not in here with your family, then outside the door."

Yetsye turned on the pallet to face the flap and watched through slitted eyes. There was no way she could sleep with all the turmoil swirling in the air. Thinking of what to do would keep her awake. Fatir's gentle voice asked, "Will you spin your tale for us?"

A solemn bunch huddled around the pot of vegetable mash and kettle of khaf'ket. Despite her resolution to stay awake, Yetsye took a brief nap. Bay'rakh woke her when the food was ready. To her surprise, Zev also sat on the blanket that served as seating.

That dusking Yuvahl wove the spin of their journey and told of the changes in Yetsye. Her heart ached as her parents' faces grew more and more grim. By the time Yuvahl finished, Zev had altered his opinion of his azho and gained a better understanding of Tsadok's earlier actions. Shira and Bay'rakh, the former softly weeping, wrapped their children in loving hugs and shared a moment of grief for Ya'el, who would never again join them. Tsadok and Zev left the tent to give them privacy.

When the tears dried, Yetsye's family set about cleaning. Bay'rakh placed her under the entry canopy of the tent and forbade her to move. So she sat, watched, and listened. The angry sounds of the crowd outside dulled, as if half were already asleep. She could pick out individual sounds better now. Two particular voices floated to her ears, though one was too low to discern actual words. The other voice she recognized as Zev Zared. She listened closer and caught enough syllables to know the other man was Tsadok. She could only guess at their conversation since they spoke in Koryu.

Zev nodded and grasped Tsadok by the shoulders before speaking again. She heard the words *azho*, *pareh*, and *morah*, and guessed they spoke of family matters. Then Zev surprised Tsadok with a brief but powerful hug. There was no doubt of Zev's pride. She tucked the beauty of that moment away, even if it meant Tsadok would return with his clan. Tsadok rumbled a reply before the two entered the gathering room.

Zev offered a brief goodbye. Had Yetsye not been watching, she'd never have heard him leave. It reminded her of the first few times Tsadok surprised her when she was calming.

Bay'rakh emerged from the central room. "Now we need to figure out sleeping arrangements," he said with a crooked smile. "We thought we'd be alone."

Tsadok nodded. "I require little. I simply wish to remain close to Yetsye to be certain she is safe."

"You have an excellent grasp of the M'Neshunnayan tongue," Shira complimented Tsadok as she came to her life-mate's side.

"Ya'el said the same thing when we first met him." Yuvahl smiled sadly.

Tsadok stared at Shira for a long moment, then said, "Yetsye is much like you."

Shira laughed, "Oh, no! She's more like Bay'rakh! They are both very kind, gentle of heart."

"No. I meant to say that the way you focus is the same, and you share the same face. Your hair is different, though."

"Yes. My hair comes from my matir and Yetsye's comes from Bay'rakh's line. We don't know where her dark eyes came from, though." Shira mused.

All was quiet for a moment, and they heard a scuffle outside. The five looked at each other and Tsadok and Yuvahl hurried to see what caused it. Yetsye waited until last to be sure her fatir didn't plant her on a cushion again.

Down the path, toward the center of Kitra, a cloud of dust and angry voices rose. No. Not angry. Afraid! A hurried discussion ended with Yetsye reluctantly going back into the sleeping area at the back of the tent to lie down and rest. Shira, Bay'rakh, and Yuvahl went to investigate further and Tsadok stayed to watch over Yetsye. Something needed to be done, and fast. With this much tension in the air, the threat of needless violence was all too close.

The chaos of Kitra invaded Yetsye's inner being. Even sleep offered no escape. The moment Yetsye lay on the pallet, she dreamed. Angry out-clanners found every hiding place she used to cover herself. She couldn't escape and the howl of a trapped tsa'gra slipped past her lips. She looked right and left, seeking an exit. Sudden flames licked at her feet, hands, and face. Rivers of sweat ran down her skin. So hot! She ripped at her clothing, seeking relief from the flamelets licking at the hems. It hurt so much! Yetsye fell to the ground. Then she felt the wetness of water and a cool hand at her neck. The relief was so welcome, she sobbed. When the tears stopped, she slept again, this time without dreams. Thanks be to Azilet'zal!

"Matir," she muttered when she woke, "water, please."

"Yes. Right here." Yetsye felt Shira hold the beaker to her lips. She gulped it, so great was her thirst, and Shira cautioned her. "You need to slow down. I know you're thirsty, but it won't help at all if your stomach is full of flut'ra."

Yetsye nodded and, her thirst now quenched, spoke hesitantly, "Matir?"
"Yes?"

"I have a task to perform." She wasn't sure how to begin this spin, wasn't sure how her matir would receive it. The only things she was certain of were her task and the help of her batir, Tsadok, and Leila, who they'd dropped off with Kven on the way to the M'Neshunnayan encampment.

"Unity. There must be more unity between the clans and the beasts, though they might not like to hear that." She took another sip of water.

"Your Visioning showed you this?" Shira was all seriousness with messages from Azilet'zal. She was also full of questions. Yetsye sighed inwardly. This might be harder than she thought.

"Yes. But it wasn't just that. Would you like to hear of my Visioning?" At Shira's nod of encouragement, Yetsye shared the three dreams. She finally looked Shira in the eyes when she was done. So many emotions flashed across her matir's features Yetsye could barely keep up. She'd never seen Shira so bewildered.

"But that's not all." Yetsye added to the spin all she'd learned at Mt. Charan and at Yacan temple. Shira was not so surprised now to hear about their visit to Yacan since she and Bay'rakh learned of Ya'el's fate. But at the news of her youngest passing Edrea's and Serafin's tests, she seemed baffled and proud and worried.

"Surely, Child of Y'Dahnndrya, you have a special purpose. I am no longer worried that a D'Koruyin warrior pledged his life to guard you. Surely that was Azilet'zal's plan, too." Yetsye felt her heart squeeze at those encouraging words.

"But Matir," Yetsye's voice faltered, though she bravely pushed on, "was there anything I should've done and didn't? Could I have prevented Edrea from taking Ya'el?"

"Does our Creator make mistakes, Yetsye?"

How many times would she have to hear that? "No," she answered, her voice small and meek.

"Then trust that same Creator to lead us well. Bad things happen to all people. But is it true they're *bad* things? Ya'el is safe, though we won't be able to see her. Serafin's message meant that she, too, has a higher purpose. Ya'el believed in you and helped you. She wanted you to succeed. Do you think she'd be happy with the way you're behaving?"

Yetsye grinned crookedly, "No," she chuckled. "She'd probably tease me unmercifully right now." Her face crumpled again as she reached for her matir's comforting arms. "I miss her so much. What will I do without her?" she whispered between the sobs. Her broken voice matched her tattered heart.

Matir murmured near her ear. "We will live, Yetsye. We'll live because it's what we must do and what she'd want us to do. She will serve her purpose and we will serve ours." She kissed Yetsye's red-gold hair and whispered, "We will live."

35

Before the Chieftain

Before the suns fully set, messengers rode out from the center of Kitra to carry the news of the meeting at the natural amphitheater on the next dawning. When the suns were three hands high, the leaders of the clans would sit at the center and answer the questions and concerns of their clansmen.

Before that happened, Yetsye thought it would help to meet with the Shinnoahn and D'Koruyin leaders. She was sure Zev Zared would come, having met him already, but the Shinnoahn High Council, who she'd only heard of, might not. She required their permission to speak to the inter-clan crowd gathered here. They'd need proof this wasn't a game.

Yetsye, the Chosen One. The Messenger. She scoffed inside at the irony as she sat in the common area of the tent. She passed the time watching people hurry by through the open flap. Her eyes glazed as she thought of faraway places and heavy responsibilities.

"What bothers you this dawning?" Tsadok's sudden question jolted her back to the present.

"I'm worried about speaking to the clan leaders. I'll say the wrong thing." She hung her head for a moment but raised it to look at him before adding, "You remember our close call at Chefvna, don't you?" She grinned wryly, her heart sorrowful. "I don't expect everyone to believe me immediately. I expect they're more like me and will have to be shown as time passes."

"If you know this to be so, and you know your purpose and plan, why does it worry you? All you need to do is share this knowledge with the Children of Y'Dahnndrya. You can only do the task given to you. To take on extra tasks would be too heavy a burden."

"What if they think I'm being prideful? Why did my bird turn to white flame first? Why—"

He held up a hand to stop the sudden flood of insecurity. "Why do you take on worries that are not yours to bear? Stay focused on your purpose and that alone. As for the words, they will come to you when you need them. Do you remember what happened when we met Kven?"

She nodded, uncertain whether to smile or frown. She was proud of her stand but uncertain whether it was proper to take pride in reminding an elder of a duty they should never have forgotten.

"Thank you for staying with us, Tsadok," she murmured, her smile brightening a bit.

"I only stay with you. Your well-being is my focus and has been from before the time I met you."

The weight of his words fell heavily on her shoulders. She shook her head sharply, "No. I can't let you do that. What about your hopes and dreams? What about life with your people? I thought you meant for the length of this journey, but," she paused and stared at her bent knees, scared to continue, "you meant forever? As in, until I die forever?" Her voice gradually faded to a whisper.

"Or until I do."

She turned toward his firm voice, complex emotions making her own reply difficult. "How can you so easily give up everything for me, who is not even of your clan?"

A fleeting frown flickered over his face and disappeared. "It was not a simple decision. I am certain Pareh also wonders." He turned toward the D'Koruyin encampment. The only sound was his steady breath for a while before he spoke again. "Yetsye," he started hesitantly, "you have your task and I have mine."

A pot crashing in the tent next to theirs startled her. She'd kept her head bowed, so she jumped again when he reached out to raise her chin. Tears burned her eyes.

"Please do not cry. I knew what it meant to take on this quest before I started. I have accepted it. My pareh has accepted it. Would you have me ignore Kai'yanga's direction?" His pleading eyes and voice were too much for her. She closed hers and shook her head. Two tears made slow tracks down her cheeks and calloused thumbs wiped them gently away.

"It's a lot for me to live with. I wonder how much more I can bear?"

"What do you mean?" His words bit like the ice storms of Glokni.

"I wasn't able to save my siveh. And now I'm responsible for taking your freedom away. Will I also fail Yuvahl and Leila?"

"You will fail if you continue thinking this way. This is not the behavior of a Messenger of Azilet'zal." He rose to his feet. "Come." He reached a hand down to her and when she placed hers in it, he lifted her to her feet. "We will go to the D'Koruyin camp. I would introduce you properly to my pareh. They will be hostile." She shrank away from the words, so he hurried to explain. "It is a test of courage. If possible, you must hold your face as still as stone and not allow their actions to break down your defenses. They will judge you based on your strength and resolve."

"What happens if I fail that test?" she whispered as she freed her hand from his.

"They will test you until you do pass. Only then will you gain their respect." His grave tone shook her. She wrapped her arms around herself and shivered.

"I'd like to see the mana first." She desperately needed calming. At his nod, she followed him to where their mana grazed on tufts of dry grass. She singled out Fhoowhsh. The faithful beast had carried her and Tsadok from Chefvna. Her thanks were long overdue.

The mana raised their heads when she clicked a greeting and replied in kind. She reached out to Fhoowhsh, and he came to her. Placing her hands on either side of his beloved face, the force of emotion emanating from him nearly knocked her over. She almost let go, but something stopped her. She rode the wild flood and sought the inner peace deep within both her and the mana.

"Worry and fear war with desire to stay calm in this strange place. Food is dry and difficult. Water is scarce. When will we return home? So tired. I want familiar fields of soft green grasses."

"Apologies! Though it is late, thank you for carrying us so far and being so faithful a friend. Soon we will return home. I will try to find more water."

As she backed away from the mana, she felt eyes on her. Many sets of eyes met her own intently. Panicking, she reached for Tsadok, who was behind her. She gazed at him in question.

"You are glowing again," he said with a mischievous glint in his eye. Her face paled slightly. "No. It is a good thing. These people will tell others and it will add another measure of truth to the spin you weave for our leaders."

She nodded and gave him a watery grin before peeling her fingers away from his tunic. "Can we walk to meet Zev Zared? Or is it safer to ride?" Fear lay in wait to steal away the calmness within her.

"It should be safe enough to walk. Do you feel well enough? You burned with fever only last evening." She read the concern in his pale eyes. The suns on their downward slide highlighted the clear blue.

"Yes. I think the walk would help." Yetsye nodded.

"This is better. Using your own strength to travel will earn favor in my clan. I am sad to say many D'Koruyin suffer under a false idea that all M'Neshunnayans are weaklings who do nothing but tend gardens and stay in one place. I am happy to have met you and your siblings. You restore my faith in the Children." Yetsye could only stare at him. "Also, it may help that I have fought against the M'Neshunnayan team in the kashklav tournament at the last Great Gathering. It was not an easy victory." After her prolonged silence, he asked, "What is it?"

"Usually, knowledge stays locked inside you. But you're sharing so freely now." His uncharacteristic chatter put her at ease, and she grinned.

"I," he halted. His pause struck her as strange. Remaining quiet was his usual choice, one she was familiar with. Being at a loss for words was quite different. He always knew what to say when he opened his mouth to speak.

"It's fine," she assured him. "I don't mind listening. I like it actually."

"Really?" he sounded uncertain. "I am sorry. Visiting my people will be good. I think we may meet Pareh as he comes this way, though."

"If that happens, we can visit another time, right?"

Tsadok just nodded with a look of disbelief and hope warring for precedence on his face. Yetsye wondered what it was all about. She hoped to help him the way he'd helped her.

They did meet Zev Zared, but not so close to the M'Neshunnayan encampment that they couldn't go back to the Chieftain's orth. Yetsye immediately felt the hostile stares and murmurs. Judgment hit her in waves, small at first but growing as they progressed deeper into the clan that was not her own. She wanted to hide, to call out to Tsadok. Her stomach twisted and burned, threatening to rebel, and she could allow none of that to happen. So Yetsye Shirasdatir focused on who she was and what lay ahead, taking one step at a time. Sifting through the whispered words pricking her ears helped her focus, and she tried to learn the sound and rhythm of Tsadok's native tongue.

When they reached Zev's home, he motioned them inside the round tent. Two other clan members arrived before them and all sat around the brazier in the center of the room. Zev offered them water to drink. That precious liquid, so rare in this place, was a sweet delicacy, and she spoke her thanks solemnly, in Genra, so the others could understand her. This seemed to open the door for them to speak in the common tongue, and the conversation began in earnest.

"When I met this *gelte*, she boldly introduced herself to me, a stranger. I knew immediately she was the person my Dremsha revealed." Zev was much more talkative in this place among his people. It surprised Yetsye, though she did her best not to show it. Zev turned to Tsadok, "What brought you here, my azho? Did you not know we would come to meet with you soon?"

"I knew. I wanted to visit my tribe and rest among my people for a time, even if that time is short." His words were low and deliberate.

Zev nodded. "I have told them of your decision. They agree with me. We will support you, though this means we cannot see you very often now. We will miss you and your contributions to the tribe and our clan." The others nodded.

The two other D'Koruyin warriors, one with hair hanging loose to his waist, the other with a short hairstyle and beard, sat on either side of Zev and across from Yetsye and Tsadok. The one with the beard spoke to her. "I hear you can speak to the beasts?" he asked.

"In a way, yes." She forced herself to look directly into his eyes. The serious beads of dark brown staring back at her were nearly her undoing. She felt her chest tighten and tamped down her fear.

"How is this done?"

"I," Yetsye paused a moment to think. "I'm not sure. It's something I've always done, though since my Visioning, the gift has grown stronger."

"Can you not explain your method?" The bearded warrior seemed adamant that she share what she knew. It set her on edge, but perhaps this was part of the test of courage.

She steeled herself and replied with boldness, "I simply place my forehead against the forehead of a beast and we talk inside our minds. I have no other way of explaining how this happens. It just does." She kept her facial expression neutral, as Tsadok had taught her and meted out her words in a slow rhythm, for good measure. "Though it's different with the Nechna. We spoke without touching."

The three D'Koruyin looked at each other and hurriedly conferred in their own tongue. Though Tsadok understood, he didn't tell her what they said. She realized it would jeopardize her chance at winning their support. Leaning on him wasn't an option now. She had to believe in herself. If she lost faith at this moment, there was no point in trying to go any further.

Zev Zared spoke in clipped Genra, "Yetsye Shirasdatir, you do us honor by sharing your knowledge with us in our own tent, despite the normal clan barriers. We will support you in your efforts to bring more unity to our world. If you call, we will come. The word will go forth to all D'Koruyin tribes."

"Thank you, Zev Zared and my thanks to all D'Koruyi." It was so hard to hold in her sigh of relief and the smile that threatened to spill out from her heart. She managed well enough and soon they were on the path back to her temporary home. As soon as they left the D'Koruyin encampment, she turned to Tsadok and smiled so brightly his eyebrows rose. "We did it!"

He smiled but shook his head. "You did it, Yetsye. If I helped, it was only in being my pareh's azho. I did nothing, really. It was that last part about speaking with the Nechna that truly won them over, though."

"That can't be true." She frowned. How could she make him understand? "My fatir always told us that even the smallest pebble can move the largest, calmest lake. All our actions create ripples which affect everyone around us. We're all connected, even if the thread is thin." She paused and thought for a moment. "What were they discussing in Koryu? I'm not familiar with the tongue and I couldn't even guess at it."

"It was nothing very special. They tested you to see if you would lose your composure. Your ability to speak with such fierce and noble creatures as the Nechna amazed them. They also said since you shared your knowledge, and had followed the D'Koruyin way during your visit to the encampment, even to earning the trust of the High Chieftain's azho, you must be worthy of their support." He chuckled. "They are a wily bunch! The other two have been Pareh's friends for many, many tsimikin. Their love for testing people is well known. The wild escapades of their younger dawnings make captivating fire-side tales."

"They sound very interesting. From a distance. People who do unexpected things are hardest for me to understand and get along with." Yetsye sighed. "Ya'el was better at that."

"You did fine with them, though they were on their best behavior."

"I was right, though," Yetsye insisted. "Your status helped them accept me." As the two came closer to the tent, the clamor of raised voices rushed out to meet them.

"You brought us here for nothing! Where is this person you wish us to meet?" Voice One was an extremely vexed male, a nasally tenor. Yetsye cringed at the obvious ire. Did she have to don the stony mask again so soon?

"Yes. We are very busy, you know." Voice Two sounded almost like Voice One and, though calm, annoyance rang in the tone.

"I am sorry. When I left, my datir was still here." That was Shira, making excuses for her. Yetsye frowned. "I'm certain she is close. Please forgive her and be a little more patient. I'm well aware of the depth of our responsibilities to our peoples." Shira's voice started out repentant and ended on a note of vexation. Yetsye was certain that was directed toward her. No time for rest. She rushed in to rescue Matir and confront the new trial head on.

36

Before the Consulate

"I'm sorry, Matir! I needed to walk." Yetsye ran and hugged Shira, who kissed her forehead in return. She turned her to greet three strangers sitting on the wooden chairs they reserved for special visitors.

"My datir, Yetsye." Yetsye nodded politely to each of the three, two men and a lady who looked so much alike she hardly believed it. Shira continued the introductions. "Yetsye, these three are the High Consulate of the Shinnoahn Clan. I present to you Kalanit, Kaleb, and Keiyn Madel." She nodded respectfully to each of them. She hoped she knew how to mask her thoughts better now. It would not do to reveal her uncertainties to these people.

Keiyn spoke in Genra and her smooth voice reminded Yetsye of the velvety ears of a tsa'gra. "It is an honor to meet you, Yetsye Shirasdatir. Your matir weaves a magnificent tale of your journey, one which took you beyond your lands and into ours." Though she was polite and graceful, the last two words cut like fine blades. She wielded the art of piercing eye contact far better than Tsadok.

"Yes. But my journey is not over. Here I am in D'Koruyin lands and I'm certain my journey will continue beyond this place." She kept a respectful tone and spoke slowly and clearly. She'd have to thank Tsadok later for preparing her to face such a formidable opponent.

"Rude! How unprincipled!" Voice One turned out to be Kalanit. He glared at Shira and continued his tirade. His high-pitched tenor grated on Yetsye's ears, reminding her of the horrible canyon winds. "I would've thought a High Priestess would train her children better." He huffed and crossed his arms over his chest.

"Kalanit!" Keiyn raised her hand, stopping him before he could say anything else. Yetsye flushed with anger and her D'Koruyin warrior standing at her side tensed, ready to deal swift justice. She could imagine the fierce glint in his eyes.

"My apologies, Yetsye. My iyaba is uncomfortable here in the hot, dry lands. It clouds his otherwise impeccable judgment."

"It's understandable," Yetsye nodded and swallowed the fiery reply hovering on her tongue at Kalanit's careless words. "The atmosphere being clouded with anger and fear doesn't help."

Keiyn nodded. "You understand deeply, Yetsye. My kyn and I have heard the tale of your journey from Shira. What proof do you offer that this fight for clan unity is a quest from Tugansol? How do we know you are the messenger you say you are?"

"If you suspect me now, then all my words will be suspect, too. I could show you my hair, which changed during my Visioning ritual. I could show you the clothes I received from Serafin at Yacan temple. Even then, you would still have doubts. I'm a shy person by nature and before my Visioning, I would not start conversations with people, nor would I continue one for long if another spoke to me. Words don't come easily for me. I doubt myself too often."

Yetsye's voice grew stronger and clearer with each successive word. "The most basic truth I can give you is this: My name is Yetsye Shirasdatir of the village of Zulima, datir of the M'Neshunnayan Clan. I am a Child of Y'Dahnndrya who wishes to see my world thrive and grow. I am blessed with, and suffer with, the same things as all other Y'Dahnndryans. My actions affect the world around me, just as all Y'Dahnndryans' do. What reason would I have to lie to anyone about these things?"

Keiyn opened her mouth as if to speak, but Yetsye raised a hand to stop her. She had to finish before she lost her courage.

"Our world groans with the pangs of unhealthy change. An entire D'Koruyin tribe is gone. We fear for the safety of our peoples, but we are all working for the same thing. Why should we work separately when we have a better chance of success working together?" These leaders of the clan, which was reputedly the most knowledgeable in all of Y'Dahnndrya, exasperated her. She jabbed a finger at them and asked, "Isn't it your people who always say when many work at a problem, the solution comes quickly? Believe in me or not. Those are your choices."

Her chest heaved with every breath she took. Yetsye folded her arms across her it and clamped her mouth shut after her outburst. The silence hung on so long she feared her temper had ruined her chances of gaining their support. But this was the path she chose. There could be no regrets.

The Shinnoahns looked at each other for a moment, then, as one, they turned to Yetsye. Keiyn's voice rang with humor and confidence when she said, "You've convinced us. We will stand with you and encourage our people to stand with yours. You weave things accurately, Yetsye Shirasdatir. A dark fog spreads over the clans, threatening to smother the light of Tugansol. We stand stronger if we stand together."

She stopped, then added one more thing. "You are a shining light, Yetsye." With a broad grin and a mischievous wink, she and her bloodkyn took their leave. The latter two apologized again and again for their appalling conduct. Yetsye looked at Shira and Tsadok in confusion. Tsadok wore a feral smile and Shira was pale.

When things quieted down and Yuvahl and Bay'rakh returned, they sat together in the common area and enjoyed a simple meal. Warm spiced mana milk calmed the body and Shira passed around beakers of it. Turning to Yetsye, she said, "Shining light? Keiyn said it well. And I would think she was entirely joking if I hadn't seen it myself. How long have you been able to do that?" She was gazing at Yetsye in amazement and concern.

"I'm not sure," Yetsye answered hesitantly, looking to Yuvahl and Tsadok for help.

"Right after her Visioning ritual was complete." Yuvahl stated. "When she communes with the beasts or counters a human opponent for any length of time, she glows. The longer or more heated the situation, the brighter she shines."

"It also happened at Yacan temple. When I finished my tests there, I looked into a pool and saw a person I wouldn't have recognized had I not known it was me looking into the water." Yetsye still wasn't sure what to think or feel about this part of her gift.

"Well, now," Bay'rakh mused. "So you glow when you use your gift and during spiritual tests. Any other times?"

Yetsye shook her head as she said, "Not that I'm aware of." Yuvahl and Tsadok confirmed her answer.

"You are gaining strength," Tsadok cut in dryly. Yetsye raised an inquisitive eyebrow. "You did not faint after your discussion with the Shinnoahns." He grinned. Yetsye flushed and bowed her head. Yuvahl chuckled.

Outside their tent, people settled down for the dusking and their noise composed an uneasy lullaby. Shira and Yetsye worked to store the leftovers while Bay'rakh cleaned and stored the dishes. Yuvahl and Tsadok brought pots of water to the mana at Yetsye's urging.

"Tsadok is always at your side." Shira opened the conversation. Yetsye nodded. "Why isn't Yuvahl guarding you?"

Yetsye hesitated, uncertain of the reason herself and equally apprehensive about how much to reveal to her matir. She couldn't lie. Shira would see through it before the words left her mouth.

"I'm not completely sure, Matir." She shrugged, "It just happened that way." Trying to change the subject, she asked, "Have you seen his beautiful tattoo?"

"His beautiful tattoo," Shira parroted with a grin. "I don't think anyone could miss something so large and intricate. It's hard to look away. I looked too long and felt it drawing me in." Her expression turned thoughtful.

Yetsye laid a hand on Shira's arm. "You're troubled. Why? Is it me? Or does Tsadok's presence bother you?"

Shira's smile was tired and worn. "No," she assured Yetsye softly. "I'm worried about things I shouldn't concern myself with. The morrowdawn will take care of itself. This dusking, we should get as much rest as possible. You will continue to sleep in the inner room with your fatir and me. Yuvahl and Tsadok will remain out here. If only we'd known you'd join us. We could have brought an extra tent."

"It will be well, Matir. As you say, you worry too much." Yetsye stood up from putting the last travel container in the proper stack. "I need to go to the mana."

"Not tonight." Yuvahl spoke up as he and Tsadok ducked through the tent entrance, grim-faced. "The mana are fine, but anger and confusion surround us. You should wait until dawning's light."

Yetsye looked to Tsadok, a plea haunting her eyes. He gave a slight shake of his head. She shuttered her emotions and moved to a basket of blankets. Removing four, she gave two to Yuvahl and the other two to Tsadok. "Matir is sorry you both have to keep to sleeping out here."

Yetsye dragged out the process. She'd never be able to sleep right now. She tried to find something that remained undone. Looking around the small area, under things, atop stacks. Everything was perfect. She sighed and turned to find Yuvahl already stretched out on his pallet and Tsadok kneeling on his, eyes closed. Yetsye waited patiently, offering a prayer for strength and the right words when morrowdawn came.

Tsadok opened his eyes, peering directly into hers. They were completely open and Yetsye read more there than she expected. She couldn't look away, but neither could she stay in the room much longer. Feeling behind her for the flap that opened to the sleeping room, she whispered, "May Azilet'zal give you good rest, Tsadok. Yuvahl." She found the flap and retreated, hearing a murmured reply in kind as the flap closed on her.

What was she suddenly afraid of? Why should his openness create such chaos within her?

She lay on her pallet and waited impatiently for sleep to overtake her. So many thoughts swirled in her mind, vying for attention. She pushed aside the question of Tsadok's feelings and tamped down her own for him. The time to delve into those would come later. For now, morrowdawn's meeting was the most important.

How would she win the people over if her request to the beasts didn't get through to them clearly? Her conversation with the Shinnoahn High Consulate ended well, but she was no fool. She still didn't know what the people of Shinnoah held in high honor. With the D'Koruyin, it was the ability to remain outwardly calm even in the heat of an attack.

Her thoughts of the D'Koruyin inevitably led her back to Tsadok. How did she really feel about him and his decision to stay with her forever? How would her parents feel about it? And more troublesome than any other thought, how much longer would she be able to cage this growing feeling for him? Was she now in the same position as Yuvahl and Leila? Or was it even more pitiable, since her feelings might be one-sided?

Oh, how she wished for a calming! If she could focus on such simple thoughts as those of the mana, the complex ones would surely fade enough to allow a good rest. She tossed and rolled and couldn't relax. At this rate, she'd be speaking to the Children of Y'Dahnndrya looking like a sickly infant. She heard a rustle at the flap and looked around. She jumped, and a strangled cry escaped her lips.

"Yetsye," she heard the soft rumble, "it is only me. You need to rest. Take my hand if it helps." His crystalline eyes peeked under the flap and he extended his hand further, palm up.

"Thank you, Tsadok." It was the quietest of whispers, but still he heard. Settling back into her pallet, she reached out toward the flap to clasp Tsadok's hand. All the chaos his eyes caused settled down with the warm connection.

37

Yetsye Speaks Up

Yetsye perched on a wooden chair set in the center of the raised platform. Ekiri stone, as Tsadok called it, reflected the light of the suns and the natural amphitheater shone. While she waited, she studied the rock surrounding her, noting its twists and turns, its lovely striations in shades of tan, red, dusty white, and orange. Holes dotted the surface and she could see tiny beaks pop out to chirp short songs. Twice two bodies followed the beaks, but the tiny flyers were so fast, Yetsye could only catch glimpses of brown and gray.

The milling crowds recalled her attention. Shira, Zev, and the Madels mingled with their people along the edges of the raised floor, offering reassurance and encouragement. Their people. She smiled to herself despite her worry.

She'd noticed a dust cloud on the horizon when Tsadok first walked her to the center of Kitra. Her people were coming. No matter the clan, no matter the form, they were all Children of Y'Dahnndrya. She just had to open their eyes to it.

Though the crowd swelled around her, she felt lonely and out of place, a youngling among seasoned veterans of life. She was a M'Neshunnayan and from the snatches of conversation she'd heard during her brief stay in Kitra, an object of scorn in the eyes of the other two clans. A frown wrinkled her brow. A scan of the area showed Tsadok returning. She couldn't help but admire the ease with which he hopped onto the raised stone. She stared openly as he spoke first to Zev, then to Shira. When he finally loped toward her, she lowered her eyes. She knew her blushing face gave her away. That would do more harm for her cause than help. He knelt on one knee in front of her, though, nullifying her evasive action.

His expression shuttered, Tsadok spoke softly in her own tongue, "I have met the beasts who are ready when you need them. I also followed the elders' wishes concerning their placement. They followed me with no trouble. All will be well. I will remain alert. You will be safe, Yetsye."

She nodded once and allowed her eyes to brush over his form. Shiny metal winked at her from within the folds of his tunic. She counted three ki'fi in his cloth belt, a kranj at his hip, and some sort of leather cloth with sharp bits of metal attached to the string ends. Folded up, it looked like a silver-edged face cloth. Surely he carried more weaponry, but Yetsye hoped he wouldn't have to use any of it.

The atmosphere in the amphitheater was better than the tense suspicions and disagreements which permeated the encampments when she first arrived. Yetsye breathed deep, grateful for the crisp air that rejuvenated her as it filled her lungs. As more and more seats filled, Yetsye's stomach reminded her she was bad at talking to one human. The multitude in front of her murmured, groaned, and shrilled, eroding her determination. She offered her fourth prayer of the dawning, once again begging for strength, courage, and a barawik's tongue before the meeting began.

Zev Zared, as High Chieftain of the D'Koruyin clan, could open the meeting at Kitra himself, or choose one of the other clan leaders to do so. When Yetsye saw him speak to the Madels, she suspected one of them would lead. She expelled a breath she didn't know she was holding when Keiyn accepted the honor. Though she didn't understand them well, Yetsye admired this strong woman. She kept her eyes on Keiyn, who glided to the front of the platform and raised her hands high, calling for silence. Random conversations died down to murmurs.

"Children of Y'Dahnndrya!" At her call, silence blanketed the auditorium. "We, your leaders, have called this meeting to address the dire happenings in our world. Each of us has experienced some form of disturbance. Rifts opened in the ground. An entire D'Koruyin tribe is lost and a river changed its course. The whole of our lands shudder. But there is another issue even more pressing than this. The Creator has seen fit to send a Messenger to us. Each of your leaders has tested her truthfulness and found her to be a person of honor and integrity. We present her to you now — Yetsye Shirasdatir."

At this, Yetsye started. She'd lost herself for a moment in the melodious voice of the speaker. Quickly, she rose from her chair and walked on bare feet to meet Keiyn, who stood several paces in front of her, while the introduction continued. She steeled herself, stood tall with feet grounded firmly beneath her, and donned her best impression of Tsadok's stone-face as she scanned the crowd.

"Yetsye Shirasdatir has attended the Visioning at Levanna, pored over the scrolls at Charan's lib'rarum, and braved the mysterious and dangerous tests of Yacan." At the mention of the forbidden island, a collective gasp of dismay and awe filled the amphitheater. "She has survived to bring us news of great import. We ask that you give her the honor and courtesy afforded to those of your own clans as we hear what she has to say." Keiyn nodded to Yetsye.

Yetsye scanned the expectant faces and flut'ra beat their wings frantically in her stomach. It was difficult, but she maintained an expressionless visage. She gave herself a mental shove, thinking of Ya'el's voice urging, *'Now is the time. Do it!'*

"Thank you, brave and honorable Children of Y'Dahnndrya, for bending your ears to this spin of mine." She'd left her hair loose today, only pulling the front pieces back so she could see. The silvery streaks showed clearly, too. "In my time at Levanna, my Visioning showed me three dreams. In two of them, one theme rang out clearly. Unity."

At the mention of the word, murmurs sprang up here and there among the throng. Yetsye faltered for a moment, doubting herself and her ability to complete this quest.

Too young. Too shy. Always saying the wrong thing. The accusations assailed her one after the other. She closed her eyes and focused on breathing until she was calm again and the murmuring crowd subsided.

"We have a saying in M'Neshunnaya." She started with her head bowed and eyes closed. "The smallest stone still has the power to stir the largest lake." She lifted her head and flashed open her eyes, bold words pouring from her lips almost unbidden. "It means that all of us have an impact on what happens in our world. I didn't understand the magnitude of this until recently. Right now, the Y'Dahnndrya we treasure is bravely enduring the pangs of growth and change. If we, her Children, do not seek to understand and support her, together, we will all crumble." Voices grumbled and picked up volume as she pushed on. If they would speak, she would speak over them. "Working together, across clan boundaries, we can learn so much more about our world and about each other. Working together in unity, we can accomplish more good for all of Y'Dahnndrya."

Yetsye let her eyes rove over the packed amphitheater and threw out her last cry for unity. "Some of you may think my words concern only the three clans before me. They do not. I have seen the way the two-legged Children treat beast-kind. This mistreatment must stop. Unity must involve our beast friends, as well as the other clans. Will you work with me?"

As she finished her speech, the first of two Nechna padded up silently behind her amid gasps. When the single tam'na sat beside them and the el'tekh soaring overhead dove to rest on Yetsye's outstretched arm. The gasps changed to murmurs of awe and fear. Fhoowhsh stepped up beside her next and turned to face the crowd.

"These are but a few of my friends, my Y'Dahnndryan family. They would be yours, too, if you are willing. I ask you again, fellow Children," she paused for effect, "will you work with me? For no one person can do it alone. Even if the stone moves the lake, the movement dies if no other pebble follows it. Will you help me unite all Children of Y'Dahnndrya?"

Kalanit spoke up first, his resounding voice snuffing the disbelieving sneers which had risen. "The High Consulate of Shinnoah stands with you. But how do you propose we work at this? What can we do differently?"

A voice from the crowd rasped, "That's right! What are you suggesting?" The dam burst with with liquid fire, spewing acidic fear and prejudice, working to smother the breath of hope. Yetsye almost crumpled under the weight of it.

Keiyn once more raised her arms for silence. When the noise died down to grumbling, she said, "If you ask a question, you must give the recipient time to think over her answer and reply. Please remain courteous to our Messenger."

At her nod, Yetsye took a breath and continued. "I have spoken with our clan leaders except for the three not represented. I believe there's a solution, a system of exchange. Three to seven members from each clan would trade places with others from different clans. In this way, we could learn about how the other clans live. There would be rules to follow. The courtesies of each clan must be observed for this type of solution to work. A test issued by the clan leaders would determine which volunteers qualify as candidates. Do we have your support for this plan?"

Keiyn raised her arms, palms open to the sky, as voices crashed upon the platform in waves. "I know you are worried! Calm your fears. Our cultures, the very fabric of who we are as clans, will not diminish. Rather, we believe by knowing more about each other, we will thrive. Everyone gathered here is a Child of Y'Dahnndrya, regardless of clan."

She stopped as a shaggy bulk rumbled up onto the platform and trotted toward Yetsye. The silence was deafening. The whe'evet knelt before her and let out its keening wail. Yetsye smiled and climbed upon its back.

When Keiyn could speak again, her voice filled with awe. "Just think of the many wonderful things we could accomplish by sharing our knowledge and ideas with each other! Our strengths could magnify, more than we can even imagine."

Kalanit spoke next. "You will have three dawnings of contemplation. Your leaders agree with the Lady Messenger and urge you to discuss this matter with us. Ask as many questions as you like during that time. We will gather here again on the fourth dawning to make the final decision. We will move forward from that point as the people wish."

The meeting concluded. Buzzing Y'Dahnndryans made their way back to the encampments. The next three dawnings at Kitra would be interesting. Was this all there was to her task? The message had yet to be carried to the Ikhel'dur and across the O'Na Sea to Bot'ha and Genzet. Would they allow her to do it? Was it safe to do so?

Maybe she was borrowing trouble. Fatir would say she must wait to see what her own people would say when the time for a decision came.

If Yetsye thought she'd be able to rest, she was mistaken. People trickled through the flaps of their tent off and on throughout the day, asking questions. Many times, a single question came more than once. Two favorites seemed to be, "What about the dangers of old?" and "What will we have to sacrifice?"

Yetsye's energy wore out quickly, but she was reluctant to ask for any help right now. To be seen as an immature weakling would threaten the success of the plan. Y'Dahnndrya couldn't afford her failure now. As the most recent visitors left the tent, she desperately scanned the space for a corner of solace.

Her eyes settled on Tsadok's hands as he worked on a piece of bone. Yetsye saw his pareh's bearded friend pass it to him the dawning before. His nimble fingers fascinated her as they wielded a ki'fi with expert ease. She couldn't help but wonder. Before she could ask, he tucked the ki'fi into his belt. He brushed the shavings away from the bone with the corner of his tunic, blew off the remaining bone dust, and threaded a hide cord through the hole he'd made at the top of it. He rose and approached Yetsye.

"This is for strength and remembrance." He held out the bone pendant to her. She took it and gazed at the intricate carving of the D'Koruyin el'tekh symbol. Tiny flames licked at the edges and at the tips of the outspread wings and tail. So much detail on so small a bone! She hardly knew what to say.

She looked up at Tsadok from her cushion. "Thank you for this," she whispered softly. "I knew D'Koruyin were excellent carvers, but I've never seen an example so close. Only on trade days was it possible. I never had enough to trade, so I've never held a piece in my hand." Looking down at the pendant nestled in her palm, she tried to stem her tears as she said, "It's beautiful. I will treasure it."

He offered her a hand up. She grasped it and stood awkwardly, grabbing his solid forearms for support. She'd been on the floor of the tent most of the dawning. It was good to stretch. When he reached out for her pendant, he surprised her. "Did you want it back?"

"No." She cringed at the hurt she saw reflected in his eyes. When would she learn to stop speaking carelessly? "I would like to help you put it on."

Blushing, Yetsye handed the pendant to him and turned around so he could fasten it. It was quickly done, but instead of stopping there, he began brushing through her loose hair. She ducked and tried to get away. "What are you doing?"

"Do you not prefer it to be confined?"

"Matir does that now!"

With a chuckle, he quipped, "Lady Shira knows how to arrange hair in the D'Koruyin way?"

She paused and looked at him for a moment. In confusion, she replied, "Probably not. But I'm not D'Koruyin."

"Hmm, I wonder." Yetsye missed seeing the teasing glint in his eye, but not his chuckle.

"Why are you laughing at me?"

"He's teasing you, Yetsye," She turned to see Yuvahl grinning as he suddenly entered the common room of the tent.

She looked back at Tsadok, who wore a crooked grin. It softened everything about his face, even his eyes. She frowned, turned away, and stalked to the sleeping room. Dropping onto her pallet, she sulked. When Tsadok poked his head through, she turned her face away. Her ears worked well enough, though. She heard the light steps stopping just behind her, heard the folding of soft hide-cloth as he knelt.

"I am sorry. I should not have teased you after such a long, hard dawning." He sighed and murmured, "Please allow me to show you a new hairstyle."

She waited for six very loud heartbeats before answering him. What happened to the calming effect of last dusking's connection? "I guess you'll have to, as it seems Matir is busy right now." She slumped a little. "I forgive you for the teasing. Perhaps it's your way of calming and if so, I shouldn't be so sensitive. Unfortunately, I can't indulge in my method right now." She sighed. The sheer number of people at Kitra would make calming extremely difficult.

"Is there any way I could help?"

"I don't think so. I think I need to do more things on my own if the people are going to believe me."

She shook her head slowly, then more vigorously. Why was she moping? She had no time for this! "What are you waiting for?" she urged him, almost roughly. The anger she felt toward herself far outweighed any amount of hurt caused by good-natured teasing.

Tsadok described several hair styles, allowing Yetsye to choose one that appealed to her. She picked an intricate style composed of three braids and several twists. One braid would wrap around her hairline, and two braids wound into buns at the back, surrounded by twisting ropes of hair.

This time, Tsadok worked silently. He separated out the strands of silver. She felt him twist and turn them up and wondered once again how he could be so proficient at this. His gentle hands didn't pull at all this time. When the next group arrived with questions, he'd finished. She didn't know what it was about having Tsadok work on her hair, but she relaxed. Perhaps it was the simple act of breathing and being still.

What would she do if she ever had to function without this man? He shattered her concentration in one moment and calmed her in the next. He'd become such an integral part of her life since her Visioning. She stubbornly refused to name her feelings concerning him. The timing was wrong. A leader could not be a rebel who cast all cares to the season of Dishi. Soft steps, slow steps, were needed concerning Tsadok's position in her life.

38

Stinging Barbs Fly

The fourth dawning arrived with clear skies and crisp air. Yetsye awoke to Shira's gentle shaking. Her arm ached. She must've held Tsadok's hand through most of the dusking again. She glanced up at Shira, who couldn't quite hide the uncertainty hovering just behind her serene mask.

"What's wrong, Matir?"

"It can wait until after the people decide." Shira slipped out of the sleeping room. Yetsye heard her waking Yuvahl. Tsadok always rose before everyone else. She missed the warmth of his hand, but pushed aside that traitorous thought and focused on what was coming.

The morning meal of fruit, grain mash, and khaf'ket warmed Yetsye and restored her energy. With a full belly, it wasn't so hard to see the positive side of things. The clans were so similar. What was most surprising was that no one had mentioned it before. Certainly, there were differences, but this was so among individuals as well. Something so obvious should be easy to see and understand.

Yetsye dressed carefully. She chose the clothing Serafin gave her. It would be good to show how variety was a blessing. When she emerged from the sleeping room, her parents stared in open-mouthed amazement at the drastic change in their datir.

The woman before them was ready for battle, strong and determined. Yetsye pasted a mischievous grin on her face, raised her chin, and crossed her arms over her chest. At her neck hung Tsadok's bone pendant. A woven cord bracelet with bright orange beads carried Ya'el's memory on her arm. Shira bowed her head.

"I'm sorry, Matir!" Yetsye hurried to Shira and placed a tentative hand on her shaking shoulder. "The bracelet gives me strength and reminds me what's at risk if I fail." Shira's tears rained down. "Would it be better for me to change?" Yetsye whispered. Shira shook her head, unable to speak.

281

Matir embraced her tightly. In her ear, Yetsye was sure she heard a whisper. "I'm so very proud of you," in tiny, broken syllables.

"I love you, Matir. I'm so sorry I couldn't bring her back with me." The cracked syllables tumbled from unwilling lips and Yetsye's tears mingled with Shira's. Then her matir released her.

"You still don't understand, and there's no time to explain." Yetsye stared at Shira, who composed herself and organized the preparations for the meeting.

Eyes bored into her from behind and Yetsye turned, expecting to see faces at the tent entrance. Instead, she saw only Tsadok. She wondered what he was thinking, but could read nothing in his gaze or the lines of his face. She admitted defeat, bowing her head and turning aside to help Shira with the preparations.

Just as no one would forget Yetsye's descent from the dais on the back of a whe'evet, neither would they forget the decision made at Kitra on that last dawning. Of the multitude gathered there, only a small band of Shinnoahns vocally disagreed with the proposed solution. The overwhelming support shocked Yetsye. She had gone dressed for a battle that never happened.

Zev Zared spoke for his people. Every D'Koruyin warrior supported the decision. Yetsye couldn't help a laugh of pure joy from bubbling up as many of their people competed to be one of the chosen exchange candidates. Finally, Zev's bearded friend, two beautiful ladies, and a young warrior around Yetsye's age followed the M'Neshunnayans to live with them for one tsimik. It would be Shira's responsibility to make sure her people treated them with the utmost respect. Tsadok remained at Yetsye's side as her aide and would live with her family in Zulima. Next, three women and two men, among them Zev's long-haired friend, moved to stand next to the Madels, bound for Shinnoah.

It took a little longer for the Shinnoahns to elect their candidates. Many were reluctant. While waiting for their decision, the M'Neshunnayans accepted Yetsye's suggestion that Yuvahl join the candidate going with the

Shinnoahn clan. Her batir frowned at first, glaring at Yetsye's grin, but accepted the honorable position. An older couple, a young male scholar, and a middle-aged female assistant healer joined him. Yetsye's Tani Ranica, that lady's eldest son, the female assistant teacher of kranj, and two sturdy young males now stood with Zev Zared, looking eager to start their sojourn in D'Koruyi.

By the time they finished, the Shinnoahns had chosen a Master Cheese-maker, a highly esteemed stable hand, and an apprentice gardener, all male, along with a female apprentice weaver and a younger female musician, to go with the D'Koruyin. Those chosen to live with the M'Neshunnayans included a male musician, an older male master weaver, a chatty female baker, an older female teacher, and, much to Yetsye's dismay, Leila. She'd really hoped by suggesting Yuvahl as a candidate for Shinnoah, he and Leila could join as life-mates.

The decisions made this dawning were final, though. If the first step of unity failed, there would be no second chance. Yuvahl and his love would live apart for now, but each could learn about the other's culture. Perhaps there was still hope for their love in the future.

The air of Kitra thrummed with the sounds of feasting and good will. Yetsye's earlier tenseness slowly faded. Ya'el was right. When bellies filled with good food and drink, hearts grew lighter. The pleasant feeling wafting through the camps put her at ease and she hop-skipped down the path toward the grazing mana. It wasn't long before her shadow caught up. His annoyance clashed with the general peace and acceptance of the crowd.

"I know. I should've said something." She chuckled. "Does it still matter since there's so much good will flowing around us now?"

"It will always matter. In good times, things can happen just as unexpectedly as they can in bad times." His serious tone clashed with the joyous revelry now filling Kitra.

"What do you mean?" she frowned.

"A few did not hide their unhappiness with the decision. They will look for ways to prevent change and silence the Messenger who speaks of it without fear."

"How? What can they do? They're only a handful of people." She shrugged her shoulders and scoffed. Tsadok caught her elbow in a fierce grip and turned her around. The grim eyes boring into her soul set off tremors of fear she'd long forgotten in his presence. His words rang with deep conviction, a sharp truth she would remember until the end of her final dawning.

"If I wished, Yetsye, among a village of unsuspecting people, before an alarm could sound, I could silence them all. Forever." He paused and the weight of truth sank deep down into her being. In the dying light of the suns, she saw a hint of regret flash in his eyes. It was gone just as quickly.

He released her elbow slowly and though his next words were whispers, the message they carried was still hard as stone. "Never underestimate the determination of a person who believes they are right. That kind of person believes their actions are justified because of their belief. People will always do what seems best to them, but it will not always be best for everyone."

Yetsye nodded as she rubbed her tingling elbow. She had hoped, however irrationally, to reach the hearts of all who attended the meeting. On the whole, this was a victory. The Children had chosen a positive path and set their feet to it eagerly. She had to take comfort in the good things accomplished this dawning. As her matir often said, morrowdawning would worry about itself.

She turned to Tsadok and smiled. It was weak, certainly not her best, for doubts crowded in once again. But she was determined to believe in herself. She would believe in Azilet'zal, her god and guide, and in the family and friends surrounding and supporting her. And she would believe in this man standing before her.

When they arrived at the grassy area, the mana crowded around Yetsye, seeking her gentle hand. She didn't commune with them this dusking. The comfort of their presence was enough. She craved the simple peace they emitted. Any more complications now might send her screaming to the ends of Y'Dahnndrya.

Two sharp clangs took Yetsye by surprise as Tsadok sprung into action. He was a whirling storm, shearing metal darts from their intended target. The mana, sensing their friend was in danger, crowded around her, cooing to comfort her and clicking loudly to distract the attacker.

"Hide yourself!" Tsadok grunted as he continued battling the ceaseless barrage of darts. He whistled high and clear, a succession of three rapidly ascending notes. He did it three times and continued tirelessly protecting Yetsye. Soon, only dead silence remained.

A sudden scuffle to her left, then to her right, startled her. D'Koruyin warriors dragged two Shinnoahn dissenters into the clearing to face Yetsye and Tsadok. They were forced to their knees, as if awaiting judgment. Yetsye looked first at their anger-twisted faces, then to the stony warriors responsible for stopping them. She wasn't sure what to do and sent a voiceless request for help to Tsadok. He just stared back at her, waiting.

She sighed and began in a low monotone, "What did you think you were doing? What did you hope to accomplish by harming someone or one of these beautiful creatures? Or did you think at all?"

She shook her head and covered her eyes with one hand. Oh, how tired she was! She tried again. "You have nothing to say?" She waited, giving them ample time to reply and received stubborn silence.

"So you choose silence as your weapon now?" Ponderous words turned brisk as Yetsye spoke plain truth to the young men. "Silence gets us nowhere. We can't reach a solution with silence as a go-between."

Suddenly, another metal dart flew, nicking its intended target on the shoulder. Yetsye yelped in pain and the culprit was soon on his knees with his brethren. Tsadok stood by Yetsye who, though she couldn't mask her pain, stood her ground before these wayward Children of Y'Dahnndrya.

"Listen to me well." She was angry now and her words were the edge of a tsa'gra's fang. "We are all Children of Y'Dahnndrya. You don't have to like me, nor agree with everything I say. You're free to make your own decisions. But you must also realize your decisions affect everyone around you. This dawning, your choice was to harm me when I've done nothing to harm you. I can't understand why you'd wish to harm another living thing when we're all in agreement to nurture our world and all living things on her surface."

As Yetsye talked, the suns said their dusking farewells to those below. Tsifi'ra shot one last ray across the land, warming her.

"I don't know what I should do in this situation. This is my matir's realm." She looked once more to Tsadok. The icy shards that were his eyes revealed what he'd like to do to them and she shivered. Turning to face her attackers once more, she clamped her lips together, hoping they would speak up in their defense. They weren't much older than her, maybe around Ya'el's age.

Could she convince them? Their palpable rage, their stubbornness, blazed out in their stiff posture and grinding jaws.

"Since you are determined to remain silent, I have no other option." She bit the words out. How frustrating! "You will be bound and carried to the High Consulate for judgment. I'm only a messenger and judgment is not for me to cast. But you should know this before you're dragged away."

She inhaled and let the breath out slowly. "I hate confronting anyone about anything, but had you harmed my friends who so valiantly shielded me, only a miracle of the Creator would allow you another breath." She warmed to her topic, her anger and contempt for their actions growing.

"Our world will never become a better place if we seek to harm others, if we seek to use our power and gifts in ways that debase others. If you think of yourself first and only, then your fellow Y'Dahnndryans will suffer. But I suppose telling you that is useless. If you think of yourself first and only, you already don't care about the rest of us. And there's the root of the problem."

She took a few calming breaths, too worked up to continue. The burning in her arm was strong enough now that she couldn't ignore it any longer. "Think on this, long and hard. Think on what you did here this dusking. How will it reflect on your entire clan? If you don't care about the other clans, surely you care about your own. Don't you?"

Using the last of her fading energy, she motioned for the warriors to take the three young Shinnoahns away. When they were out of sight, Yetsye grabbed for Tsadok's arm, missed, and fell against his chest. "Help," she whispered, and a whimper escaped her trembling lips.

39

Pain and Forgiveness

"Hold tight to me." Tsadok took Yetsye up in his arms and carried her quickly to their tent. Yuvahl met them just outside the entrance. Tsadok went straight to Yetsye's pallet while explaining what happened. He tried setting Yetsye on the pallet, but she couldn't open her clenched hands. Every muscle had drawn as tight as a *taval*. Tears of helplessness dampened his tunic. She shuddered.

"Yetsye, you must let go." She could barely shake her head. "Are you so afraid?"

Between choked sobs and gasps, she spoke through clenched teeth, "Poison. Fro-zen. Can't let go!"

He brought her out again into the main room and sat cross-legged on the blanket-covered floor. He grabbed his own flask and popped it open. Lifting it carefully to her lips, he encouraged her to drink. The shuddering was so bad she couldn't force her mouth to obey. Her temperature rose. She felt more than saw Tsadok take a swig. She was too weak to protest when he slowly force-fed her the water. When he finally raised his head, her family knelt around them. Together, Matir and Yuvahl pried open her fingers while she whimpered in pain. They settled her as gently as possible on her pallet. Worry lines etched Shira's face more deeply than ever before. Then the pain spiked and Yetsye writhed.

"What do you need? Is there any help I can offer?" Tsadok's agitated baritone crept to her ear as if through a fog.

"Go to the Shinnoahn High Consulate. They should know what to do." Her hasty words chased him as he sped from the tent.

Yetsye whimpered as Shira bathed her face and brow with cool water. "What kind of poison leaves you fully conscious while it kills you? How would someone know of such terrible things? And why would anyone wish to use such a terrible poison, anyway?" Her matir was angry.

287

Before she had time to fall further into despair, Tsadok burst through the tent flap. Keiyn and a gray-bearded stranger kicked up dust behind him in their hurry.

After a brief examination, the short, stout man raised shocked eyes filled with worry to Shira and Keiyn. "I need many things to reverse this, and we have little time. This is indeed one of the strongest known poisons in Shinnoah." He rattled off a list of items to Tsadok and Yuvahl. D'Koruyin warriors came at Tsadok's call to help gather the items necessary for the antidote.

Time passed so slowly. Pain spasmed through Yetsye's bones. Her stomach clenched and the small trickle of water Tsadok gave her was long gone, leaving her throat dry and cracked. The poison intensified all feeling. The cloth covering her was glass shards scratching her skin, no matter how gentle Shira was. Where was her relief? Would she ever feel comfortable again? She was far too busy fighting the pain to consider hating the angry men who forced it on her.

Yetsye heard a shriek and whimpered again. Was that the tent flap? The tapping that followed told her the healer was hard at work in the outer room with his mortar and pestle. When the last ingredient arrived and the antidote was complete, she almost refused it. Thoughts were so hard to hold on to and her eyes refused to open. The smell of wood and leather cut through the pain and calmed her enough to swallow the bitter, chalky syrup.

"She's glowing!" A voice she didn't recognize fought its way through the painful haze.

Yetsye burned from the inside. She found it easier now to make complete thoughts in her head. A familiar hand on her chest made her heart leap in response even as pain exploded through her ribs.

"Her heart is racing!" Was that fear in Tsadok's voice?

His soothing scent wafted over her as another hand took Tsadok's place. She simply tried to keep breathing. How could she reassure them? Her mouth wouldn't work and helpless tears leaked from beneath her sealed eyelids.

A warm tenor voice said, "Peace, warrior. We will wait and see. Tugansol takes us down the best path. Always." The voice was fuzzy, but it spoke the truth. She wished Azilet'zal would end this misery soon.

Shira, Tsadok, and the healer were the only ones in the sleeping room when Yetsye forced her eyes open. Her heartbeat was almost normal. Though they sounded raw, each breath was slow and steady. The healer deemed her out of danger after checking her over thoroughly.

"Well, Lady Messenger! You gave us all a scare. Are you satisfied now?" He smiled and sparks danced in his pale brown eyes. He spoke to Shira, Bay'rakh, and Tsadok as he gathered his things.

"She'll be very sore and her skin will be tender to the touch for several hesps. Keep her here from one suns-rise to the next. She is to have no visitors until she can tolerate a gentle touch against her skin. You'll notice I removed her coverlet. But I cannot stress enough the importance of waiting one whole dawning before testing it."

Tsadok gave thanks while Shira nodded. The healer briefly bowed in return and exited the sleeping room. Yetsye heard him repeat the instructions to Yuvahl. Strange! She expected to hear one voice, not eight! She shifted questioning eyes to Tsadok.

"The warriors who gathered the ingredients for your antidote stationed themselves around the tent, determined to keep watch. My charge is their charge as well, it seems." His glassy, red-rimmed eyes spoke volumes. How long had it been since he slept?

"I'm sorry," she rasped and winced with the pain of speaking. "Sorry I made you worry." And then she had to remain silent. Talking hurt too much. Tears once again tracked down her cheeks to dampen her pallet.

"You do not have to be sorry. None of this was your fault." The mask fell from the warrior. He dropped his guard and wept. How could she ever repay him?

The waiting irritated her. When the suns settled below the horizon, heralding the beginning of the prescribed dusking, the healer returned to check on his patient and oversee the test. Shira slowly reached out one finger to stroke Yetsye's hand, which lay palm down beside her. Yetsye flinched, but soon relaxed. Shira tried again and this time, Yetsye sighed.

"Matir, I'm fine. It doesn't hurt."

"Yetsye!" Shira's voice caught as her emotions overflowed. "I was so scared!" She moved as if to hug her but pulled up short, uncertain if her skin could tolerate that much pressure.

Yetsye reached for her anyway, needing the reassurance of her presence. The memory of the wayward Shinnoahns had come back.

"Where are they?" she asked aloud.

"Who?" Shira's brow furrowed in confusion.

"The three young Shinnoahns."

"Keiyn has planned, but postponed, their punishment. She thought you should be present. They'll join us here. If you're willing, that is."

Yetsye nodded.

Tsadok's grim face promised swift retribution if they dared ever do such a thing again. He moved forward to reassure her. "They will not harm you. I will make certain they do not."

She gazed at him for a long moment before she whispered, "I know. I know you will."

As the Shinnoahn healer, her family, and Tsadok gathered around Yetsye to eat the mid-dawning meal, a D'Koruyin warrior popped his head through the flap of the sleeping room and muttered to Tsadok in a D'Koruyin dialect Yetsye hadn't heard. She thought only M'Neshunnayan defenders had a secret war language, but maybe others did, too. It was helpful to keep some things hidden. Not all knowledge needed to be spread around so freely. As in their current circumstance, when a person's life was in danger, such a valuable tool was necessary. That they spoke it in the presence of out-clanners was a great honor indeed.

Tsadok nodded to the warrior and turned to address them. "They are here."

No need to ask who. Yetsye waited for the Shinnoahn healer and Shira to exit the sleeping room before attempting to rise. She knew they'd try to stop her. She groaned with the effort, but wouldn't lie here like a helpless infant. When she tried to stand, her weak muscles shook like a newly birthed mana.

She set her focus, opened her eyes, and, seeing the tan clad legs in front of her, raised determined brown eyes to meet icy blue ones.

He chuckled. "You scared me," he said as he slowly squatted in front of her. "There has not been one thing which has so scared me for more tsimikin than I care to recount. Yet you managed it." He seared her with eyes now on fire. "You will pay for that later, when your strength has returned."

If she was shaky before, she was even more so now. She wasn't sure what Tsadok meant, but she was already thinking of ways to avoid the promised punishment. Unfamiliar voices outside the flap drew her attention.

"I want to go out there." Her determination was back. She whispered to save her voice and hide her intent from Matir. "Please, Tsadok." Ugh! It was frustrating to have to ask for help. "Help me get out there!" she begged frantically. If they saw her as helpless now, it might end all possibility of convincing them she was Azilet'zal's Messenger.

Tsadok nodded, but rather than helping her stand, he simply gathered her up in his arms and carried her out. This was not what she had in mind. She flushed in anger and embarrassment, unable to protest at all. They exited the sleeping room to gasps of awe and dismay. Tsadok set Yetsye gently on a pile of cushions Shira set up quickly for her. He crouched nearby, in case she needed a quick rescue. She wouldn't.

Once settled, Yetsye contemplated the three Shinnoahn younglings sitting cross-legged in front of her. "What are your names?" Her raspy voice cracked on the words.

Silence.

"Are you still refusing to speak to me? Then why are you here?" She didn't bother to hide her anger or her sadness. Those she hoped they could see clearly.

Silence hung like a thick fur inside the tent. But Yetsye was prepared to wait them out. "Matir, would you prepare some warm spiced mana milk, enough for all, please?" Shira nodded. When a warm mug sat in front of each person, she began again.

"This time you will answer me." Her voice did not crack now and her meaning was clear. "We must get around this stubbornness of yours. If you choose not to answer this time, you will lose something precious to you." Her eyes bored into each of the three Shinnoahn men, her resolve plain to see.

The one on the left twitched. Ah! "Now," she continued in her most regal voice, "What. Are. Your. Names?" She focused on Fidget and turned on her charm. At the best of times, her charm was scary. At least, that's what Ya'el used to say. Maybe it would help her now.

Fidget gulped and squeaked out, "M'veta."

She nodded and inhaled. "Thank you for answering my simple question, M'veta of Shinnoah." Turning to the man in the center, she repeated her question. Having cracked the shell of one, the other two quickly relented and shared their names, Habti and Joran.

"Now we can get somewhere. M'veta, Habti, and Joran, I am Yetsye Shirasdatir of the village of Zulima of the clan of M'Neshunnaya. I hope that our association from this time on will bring much honor to our world." A weight lifted visibly from off the shoulders of the three. They gasped for breath, but it was Joran who spoke freely first.

"Why are we still alive? We tried to take the life of another being. We know the penalty and are prepared to accept it. I don't understand."

"You don't understand the purpose of life. One thing I can teach you is this. Your purpose is bigger than your own desires. If this conversation with you wasn't necessary, I wouldn't be having it. If my siveh had not pressed me to visit Yacan, I would never have gone. But if these things had not been done, something would be missing from my life that I would never have. Do you know what it is?"

The three offered the most banal of answers. Words like honor, fame, pride, and adventure, but Yetsye shook her head.

"Experience." She paused a moment, waiting for the realization to strike.

M'veta caught it first, and his eyes widened. "Ah! If we don't experience things, new things, we can't go forward. We can't learn or grow."

"That's it exactly. I wish to grow into a better human being, making a positive difference in my world, M'veta. Isn't that what all Y'Dahnndryans truly wish for?"

They nodded, making Yetsye feel like an Ancient. Who had encouraged these innocent younglings to do something so deadly? "So, what have you learned?" She was pushing the 'wise old teacher' mantle too far, but they dutifully mumbled replies.

"Please speak up!" she encouraged them. "I do want to hear your answer," Yetsye gently chided.

"I learned you can't judge a person by what you're told about their clan." M'veta was certainly talkative. "I humbly apologize for shooting you with the arteh. I thought I was doing the right thing. What you said that dusking sliced through my resolve. I don't want to hurt my clan. And I didn't really want to hurt you. I just wanted to stop the changes that scared me."

"It's the same for me," Joran piped up. "I always thought the other clans were against us, against our way of living. But I never asked." He hung his head and whispered a soft apology for his own part in the attack.

"I'm sorry, too," said Habti reluctantly. "I hate to admit when I'm wrong. You're strong, Lady Messenger. You sit there with the power and the right to take our lives. Yet you don't! You would rather try to teach us. I don't understand why. We deserve death." He never took his eyes from Yetsye's as he shook his head in disbelief. "You've convinced me. I'm willing to learn a new way."

"Wonderful news, indeed!" When Yetsye smiled this time, she beamed. "Then our talk here is done. You should go now and try to talk to the other dissenters and encourage them to think of the well-being of their clan and how every single part of Y'Dahnndrya connects with the others."

At this, their faces fell. "I'm sorry, Lady Messenger. I don't think we can do that." M'veta spoke hesitantly. "The rest of them left the encampment as soon as our attempt failed. We don't know where they've gone."

Yetsye shrugged. "When you see them again, and I'm certain you will, you can tell them then. Until that time comes, do all you can to improve the world around you. Learn more. Be more active in sparking positive changes. Help the D'Koruyin and M'Neshunnayan visitors who stay with your people for a time. This is the best way to serve Y'Dahnndrya. At least for now, until you receive your own quest from our Creator."

Yetsye shifted, and Tsadok set a hand on her shoulder. She was certain he felt her shaking, but hoped it wasn't visible. "I think I should rest now. Please enjoy your mana milk before you go. I wish we could talk more." And with that, Tsadok lifted her easily and carried her back to her pallet.

"Thank you, again, Tsadok. How many times will you make me say those words?" She teased him, but her fading voice betrayed how tired and weak she actually was.

"I will make you say it many times." He teased in kind. He rose to leave, but Yetsye tugged on the hem of his tunic. "I must go. There is no one else in this room and I will obey the laws." She sighed and a lone tear escaped. He bent and wiped it deliberately away before exiting the sleeping room. It wasn't right to ask him to stay, anyway. She kept forgetting she'd have to say goodbye to him one dawning, despite what he kept saying.

Her parents, Yuvahl, the three young men, Keiyn, and the healer spoke together. Every now and again, Tsadok's low voice would join in, but only rarely. She knew he was observing. It would be lovely to hear him sing for her again.

40

No Going Back

Yetsye closed her eyes and breathed deep. It was good to be home, nestled in her special place. Azilet'zal's hand was as discernible in the glade as the Most Holy Voice singing within her spirit. Tsadok attended the weekly candidate meeting. He hated going, for he couldn't shadow her then. She always promised to take care and stay alert, but it seemed impossible to convince him.

Yetsye knelt. Was it her imagination? The little clearing seemed smaller than before. She'd been gone a little less than a dahlsik, but nothing would ever be the same. The temptation to close her eyes and immerse herself in the soul of Y'Dahnndrya drew her. Neither Yuvahl nor Tsadok were here, but it was worth the risk.

She laid back, steadied her breathing, and rested her hands palms down on either side of her, nestling them in the soft green grass. Her eyelids fluttered and closed. At first, the rushing tidal wave of feelings and senses stole her breath. She retreated deep into herself, seeking that small coal that was her inner essence sprinkled with a minuscule portion of Azilet'zal.

The more she settled in, the sharper her vision became. She didn't just feel the breeze, she heard the spin of its journey. The sounds fluttering down from the tree branches sang an intricate composition for which she now knew the words. She could sense every nook and cranny in the glade, from the tiniest crack in the kho'ni bark with its line of bet'ihs carrying food to their leafy nest, to the many burrows dotting the ground under her.

Her senses opened even more, reaching out from the tiny glade to the village center. She heard the voices of her people going about daily life. If she focused well, she could pick out particular conversations, but the thought of doing so disgusted her.

Yetsye shifted her focus to the temple. The harmonic bells signaled the end of the candidates' meeting. She watched from above as they filed out of the main entrance. Shira oversaw the meeting this time instead of handing the task to one of her aides. Yetsye watched as she spoke with an attendant, gesturing toward the ceiling. Yetsye smiled to know that at least in M'Neshunnaya, the spark of unity had become a strong flamelet.

A black cloud of anxiety drew her attention. She honed her focus. The cloud lifted and a powerful determination raced toward her. "Tsadok." She whispered his name in her mind, savored the rhythm of it. He paused and his black hair swished as he searched left and right. Not finding what he sought, he looked up and his eyes bore into her soul. Fear and astonishment flashed across his face before he shuttered it once again and opened his mouth.

"YETSYE!" His voice boomed louder than the thunder of Ikishi's storms, shattering her concentration.

She bolted upright in the glade, shaking her head. Her ears rang, so she tapped on them. The ground vibrated. He was close. She tried to rise and lost her balance as she stepped into a hole. But when Tsadok arrived at the edge of the clearing, she'd regained her footing. She waited calmly while he paused and scanned the area. Finding nothing amiss, he stalked over, glowering. She cringed inwardly. He was definitely angry.

"What was that?" he asked as he studied her for signs of distress.

"That was what I can do when I focus properly." She paused and ducked her chin a bit before teasing him, "You shouldn't yell at me when I'm doing that. I could've gone deaf for the rest of my tsimikin. Or I might've died right then." She could no longer hold in the smile. It rang in all its glory, as clear as the temple bells, when she raised her eyes to his.

Her joy was short-lived, dying under his fierce glare. Yetsye kicked herself for not thinking her words through. She'd never seen him so pale. Why couldn't she remember not to tease others? She viewed him as dear as her own family and had been treating him the same. Why was she still making stupid mistakes?

"Now, who is the worried one?" He hissed and grinned, giving her the impression he'd roast her in the fire for taking death lightly. "I believe I still owe you for the scare at Kitra, too. There is no time like the present."

She panicked and backed away, forgetting the hole she stepped in moments ago. It knocked her off balance again, and she thought to use the backward momentum to her advantage. She should have known better. He caught her before she took two steps. His arms trapped hers at her waist and since she couldn't win by strength, she froze, seeking vainly for a weakness she could use.

His voice rumbled beside her ear. "Just when I think I understand you, you do something different. Then I have to refit the puzzle that is Yetsye Shirasdatir." He waited to see if she would respond. She didn't. "Do you even consider the effect of your words and actions?" Those last whispered words were her undoing.

His heart pounded directly behind hers. Scared? Worried? Tsadok? "I'm sorry." She hung her head. How could she forget his intensity? Tears pressed against her eyelids. She fought them, and whispered again, "I'm sorry, Tsadok."

The rhythm of his breath passing her ear didn't change. By the Creator's Voice! He hid too much! How could he expect her to know what affected him and what didn't? And what kind of punishment was this, anyway? Her anger blazed, and she snapped, "Let me go."

"I do not believe I can ever do that, not as long as Azilet'zal gives me breath." But he relaxed his grip.

Yetsye wrenched away from him and stalked home. He dogged her steps, but she refused to look at him. His words broke her resolve even more than his actions. She'd decided not to allow her feelings to grow for this person. But at every turn, her heart ignored her head. Society's demands vied with what felt right. She loved him. Azilet'zal help her, but she loved him very much!

When they reached home, she went straight to her room and closed the woven grass curtain. Running to her pallet, she collapsed on it, muffling tears of frustration in her colorful blanket. Churk nuzzled next to her and wrapped his long body in a coil beside one clenched hand. His gurgles and whistles offered comfort. She patted his downy head softly in thanks. Another choice of paths loomed before her and this might be her greatest challenge yet.

By the time Matir came home, the path seemed no clearer to Yetsye. She swallowed her discomfort and joined the family for the dusking meal. Tsadok filled Yuvahl's space across from her at the table. Ya'el's favorite flower sat in a tiny jar in the center. Yetsye barely glanced at it, her grief still too raw to linger. Her eyes lit on a small platter of bon'jiis, but she couldn't eat them without thinking of Tsadok. She dared a small glance in his direction and was immediately sorry. He hid nothing and what she saw tore at her heart — deep sorrow, pain, and worry.

"Yetsye," he said, his voice heavy with self-recrimination, "I am sorry. I—"

She held up her hand, halting his apology. Forcing down the small bite in her mouth took more effort than it should have. "I'm the one who should apologize. I should know by now I'm not able to tease anyone. Someone always ends up hurt." She paused to breathe, but continued before anyone else could speak. "I am more sorry than you could know. To hurt the person who has given up so much for me." She couldn't continue. She rose and fled once again to the only place she could be alone, her plate of food forgotten.

She sat in one of the two corners of her room. The acute angle cradled her back and Churk curled in her lap, rumbling as he breathed. Her eyes were so dry they burned. Had her well of tears finally emptied? She knew the path she'd choose. Even this short time had proved the necessity of his presence in her life. His pain was hers.

Running away again would allow her to avoid the issue this dawning. Or she could tell him now and maybe ease some of the tension. When she emerged for the meal earlier, she'd almost tripped over him. She sighed, certain he was nearby. All she had to do was call.

"Tsadok?" Her voice trembled, but she was determined now that she'd chosen.

"I am here," came the weary reply. She took a deep breath.

"I need to say something." It was a long moment before he popped his head through the door. He was sitting on the floor again. "Please, open the curtain and come in. What I have to say, if they hear, it might be easier, though I think Matir already suspects." She barely got the words out. It would be amazing if he actually understood her.

He came in, but stayed by the door. She looked up at him, pleading silently, sorry that she'd created such distance by her actions. "Please," and she bowed her head as her voice broke on the words, "come closer. It's hard to speak."

He knelt in front of her, formally, throwing her emotions into further disarray. "And you say I confuse you," she began, her voice low. "You should consider how much that applies to me, too." This was so hard. She was happy with her choice but scared of the stir it would cause. She risked everything. Home, family, clan, everything could disappear forever, all but Azilet'zal's presence, her beloved Y'Dahnndrya, and Tsadok's promise.

He reached out a hand, but she held up her own, stopping him. "You shouldn't. I don't know if I can control my gifts right now." He rested his palm against her uplifted one, hooking his fingers to clasp it. She gasped and raised her eyes at the same time he opened his heart.

Her spirit tumbled first from image to feeling and back. She fought her way to the little ember of her soul and clung to it. In the midst of the tempest Tsadok usually kept prisoner, she learned it was acceptable to tell him the words she needed to say. He was more than ready to hear them. She opened her eyes and looked directly at him.

"I love you," she said simply. Simple was best, right? Complications caused more trouble. He nodded but said nothing, waiting. He obviously expected more. She wasn't sure what to say, so she tried to explain herself. "I had to think. I had to determine if I really wanted to take this path. You are definitely worth the risk." Her free hand fluttered, betraying her nervousness. "But it's a scary step, to risk separation from all you've ever known." He nodded again. Hadn't he fought the same battle before choosing his path? "Why won't you say something? Where am I supposed to go from here?" came the whispered plea as she hung her head.

He lifted her chin with his free hand and said, "With me, Yetsye. You will go with me. Love is a hard word, difficult to describe, like grasping at a mist. But yes, I do not wish to be separated from you. I could not approach you with these feelings because I was the stranger among your clan." It was his turn to drop his eyes, but only for a moment. And when he raised them again, they blazed as bright as the sister suns. "You understood my feelings, then?"

She nodded, unable to speak past the knot lodged in her throat. She shifted to stand and Tsadok rose, pulling her up along with him. When she'd worked out that painful knot blocking her voice, she spoke up for the benefit of the two standing at the door. "Matir, Fatir, you know now. Your guidance would be helpful."

Bay'rakh ushered Shira into the room by her elbow and turned to Yetsye. "You know the complications. You're aware of the risks." These were statements, not questions. She nodded, solemnly.

"I've run every life path I could think of through my mind. I believe I've done that since our stay at Mt. Charan temple. But I know now this is the right choice, even though I'm afraid." Her voice shook, but Yetsye's eyes didn't waver from Bay'rakh's. She stood her ground.

He nodded at his youngest child and murmured, "I see you are determined. Shira and I will think of how to present this to the elders of M'Neshunnaya."

Turning to Tsadok, he voiced another worry. "How do the D'Koruyin view an inter-clan life-mating? I thought they were of the same mind as both M'Neshunnaya and Shinnoah?"

Tsadok stood tall, wavering in neither stance nor speech. "It is the same. They will not like it. I, too, know the risks, and have had more time to think on these things than Yetsye. She was my quest long before I met her. I made my decision at the time of my Dremsha."

Yetsye turned to him, mouth agape in surprise. He looked down at her, reached out a finger to her chin, and closed her mouth. A grin flashed across his face. She would've missed it entirely if her eyes hadn't been on him. Composed, he faced Bay'rakh again. "I also value your thoughts concerning us and the connection we share."

The men agreed to talk more the next dawning. It was late, and the dawning had been long and tiring. Yetsye's knees gave out. She collapsed on her pallet. Churk once again curled up in her lap. His rumbly breathing soothed her nervousness and helped her focus.

"I wish I'd known how you felt from the beginning," Yetsye mused.

"Would that have made some kind of difference in how you treated me, then?" She wasn't sure, but she thought she could detect a bit of wry humor in the question.

"Probably not." She was ashamed now of the fear she harbored of the tall stranger with the long braids and the captivating tattoo.

He knelt in front of her again. "I will not stay here long. It would be a strike against us to anger your people with careless actions."

"They will be your people, too, if they allow our joining." She sighed heavily. "We will belong to no people if they don't."

"Perhaps not. Mikot once told me there were those among the Ikhel'dur who were life-mated to out-clanners. If we cannot live here, then we will go there. If we lose home and provision, it will not be for lack of diligence." The confidence in his eyes comforted her.

"Alright. Let's continue this journey together, then." She added in a chipper voice, "I should go to the islands, anyway. They need to know what happened at Kitra. I still have work to do."

He nodded. "You need to rest now."

As he leaned forward to rise, Yetsye stopped him. "Not just yet. Please?"

He shook his head. "It is unwise. Surely you are aware." At her reluctant nod, he reminded her, "I will be near. You have only to call."

"Thank you, Tsadok." She closed her eyes and settled into her blanket, Churk at her side. She felt a quick rush of air and a light pressure on her forehead. Her eyes shot open to see Tsadok's braids swing over her while he rose to his feet once again.

Was that a kiss? She was certain she'd have a hard time sleeping now. How would things turn out on the morrowdawn? Causing her parents trouble saddened her. But there was no other choice than joining herself to Tsadok, even if he jumped into the fiery rift. The strong bond subtly knit over the course of their journey couldn't be ignored any longer.

Yetsye rose, knelt, and bowed over her knees. She poured out all the chaos in her heart to Azilet'zal, who guided her. She didn't need words. The Creator read her heart easily.

She raised her head when Tsadok's hand gently rested on her back. He knelt once again beside her, lifting his own prayer. She smiled and as she did so, he looked down at her.

"It will be well. You will see."

She nodded, and they returned to their pallets to await the dawning. Yetsye knew it wouldn't matter what the clan leaders decided. From this point on, she and Tsadok would be life-mates. Even if the ceremony had to be performed secretly, they'd do it.

She thought back to when she first left all she knew to make her Visioning pilgrimage to Levanna. Seth Yi'in of Mt. Charan, in his condescending manner, encouraged her with words and actions. Serafin of Yacan made certain she knew what was necessary to make it through trials. Her steadfast support bolstered Yetsye during her grief at Ya'el's sudden absence. She thought of her speech at Kitra and the dissenters who dimmed her hope.

Thoughts of Ya'el brought tears to her eyes, but this time, they comforted. Her siveh would be proud of how she'd spoken up at Kitra and for finally choosing Tsadok as her life-mate.

The familiar, gusty laugh echoed in her mind, asking what took her so long. She missed Ya'el dearly, but her memory would live in the spins they wove about her each Mem'ram.

Yetsye forced her mind to a happier plane. What would life with Tsadok be like? Restless, she moved her pallet to the door of her room. Slipping her hand under the bottom of the grass panel, she hoped he wasn't asleep yet. The warmth of his hand clasped hers. She smiled and settled into her blanket, content in his presence. The dawning could not come fast enough.

41

Her Precious Treasure

(*Two minsik later...*)

Yetsye knelt by the brazier and stared at the travel pack sitting in the orth's corner. They'd been traveling for a nainda since leaving the outskirts of the hunting grounds. Zev graciously provided all they would need for many dawnings in the dry lands of western D'Koruyi. But this pack was not part of Zev's provisions.

Tsadok set out earlier to scout the area and forage for anything useful. Yetsye hated the silence he left behind. She couldn't stop the thoughts then.

She looked at the closed door of the orth, sighed, then turned toward the travel pack once again. When Matir tried to add secret provisions, Yetsye usually noticed. She'd given this pack to Tsadok, though. He'd kept it secret and surprised her with it. And what a surprise! It left a bittersweet taste in Yetsye's mouth. Knowing Ya'el was alive, though they would likely never see her again, had been a fact she didn't want to face. Not now. Not ever. It would've been easier to overcome the grief of her death than this awful separation.

"You are such a myeta, Yetsye! When will you burn fierce and bright?" Yetsye jumped and looked around the orth. No one was there, but she heard the words as if Ya'el sat next to her.

"A challenge, then?" Her voice cracked. "One last challenge from my siveh."

She rose slowly, her eyes never leaving the pack. Step by hesitant step she walked, the pack drawing her as the falls draw one to death. She stopped in front of it and slowly sank to her knees. With trembling hands, she reached for the lacing, barely able to loosen the knots. The flap swung free and Yetsye released the breath she didn't realize she was holding. Her hands shook so badly when she reached for the maw of the pack, she wasn't sure she'd be able to hold on to anything inside. She grabbed the opening with one hand and plunged the other in.

The first thing she touched was a bit of stiff cloth. She drew it out slowly to find it was an old painting of the setting suns. Ya'el's sign marked the lower left corner. Yetsye ran shaky fingers over the pinks, oranges, and deep reds, the cracked paint scratching at her fingertips. When the colors blurred, she rolled the painting and set it aside.

This time when she reached in, her hands closed over something smooth and solid. She paused and looked upward. She'd held this before. Her hands hadn't forgotten the feel of Ya'el's pa'pukh. She drew it out quickly and held it close until the sobs calmed and she could see well enough to untie the leather cord and open it.

A folded page fell out and Yetsye read her name written in Ya'el's familiar hand. She set it aside. She wasn't ready yet. But the pages of the pa'pukh called to her.

As she turned them, the bush'ka with the thorny branch tangled in its fur came to life, a golden light hovering near its head. She looked closer and realized the light had a face and two tongues of curling flame as eyes. There was the vague impression of arms soothing the bush'ka, and Yetsye realized it was her. At the bush'ka's side, Yuvahl worked. Every line of his form spoke loudly of his dedication and purpose. Though she couldn't see his face, there was no doubt this was her batir. Ya'el was more expert with shape and line than Yetsye ever imagined.

Turning a few pages more, she found a portrait. Ya'el captured Tsadok's feelings so clearly and Yetsye almost sobbed again at the hurt deepening every line of his beloved face, shadowing his eyes. It was their first meeting. She couldn't even raise her face to him. She had hurt him. In the background, her siblings looked on with hope and wonder. How did Ya'el convey so much in simple lines and shapes?

A few more pages took her to the Nechna, then to their meeting with the whe'evet and Kven's band. Once again, golden light surrounded her form, though this time her hair was a mass of flames. There was a gentleness in the arms reaching out to the whe'evet, which puzzled Yetsye. Was she capable of such beautiful compassion?

Tears filled her eyes again, and she closed the pa'pukh until she could control them. Her beautiful siveh saw her as beautiful, too. Overwhelmed and amazed, Yetsye hugged the pa'pukh to her chest and bent over her knees as she wept quietly.

Sudden warmth spreading over her back startled her at first, but she sat up and leaned into Tsadok's embrace.

"What is it, my Yetsye? What have you found?"

In reply, Yetsye reopened the pa'pukh and turned the page to reveal the portrait of her cradled in Tsadok's arms on the ride to Chefvna. Love was a tangible shield surrounding them with its glory.

"She knew of my love for you before I did." Yetsye's voice wobbled, but she continued. "In every picture of me, there's a beautiful image I could never see, no matter how long I stared at my reflection. Even my true spirit reflection in Edrea's lifeblood didn't show this picture of me." She closed the pa'pukh and set it reverently back in the pack, then turned fully into Tsadok's arms. She could finally release the grief which had piled up since losing Ya'el at Yacan.

After a long while, Tsadok spoke, "What is this?"

She pushed away to see the folded page in his hand. "I don't know. I saved it, wasn't ready."

"And now?" he asked as he held it out to her.

She sniffed and rubbed her nose with a cloth she kept in her pocket. With shaking hands, she unfolded the letter.

"Little Siveh, Yetsye, this pa'pukh is for you.

I documented it all.

The journey from home to Yu'ul Forest and the bushes where you found Tsadok.

Your work to relieve the raging bush'ka and save the confused one.

The glowing apparition that was once a simple maid but now has a higher purpose.

The confused Little Siveh who didn't want to recognize the love which grew stronger with each dawning.

The excitement of your face at each victory, no matter how small.

The love and care you show for all those around you, whether they see or not.

I'm sorry my last words to you were harsh.

I have my own calling. My own purpose.

I regret not telling you goodbye, though I had little choice.

This will have to do.

If I never see you again, know that I love you as much now as I ever did.

And know that I will lift your name up to Azilet'zal in prayer every dawning, as I do for all our family.

I'm sorry I had to hide my silver from you.

I am Edrea. And Edrea is me. Or that is what I believe will happen now.

I couldn't tell anyone before coming here.

So you can't ever tell anyone that you know.

I will serve where Azilet'zal has sent me.

Take care to serve well wherever you go.

As for Tsadok, take care of the brave warrior who sacrificed everything for you. You know he'll refuse to go back to his old life.

My love to you both.

Ya'el Shirasdatir

Guardian (to be) of Yacan"

Glossary

- Aljis - a plant whose juices are cleansing, used to disinfect wounds and as a mouth cleanser; like mouthwash and toothpaste all in one substance

- Anzha - Shinnoahn vocal performances

- Arteh - small hand-thrown dart which can be tipped with poison; used mostly for hunting food by the Shinnoahns

- Auzi'ide - (ow ZEE ee deh) - D'Koruyin word for a person not of their clan

- Babete - D'Koruyin word for infant

- Bansan - Vining plant producing fuchsia-colored berries, similar to a blackberry but twice as large

- Barawik - A historical, lyrical poem or chant performed in M'Neshunnayan society

- Bit'tehs - Similar to ants, they are small insects, live in colonies, and are constantly working. But they are strictly vegetarian and nest in treetops

- Bix'n - Large mammal similar to an ox and used by the Shinnoahn Clan in the same manner.

- Bizhal - a small, fluffy mammal, colored black, white, gray, or any variation of those colors; eye color varies in shades of blue, green, and gold; no tail; round ears; two iridescent antennae in the center top of the head

- Blud'ig - Similar to a dog in face and manner, having four legs with three toes on each foot, a long whip-like tail and large erect ears. They are easily domesticated and make good pets.

- Braka - Bardic lay used by the M'Neshunnayan Clan; preserves the memory of historical events and special people. When a family member dies, it is common practice to compose a braka in their memory.

- Bumbir - A dunce, one who isn't very knowledgeable.

- Bush'ka - Land mammals, leviathans across between elephants, giraffes and cows; mild mannered with round heads; pudgy muzzles perched atop a tall, trunk-like neck, having bony ridges running up the spine to end in backward curving horns on either side of the face. Their nut shaped eyes are the color of their shaggy coats, ranging the scale of blue-gray to deep turquoise. Ponderous walkers, their four legs the size and shape of tree trunks only speed up if in pain or startled.

- Chimah - a sweet herb whose pea-sized, purple, bell-like blossoms are used for making perfumes; conical flower clusters are also used as decoration; roots can be ground up and used as a poultice for calming rashes

- Chippit - Vaguely resemble canaries; have a beautiful, complex repertoire of songs; Used as messenger birds; alert to danger, making them excellent alarms; decorative yellow-white plumage; easy to spot in the trees of M'Neshunnayan and Shinnoahn Territories; lay no more than two 3" pale blue eggs once every rainy season, nest in the same place every season.

- D'gut - Rounded; partly subterranean; earthen/clay bricks; homes of the M'Neshunnayans; built to fit the space available; central brazier with smoke-hole at the center of the rooftop; high, organically shaped windows; Yetsye's d'gut has one central room where the cooking and visiting take place with five surrounding rooms branching off from it.

• Dimin - M'Neshunnayan word for 'monster'

• Dirksh'n - Like a compass, it points travelers in the right direction.

• D'nagze - Goat-like animals that live in the mountains of Shinnoahn Territory

• Dozhi - Yellow flowers with burgundy centers and nine petals; grow on long, thin stalks; sport tiny, three-lobed leaves; fragrance is crisp like citrus and grass.

• Draconisi - Eel-like ocean dwellers; travel in retse (a family group); long, thin, shimmering blue bodies tipped with spines; long snouts; large, round eyes; eat a variety of free-floating ocean plants; only dangerous to humans during mating season.

• Dremsha - Prophetic visions given to the D'Koruyin Clan at Mesna'ya

• Dyr'kunfi - Similar to dragonflies; have 3 pairs of iridescent wings; long bright green bodies; grow no larger than 2 inches long.

• Ebit'n - D'Koruyin word for baby

• Edjig - Long-bodied; feathered mammals; have six pairs of 3-taloned feet; they're like miniature Chinese dragons in body; have a stubby snout meant for munching leaves and fruit; one set of fragile wings helps them glide through the treetops, though they don't actually fly; can be tamed.

• Ekiri - sedimentary stone whose layers range from red to yellow

• El'tekh - Predatory bird like an eagle with brown/gold feathers; has excellent vision and large nostrils; has three long tail plumes; males have a curving feather crest of red and white

• Flut'ra - Similar to a butterfly; has three sets of wings and a squat body; have eight legs; pattern of the wings is random overall; colors range from yellow-white to deep red.

• Fyryan - (FYIR yahn) - a flowering shrub having multicolored leaves of red, orange, and yellow smoothly curved on one side and jagged on the other; tri-petaled red-orange blossoms are cloven making them look like tongues of flame; smoky and heady scent

• Geilin - Seal-like creatures; land dwellers but play in the sea; a little smaller than mana; bear pups on the northern shores of Shinnoah and Genzet, usually 2-3 at a time; stay nearby while the pups learn to swim safely; range in color from pale blue on the underbelly to brown-blue mottled on their backs; have four fin-like feet and a stubby paddle-like tail.

• Gelte - D'Koruyin word for a girl who is not of their Clan

• Ghem - a measure of weight, similar to the gram. Ghema is a modification similar to the kilogram.

• Glashiin - equivalent to our glass, but much stronger

• Graida - brown, tan, and gold variegated stone; metamorphic stone; the gold veins have a sheen and are slightly translucent

• Grekh - an aromatic green herb used in making a purifying skin tonic

• Hahne'en - The M'Neshunnayan equivalent of honey, but made from cooking down the nectar of certain flowers; can be fermented to make a mild alcoholic beverage called wazha

- Hawikh - Bird of prey; built small and lean for speed; red-brown feathers; black curved beak; do not mate for life like the el'tekh.

- Hesp - A measure of time, sort of like hours, arrived at by using the hand to measure the distance from the horizon to the largest sun.

- High Priest/Priestess - Leader over all the M'Neshunnayan Clan; resides in the capital village of Zulima; is elected by the people; can be male or female.

- High Chieftain - Leader of the D'Koruyin Clan; always a male; must pass through rigorous trials to gain the position; Any male strong enough in body, mind, and spirit can earn the right to hold the title.

- Himmer - (HEE mehr) small, short-haired mammals having four legs each ending in three talons and having one set of leathery wings; about the size of a mouse; color varies in shades of brown and darker greenish grays

- Homish - one of the grain plants that grow in M'Neshunnayan territory. The bluish seeds are ground to make meal and flour of the same blue-gray color. The meal can be stewed with seasonings and herbs to create homish gruel, which M'Neshunnayans will usually eat for the morning meal.

- Hon'chi - Tiny white birds, about the size of a woman's palm; males have a five-feathered crest tipped with shades of green; sing a complex range of shrill chirps; travel and nest in flocks. Native to the Shinnoahn Territory.

- Iscael - Shinnoahn community dances

- Jiban - A low-growing shrub producing small edible nuts; can be found in Shinnoah and in the northern reaches of D'Koruyi

• Jinj - Flowering herb; flower heads, leaves and stems used to spice food; flavor is hot and sweet.

• Jin'ya - A leafy weed; only grows wild in certain types of soil in temperate zones; cannot be cultivated; prized among pipe smokers for its calming effect and slightly sweet, nutty aroma; has several medicinal properties; anti-fungal; anti-viral; anti-bacterial.

• Kashklav - a team event, part sport and part battle tournament; a game of team strategy and tactics

• Kez - a measure of length, similar to the meter

• Kho'ni - Tallest trees of Y'Dahnndrya; record height of 345' reached; trunks wide at the base; roots grow in jumbles which sometimes peek out of the ground; bark is rough to touch but good for medicinal teas and tinctures; hand-sized, 5 lobed leaves and palm-sized nuts are edible; a staple of M'Neshunnayan diet; nuts resemble scallops, round and flat with hinged halves.

• Ki'fi - A thin, leaf-shaped, double-edged dagger; blade is 8" long and 1.5" wide at the hilt; leather-wrapped hilt is 4-5" long; designed to fit the owner; commonly used by M'Neshunnayans and D'Koruyin.

• Kranj - A long length of supple chain whose links are barbed; a favorite weapon of M'Neshunnayan defenders; difficult to master.

• Krichte - mostly nocturnal mammal which uses its chirping call to attract prey and impress prospective mates; about the size of a guinea pig; fur ranges several shades of green; live in burrows; extremely shy;

• Lib'rarum - library; each shrine has one, as well as each clan capital; some larger villages may also have one.

- Liilum - Flowers resembling lilies; colored in shades of white, pale pink and pale yellow; fragrance is strong and very sweet; a favorite for gardens and bouquets.

- Linnel - a rough fabric used like paper made from plant fibers

- Mem'ram - a memorial song written to honor a dead loved one; particular to the M'Neshunnayan Clan; Mem'ram Day is held on the last day of the year and is a day of happy remembrance

- Mana - Grazing animal; has four paws; thick, elongated heads; shaggy fur; resemble equines, but for their feet; manes and fur grow short but thicken in colder seasons; tails are long whips tipped with a tuft of fur; extremely docile; colors range from bright red, to golden yellow, to coppery brown and any mix of those colors; eyes most often rich brown but blue or green on rare occasions.

- Met'cha - Similar to midges and gnats

- Mid'jin - Four-hoofed plains grazers; like antelope; the D'Koruyin tribes follow them as they migrate; are light of build; sport a pair of filigree horns which grow close together atop their heads and directly between their pointed, erect ears; horns often so close together the branches of one entwine with the other; very short tails; short-haired coats range from a deep golden brown in the warmer seasons to grow long and shaggy, medium gray to black in the colder ones; D'Koruyin use them for transportation

- Min'gif - A fish similar to a salmon; has whiskers like a catfish and a tall dorsal sail; have a series of short, sharp spikes that run the length of their spine; tails have long trailing ends; colors are varying patterns of white and gray but their eyes are ringed in bright green.

- Mijiwa - similar to a field mouse but about the size of a rabbit; main prey of the tam'na; colors range in sandy browns, cream, and grays

- Miritasi - Flammable fibers of the mirita plant (a water grass) used by the M'Neshunnayans to make candle-like light fixtures.

- Mir'ir - a mirror

- Muffit - Lizard-like creatures with scales and curly tails; have a frilly ruff around their necks for frightening predators; have 4 legs with three toes on the end of each; toes have sticky pads; can climb trees easily to catch insect prey; small enough to ride on a human's shoulder, can be domesticated.

- Myeta - like saying someone is a scaredy-cat or is scared of their own shadow.

- Nechna - Very large, four-legged plains animal; muscular build; silky fur that ranges the shades of gray and black; sport a mane around their elongated cat-like heads; males' manes are much more full; stealth hunters; travel in packs; oldest male is the leader; older Nechna have silvery streaks appear in their manes; telepathic.

- Opin'e - (OH pee neh) - clear to pale translucent white gem having iridescence; prized among all Y'Dahnndryans, but especially the Genzet and Bot'ha Clans

- Orif - wax-like substance made from kho'ni tree sap used to seal small openings, shine and protect leather boots and accessories

- Oukaan - (OW kahn) - Shinnoahn term used to refer to a person not of their clan.

- Pa'pukh - A leather-covered sheaf of linnel (papers) to which more linnel can be added as needed

• Pik'teh - A long-toothed comb

• Pinya - Smallish tree of the mountains of Shinnoah; spindly branches tipped with tufts of blade-shaped leaves; dual-layered outer bark; topmost layer is flaky and gray; under layer is darker gray with rougher texture that's somewhat spongy

• Pitikeli - flowering mountain herb of Shinnoah having gray-green blade-shaped leaves, and fuzzy white orb-shaped flowers on thin stems

• Pixet - Similar to a Galapagos turtle in size; wears a segmented shield on its back; the segments are lined with sharp spikes; four paws with three toes and sharp claws; an omnivore eating a wide range of small mammals, insects, tender plants, and shoots.

• Saghitan - A low-growing ground plant with diamond-shaped leaves used to create a healing ointment for open wounds

• Senya/Senyani - (male/female) Shinnoahn elder, not elected but a position of understood honor, like an honorific title

• Skal'kekt - The M'Neshunnayan name for the place where the souls of evildoers go when their bodies can no longer contain them. Some say it is a fiery place. Others say it is a place where you dwell within your worst nightmare for the rest of your soul's existence. This varies by clan, as does the name of the place.

• Shi'iket - a short tree, growing three daughter-trunks out of a central trunk stub, whose sharp blade-like leaves grow along central stems in sets of five

• Shiitha - Similar to groundhogs but rounder and slower; have poisonous mucous deadly to their prey and painful to beings larger than themselves; live in burrows in the plains of D'Koruyin Territory; fur is golden brown like the plains grasses; unfriendly.

- Shinahli - (shee NAH lee) The M'Neshunnayan word for the paradise their souls go to when their bodies can no longer house them. It means "Pure Lands."

- Skiiv - Shinnoahn boat strong enough for ocean travel but small enough to use in lakes or on rivers; two masts with single sails; two sets of oars

- Shwi'ich - similar to a weeping willow tree, but having tiny, white, tubular, blossoms which emit a soft, sweet perfume

- Sich'ik - Tree-dwelling mammal; similar to a squirrel; sports two short horns on its head; ranges in color from mottled green to mottled brown-gray; preys on insects and small reptilians.

- Slitchit - Snake-like reptiles, travel in knots no fewer than 10; only grow to a length of 12"; poison is strong enough to take down a bush'ka; satiny gray skin is great camouflage; hard to spot; live in underground dens; lay large numbers of eggs in a communal nest.

- Spin/Spinning - A story; The telling of a story; usually historical in nature; often has a moral; words are spoken in a sing-song way; a blend between rap music and poetry which is read aloud.

- Stiil (STEEL) - a soft mineral used in lump or tube form to write or draw

- Tam'na - Desert mammals; resemble cheetahs most closely, but they aren't quite as fast; coats are mottled in gold and pale browns to blend with the grasses in their hunting territory; hibernate in rocky dens during coldest seasons; large rounded ears, tipped with black pick up the tiniest of sounds from miles away; hard to domesticate but it has been done; hunt in packs.

- Taval - a small M'Neshunnayan drum having a slight tinny sound

- Tsa'gra - These cats live in family groups, anywhere from two to five members; coats are brindle and all shades within brindle; well camouflaged; sire and dam defend their kits faithfully; have been known to kill a human when provoked; known for speed and accuracy; two six inch incisors descend from top jaw; sharp claws; hard to domesticate but possible.

- Tseta - Pink flowering vine; grows in the woodlands all over Y'Dahnndrya; a favorite food of bush'ka; extremely sweet, heavy perfume; known to cause allergic reactions in some humans.

- Umb'el - Tiny wild-flower with a grouping of six complex flower heads; leaves are round and set in fronds on either side of the stalk; more decorative than fragrant.

- Visioning - A dream or a waking prophetic vision particular to Levanna Stone Temple

- Whe'evet - Across between a wolf and an ox; shaggy, ropy, mottled gray fur; long elegant muzzles; cloven ears; sharp and curved fangs; dinner plate sized paws; a single short curving horn growing between their ears; have 3 sets of dark red eyes sometimes hidden in their shaggy fur; can only see in infrared; travel in packs; move silently; native to northern mountains of Shinnoah; known as vicious predators

Index

Time Flow On Y'Dahnndrya

There are 684 days in a Y'Dahnndryan year. Each year, or tsimik, is composed of six dahlsikin (seasons). Each of the dahlsikin lasts for three minsikin (moon-cycles). Each minsik is composed of four nainda (weeks). A day is most often referred to as a "dawning" and a night, a "dusking."

List of the Seasons and Their Months

Ikishi - Season of Storms - harsh/cool - The stormy months are Koziki, Domiki, and Grokiki.

Yima- Season of Planting - mild/warm - The planting months are Yarma, Memma, and Hanma.

Ekishi - Season of Rains - mild/warming to hot - The rainy months are Zazinek, Fezek, and Shizek.

Iyaam - Season of Harvest - mild but drying/ hot to warm - The harvest months are Yannat, Yappat, and Yarrom.

Dishi - Season of Wind - dry/cool - The windy seasons are Nondi, Ragadi, and Maradi.

Nishi - Season of Ice - harsh/cold - The icy months are Shiini, Iriini, and Glokni.

Dawnings of the Nainda

Koz, Mem, Ara, Zet, Mut, Za, Ki, Irsh, and Gok are the generally accepted names for each day of their nainda.

About The Clans

Y'Dahnndrya is divided into six clans. Three of them have territory on the Eastern continent, Sheromoth. Two are located on the western continent, Emidar. The last clan inhabits the islands of Y'Dahnndrya.

The Three Clans of Sheromoth, Their Languages,& Familial Titles

M'Neshunnayan Clan - Language: Shunya (SHOON ya) - [Grand]Father: [Zat']Fatir (FAH teer); [Grand]Mother: [Zat']Matir

(MAH teer); Daughter: Datir (DAH teer); Son: Shoneh (SHOW neh); Sister: Siveh (SEE veh); Brother: Batir (BAH teer)

D'Koruyin Clan - Language: Koryu (KOR yoo) - Father: Pareh (PAH reh); Mother: Morah (MORE ah); Daughter: Oori (OH ree); Son: Azho (AH zho); Sister: Mireti (mee RET ee); Brother: Bramet (BRAH met)

Shinnoahn Clan - Language: Oahn (OH ahn) - Father: Babeiya (bah BAY ya); Mother: Moyri (MOYi ree); Daughter: Daula (DHOW lah); Son: Abei (AH bayee); Sister: Sadau (sah DOW); Brother: Iyaba (ee YAH bah)

The Two Clans of Emidar, Their Languages, & Familial Titles

Genzet Clan - Language: Enzi (EHN zee) - Father: A'ada (AH' AH dah); Mother: imi'I (ee MEE' ee); Son: O'oso (OH' OH soh); Daughter: ulu'U (oo LOO' oo); Brother: O'boer (OH' boh AIR); Sister: luer'U (loo AIR' oo)

Bot'ha Clan - Language: Othwa (OHTH wa) - Father:Baba'ir (BAH bah eer); Mother: Madri (MAH dree); Daughter: Lenal (leh NAHL); Son: Fari (FAH ree); Sister: Eisys (AIS yis); Brother: Fibyr (feeb YIR)

The Island Clan

Ikhel'dur Clan - Language: Keldu (KEL doo) - Father: Peliir (peh LEEER); Mother: Amarin (ah mah REEN); Daughter: Arini (ah REE nee); Son: Eliir (eh LEER); Sister: Bemin (BEH meen); Brother: Fimir (FEE meer)

Pronunciation Guide & Other Helpful Information

1. Y'Dahnndrya - pronounced (yi DAHN dree ya) - think of the initial 'Y' as you would in the name Yvonne or Yvette and the ending syllable is clipped.
2. M'Neshunnaya - Pronounce both the 'M' and the 'N' but together (muh NEH shuh NIGH uh)
3. D'Koruyi - Pronounce the 'D' and the 'K' together so that the 'd' is clipped (dKOR oo yee)
4. Shinnoah - (shee NOH ah)
5. Genzet - (GEHN zeht)
6. Bot'ha - (BOAT hah)
7. Ikhel'dur - The 'h' is a slight breath in the second syllable (EEK hel door)

8. Y'Dahnndrya has two suns, Tsifi'ra (the greater) and Mit'ra (the lesser).

9. Y'Dahnndrya has five moons. Min and Dahl are called the Guide Moons since their paths are regular. The calendar was created with their help. The other moons are Go'it (GOH iht), Yur'e (YOOR eh), and Shoth'a (SHOWTH ah).

10. Though each clan has its own tongue, and some have a secret warrior language, all the clans speak Genra (GEHN rah), the common tongue, when there are inter-clan events.

11. Since the deity most focused on in my books up to date is a creator god, I searched for words in various languages that fit the description. Each clan calls this deity by a different name, but they all mean 'Creator' in some way. I simply chose a pronunciation that looked like it would match each clan's personality to write the name out.

Clan - Name of the Creator and Pronunciation - General Meaning

Shinnoahn Clan - Tugansol (TOO gahn sole) - Life Giver
M'Neshunnayan Clan - Azilet'zal (ah zee LET' zahl) - Thread of Life
D'Koruyin Clan - Kai'yanga (kie' YAHN gah) - Creator
Ikhel'dur Clan - Kwikrei'ya (kwee KRAY' yah) - One Who Creates
Bot'ha Clan - Changjo'ja (chahng JO jah) - Creator
Genzet Clan - Andurdrao (ahn DOOR drow) - Breath of Life

When Reading Names of People, Places and Unfamiliar Things:

- A's most often say 'ah'.

- E's most often say 'eh'.

- I's most often say 'ee'.

- O's most often say 'oh'.

- U's most often say 'oo' like 'moon'.

- When vowels are combined (like - 'oa' or 'ai' or 'ei') simply combine the above sounds.

- Doubled letters denote a slightly elongated sound, such as 'ii' = 'ee+ee'.

- R's are slightly rolled, unless doubled when the rolling is more pronounced.

- G's are always hard, as in 'garden'.

- TH's are always voiced, such as in the word 'than'.

- Apostrophes denote a clip or short break between syllables, not always an accent on the preceding syllable. For example: Sari'i would be pronounced "sah REE ee" and Kai'yanga is pronounced (kai YAHN gah).

- Otherwise, if a name or word looks familiar, use a familiar pronunciation.

Author's Thanks

Thank you so much for reading my work. You made my day when you picked it up and cracked open the cover or flipped/scrolled that first digital page. Because you've given me something special, I'd like to share something special with you.

It wasn't easy for me to write. I'd thought about doing it for years. And to be completely honest, I might never have started writing still if it hadn't been for the need to change up our home school curriculum a bit.

In October of 2016, I started putting fingers to the keyboard and pen to paper. The goal was to have my novel completed and published in a year. Oh, my! Did I have a lot to learn! It took about two years, but the time came and went. Ripples is complete and I can move on to more of the books in the series, Surge, Over Land & Under Stone, Bid the Fallen Rise, and The Crash of Waves.

I couldn't have done any of this if it hadn't been for my supportive family and friends: John, Noah, Judy, Randy, Shiloh, Rowan, Ruth, Robert, Christina, Brenda, Denver, Nancy, Aliz, Amber, Jay, Julie, Danny, Jeff, Mrs. Laura, the ladies of my church, the Plotter Life Writing Group on Facebook, the Writers Block group on Discord, the Camp Nano Warriors group also on Discord, the Alliance of Independent Authors, and of course, the creators and mods of NaNoWriMo. I also want to thank those who proof-read the first awful draft of my prologue and chapter one on Scribophile back in 2016. Y'all opened my eyes to many things.

But there's one person I could do nothing without, and that's my savior, the Messiah Yeshua. Yes, my religious beliefs shape who I am and how I conduct myself. Yes, those beliefs affect my writing to a certain extent. But my prayer is that every person who picks up this book will be able to enjoy it and gain something positive from the reading of it. Know that all my readers are in my prayers.

Author's Special Note

In the first edition of this book, I had planned to include more of my story. Then I talked myself out of it, using awful reasoning. How can the light shine into the darkness if it's hidden?

My Plan B was to have a webpage which could be linked to any book I wrote so people could just visit that page. Well, that didn't work out as planned, either, so I'm going back to Plan A.

My intent is to inform, not to offend. I do realize some choose to be offended because it's their habit to do so. It's unfortunate and discouraging, but I need to move in the way my God points me. Keep reading if you want to know more of my story.

More About the Author

Introduction

It took me quite a while to determine whether or not I should actually put this out there. Some folks are quite adamant about not reading books by Christian authors, no matter if they are preachy or not. However, I think there are some readers who'd like to know more about me, what I believe, and why I believe the way I do. This is for those readers.

My History

One reason I don't say much about my faith journey is because I feel like there are few who can relate. I was raised in a relatively happy home, supplied with all I needed to grow properly, achieve goals, and thrive. My parents have always been together and I have never doubted their love for me. We weren't rich, but we had what we needed and it took me a while to understand that, to understand that what a person needs often differs greatly from what they think they need. I often bemoaned the fact that I didn't wear the same clothes as the cool kids or have the same kinds of toys or gadgets. My dad was a farmer on a small farm. As such, there was never really enough money for those upper middle class items and certainly none for luxury items. We didn't even have a Nintendo until I was well into my teenage years, and we got that one used and only had two games for it. Still, I knew I was loved. I knew I had a warm bed to sleep in and good, sturdy clothes to wear. I never went to bed hungry. And I occasionally got to have special treats, usually a favorite snack or something equally inexpensive.

Another thing I grew up with was music. Music is my first true passion. I love to sing and will take every opportunity to do so. I especially love to sing with my family or anyone who can sing harmony and improvise. I can play the piano, mostly like Elizabeth Bennet, "...a little and very poorly, I'm afraid." I can also play the guitar in a similar fashion. But singing, ah! I wish I'd been able to do something with that earlier on in my life. I considered majoring in it in college but my mom talked me out of it. It's probably a good thing. I didn't like opera until much later in life and if they'd made me sing such things in college, I'd likely be biased against it now. Music is a huge part of my family life. Most of my family sings and we usually sing when we get together.

One place music really came alive for me was in church. I was in church from day one. My mother has been playing the piano in church since she was twelve and my dad was the worship leader for years before PTSD pulled him away from it. They were part of a traveling gospel music quartet and we visited churches all over southern Louisiana during the younger years of my life and until I was into my teen years. Their music used to be on YouTube, but I can't find it anymore. I used to sing in the middle of their performances to give them a break. I loved it!

Then I became a teen and it was just "old hat." I wanted to sing more contemporary songs which didn't really fit in with southern and country gospel. I also lost focus for a while. But I'm getting ahead of myself.

Hearing God's Call

At a summer evening service in a small Southern Baptist country church, the sun shone gold through the westward-facing, rectangular, colored glass panes of the church windows. The air conditioning was working hard to keep up with the southern Louisiana heat and humidity. I was sitting with friends of my family, I think, listening to the sermon. At the end, when the pastor gave the altar call, he asked if there was anyone who wanted to be saved, encouraged them to step forward, and asked them to come pray with him. I surprised everyone, I think, but I stepped up and prayed that prayer.

"Dear Lord,

I know I'm a sinner. I've done some awful things in my life.

I believe You died on the cross to wash away my sins.

Please forgive me.

Please help me live the way You want me to live.

In Jesus Name,

Amen"

I was in fourth grade, or getting ready to go into fourth grade. Young, yes, but I knew right then God was calling me. I felt Him nearby everywhere I went. I still do because I see His hand in every part of the creation.

I'd always felt like an outsider before, but after making this decision, I really felt like a misfit. I was fanciful as a child, with a good imagination, but there was still something, some kind of wall, between me and the other kids I knew, like it was impossible to really connect with them.

This got worse as I got into my teenage years, as you might expect. Those are rough years for anyone. It was a good thing I had my Savior to lean on and the guidance of the Holy Spirit. I wouldn't be here now if it wasn't for Him. I never had an easy time making friends and in 9th grade, I changed schools. I had to make new friends and most of them were Catholic. I loved them, still do, but it was more difficult to connect with that difference in the spiritual doctrine hovering between us. In the middle of that year, I asked my mom to get me out of that school and help me find another one because I felt smothered. But I think back on my time there and I do smile. It was an experience I'm glad I was able to have.

I moved to a new school the following year. It was no easier to make friends and the one friend I made before the school year started, turned out to be a malicious person. The one good friend I made during that year hated me and ignored me after I asked (and was rejected) a friend of mine, who she happened to have a crush on at the time, to attend a banquet with me at my church. I only asked him because I was pushed to do it by a teacher I respected. I would've gone alone like I usually did. No one really paired off at those events anyway. But it was a serious blow to my confidence. At that point, I didn't really try to befriend anyone. My faith was growing, though, and rather than take my life (the thoughts were fleeting but they were there), I stuck it out.

School had always been a drag, though I did well enough in my studies. But church and the youth group were my salvation when it came to socializing. I lived for those moments in Sunday School, Discipleship Training, and youth events. I was part of the cool kids for a little while and it was pretty heady stuff.

Not only did I get to sing with our youth group at church, I got to sing in the choir and the specialty concert choir at school. In doing the latter, I finally made a few friends. Some of them, I still keep in contact with. It was in those moments, chapel, Bible study, youth events, where God was really working on me and convincing me of the certainty of His presence. I still had moments where I knew I was a misfit and an outsider in all those places, but I got to participate in so many things, it wasn't such a big deal.

It was also during my teenage years that I started to doubt my conversion. Some religions teach that you can lose your salvation, but that never made any kind of sense to me. I believed then, and still do, if you have felt the Savior's presence and heard His call, there's no going back. You either respond with a willing heart and mind, or you reject Him utterly. Your life, the decisions you make from that point on will show whether or not your conversion was true. The Bible even says that in Matthew 7:16:

16 You will recognize them by their fruit. Can people pick grapes from thorn bushes,

or figs from thistles? 17 Likewise, every healthy tree produces good fruit, but a poor

tree produces bad fruit. 18 A healthy tree cannot bear bad fruit, or a poor tree good

fruit. - Complete Jewish Bible1

I started wondering whether my fruit was good or bad, whether I was right with God for real. I recommitted my life twice over the three years I spent at the prep school. One teacher helped me see clearly that my conversion as a young child was a true conversion, that the moment I heard God's call and responded was the moment I surrendered to Him as Lord over my whole life. I didn't need to be baptised again. I just needed to be sure I was staying connected to Him in prayer and Bible study, and working to follow His commands.

Walking With God

My walk with God has never been what you'd call easy. But neither has it been as difficult as that of Corrie ten Boom, or Saint Peter, or Stephen, or Paul. I'm a pray-er, though. When I pray, it takes time to get everything I want to say out there. My kids dread it when it's my turn to pray at night because they know I just have so much to say. And I don't want to miss anything.

As a child, I used to pray for blue eyes and blonde hair. It's OK. You can laugh if you want to. It's a rather silly prayer, but it was the cry of my heart. I felt my brown hair and green eyes were ugly compared to my gorgeous friends, one of whom had beautiful, long black hair and cool blue eyes, and

---

1. https://www.messianicjewish.net/pages/copyright

another who was of German heritage and had sun-gold hair with natural large curls and clear blue eyes. Now, you may laugh at this, but when I got to my second year of high school, one of the older guy students mentioned my eyes, asking what color they were. I said green and he said he'd thought they were blue. I noticed at that point that my eyes change color in different lighting and with different colored shirts. It had probably always been that way, but I never noticed at the right time. My hair is still brown, though sprinkled with lots of gray, but I've learned to love my natural state since then.

Another major thing I prayed for was a boyfriend. I had made it all the way to my senior year of high school without dating anyone. And I knew years before then that I would not be dating anyone in my class or age range, and that I would not be dating anyone I knew while growing up. I don't know how I knew. I just did. We didn't have the same ideals. We didn't have many common interests. I just knew it wouldn't work. And dating for me was a serious thing from the get-go, never a game. See? Misfit.

God heard the cry of His little misfit and sent my husband. He wasn't interested in me at first. Why should he have been? There's an eight year difference between us. He was already working in the US Air Force and I was still finishing high school. So you may be wondering how that all came about. He was actually working with our youth group and coming to church regularly. He'd made a profession of faith and felt he'd been called into ministry. We hung out within the youth group and that was the extent of our connection. Then it was time for prom and I needed a date. My parents actually suggested I ask him, so I did. We're still together.

But that wasn't easy, either. He came with his own terrible inner struggles which had to be overcome through years and years of battles. God knew I needed him as much as he needed me. God knew I wouldn't give up on him, no matter how painful it was in the process. I was determined.

Through all those ups and downs, God has been faithful. Some of my dear friends say God has never done that for them and they can't really believe in Him. To them, I want to say, God is faithful to the faithful. If you haven't dedicated yourself to living His way, then you can't really expect Him to bless you. I don't expect that from Him.

Want an example? In our faith, we tithe ten percent of our earnings. Anytime I skipped paying tithe because the bills seemed too large to cover, we surely did not have enough to pay for everything. But when I was faithful to pay my tithe, we had an adequate supply of all we needed. Not overmuch, mind you! Just enough to make certain we had what we needed. God is faithful to the faithful.

Conclusion

So much more happened to me over the course of my life. It may look easy to you, but I guarantee you my life has been no walk through a rose garden. The one reason I keep pressing on is the thought that one day I will be able to live eternally with God, the Creator of All That Is, with my Savior, the Messiah Yeshua, who rescued me from my sinful self.

When I write, I want to do so in a way that is pleasing to God and pleasant for humankind. I hope I'm doing that and I hope you are enjoying my efforts. God has prepared me for this writing journey. He's filled me with all kinds of knowledge, gleaned from many different experiences throughout my life. More than anything, I want to give back. I've been given so much, I want to share what I have with others who are interested.

So if you read something in this essay that has you wanting to know more about the God I serve, I would like to point you to the book of John in the Bible[2]. It's an excellent place to start and includes some of my favorite verses. Once you've finished there, you might want to take a look at what Southern Baptists call the Roman Road to Salvation[3]. There are several specific scriptures in the book of Romans that teach how a person can begin their own walk with God. I hope you're in the family of God with me. But if not, then I hope you'll take a little time to learn what this is all about. Know that either way, I prayed for you even before you opened this document and someone cares about your spiritual well-being.

There's one other thing you should know before embarking on this journey. It won't be easy. Nothing in life is easy, after all. Jesus even warned the people who heard him.

---

2.   https://www.biblegateway.com/passage/?search=John+1&version=CJB

3.   https://www.biblegateway.com/blog/2016/09/evangelism-the-romans-road-to-salvation/

24 Then Yeshua told his talmidim, ⁴"If anyone wants to come after me, let him say 'No' to himself, take up his execution-stake, and keep following me. - Complete Jewish Bible⁵

But having God on my side has made the difficult things in life much easier to bear. I don't always understand the why, but I believe God has a plan and it's a good one because He is ultimate good and can be nothing else. Please don't let thoughts of what-ifs and possible future difficulties keep you from experiencing the beauty and love of the Savior who gave all to wash you clean from your sins.

My Prayer for You

"Dear Heavenly Father,
My prayer for each person who reads this is that You would speak to their hearts.
I pray that you would supply them with what they need.
For those looking for something to fill the void within, I pray that these words will open a door to knowledge of who You really are and what You really offer.
And I pray that You would keep them in the best possible health and safety according to the plan You have for each of their lives.
In the name of Yeshua, the Messiah, I pray.
Amen"

[1]. To share the yellow strands" is a M'Neshunnayan saying which means to tell someone the truth. M'Neshunnayans call storytelling "spinning" and liken it to weaving a tapestry. Yellow threads are most often used to portray light and light reveals what darkness hides.

[2]. The hesps turn - time passes faster than it seems

4. http://www.messianicjewish.net/pages/copyright

5. http://www.messianicjewish.net/pages/copyright

Don't miss out!

Visit the website below and you can sign up to receive emails whenever Robin McElveen publishes a new book. There's no charge and no obligation.

https://books2read.com/r/B-A-LNLG-IEIEH

BOOKS 2 READ

Connecting independent readers to independent writers.

Did you love *Ripples*? Then you should read *The Tale of Outh'n Durr*[6] by Robin McElveen!

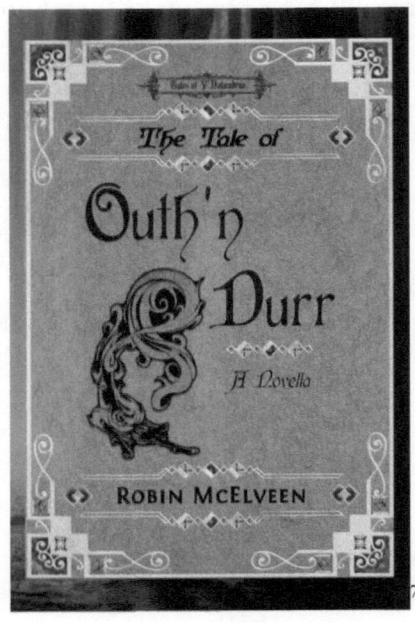

When Outh'n Durr's path darkens and giving up is the easiest way out, will determination be the light that leads him to true freedom?

Wuveia. It had to be. And this close, the pack would already have his scent. They'd probably picked up his conversation with the bizhal moments ago and were biding their time. Deciding it was now or never, Outh'n made his move and rose from the thorny thicket. Coming to his knees, he met the golden-eyed glare of one ot the beasts.

Dear Tugansol in Zoleta, it was massive! He'd never seen one up close, only from a distance as he'd watched over his babeiya's cattle. The domesticated wuve, relatives of these forest dwellers, never grew this big.

Outh'n sat back on his heels, resigned to a fast, bloody death. Shaking violently, he closed his eyes and bared his throat. If he made himself an easy target, maybe death would be swifter, less painful. He'd had enough of pain

6. https://books2read.com/u/bWpOdx

7. https://books2read.com/u/bWpOdx

over the course of his life and what did he have to live for, anyway? He was more than ready to die.

Read more at https://www.authorrobinmcelveen.com/.

Also by Robin McElveen

Children of Y'Dahnndrya
Ripples
Ripples

Tales of Y'Dahnndrya
The Tale of Outh'n Durr

Watch for more at https://www.authorrobinmcelveen.com/.

About the Author

Robin McElveen is the author of the *Children of Y'Dahnndrya* YA fantasy series, of which *Ripples* is the first tale. She lives in Louisiana with her family. In addition to writing, she enjoys singing and playing music, creating art, and sewing costumes. As a Christian, she tries to keep her books in line with her faith. Faith and family come first. She's taught her children at home since 1998 and feels there's a growing need for quality books which promote good morals. She's doing all she can to help meet that need.

Read more at https://www.authorrobinmcelveen.com/.

About the Publisher

MKRM Author is the exclusive publishing imprint for books by Robin McElveen and Melody Kittles. Find out more here: https://www.authorrobinmcelveen.com

RHONDA PARRISH ANTHOLOGIES

Available Now

A IS FOR APOCALYPSE
B IS FOR BROKEN
C IS FOR CHIMERA
D IS FOR DINOSAUR
E IS FOR EVIL
F IS FOR FAIRY

FAE
CORVIDAE
SCARECROW
SIRENS
EQUUS

MRS. CLAUS: NOT THE FAIRY TALE THEY SAY
TESSERACTS TWENTY-ONE: NEVERTHELESS
METASTASIS
NITEBLADE MAGAZINE

FIRE: DEMONS, DRAGONS AND DJINNS
EARTH: GIANTS, GOLEMS AND GARGOYLES

GRIMM, GRIT AND GASOLINE

Coming Soon

HEAR ME ROAR
SWASHBUCKLING CATS: NINE LIVES ON THE SEVEN SEAS